**When he looked up, his friends stared
at him. "What?"**

"I asked you what you saw that last night," Beth said.

Far away, a red glow outlined the crown of Red Peak.

Gaunt from hunger and hard labor and pain, the congregation shambled out of the darkness for their final act of worship . . .

David winced at this flashback, which appeared as sudden and real as if he'd physically transported to the past. "I'll tell you the same thing I told you at the mental hospital. I didn't see a damn thing. When everybody went to the Temple, I hid in the supply closet. I didn't come out until the sheriff's deputy found me."

"I saw something," Deacon said.

"Please." Back when they were institutionalized, David had heard the horrifying story of what happened to Wyatt and had no wish to ever hear it again. "You don't have to say it. I remember."

"You didn't hear everything, David. I never told Dr. Klein what I saw because I thought if I did, he'd never let me out of that place. I never told you either."

"All right. What?"

"When the end came, when everybody was dead? I saw—" His face pale and taut, he hesitated. "I saw a pillar of fire on the mountain, shooting straight up into the sky."

By Craig DiLouie

The Children of Red Peak
Our War
One of Us
Suffer the Children
Tooth and Nail
The Alchemists
The Great Planet Robbery

CRASH DIVE
Crash Dive
Silent Running
Battle Stations
Contact!
Hara-Kiri
Over the Hill

THE INFECTION WAR
The Infection
The Killing Floor

THE RETREAT
Pandemic
Alamo

THE
CHILDREN
OF
RED
PEAK

CRAIG DiLOUIE

REDHOOK

Copyright © 2020 by Craig DiLouie
Excerpt from *One of Us* copyright © 2018 by Craig DiLouie

Cover design by Lisa Marie Pompilio
Cover images by Getty Images and Shutterstock
Cover copyright © 2020 by Hachette Book Group, Inc.
Author photograph by Jodi O

Hachette Book Group supports the right to free expression and the value of copyright. The purpose of copyright is to encourage writers and artists to produce the creative works that enrich our culture.

The scanning, uploading, and distribution of this book without permission is a theft of the author's intellectual property. If you would like permission to use material from the book (other than for review purposes), please contact permissions@hbgusa.com. Thank you for your support of the author's rights.

Redhook Books/Orbit
Hachette Book Group
1290 Avenue of the Americas
New York, NY 10104
hachettebookgroup.com

First Edition: November 2020

Redhook is an imprint of Orbit, a division of Hachette Book Group.
The Redhook name and logo are trademarks of Hachette Book Group, Inc.

The publisher is not responsible for websites (or their content) that are not owned by the publisher.

The Hachette Speakers Bureau provides a wide range of authors for speaking events. To find out more, go to www.hachettespeakersbureau.com or call (866) 376-6591.

Library of Congress Cataloging-in-Publication Data
Names: DiLouie, Craig, 1967– author.
Title: The children of Red Peak / Craig DiLouie.
Description: First Edition. | New York, NY : Redhook, 2020.
Identifiers: LCCN 2020007118 | ISBN 9780316428132 (trade paperback) | ISBN 9780316428101 (ebook)
Subjects: GSAFD: Suspense fiction. | Mystery fiction.
Classification: LCC PS3604.I463 C48 2020 | DDC 813/.6—dc23
LC record available at https://lccn.loc.gov/2020007118

ISBNs: 978-0-316-42813-2 (trade paperback), 978-0-316-42811-8 (ebook)

Printed in the United States of America

LSC-C

Printing 6, 2023

For my wonderful children: May you always smile at the past and find meaning in the present.

After these things, God tested Abraham, and said to him, "Abraham!"

He said, "Here I am."

He said, "Now take your son, your only son, whom you love, even Isaac, and go into the land of Moriah. Offer him there as a burnt offering on one of the mountains which I will tell you of."

Abraham rose early in the morning, and saddled his donkey, and took two of his young men with him, and Isaac his son. He split the wood for the burnt offering, and rose up, and went to the place of which God had told him.

—Genesis 22:1–3

ENTERTA

10 Cults to Know Before Wat New Way

By KATIE WALMA

The highly anticipated new cable series *New Way*, starring Jacob Marsh and Donna Salidas, takes us inside a doomsday cult in an examination of fulfillment and fear. As the portrayal of the fictitious *New Way* cult draws from real-life groups, here are 10 infamous cults to know before you catch the season premiere on Sunday.

The Peoples Temple: Founded in 1978 by Jim Jones, the Peoples Temple of the Disciples of Christ drew a large membership in Indianapolis before moving to California and then Guyana, where it founded the Jonestown commune. After ordering the murder of a visiting Congressman, Jones next commanded his followers to drink cyanide, resulting in the death of 918 people.

police discovered 39 bodies in the mansion, the largest mass suicide in the United States.

The Family of the Living Spirit: In 2005, a teenager burst into a sheriff station in Medford, California, with a bizarre story: More than 100 members of the group founded by Reverend Jeremiah Peale had committed mass suicide and murder at its commune at nearby Red Peak, preceded by months of ritualized mutilations. The sheriff drove to the site to discover the group had vanished, leaving behind five children in all to be rescued. An extensive search turned up no other survivors or bodies, resulting in the "Medford Mystery" that has endured 15 years.

Manson ___ *ly:* In 1969, the

"Helter race w Tate, ar As for M 2017.

Branch D siege in 1 apocalyps his follow believin of Chris Koresh d stockpile Waco rai the ra gun batt 51 days. consumir died in th

Aum Shi Asahara mixed E "Suprem 1995, th sarin gas 5,500 pe

1

REMEMBER

After years of outrunning the past, David Young now drove straight toward it.

His Toyota hummed south along the I-5 as the sun melted into the coastal horizon. The lemon trees flanking the road faded into dusk. Most nights, he enjoyed the solitude of driving. He'd roll down the window and disappear in the sound of his tires lapping the asphalt, soothing as a Tibetan chant.

Not this time. California was burning again.

The news blamed the wildfire on a lightning strike in the sequoias. Dried out by the changing climate, the forest went up like a match. Outside the car, the air was toxic. A crimson glow silhouetted the Sierra Nevadas like a mirror sunset.

Red Peak called to him from all that fire and ash.

David turned on the radio to drown out his memories. He'd spent years forgetting. In all that time, he hadn't kept in touch with the others. He hadn't even told his wife about the horrors he'd survived. Claire believed he was visiting a client and not on his way to the funeral of an old friend to whom he owed a debt.

He didn't want to go, but Emily was dead, and he had her letter.

I couldn't fight it anymore, she'd written in flowing cursive.

All those years ago, five children survived. Now there were four.

He found a parking space at the All Faiths Funeral Home and cut the engine. Cars filled the lot. A sizable crowd had come to attend Emily's wake, friends and family who wanted to say goodbye.

Whatever happiness she'd found hadn't been enough for her.

He turned on the overhead light to inspect his appearance in the rearview. People said he had both charisma and looks, a genetic gift from his mother. Under dark, wavy hair, his angular face was sensitive and inspired trust.

Tonight, wild eyes stared back at him, the eyes of a man he didn't know or had forgotten. The eyes of a scared little boy.

You have children you love more than anything, he told his reflection. *You have a job that allows you to help people escape the worst of what you suffered. You're alive. The past isn't real. It's dead and gone.*

"I'll be okay," he thought aloud and opened the car door.

The warm night air smelled like an old brick fireplace. The mountains burned in the east, bright and close.

David turned his back on the view and lit a cigarette, a crutch he revisited in times of stress. He took a long drag, but it tasted terrible and only made him fidget more. He ground it under his shoe and went into the funeral home.

▲   ▲   ▲

Black-clad mourners filled the foyer and lobby, mingling in the air-conditioned atmosphere heavily scented with fresh-cut flowers and sharp cleaners and the acrid tinge of wood smoke. Organ music droned over the murmur.

Stomach rolling, David scanned the faces. There was nobody here he recognized. He stood in awkward tension on the thick carpet. He should visit Emily's body and say goodbye, but he wasn't ready for that, not yet.

Then he saw her. Emily, still a child, reaching to tuck her long blond hair behind her ear, a frequent gesture he remembered well.

His heart lurched. He was seeing a ghost.

A man sat on the folding chair next to the girl and stroked her hair while she frowned at a tablet resting on her lap. On her other side, a towheaded boy played with his own device.

Her children, he realized. Around the age of his own kids. The girl was about the same age as David when he first met Emily in 2002.

They slouched in their chairs, miserable and bored. They didn't understand how profoundly their world had changed, not yet. After his mother died, David had taken a long time to process as well. A stabbing pain of homesickness stuck in his chest. He missed his own children back in Fresno, safe in Claire's care, still naive to how cruel the world could be.

The man caught him staring and rose to his feet with a scowl.

David held out his hand. "You must be Emily's husband."

"Nick." His breath was thick with whiskey. "Who are you?"

"David Young. I'm sorry for your loss, Nick."

Still protective, distrustful. "How did you know Emily?"

"We grew up together."

The man's scowl softened until he wasn't looking at David at all. Emily's suicide had broken him. "Where did...?"

David waited until the silence became awkward, then said, "She was a very good friend. In fact, I was just thinking how much your daughter resembles her back when I knew her."

He and Emily used to talk about how all they had was each other, how they'd spend the rest of their lives protecting each other.

"She never mentioned you." Nick shambled back to his kids.

David released the breath he'd been holding and retreated as well. He found himself walking without direction among the black-clad mourners, who murmured in small groups and shot him curious glances as he passed. He'd always had a difficult time sitting still, but now he had a purpose for it. As long as he appeared he had somewhere to go, nobody could draw him into conversation, and the mourners would remain raw impressions instead of real people.

He reached into the pocket where he kept his phone. He thought about going outside to call Claire and tell her he'd arrived safe at his hotel. If he did, however, he might not come back inside. Instead, he edged closer to the viewing room.

On the far side, Emily's white casket lay surrounded by arrangements of lilies, carnations, roses, orchids, and hydrangeas. He glimpsed slender lifeless hands clasped over her breast. At the doorway, a large poster mounted on an easel displayed photos of her life. Emily smiling at the camera, holding a baby, hugging her children, posing with her family.

David found it jarring to see her grown-up. She was still

so familiar, but the intervening years had turned her into a stranger. His breath left him in a gasp as nearly fifteen years rushed past in an instant.

Her smile was still the same, however. A smile that lit up the room. He leaned for a closer look at a photo of her on a windy beach at twilight.

How did you fool them all for so long? he thought.

Or maybe she'd fooled herself.

A familiar voice said: "I thought I was gonna find you hiding in a closet."

Again, a strange sense of vertigo. He wheeled to find a teenage boy wearing a comfortable grin. The boy morphed into a man.

David shook his head and smiled. "You're still an asshole, Deacon."

Now in his late twenties, Deacon Price appeared much the same skinny kid with his boyish face and easy smirk. But he'd styled his shaggy hair into an emo swoop that shadowed one eye, and he wore a black T-shirt, leather wristbands, jeans, and Chucks. His shirt advertised he liked HOT WATER MUSIC. An odd choice for a funeral. Then again, Deacon's outfit struck David as some kind of uniform.

A long time ago, they'd been best friends.

"You dyed your hair black," David said after a tight hug. He didn't mention the tattoos that covered his friend's arms.

"And you got older."

"Okay, let me guess." He made a show of studying Deacon. "Stock broker."

"Nice try." Deacon chuckled. "Musician. My turn." He took in David's black suit, white dress shirt, black tie, and shiny shoes. "Bible salesman?"

David snorted. "Hardly."

"Then you must be a cult deprogrammer."

"Wow, how did you know?"

His friend rolled his eyes. "It's called Google, dude."

"Right." David flushed with a little embarrassment. He'd never checked up on his old friends. "I'm an exit counselor, though, not a deprogrammer."

Usually paid by the family of a cult member, deprogrammers retrained a person out of their belief system, and some used kidnapping and confinement. Exit counseling was voluntary, more like an addiction intervention.

"Whatever you say." Deacon shrugged, the difference lost on him. "Did you think I wasn't coming? I assume you got the same letter I did."

"I don't know what I was expecting." David thought about it. "Now that I've come all this way, I feel funny, like I don't belong here. Don't you? Whatever life Emily made for herself, I wasn't part of it."

Deacon's eyes roamed the room until settling on Nick. "On the other hand, these people weren't a part of her life with us. I don't think they even know."

"You talked to Nick, her husband?"

His friend ignored the question. "Which do you think was the real Emily?"

David shook his head, which hurt just thinking about it. He was having a hard time processing who he even was right now. "I need a smoke."

"Excellent idea."

They emerged in the dim parking lot.

Deacon lit a cigarette. "Is Angela coming?"

David leaned against the funeral home's brick wall and blew a stream of smoke. "I seriously doubt it."

"Why not?"

"She's angry."

Deacon snorted. "So some things don't change."

"Only she's a police detective now, so it's even scarier when she gets mad."

"I wonder what she made of Emily's letter."

"I know she's mad at Emily for doing what she did." David didn't want to talk about his big sister, with whom he rarely kept in touch. He gazed across the parking lot toward the distant red glow. "Jesus. Look at it. I hope it rains soon."

Deacon cast his own eyes toward the fire. "Two million acres going up this year, all thanks to climate change. The ol' Reverend was right. The world's coming to an end. Only it's happening so slowly, hardly anybody is noticing."

He didn't want to talk about the Reverend either. "So how are you, Deek? How's life been treating you?"

Deacon pursed his lips. "Uh, good, David. How about you?"

"I'm doing good. Real good."

They smoked in silence for a while, which suited David just fine. Nothing stirred among the cars parked in the dark lot. Deacon seemed to want to pick up where things left off years earlier. David was one bad vibe away from fleeing to his car. A little small talk wouldn't hurt. A little quiet.

His friend had never known how to take things slow. He seemed ready to talk everything out. He'd read Emily's letter and found some hidden meaning.

David gazed toward his car, which promised the safe routines of home.

A woman emerged from the gloom to pose with her hands on her hips. "You boys. I leave you alone for fifteen years, and look what you get up to."

▲   ▲   ▲

Beth Harris was still petite, though she'd filled out in womanhood, and her long, straight, sandy hair was pulled back in a bun instead of flowing free around her shoulders. Otherwise, the years had done little to age her pixie face.

David hugged her. "It's really nice to see you."

She patted his shoulder. "You were brave to come."

He released her, and she and Deacon regarded each other with goofy grins. They stepped into an embrace that was far friendlier than the one she'd given David.

Get a room, David heard his twelve-year-old self say.

At last, they let go, though the tension between them hung in the air.

"Look at you." She appraised Deacon. "Rock 'n' roll star."

"You'd never guess what put me on this path."

"We're going to talk," she said and turned to David. "But we're going to take it slow." She reached into her purse and produced a silver flask. "I brought a little bottled courage to guide us on the path."

David smiled as Beth handed it over. The strong scent alone braced him. Rum. The alcohol burned down his throat with a warm, fuzzy aftermath. He passed the flask to Deacon, who tossed his head back in a long swallow.

Beth shot David a questioning glance. "No Angela, huh?"

"Nope."

Deacon stared at the distant fire. "God, look at it now." The fiery glow shimmered and pulsed in a natural light show. "It reminds me...Listen. Can I tell you guys something about the last night at the mountain?"

Beth raised her hand. "Going slow, remember?"

Deacon shuddered and took another long swig. "Okay."

"So. Have either of you visited Emily yet?"

They shook their heads.

"Then we should tear off that Band-Aid first." Her large brown eyes flickered between them. "We can visit her together."

David produced his box of Marlboros. "I need a quiet moment. You guys go ahead."

"We have to say goodbye." Beth rested her hand on his arm. "Once you do, you'll take all that weight off your shoulders."

He put away his cigarettes. "All right."

They entered the funeral home and threaded the crowd toward the viewing room. David's heart crashed like a rock flung at a brick wall.

Beth slipped her hand into his. "I'm right here with you."

He answered with a vague nod. There was no controlling his legs anymore. He simply floated toward the casket. Emily lay with her hands clasped as if to hide where she'd parted the flesh of her arms with a razor.

Memories flashed across his vision, which fragmented into puzzle pieces. Emily sat next to him in a dark supply closet. Gripped his hand while his mother purified herself in the Temple. Said goodbye the day they left for separate foster homes and promised they'd be together again, as it was meant to be.

He groaned as Emily's corpse rematerialized before him. Sweat soaked through his dress shirt. He was shaking. Was going to be sick. The stress of revisiting the past. All the smoke in the atmosphere. Something he ate.

Beth guided him out the door into the open air. "You're having a panic attack."

David stood outside on trembling legs. His blood roared in his ears, his heart about to burst. His car seemed miles away. He spotted a row of camellias planted around the base of the funeral home and burrowed into them to sit on the mulch with his back against the rough wall.

"Look at me." Beth crouched to face him. "There's nothing to be afraid of. You're safe. Just breathe, okay? In through your nose for a few seconds, now out through your mouth, nice and slow. That's right. You've got it. It'll pass soon. I'll stay with you as long as you want me to."

David wiped cold sweat from his face. His tears were warm. "I'm stupid."

"No, you're not."

"I thought I was safe."

"You are safe."

He wagged his head. "All I did was find a bigger place to hide."

2

RUN

The orange U-Haul truck chewed long miles along the endless highway, bound for California from Idaho. The vehicle was a fifteen footer, the biggest vehicle David had ever ridden in. After sitting half the day in the middle seat between Mom and Angela, however, the novelty had worn off, and he was carsick and bored and worried about the future.

Mom tapped the steering wheel, singing along to a Christian radio station. She wore a T-shirt and jeans. Sweat glistened on her forehead despite the air-conditioning. She'd tied her hair into an austere ponytail. She shook her head as she drove past an exit leading to a small town.

"Another dead end," she said. "Dead and don't know it yet."

Mom talked a lot about the war that was coming. Eleven months earlier, terrorists flew planes into the World Trade Center. The coming war would be the big one, she said, and the start of even bigger wars to come. Millions would die, heralding a dark age leading up to the end of the world.

"Who's dead?" David said.

"Nobody, Davey." Her mouth formed a grim smile. "Right now, they're just sleeping. They'll wake up soon, you can count on that. They'll be wide awake when it all goes down."

When she talked about the apocalypse, she sounded strangely happy.

For David's nine-year-old brain, it was the stuff of nightmares. God loved him, and he was therefore safe, but he didn't like the idea of God hating everyone else.

Mom had told him the next time God destroyed the world, he'd do it with fire.

She nudged him with her elbow. "You ready for it, Davey?"

He shrugged. "I guess so."

"When Jesus comes, you have to be prepared."

"I'm ready." He liked this part. While God was scary, Jesus was kind. David prayed to him every night. No matter how much his parents fought, Jesus had kept him safe.

"Can I get an amen?"

David grinned. "Amen!"

"Praise God."

Angela sighed as she gazed out the window. "I don't see why we can't get ready in Twin Falls, where I have friends and a life."

"When are we going to see Dad again?" David said.

Mom's face turned dark with alarming suddenness. "Don't make me the bad guy for taking care of you the best way I can."

"I was happy," Angela said, leaving the rest unspoken. She believed Mom was taking care of herself. David had heard it all before.

Mom gripped the wheel hard enough to turn her knuckles white. "Your father's starting a new life. It's about time we did the same."

This was news to David. "What new life is Dad starting?"

Mom turned up the radio and didn't answer. In a gravelly voice, the radio preacher said the world's sinners didn't listen any better than Pharaoh did when Moses warned him, and for that they'd suffer, just as the Egyptians had.

Mom's smile returned full force as she said, "Amen."

Outside of Reno, the U-Haul pulled off the interstate. Mom drove toward a Chevron and maneuvered the truck next to the pumps. The hot, dry air reeked of gasoline fumes and desert dust.

She shoved her credit card into the slot and removed the pump handle. "They have restrooms here. Anybody who has to go, do it now, and don't be long."

Angela said, "Can I go in and buy a drink?"

Mom thrust her hand into the pocket of her jeans and handed over a few crumpled bills. "Nothing with caffeine. Get something for your brother too. And take the thermos and fill it up with water."

David climbed out of the cab, happy to stretch his legs. He'd been holding his bladder in check since Winnemucca. His body broke out in sweat from the day's scorching heat that waved above the asphalt. He followed Angela into the air-conditioned convenience store and stopped in front of the candy racks.

"You can't have any of that," his sister said.

"I can look."

"I'll buy you some peanuts."

"Okay." David walked off to find the restroom.

Inside, fluorescent lights glared across white tile. A man wearing a baseball cap and jeans stood shaving at the sink with the water running. The man's eyes flickered in his reflection to gaze back at him. He winked, then went back to pulling a razor over his lathered jaw.

David put his head down and entered one of the stalls. He locked the door and raised the seat. Outside the stall, the water turned off. The bathroom became dead quiet except for the man humming while he shaved.

He couldn't go. Peeing would make noise, which would call attention to himself. He waited for the man to either leave or turn the faucet on again, but neither happened. Pushing it out didn't work. It was stuck.

"Niagara Falls," he whispered.

Nothing.

He thought about what his best friend Ajay Patel might be doing back home. Ajay's parents stayed together and didn't fight. Nobody dragged him on a boring car ride to a whole other state to start a new life. He wondered if Ajay was one of the sinners who would be destroyed.

David wished he was Ajay.

Outside, the bathroom door cracked open. "Davey?"

Fear paralyzed him. The man could hear everything. A fierce heat blazed across David's face and chest, leaving him miserable and nauseous. His bladder about to burst. If he stayed quiet, they'd all go away, the man and his mom both.

"Davey, answer me right now."

"I'm peeing," he managed.

"Come on out. I'm not asking twice."

He zipped up and emerged weeping from the stall. The man turned toward him with a surprised expression, but the tears poured out in a flood, melting David's vision to a hot blur.

Mom grabbed him by the hand and yanked him through the store and back into the sun.

"I have to pee," he sobbed.

Angela chased after them. "What happened?"

Mom kept pulling. "You don't have to go."

"I do!"

"Then you'll have to hold it until Sacramento."

David wailed with fear and shame and self-pity. "I can't! Please! I'm sorry!"

"Just let him go to the bathroom, Mom," Angela said.

Mom stopped near the pumps and growled. "Lord, give me strength."

She led him around the back of the gas station, where he did his business against the white cinder-block wall, moaning with relief.

When he came back, Mom was pacing out in the desert scrub, smoking a cigarette and muttering to herself. David's shame deepened that he'd troubled her enough to smoke, something she shouldn't do. She'd changed so much in the last year, when she and Dad started fighting all the time.

He didn't want her to be upset. He didn't want her to smoke. Mom had become God and Jesus rolled into one, angry and loving in equal measure. He crossed the dirt lot and said, "I'm sorry, Mom. I'll be good."

She quit her pacing and forced a smile. "I know you will, Davey. You're a good boy in your heart."

He tramped back to the truck, where Angela waited.

She handed him a bag of peanuts and a cold can of ginger ale. "You okay?"

"Yeah."

His sister glared across the lot toward their mother. "She shouldn't get so mad. It wasn't your fault."

David flinched. "It was."

"Hey. Hey, stupid."

"I'm not answering you because I'm not stupid."

She cupped his chin. "Next time you have a problem you can't handle, you come to me, okay? You're too little to take on everything."

Before his parents' breakup, David would have yelled back at her that he wasn't little and that she wasn't the boss of him. Now he accepted her comfort with a grateful nod while he chewed his peanuts into a dry paste.

David awoke in the parking lot of a Super 8 motel.

"Wait here," Mom said and got out.

Wiping drool from his mouth, he looked around at cars and asphalt lit by the glow of pole lights. "Where are we?"

"Sacramento." Angela sighed. "God, this really and truly sucks."

He stretched. "I'm hungry. What time is it?"

"Just hang tight."

"Do you think there will be kids there? Where we're going?"

"It'll be like going to church every day. It's all Mom cares about now."

"Sunday school can be fun sometimes."

"Yippee."

The truck door creaked open, and Mom leaned inside. "We're checked in. Let's eat some supper before we head up to the room."

She led them across the street to a bright Denny's. The host got them seated in a booth and passed out menus and crayons.

David opened his kid's menu and started coloring the woolly mammoth from *Ice Age*. "Can I have the chicken tenders and fries, Mom?"

"Spaghetti for me," Angela said. "And lemonade."

"Oh, me too, please."

"You got it." Mom smiled at them. "Look at us, having an adventure."

"Can you tell us about this place we're going now?" Angela asked.

"It's a community near Tehachapi. They call themselves the Family of the Living Spirit. They're very selective about who they let in. I sent a letter to Reverend Peale, and he wrote back personally to invite us to join."

David chewed on the word in his mind. *Tehachapi*. Mysterious and old. He pictured buffalo and little tendrils of smoke wisping above tepees.

"Where is this place?" Angela said.

"South east of Bakersfield. Not too far from Los Angeles. They live a pure life there, simple and close to God."

"God kills people," David blurted.

The smile wavered. "Not us, Davey."

"Angela said we'll have to go to church all the time."

His sister kicked him under the table, but he ignored her. She *did* say it.

"We're going to live off the land," Mom said. "You can grow anything in the Cummings Valley, year round. Lettuce, tomatoes, herbs, spinach. The weather is always gorgeous. It's a wonderful place for children to grow up."

David wrinkled his nose. "Spinach?"

"Why is Tehachapi better than Twin Falls?" Angela said.

"The people," Mom answered. "Everybody at the community lives in harmony with each other and God. I want to be surrounded by people who love me no matter what and won't hurt me just because they can."

"Sounds like the life I had back home," his sister muttered. "Minus the part where we have to grow our own food."

The server arrived to take their order. While Angela slouched in moody silence, Mom ordered their suppers with a bright smile. David hoped she'd forget what Angela said and remain in a good mood.

After the woman left, the smile vanished. "Your life wasn't as great as you think it was. The world is chock-full of people who'll try to take everything from you. They say they love you, but they only love what you can do for them."

"You don't know my friends. And you don't know these people either."

"The Reverend Peale's community doesn't just talk the talk," Mom said. "They live spiritual lives in accord with God's laws. Every day is planned out for them, they know exactly what comes next, and they want for nothing. We'll be happy there. The wilderness will be the safest place to be when it all goes down. In any case, a little hard work in fresh air and a little less TV will do you a world of wonder, Miss Angela."

His sister slouched even further in her seat, quietly fuming.

"Why does God want to kill everybody?" David asked.

"He doesn't. Men will destroy the world with their greed and sin. The end will be a time of tribulation and testing."

"He can stop it, though, right? Why doesn't he?"

"So Jesus can return to his chosen people in all his glory."

Put another way, if everyone was good, Jesus wouldn't come back, though Jesus coming back was what God promised and Mom wanted.

He frowned. "Okay."

"Don't think too hard about it," Mom said. "Feel its truth in your heart."

The truth was he depended on his mother for everything, and God and Jesus made her happy. As long as they did, he'd love them too. And if he was good enough, maybe God would leave the world alone.

In the blazing heat of day, Mom pulled off the road and parked in the shade of a stand of blue oaks. She unfolded her road map and scrutinized the markings she'd made on it.

"I think we passed the turnoff," she said.

She frowned at her children as if getting lost was their fault. The black discs of her sunglasses covered her eyes. David didn't like when she wore sunglasses. Whenever she did, he never knew which mom he was going to get.

"So let's go back and find the turn," Angela said.

The U-Haul growled as Mom yanked the wheel and nudged the gas pedal. "We can't be late. They gave us a very specific time we should come."

"Why can't we be a little late?"

"Because," Mom grated, "they have a small community that is very picky about who they invite to join, and I want to give them enough respect to show up on time. Like you should give your mother respect."

"Respect goes both ways."

She regarded Angela from behind her sunglasses. "Respect starts with you, Miss Angela, and any respect you receive in return is earned. So mind your manners when we get there. We'll be on probation for the first six months. If that mouth of yours gets us thrown out—"

Angela glared out the window. "I don't care if—"

"We'll be there on time, Mom," David said.

"From your lips to God's ears, Davey—aha! Here's the turn."

The dirt road cut through woodland. Nobody lived here except the Family, far from civilization. Mom had said they were going into the wilderness, and she wasn't kidding. The U-Haul's tires crunched stones and banged across ruts.

The drive went on and on, taking him farther from everything he knew and closer to a new life among strangers. Nothing but the dark trees and the dirt road. David shrank in his seat. He imagined himself caught in a steel trap, unable to move until the hunters arrived.

At last, the trees opened to broad fields on which green plants grew from dark soil. Men and women worked the rows with baskets, harvesting vegetables. Beyond, David glimpsed a cluster of white buildings. The one with the tall steeple, he guessed, was their church.

"Oh, my Lord," she said. "It's like Eden. I can't believe we're here."

He squinted, trying to view it as she did and with the same excitement. It was pretty cool, he guessed, but nothing special. All he saw was a bunch of people farming. No children. Who were they? What was this place?

"Oh, no," Angela said. "I don't like this. Mom, let's go. Please."

"Where?"

"Anywhere! Back home!"

"Angela, do you believe in God?"

"You know I do, but—"

"Try to remember before you were born."

"I can't."

"Do you think that's what it's like when you die?"

"No, but I was—"

Mom parked the truck on a patch of gravel in front of the church and turned to her daughter, her face fierce and rigid. "God loves you and wants you to go to Heaven. All he asks in return is that you live by certain rules to prove you're worthy of it. The choice is yours. You can either go to Heaven or Hell. Forever and ever. Right now, your life is writing a check that your soul will have to cash. Do you think you should learn the rules and abide by them, or take your chances?"

Arms crossed, Angela glared out the window.

"These people have the best life insurance policy in the universe, and they're paying attention to the fine print." Mom turned to smile at the church, where a woman waited. "Stay here until I come back."

She got out of the truck and closed the door with a loud thud.

"Maybe she's right," David said.

"Shut up, stupid," Angela snarled. "She's just repeating stuff she read online."

"Well, God makes her happy. Maybe we'll be happy too."

He wanted to believe it. He had no choice.

The woman hugged his mother, who laughed and burst into tears at the same time. Then the woman held out her hand. Mom hesitated before digging into the pocket of her jeans. She produced her cigarette pack and handed it over.

Angela watched her mother surrender her habit in an instant. "I guess it depends," she said carefully, "on what the rules are, and what happens when you break them."

Through the dusty windshield, David watched men and women stream out of the fields to gather around. Mom's entrance to the community had been timed with the end of the workday, so they could give her a warm Christian greeting. The men all had short hair and simple farming clothes, while the women wore long dresses. All had broad-brimmed hats or scarves on their heads.

"I'm starting to think we joined the Amish," Angela said.

David let out a nervous chuckle, though he had no idea who the Amish were.

With warm smiles, the people crowded around Mom and bowed their heads as if praying. Those closest to her laid their hands on the top of her head.

"Thank you, Jesus!" Mom started to cry, her racking sobs punctuated by bursts of laughter. "I'm home!"

"Oh, Mom." Angela sighed with something like pity and nudged David. "Hey. I'm pretty sick of this truck. You want to have a look around?"

Staring at Mom with wide-eyed dread, David shook his head, too afraid to move. Then Angela grabbed his hand and pulled him out of the cab.

On the ground, he couldn't see anything except the backs of adults crowding around his mother. She bawled at the top of her lungs over the rumble of prayer.

He broke away from Angela and ran.

His legs took him toward the trees, but the woods struck him as dark and ominous and all too easy to get lost in. He veered into the church and stood panting among the simple oak pews. His eyes roamed across the windows, altar, organ, pulpit, choir seating, and a massive carved wood dove mounted on the wall behind them. Nowhere to hide. A door beckoned to him. He raced to it.

In the hallway beyond, David found an office and bathroom. The last door revealed a supply closet. He stepped inside and slammed the door and sat on the floor in the dark. The scent of dust and cleaners hung in the air.

Safe at last. But lonely. All he had to do was wait.

Any minute now, Mom would come and pick him up the way she used to when he was smaller. She'd tell him everything was going to be okay, and he'd believe it. In her warm arms, he'd have unconditional love and real safety. Then they could leave and go back home.

His heart sank with each passing moment as she didn't show.

Noise outside, the voices of children.

"We shouldn't be back here," a kid said. "We could get in trouble."

"I saw him go into the church." That was Angela talking. "He didn't come back out, so he must be here somewhere."

"Check the bathroom. Maybe nature called."

"I know where I'd hide if I was scared," another voice said.

David flinched as the closet door opened. Framed in light, a girl stood in the doorway, hands planted on her hips. His eyes adjusted to focus on her warm smile.

"Hi, Davey," she said. "I'm Emily."

3

MOURN

Stained-glass windows washed the funeral home's chapel in soft morning light. Sitting on a cushioned pew, David listened to the pastor assure Emily's family that her soul was bound for the afterlife. Wearing a wide-brimmed black hat, Beth sat between him and Deacon, holding their hands. Her fingers felt cold in his; the air-conditioning was freezing.

The pastor was a spindly, gray-haired woman in bright white vestments. She stood earnest and consoling behind the pulpit. "Every faith in the world attests to life after death," she said. "We don't know what the afterlife is like, but we have our hope and belief it is one of peace and reuniting with loved ones."

After spending part of his childhood in the Family of the Living Spirit, David found the sermon soothingly boring, the religious staging comfortably antiseptic. At the Temple, the Reverend's sole concession to clerical costume had been a black suit jacket worn over a gray or black T-shirt. He'd bound across the stage powered by electric faith, preaching straight to the heart about glory and fire. The congregants

would wave their hands and little black Bibles and yell *Amen!*
Seized by the Spirit, they'd rave and speak in tongues.

Right now, boring was okay. Boring suited David just fine.

"For Emily, her journey is beginning," the pastor said.
"For us, there is only the loss of her passing. This loss hurts
because her life touched the life of every one of us here,
either in some small way or by completely transforming it."

He tried to focus on the woman's words, but the platitudes
turned to mush in his brain. Instead, his mind flashed to last
night's dream as he'd tossed and turned in his hotel bed.

The nightmares had stopped at some point in his early
twenties, and he hadn't dreamed of the Family in years. Last
night, he did—a new dream this time, however, not one of
the recurring horrors that once plagued him in the dark.

In this dream, he roamed through the windy night around
the base of Red Peak. A black cross burned energetically on
its summit. David wanted to climb to the top but couldn't
find the path.

In the morning, he'd woken up sweating, anxious, frustrated.
After checking out of the hotel, he found a hawk perched on
the hood of his car, a refugee of the great fire still burning in
the east. The hawk studied him before spreading its wings and
soaring across the parking lot. Smoke blanketed the morning
sky in a gloomy yellowish overcast that set David coughing.

The memory faded to an unsettling murmur in the back
of his mind. Deacon had let go of Beth's hand and now
traced a circle on her knee. The tattoos covering his arms
were mostly words, phrases in Latin and what appeared to be
ancient Greek. A flaming cross decorated his forearm, as if
to remind himself daily of things David had spent his entire
adult life trying to forget.

"As night follows day, death follows life," the pastor said.

"We are all leaves on the Tree of Life, which replenish each year. We who remain can mark this moment by loving one another and doing our own part to make the Tree stronger."

Beth brushed away Deacon's exploring fingers and dabbed a tear with a tissue. "She was strong."

David squeezed her hand. Yes, Emily was. She'd been the calm center of his world at the commune and later at the institution where Dr. Klein had treated them. Without Emily, their scattered little tree was even weaker.

Some fundamental stress had built up in her over the years, or she'd just snapped one day. If she hadn't been strong enough to fight it, whatever *it* was, then quite possibly none of them were.

"May the Lord bless you and keep you," the pastor said. "May the Lord make his face shine upon you and be gracious unto you. May the Lord lift up his countenance upon you and give you peace. Amen."

While the mourners prayed, David again drifted into the past.

He didn't know the name of the place where the adults had brought him, which he'd guessed was some kind of hospital. Since the sheriff's deputy led him out of the Temple, David's world had been a blur of strange people asking him questions and shuttling him from place to place. Now he wore pajamas all day and took a pill called Prozac and had to talk to a man named Dr. Klein about how he was feeling.

He hadn't seen his sister and friends since they'd arrived here, but today, the psychiatrist had good news. They were all allowed to go to the rec room. A large space with Ping-Pong tables, board games, and the same white walls. There, he found Angela sitting at a table, glowering over a puzzle.

Hunching his shoulders to make himself as small as possible, David sat in the opposite chair. There were other people in the room, all teenagers in pajamas except for a big woman wearing a uniform. He wanted his sister to hug him and tell him everything was going to be okay.

He scanned the room one last time for threats. "Hi."

Angela didn't respond as she fitted a piece. When finished, the puzzle would make a picture of dogs playing on a beach as if they were people.

He leaned in to murmur, "Are you okay?"

Angela spun another piece in her fingers, her face a mask of frustration. "I don't know who to be mad at. Maybe it's you."

David sank even lower. "Please don't be mad at me."

Emily, Deacon, and Beth entered the room. David smiled at them and ventured a wave. They pulled up chairs around the table.

"They think we're crazy," Beth said. "Like what happened is our fault."

David struggled to hold back a surge of tears, another round in a losing battle he'd been fighting ever since the police officers had brought him here. "I'm just twelve. I didn't do anything wrong."

Angela glared at him. "You didn't?"

"You didn't," Deacon assured him. "None of us did. We're alive, that's all."

"We aren't supposed to be," Emily said.

"The world isn't supposed to be here either," Deacon pointed out.

"Nobody died," David said. "They're all in a different hospital."

His friends said nothing, pretending to be interested in

Angela's puzzle. Beth picked up a piece and pressed it into its proper place.

"When I came out of my hiding spot," he added, "everybody was gone."

Beth's hand froze as she reached for another piece. "They…"

"You don't know anything, *Dave*," Angela growled. "You were *hiding*."

"I was scared."

"I didn't see much either," Emily said. "My mom locked me in a storage shed. I could only see outside through gaps in the boards. Just…"

Angela eyed her. "Just what? What did you see?"

"I don't know. Nothing."

Beth shuddered. The puzzle piece she was holding dropped to the tabletop, seemingly forgotten. "They…Everybody's dead."

"That's not true," David said.

"I was with Mom when *she* died," Angela said. "Where were you again?"

"You're a liar!" He leaped to his feet. The chair tilted to crash against the floor. "She's not dead! Stop saying everybody's dead and that it's my fault!"

Across the room, the other kids cringed or paced. The nurse locked eyes with his. Heat bloomed in his cheeks.

"Sorry," David said.

"Do you need a time-out?" the woman said.

"I'll be good." He sat down, shivering.

Emily wrapped her arms around him. He gaped at the puzzle, seeing not the materializing picture but the empty spaces that riddled it.

"If they're gone, it's not your fault," she murmured. "If

they're gone, they're across the black sea now. They're with the Spirit."

"I want my mom." He covered his face and wept. "I want to go home."

Angela said, "If they're with God, then maybe that's who we should be mad at."

The remainder of the funeral service saw a parade of Emily's family and friends stand behind the pulpit to share stories about her. David listened with interest, learning about the life she'd led after leaving the institution. Otherwise, he stayed seated, doubting they wanted to hear his own stories. When her husband, Nick, went up to talk about how important she'd been to him and their children, the man broke down so completely he had to be escorted back to his seat, a heartbreaking sight. The mourners sang a final hymn, and the pastor turned over Emily's soul to God.

After the service was over, the organ played, family members carried her casket to the waiting hearse, and David needed a stiff drink.

Outside, Beth coughed on the smoky air. "I'll drive us to the cemetery."

David reached her Mercedes first and climbed into the front passenger seat. "Do you still have that flask?"

Beth started the car but let it idle to allow the other mourners to leave the parking lot first. "In my purse."

He unscrewed the cap and took a long belt before passing it to Deacon.

"I still don't understand." His friend tilted his head back to drink and sighed. "Why she did it."

"She was the last person I ever would have expected to do it," Beth said. "Back when we knew her, nothing ever seemed to get her down. In her new life, she was surrounded by people who loved her. She volunteered for groups helping battered women and abused children. She had plenty to live for."

"Maybe the reason is something ordinary. Like she found out she had cancer, or her husband was abusing her."

"I don't think so. Whatever got her, it started in her core. The anniversary of the Medford Mystery is coming up in just a few weeks, and this year is a big one. Fifteen years. I think that's significant. People living with trauma often have what's called an anniversary reaction."

David sighed. "Can we do this later? Just drive."

"We took it slow for you," Beth said. "Now we're going to talk."

He gripped his head in his hands. "What difference will it make?"

"If you don't like us talking, then don't listen," Deacon said. "And if you didn't want to talk, why did you take the front seat next to Beth?"

"Because children sit in the back," David answered. "Plus, I didn't want us getting in an accident because you two were making out."

He wanted to say a lot more about what he thought of Deacon fooling around during the chapel service, but he didn't. In fact, he regretted what he'd already said as soon as the words flew from his mouth. But his friends only laughed.

"Sorry, that was rude," he said anyway, as if they'd scolded him.

"No, I loved it." Deacon grinned. "It's nice to see the old Dave again."

Outside, it was raining ash. Beth sprayed her windshield with fluid and turned on the wipers, producing a gray smear.

Then she shifted and backed into the parking lot before driving off toward the funeral. "Boys, we're getting off track again. I assume you both got a letter, and that's why you're here?"

" 'Dear Deacon, I'm sorry. I couldn't fight it anymore.' "

"Same here. David?"

"About the same," David said.

"What was different about yours?"

He tossed his hands. "For God's sake."

"Beth is a psychologist," Deacon said, adding, "which I hope is working."

Beth shot a look at him in her rearview. "What do you mean?"

"Oh, you know what they say. The most messed-up people become psychologists so they can find out what's wrong with themselves."

Beth chuckled. "I'm the sanest person in the world, Deek." She glanced at David. "Come on, tell us."

"I hope you're not charging me by the hour." He sighed. "She said she loved me. That's the only difference."

Beth nodded as if she'd expected this. "She always did."

"There wasn't any way." He crossed his arms and gazed out the window at the flakes of ash fluttering out of the gray sky. "What happened isn't my fault."

"Of course it isn't," she agreed. "But there might have been a way."

David said, "I wanted to put everything behind me."

His words hung in the air like a confession. He'd sworn to reunite with Emily after they left the foster system but had never made any real effort. Thanks to Dr. Klein's therapy, he'd woken up a little stronger each day, a little more in control. A part of him understood that if he saw Emily again, she would bring the past with her, which might drag him back down into the dark place. The hardest thing about escaping a cult wasn't leaving but making sure it had left *you*.

Whenever he thought about finding Emily or any of the other survivors, his mind put up one roadblock after another. *Tomorrow* became *I'll do it after I'm settled in my new job* became *I really should do that sometime*. He was busy, always busy, with too much going on to commit to something as significant as reconnecting, and the more time passed, the more daunting it became until he'd stopped thinking about it altogether.

Then Emily died to remind him that besides Angela, Claire, and his children, these people remained the closest thing to family he had left.

Hot, dry winds blew the ash of ancient forests across the cemetery as Emily's body descended into the ground. The sun was a yellowish disc in the gray sky.

A reception at a local restaurant had been scheduled to follow the funeral. A few more hours, and David could go home.

He already had his exit planned out. He'd tell Beth and Deacon this was a sign they should stay in each other's lives. He'd promise to keep in touch and propose ways they could do it, perhaps an annual retreat somewhere to talk and catch up. Then he'd stop thinking about it.

Old wounds never really healed. They opened again at the slightest cut. He'd never even told Claire about his years with the Family of the Living Spirit. How could he tell her about the nightmare he'd survived? Harder still would be explaining the joys. The raw happiness he'd experienced before it all went bad. How even now, after all these years, he still missed the Family. People only knew the stories about the murders, mass suicide, mutilations, and how everyone disappeared. They didn't know that before Red Peak, the Family was a happy, safe community of people who'd simply wanted God in their lives every day, not just on Sundays.

Shortly after David had left the foster system, he'd met Claire in a trauma counseling group. She'd shared her story about her parents' divorce and how her stepfather sexually abused her as a child. David told them that his parents had divorced due to his father's infidelity, and his mother had moved them to another state to join a church, where he'd suffered a different type of abuse. Not a full description of the disease, but the symptoms were the same.

Over coffee, he and Claire discovered they both felt out of control, anxious, worthless, easily startled, and plagued by depression. Both were workaholics and prone to addictive behaviors. He couldn't believe this intelligent and stunning woman was spending time with him. They saw themselves in such a negative light that they were surprised at their mutual attraction. A relationship with another person living with post-traumatic stress disorder presented obvious risks, but at least they understood each other's demons.

Six months later, they were married. They didn't know it at the time, but Alyssa, their daughter, was already on the way.

At the time, he'd started work as part of a security team hired by a cult deprogrammer operating in San Francisco. The deprogrammer achieved positive results with two out of three cultists, but the methods troubled David. Civil rights issues aside, he risked arrest for kidnapping. He worried whether the ones they saved were true successes, whether they came away from the experience possessing real freedom of choice. And for every cult member they lost, their relations with their family—the only lifeline they had to return to a life over which they had control—was severely damaged.

Claire had wondered why he didn't just talk to them. For David, the answer was the same as to why you couldn't reason a person out of a severe mental illness. Groups that practiced mind-control techniques rewired brains. They distorted reality. If a man thought he was Jesus, a simple solution seemed to be to quiz him on the Bible and then present his wrong answers to show him he was not in fact Jesus. But the man would simply answer, *You have the wrong Bible.* The same way the diehards in the doomsday cults doubled down on their belief every time their leader screwed up the date of the apocalypse.

No, one couldn't simply reason with them.

Or perhaps one might, with the right approach. David began to seek out people calling themselves exit counselors to learn their methods. Several years later, he started his practice. After a few false starts and speed bumps, he achieved his first big successes, recommending deprogramming to his clients as a last resort if exit counseling failed. Everything in his life finally started to come together. Alyssa had already been born, followed by Dexter, and when he wasn't working, David devoted time and energy to provide as loving and warm a home as he was able, a safe cocoon armored against the horrors of the world he knew too well.

Driving through a smoky haze, they agreed to skip the reception and pulled into a restaurant parking lot. Most people were staying home because of the fire and the unhealthy air, and David and his friends about had the place to themselves.

After ordering lunch, Beth removed her hat and said, "I guess that's it. What are you boys doing after this? What's next in life?"

"My band has a gig tomorrow night," Deacon said. "Back in LA."

"It's wild you're like this rock star now. Not at all surprising, though."

"Rock, sure. Star, meh. Our fan base is devoted but small." He trembled with restless leg syndrome, contrasting against Beth's poised calm.

She gave him a practiced smile. "What about you, David?"

David worried the cloth napkin from his place setting, still a little anxious himself. "I'm going to return to my family and get ready for my next client."

"You convince people to leave cults," Beth said.

"Every single one of them, if I can. I practice exit counseling, though, not deprogramming."

"I'm aware of the difference. It's a perfect job for you."

"Thanks." David smiled and let go of the napkin. This was the conversation he'd imagined having with them, small talk and catching up and a little banter. "How about you? What's next?"

"First, a long bath. After that, there are plenty of heads to shrink. Humanity is a spectrum disorder."

Deacon chuckled. "I like that. What's it mean?"

"It means very few of us are playing with a completely full deck, though there's a huge variation in the number of cards each of us are dealt," she explained. "That's how you end up trusting the pilot flying the jumbo jet you're on, while he thinks the moon landing was faked and plays lucky lottery numbers recalled from dreams. If delusions become destructive, that's where I come in."

The server returned with a glass of wine for Beth and coffee for the men. Deacon drank it black and bitter. David poured milk and sugar into his and stirred, already making mental notes of what he needed to do when he got home.

He'd mowed the lawn before he left, but the flower beds required weeding. He wanted to expand his backyard garden. A few unpaid bills waited on his desk. He had to practice the talk he was scheduled to give at the conference after the weekend and prepare for his next counseling session, a young man in a group called The Restoration, another lost soul needing salvation.

He sipped the hot coffee and longed to get back to these problems. The only thing better than leaving a routine was returning to it. Juggling the demands of work and children would snap him out of this anxious sense of hanging suspended between worlds. Having too much to do had always been a good way to avoid thinking about what had been done to him.

When he looked up, his friends stared at him. "What?"

"I asked you what you saw that last night," Beth said.

Far away, a red glow outlined the crown of Red Peak.

Gaunt from hunger and hard labor and pain, the congregation shambled out of the darkness for their final act of worship . . .

David winced at this flashback, which appeared as sudden and real as if he'd physically transported to the past. "I'll tell you the same thing I told you at the mental hospital. I didn't see a damn thing. When everybody went to the Temple, I hid in the supply closet. I didn't come out until the sheriff's deputy found me."

"I saw something," Deacon said.

"Please." Back when they were institutionalized, David had heard the horrifying story of what happened to Wyatt and had no wish to ever hear it again. "You don't have to say it. I remember."

"You didn't hear everything, David. I never told Dr. Klein what I saw because I thought if I did, he'd never let me out of that place. I never told you either."

"All right. What?"

"When the end came, when everybody was dead? I saw—" His face pale and taut, he hesitated. "I saw a pillar of fire on the mountain, shooting straight up into the sky."

David recoiled. "What the hell?"

"That's incredible," Beth said.

"To put it mildly!"

"Incredible because Emily saw it too," she clarified. "A fire that went all the way up into the air. She told me about it at the hospital but swore me to silence."

"She never told me about it," David said.

"You were already upset enough. She didn't want to make it worse."

Deacon nodded. "All the way up to the sky. Glowing red just like that forest fire out there. And that horn. It was so loud."

She shivered. "The horn I remember. And…"

"What?"

"Nothing," she said. "It's just a fragment, like a dream. It's crazy."

"Crazier than a pillar of fire?"

David shook his head. "The light was playing tricks on you or something. The cross on the mountain was on fire, remember? Beth, I'm surprised at you. Surely, you know what Occam's razor is and how it works."

"Occam what?" said Deacon.

Beth filled him in. "Occam's razor. Another way of saying the simplest explanation is almost always true."

"You suffered a visual and auditory hallucination," David went on. "Guys, I hate to break this to you, but whatever the Family was at one time, it turned into a cult at Red Peak. We were all brainwashed."

"It doesn't explain how me and Emily had the exact same hallucination," Deacon said.

"Of course it does. On the last day, Reverend Peale said we weren't waiting for paradise, it was waiting for us. And once everybody shed their mortal coil, as he put it so quaintly, we'd all beam up to paradise. The terrible things you saw, I can't even imagine. These are extremely traumatic memories. The brain reacts in strange ways to trauma, especially a child's mind."

"He's right about that," Beth conceded. "But...I don't know."

"Okay, fine," said Deacon. "Then where did the bodies go? How do you explain that?"

When the sheriff's deputy took him by the hand and led him out of the shattered Temple, only bloodstains remained on the wrecked pews and mountain slopes. Not a single body was ever recovered, and what happened in the desert near a little nowhere town called Medford became forever infamous as the Medford Mystery, the subject of *Unexplained Mysteries*–style documentary shows.

"Somebody had to have taken them and buried them in the mountains," David said.

Deacon laughed. "You actually think somebody found and moved over a hundred bodies in the dark and got them all out of there in just one night." He snorted. "And I'm the one who's hallucinating."

"I agree that part is a mystery."

"Occam's razor," Beth said. "The simplest explanation is usually true."

"I see you have a theory," David said.

"More like playing devil's advocate. Let's say the Reverend was right."

"A psychologist saying this." David sputtered in disbelief. "You've completely lost it. You know that, right?"

"I'm not saying what I believe," Beth said. "Though yes, one might, as you put it, *lose it* if one accepted it as truth."

Deacon stiffened in his seat. "Oh, you think..."

"Emily was always a true believer. I think she couldn't handle the contradiction of loving a God who would do this to his followers, even with paradise as the reward."

"Or maybe she thought she was fulfilling the deal the Rev made," Deacon said. "The covenant he always talked about. She wanted to cross the black sea."

The black sea. David shuddered. A term Jeremiah Peale started using after the Family moved to Red Peak in 2005.

"Yes," Beth said. "That works too."

"Stop," David said. "Just stop. Please. Let her go and rest in peace."

The server approached with their lunches and delivered them with brisk efficiency, as the tension at the table was obvious. David stared bleakly at his grilled chicken salad and wondered if he was going to be attending two more funerals soon. His friends had taken a long dive off the deep end.

One thing bothered him, though. Safe in his hiding place, he hadn't seen any light show on the mountain, but he remembered hearing the rumbling blast, which rent the air like the horn of a giant ram. The noise had been so powerful, he'd felt it vibrating through his chest and heard the windows shivering in the panes, followed by a loud series of bangs, the pews being thrown around. Later, he'd assumed it was an earthquake, this being California, but the timing was a bizarre coincidence.

A coincidence, yes. Nothing more.

Even if the impossible were true, it didn't matter to him anyway, not anymore.

4

CREATE

In the funeral home parking lot, the three childhood friends hugged.

Deacon Price was glad it was over. Burying Emily had left his soul raw, as if a cheese grater had run over it. His friends didn't understand that when he was flirty or insensitive or cracking jokes at inappropriate times, he was holding back a scream.

Now he couldn't wait to turn that shriek into music.

He offered David a lopsided grin. "Stay in touch, okay?"

"I was thinking we should try to meet up at least once a year. I'll drag Angela along next time."

"Sure thing." Deacon knew his friend was full of it.

Beth fished in her purse and handed David a card. "If you can't see us socially, see me professionally. If you ever need to."

David smiled as he got into his car. "I've gotten very good at taking care of myself. But thanks."

Deacon waved him out of sight, something inside him

breaking. They'd once been best friends. He was glad the reunion was over, but a part of him wanted it to never end.

"Are you okay?" Beth said.

He appraised her. God, she was beautiful. Still Beth, but now all grown up. The same large dark eyes a boy could fall into. So much stronger now. And smart as hell. Alone of the survivors, she'd been able to go on to college, all the way to a doctorate in clinical psychology.

"You're pretty awesome," Deacon said. "How is it you never got married?"

She pursed her lips. "That's not a polite question, you know."

"I'm just surprised."

She gestured to the gray snow fluttering around them. "If you'd like to keep talking, can we get out of this?"

He pointed out his battered Honda Civic coated in ash as fine as powdered sugar. "We could hop in Honey for a bit."

Beth scrutinized his car, no doubt imagining grimy floors and seats covered in rock band detritus, which wasn't far from the truth.

"Mine's closer," she said.

Deacon climbed into the immaculate interior of her Mercedes. *You could eat off her seats,* he mused, *while mine look half-eaten.*

She gazed through the dusted windshield at the funeral home. "Do you think Emily is in a better place?"

"Sure. Why not."

"That's not very convincing."

"You heard the pastor. We really have no idea what comes after, so yeah, it'd be great. You want me to believe anything else, forget it. That's how you end up with people singing hymns one minute and drinking Kool-Aid the next."

Or in the Family's case, communion wine mixed with cyanide, but not far from the method the Peoples Temple had used to kill themselves in Guyana back in the '70s. He glanced down at a Latin proverb tattooed on his arm: *A diabolo, qui est simia dei*. Rough translation: Where God has a church, the Devil has a chapel.

"I struggle with it myself," she said. "Being raised a believer while seeing what taking belief to its limit did to the Family."

"So." He smiled.

"What?"

"Why didn't you ever get married? I don't see a ring."

She sighed. "Because nothing lasts."

His heart thudded now, pounding pure bass in his ears. *Beautiful.* "Some things do. Some things last a lifetime."

He leaned in to kiss her, and she returned it in a surprising burst of eagerness, devouring him. She tasted like wine and peppermint. His restless mind zeroed out into the strange nothingness one finds at the dead center of a startling noise. They broke for air, and he dove into her slim, soft neck, sucking and biting.

Beth moaned and gave him a gentle push back toward his side of the car. "Not the time or place." She reached into her purse and produced a business card, onto which she wrote something.

Deacon took it. "Social or professional?"

"That remains to be seen." She smiled. "I checked out some of your songs on YouTube. They're dark as hell. I could give you a couple months of therapy on 'Shadow Boxer' alone."

He chuckled. "Music is my therapy." He didn't add that this was close to being the literal truth. His interest in songwriting had started a long time ago, an offshoot of Dr. Klein's poetry therapy.

Then he checked the card, on which she'd scribbled an address. An invitation? The heartbreak of another separation didn't have to last.

"Santa Barbara," he said. "That isn't too far. You should come down and catch one of my shows."

"Actually, I was thinking of something else. An expedition."

"This sounds intriguing."

"We should go back. To Red Peak. It's been fifteen years. I'd like to see the place again for myself. See if anything surfaces that I don't remember, or don't *want* to remember."

"You want to see if we hear the same voice the Reverend did. Like Angela wanted us to do—remember that trip she was on for a while?"

She shook her head. "David was right about the hallucinations. He's wrong, though, about suppressing his feelings. I'm thinking of the trip as therapeutic. For him, in particular. Confront the source of our trauma, clarify our memory in safety, and put it behind us forever. We should all go together."

"You really do like to tear off the Band-Aid. Hell, lady, there's only one answer I can give. Fucking yes."

"I thought you might think it was stupid or weird. It's been so long."

"It's pure genius. It may just be us, though. David wants to pretend the whole thing never happened. As for Angela, who knows. It's been a long time since she wanted to go back. Knowing her, she'll yell at us over the phone and hang up."

"Use that card. Personal or professional, your choice."

Beth turned the ignition, and her Mercedes purred to life. "And give the trip some thought. I think it might be good for you."

Deacon winced at the idea of them parting. He'd only just found her again. He could stay in this car and talk all day and night. But he had a gig to get back to, and she had a life.

He swallowed hard. "It was really, really nice seeing you again."

Beth leaned in to plant a soft kiss on his cheek. "Take care of yourself, Deek."

She drove away, taking his breath with her as the heartbreak returned full force.

Sad, realizing the best years of your life happened before you turned fifteen, that everything after felt fake, one scene after another in a long dream.

So good too, like a long, excruciating tattoo on the soft flesh covering the jugular, where a single flinch could ruin the permanent mark.

Buzzing with ideas, Deacon raced to Honey and got in. The seat behind the wheel, its fabric ripped with bulging yellow foam, welcomed him with a sense of home, which made sense for a man who had none.

A long drive awaited him.

First, he had to write these feelings down.

He caught another Latin proverb on his arm: *Abyssus abyssum invocat.* Deep calls to deep. In the Bible, *deep* meant the Word. The Living Spirit.

Under that, NO PAIN NO GAIN.

"Amen, motherfucker," Deacon said.

He reached under his seat, his hand brushing against empties and ancient McDonald's wrappers, and gripped his songbook, a black faceless thing he poured his howling soul into when the muse struck. Next he thrust his hand in the glove compartment for a pen, which turned out to be dry. He flung it away and got another, a flowing black marker whose scrawl would bleed through the page.

Deacon wanted to write a song. No, make that an album. Actually a concept album, a rock opera in which he would reveal to the world the beauty and horror of the Family of the Living Spirit. *The Gospel of Deacon*. Better yet, *The Gospel of the Sad Cat*, an homage to Cats Are Sad, the name of his band.

In this opus, he'd finally share the thing that for fifteen years had lived under his skin. Share his pain in a way that weeviled into his listeners' flesh, like an auditory tattoo or a new type of STD. By the time they finished listening to his story, they'd never forget it, and some might even join a cult themselves.

Part of him believed.

David could deny all he wanted, while Beth wanted to have it both ways by attributing the phenomenon to a glitch of mental perception. Barking up opposite trees, and both of them were wrong.

Deacon believed *something* had happened up on that monolith, something that defied rational explanation.

The Gospel of the Sad Cat would be his way of starting a dialogue.

He was due in LA in a couple of hours. The band was getting together for a rehearsal to tighten up their set before tomorrow night's club gig. They'd have to wait, which would piss them off.

Oh well. This was art, which trumped everything. That included eating and sleeping, not to mention rehearsals.

Pen poised over blank paper, he gazed across the ashfall and breathed the poisonous atmosphere that reeked like a chimney's sooty asshole. In the distance, the crimson glow outlined the mountains under a pall of white smoke. Since the wildfire had started, it had grown to become a breathing god, its cloud spinning clockwise like a hurricane when seen from space.

Slowly, reality collapsed around his own fresh burns. The heartbreak of seeing his childhood best friend Stepford Wifeing himself, the exquisite pain of loss when he saw Beth again, the horror of facing Emily in her casket.

And the church organ. Its droning and haunting sound being the worst of all.

Organs always reminded him of his mother.

We played so beautifully, he wrote. His ode to Beth.

The pen paused over the page before scribbling again.

We played so beautifully, but the wall fell down.

We played so beautifully, but the wall came round.

He'd write a song for each of his friends, render a few classic spirituals like "Nothing but the Blood" in moody Goth, and build toward a dirty, howling climax followed by a triumph—a vast choir of sopranos discordantly heralding the resurrection of the dead, leaving behind only bloodstains to bury.

Time blurred. His phone rang. He ignored it.

The second time, he answered it.

"I'm working."

"So are we," Laurie said. "Unfortunately, we seem to be missing our singer."

"Screw your singer. I'm *working*."

Silence on the line. Laurie knew what he was like when the muse burned him alive, and that he always produced his best lyrics in this state. On the other hand, she was in a band, the band had a gig, and the gig was tomorrow, and this weighed equally in her mind as she was a practical person who lived in the real world.

"All right," she said.

"All right," he echoed.

"Just hurry your ass up."

"Hurrying my ass up. Right." He terminated the call. "Shit."

His fugue was over. Deacon inspected the pages he'd filled with black ink violent as flame. His hands were smudged with it. He had no idea what he'd written or how strong it was. When he fell into the zone, his hand caught a fever and did its own thing, like automatic writing.

Good enough. Okay. The new album screamed for birth, but he had a gig first, and in the end, the gigs trumped all. Standing in front of a crowd and ripping himself to shreds. Inviting them to share in his pain, and survive it together.

He read the last line of his hurried scrawl.

The meaning of life should transcend the meaning of death.

Amen. Deacon closed his book and roared out of the parking lot, bound for the City of Angels.

He drove down the Golden State through Los Padres until turning west along the 110. The great city's roaring heart and clogged arteries absorbed him as just another red blood cell among ten million. The 110 brought him to the Santa Monica Freeway, an autobahn of hurtling glass and steel where speed limits flickered past as mere suggestion, and which dropped him in Crenshaw. There, Cats Are Sad rented rehearsal space in a self-storage facility for twenty-five bucks a night.

With his rural childhood followed by years living in sub-
urban foster homes, the city had baffled Deacon when he'd
first shown up with little money and no plans other than to
see the world and then disappear into it. For the first few
months, he learned the geography, the value of resilience,
the treasures buried among the homogenized sprawl, and
how the metropolis was in reality a confederation of smaller
cities forming a tapestry of different cultures, ethnicities, and
economies. They were the real Los Angeles, Los Angeles
itself being a fantasy projected by need and want and hunger.

Odd jobs, roommates, music lessons, and open mic nights
and jams got him into the music scene. Deacon would walk
onstage and sing old spirituals like "Go Tell It on the Mountain" to whatever jam the ad-hoc band cooked up. Following Dr. Klein's therapy, he'd never stopped writing poems to
process the trauma he now called his muse, and he started
singing them onstage as songs.

This got him into Sweet Frostbite, a neopunk band that
shattered after the bassist's messy suicide. Then the post-
metal blackgaze band Night Broadcast, which came close
to hitting with "Love to Hate," and which fell apart over
ego and burnout. After that, Deacon found a new home
with Cats Are Sad, a Goth band that with him as frontman evolved into something new, something that might best
be described as nu gaze, but with the vocals out front and
a dark-brewed Goth flavor. Their songs were packed with
grunge lyrics dedicated to classic themes of alienation, low
self-esteem, trauma, and the raw want of being young.

During these years, he lived with bandmates. Anytime he
got money, he gave it to the band or blew it. He wasn't starving for success like so many other musicians, didn't need
anyone's validation beyond them watching him sing onstage

until he'd self-cauterized his way into numb and peaceful nonexistence. He mapped a new geography where he could become lost and found, one consisting of music theory and song recipes and the enormous range of equipment and software used to alter sound. He lived in perpetual surprise that he was alive. The band's gritty black-and-white promo posters showed him grinning among bandmates who glared youthful defiance at the camera. A dark grin that made you wonder. People like David might see him as a Peter Pan, a nearly thirty-year-old boy who never grew up, but that wasn't true. Deacon's childhood had died screaming when he was fourteen. His music and performances were all about expressing its loss.

He wasn't going anywhere, but he'd achieved something like happiness amid the constant melancholy. He'd become a cat.

Honey rolled up to the band's rehearsal space for the night, storage unit 27, and Deacon smiled at the angry faces of his bandmates reflecting the glare of his headlights.

He cut the engine as Laurie walked over, tall and skinny and dressed in her rocker uniform of black choker collar, tight tank top that showed off her boobs, and ripped sweatpants. Her long, frizzy blond hair was tied up in pigtails, her doll face shadowed with black eyeliner and lipstick. The Joker's Harley Quinn without the color. She was the lead guitarist and the band's sound witch, a real savant with the effects pedals, an artist by choice but an engineer and nerd by birth.

Laurie was your gal if you wanted a specific juxtaposition of frequencies across the ears that biohacked the listener's head by synchronizing their brain waves to three to eight hertz, the operating frequency of dreams and meditation. Or if you needed reverberation to express a binaural beat entraining gamma waves to inspire insight and expand consciousness, which was always part of their opening and closing numbers.

Stain the brain was Deacon's motto. Laurie's was to *train it* with music mainlined like a drug. She wanted to re-create the Mozart effect—an escalation in spatial-temporal reasoning among some people after listening to the great composer's music—as the Sad Cat effect with her own secret recipes. She was a disciple of My Bloody Valentine and studied everything from chakras to Tibetan chants to the punk band Vision Quest. She played with pedals, whammy bars, didgeridoos, and singing bowls, always searching for the perfect mind-altering frequencies.

"Christ," she said as he rolled the window down. "You smell like Auschwitz."

"Nice," sighed Deacon. This was how Laurie talked. He was used to it.

"We're pissed off."

He held up his songbook. "And I wrote a concept album about a cult."

"What?" She reached for it. "Let me see—"

"With your eyes, not your hands, lady. It's raw." He opened the door and got out to arch his back in a dramatic stretch. He was bone tired.

"Then how are we going to work together?"

"I have to do this one alone," he said.

"You're writing an album about a cult without me?" Laurie looked like a kid uninvited to a birthday party.

"The music is all yours. But the *words* are mine."

She scrutinized him with her Kewpie-doll face. "This one is personal for you, isn't it? That funeral you went to up in Bakersfield. You're holding out on me."

He smiled. "Good things come to those who wait."

She sighed. "All right. Now face the music, or they'll pout all night."

"Sorry, guys!" he called out. "Foreal!"

"Fuck you, Deacon," the keyboardist shouted while the drummer raised his sculpted, tattooed arms to give him the double finger.

"Real nice," he said. "Hey, Laurie. Quick one for you. Joy's Yamaha can do organ sounds, but how close is a keyboard to the real thing?"

"You mean like a Hammond B3 with a rotary speaker cabinet?"

"I'm thinking more like a pipe organ." The B3 used tone wheels instead of air moving through pipes to produce sounds.

"I don't know. Tone wheel, though, yeah, you can get real close. You could play around with the Yamaha Reface. You could also check out Hammond's XK-3c, which is pretty good at imitating a tone wheel. There are some others."

Deacon thought about it. "So with the right gear it's possible to at least approximate the same ambiance."

"Unless you want to buck up and buy a real pipe organ and then lug it to gigs, yeah. Why are you so interested in organs now?"

"Because the album tells the story of a doomsday cult. The type that makes the apocalypse a self-fulfilling prophecy. I'm thinking we might need a church vibe for some of the songs. The kind of sound that fills a room."

"What's the message here, with this album? What are you trying to say?"

Deacon considered how to put it. Like his friends, he didn't regard the Family of the Living Spirit as a cult, not before it moved to Red Peak, anyway. The contradiction had always fascinated him, leading him to believe maybe there wasn't a contradiction at all.

He said, "A Christian group becoming a death cult has a terrible beauty to it. A certain logic, if you take it all seriously."

Laurie's face lit up at the idea. She put a high value on anything that stuck society in the eye and made people uncomfortable about their treasured myths. She especially enjoyed anything creepy and dark, and doomsday cults neared the top of the list.

Deacon didn't care about that. He wasn't even sure he believed the contradiction anyway. What he really wanted to do was capture the essence of an even deeper, far more terrible contradiction, one that had possibly nudged a childhood friend inch by inch into a spiral of suicidal depression. A question he wanted to ask every single person who would one day listen to his new album.

If God appeared in front of you and told you to sacrifice your own child with a knife, the way he told Abraham to kill Isaac, would you do it?

5

PRAY

Deacon squirmed with excitement as he finished his breakfast. Today was going to be the best day ever. A new family was coming to the farm, which included two kids about his age. More kids multiplied the drama, the complexity of alliances, the range of games one could play after finishing the day's chores.

Mom fluttered around him, tidying up for the Reverend's visit. Physically, mother and son made an odd pair. Deacon was lanky and tall for almost twelve, Mom short and round. The main thing they shared was a love of music. Deacon sang and was already a fair hand at the guitar. While his talent was budding, Mom's had fully grown. When she played the organ in the Temple during worship, people felt the Holy Spirit. As for the Spirit, she could make it dance.

Mom eyed the remains of his breakfast. "Finish up so you can get to your chores."

"Almost done." Deacon raised his glass, which was still half full of milk.

She pursed her lips, as she was onto him stalling on the days Jeremiah Peale visited, and returned to making everything perfect. While her back was turned, he set his glass back down. She started to sing, delicate and clear as crystal, though hearing her required some intimacy, as she had a quiet voice.

The cabin's front door sounded with a polite rap. Mom again pursed her lips at Deacon, who raised his glass and made a show of slurping. Taking a moment to fuss over her appearance, she answered the door.

"Good morning, Reverend. Come in. We're just finishing breakfast."

Jeremiah Peale stomped into the house. "Am I too early?"

"Not at all. Would you like some tea?"

"Thank you, no."

Deacon stared at the Reverend. The man was physically big, with a barrel chest and large hands calloused by farming. His presence was even bigger, filling whatever room he was in, whether it was a cabin or the Temple.

He'd combed his hair in a neat side part that was already threatening to break loose over his forehead as the day's heat rose. On his wide face, he wore a Cheshire cat smile, half choir boy and half rascal.

He beamed that smile on Deacon. "How goes it, boy?"

"I'm well, thank you, sir."

"Not to mention taller. Every time I turn around, you young ones get bigger."

The Reverend founded the Family after the 9/11 attacks, which he'd interpreted as a sign. History was coming to an end, and Jesus was on his way back after being gone two thousand years. He didn't know the exact time and date of Christ's return, only that he was certain it would happen.

After all, Jesus had promised he'd come back, it said so right in the Bible, and the Bible never lied.

Here in this lush valley in the Tehachapi Mountains, the border of the San Joaquin Valley and the Mojave Desert, this man had built a community that would serve as a fortress and model of joyful Christian living in a dying and sinful world. If nothing else, he always said, that was something worth doing.

"Finish your milk, Deacon," Mom said, her eyes on Jeremiah, "and then you can go outside and get to your chores."

Deacon picked up his glass again. "Okay, Mom."

The grown-ups went into the adjacent living room. The Reverend settled into the easy chair while Mom perched prim and proper on the edge of the couch, pen poised over her notebook. They talked about the hymns he wanted in this week's services. As the Temple organist, she needed to know what he planned for music.

Whenever she looked up at the Reverend, she blushed all the way to her roots and glowed. Deacon liked how happy he made her. After a texting teenager ran a red light and smashed into Dad's car when Deacon was little, Mom had been sad until she and the Family found each other. The group had given her faith that Dad's death had purpose and meaning and mystery, and belief he was still alive.

The Reverend smiled at him again. Busted. He gulped the last of his milk.

"Something on your mind, boy?"

He froze like the proverbial deer in the light. He'd been thinking that if Mom ever married the Reverend, he'd be just fine with it.

"When I grow up, I want to be a preacher too," he blurted.

"It's a noble calling. The hardest job you'll ever love."

"Maybe I could help the new family feel at home. Is there

anything special I could do?" He could write a song for them, play it on his guitar.

"You have a fine heart. You care about people, like your mama. So just be yourself, boy." The Reverend winked.

"Run along now, Deacon," Mom said. "The day's waiting for you."

"Okay!" He ran to the door to slip into his runners, and bolted.

When the new family arrived, the mom had received a warm welcome, while the kids got drama. David, the new boy, ran off and hid until Emily found him in a supply closet. She'd gone inside and closed the door, and they'd talked so long that Deacon grew bored and went home for supper.

Over breakfast the next morning, he had a brainstorm and gained permission from his mom to act on it. He'd give the new kids the welcome *they* should have received. After clearing his plate, he went to his room to put on the suit jacket he wore to church.

In the bathroom, he admired himself in front of the mirror. "I just wanted to see how you were all doing," he told his reflection. "So, how are you settling in?" He cleared his throat. "Oh, hey, how are you? How's everything going so far?"

He reached to comb his shaggy mop into a side part with his fingers, but stopped himself. No need to overdo it. The Reverend had told him to be himself.

Another great day waited, the best yet.

Outside on the grassy commons, he greeted the sunrise with a grin. Few people wandered about, as most had started work for the day. He had about an hour before he had to start his chores.

"Good morning, Freddie," he called out sunnily.

Freddie Shaw was seventeen and therefore didn't have to

be called *mister.* The kid was a mechanical genius and kept the farm's machinery working. *From each according to his ability, to each according to his need* was a Family motto.

Freddie looked up from the engine of the truck he'd been servicing, and chuckled as he wiped his forehead with a grimy rag. "Morning, Reverend."

Deacon faltered but kept walking. Maybe he didn't look as cool as he thought. He'd wanted to impress upon the new kids that he was an aspiring spiritual leader, but now he wondered if he looked silly. Maybe he should go back to put on his normal duds, but then Freddie would see him and know why he'd changed.

He grinned again and put it behind him. Jeremiah Peale had envisioned the Family as a joyful community ruled by the carrot not the stick. He believed if a believer was happy, that meant the Living Spirit was near. Deacon could be anything he wanted, as long as he did it with joy and a loving heart.

"Hey, Deek!"

He turned to find Beth running toward him in one of her flower-print dresses. Because she was still a kid, she didn't have to wear a headscarf, and her long hair flew around her head as she ran.

Deacon groaned. With her little chin and huge eyes, she was so cute it sometimes hurt just to look at her, but she was as annoying as gum on his shoe.

Panting from her run, she caught up. "What are you doing?"

"I'm going to give the new kids a tour of the farm," he said.

"Can I come too?"

He didn't need to feel even more self-conscious, which was certain with her tagging along, but he couldn't say no. "Sure, I guess. But I'm in charge, okay?"

"Is that why you're wearing your jacket?"

"I wanted to look nice."

"You kind of look like the Reverend." She smiled as he deflated a little further. "I think it's cute."

Cute wasn't what he was going for, but he thanked her anyway. He thought about taking the jacket off and carrying it, but that would only make him feel sillier. He'd have to go all the way with his plan.

"We should show up holding hands," she added. "Like we're married."

His face turned hot. "No!"

Beth bent over cackling. "I was just kidding. Jeez Louise."

"Quit fooling around." God, this was what he was talking about. Annoying.

"Okay, okay."

After he knocked on the new family's door, Angela answered and stared down at him. "What do you want, small fry?"

"I—" He stopped, caught off guard by the cell phone in her hand. The device that had killed his father. He hadn't seen one in almost a year. "How's everything going so far? How are you settling in?"

"I'm so happy I could die," she deadpanned. "Is that it?"

"Is your mom home?"

Behind Angela, the cabin's main room was a mess, filled with furniture and half-unpacked cardboard boxes. No sign of Mrs. Young.

"She's out," Angela told him. "Whatever you want to ask, ask me."

"Well, okay. I was wondering if you and Davey wanted a tour of the farm."

"Really?" The girl smirked. "I thought you were Jehovah's Witnesses."

Deacon opened his mouth, but nothing came out. The

new girl was sure of herself in a way he wished he was. He found her intimidating.

Beth was cracking up. "We are. And we're married."

He wheeled on her. "Shut up, Beth!"

She stuck out her little chin and gave him the stink-eye.

"Sorry," he mumbled. "I didn't mean it."

"You two make an adorable couple," Angela said. "Sure, I'll take the nickel tour." She turned and yelled, "Davey!"

"What?" the boy yelled back from his room.

"Come on out here."

"I don't want to get baptized!"

"Now, Davey."

"You're not my boss!"

Angela sighed. "Two kids are here! They want to say hi."

A few moments later, David appeared, looking past them. "Is Emily here?"

"Get your shoes on and prepare to be amazed," Deacon said, trying to regain some control. "Beth and I are going to show you around."

Along the tour, he pointed out the Temple, mess hall, smokehouse, and root cellar, all of it built by the Family with their own hands and sweat. The more he talked, the more he enjoyed seeing it as if for the first time, as they did.

Deacon remembered cartoons, video games, movies, Hershey bars, and Halloween. His imagination had warped it all into a child's Babylon of temptations and awful comeuppances, but he didn't miss much of it anymore. Out in the dying world, kids shot each other at school and got hooked on drugs and had babies and got stalked by creeps on the internet and killed dads while texting and driving. Not here, where people looked out for each other and God watched over them all.

Despite its hardships and petty squabbles and whispers about bad behavior in this house or that, the farm was a good home, where one could live with the Spirit and without fear. Each night, Deacon crossed over convinced that his father was watching over him as well, and was glad to be at the farm, because if he were anywhere else, Dad might not be able to see him.

He wanted very much for them to look at it the way he did.

"Soon, we'll have a leather workshop and a forge," Deacon said. "We'll be able to make everything we need. We won't need the outside world for anything."

"Cool," Angela said, this time without sarcasm.

Her brother remained a lost cause, his gaze darting around as if searching for an escape.

"Hey, Davey," he said. "What do you think?"

The boy mumbled something he couldn't hear.

"Don't you like it?"

David shrugged.

"He's nervous about being baptized," Angela said. "Right, Davey? Ask this kid about it. He'll tell you what I told you."

David said, "Does it hurt?"

"What?" Deacon couldn't believe his ears. "Of course it doesn't hurt! It's supposed to be fun, for Pete's sake."

"You get forced under the water."

"Just for a second. And you're being helped, not forced."

Another shrug. The kid didn't sound convinced.

"Do you want to see the animals, Davey?" Beth asked him.

This time, he responded with an enthusiastic nod.

The animal pens consisted of several small buildings surrounding a yard partitioned by fences. In these pens, pigs, chickens, and sheep roamed and grazed. Angela wrinkled her nose and made a disgusted sound at the smell, but David grinned at the sheep.

"Hey, Deacon," Mr. Preston called out. "Giving the new kids the grand tour?"

"Yes, sir."

"Well, come look," the man told David. "They won't bite."

"Can I pet them?" David asked.

"Of course you can."

They approached a section of fence where one of the sheep stood. David reached and stroked its coat. "I think this one likes me."

"We get a lot of wool from her," Mr. Preston said. "How about you, miss? Do you want to pet her?"

"No, thank you," Angela said. "I'll just watch."

"What does she eat?" the new kid asked.

The man jerked this thumb at a metal box on the other side of the pen. "We don't have enough land for a good-sized paddock, so we set up a lick feeder. The sheep have to lick the feed, so their tongues tire out after a while. When they go off to get a drink of water and rest, the other sheep can take their turn."

A gray-haired man approached. "Don't you kids have work to do?"

Deacon froze. Mr. Wright was one of the Family's shepherds, a title given to the men on the Family's spiritual council who tended its human flock.

"Deacon is showing the new kids around," Mr. Preston said. "There's no harm in it." He reached into the pocket of his overalls and gave David a handful of carrot and dried apple slices. "You can give her a snack if you want."

David laughed as the sheep licked the treat from his palm. "Her tongue's really rough. Does she have a name?"

"I wouldn't name her," Deacon said. "We eat the animals, you know."

The kid stiffened. "Oh."

"See that building near the trees? That's the slaughter-house. A lot of the animals end up there." He added in a stage whisper, "Along with the kids who don't say their prayers."

David flinched this time. "Oh."

"No, no." Deacon laughed. "I'm just kidding."

The kid blushed a deep crimson. He gave his head a slight shake.

"Hey. Deacon." Angela fixed him with a menacing glare, shaking her head slowly. "Not a good move."

"Yeah," Beth said, playing it up. "Jeez Louise, Deek. Are you okay, Davey?"

"Come on! I was obviously joking." He gave up with a sigh. "Sorry, Davey."

"Maybe the shepherd's right, and you kids should get to your chores," Mr. Preston said. "The baptism is in a few hours."

The rest of the day promised a spiritual event, good food, and an afternoon off from school to play and explore, but Deacon wasn't sure he was up to any of it anymore. The tour had gone better than he'd imagined, but then he'd blown it. And in front of Beth, whose mom was a gossip, which meant everyone would know.

The Reverend had called it the hardest job. He wasn't kidding.

Mom looped the tie around Deacon's neck and gave him a sloppy kiss on his forehead before starting to knot it. Usually, he'd groan as loud as possible at this kind of attention, but now he stood rock still, feeling glum.

"Mom? Do people go straight to Heaven when they die?"

She smiled. They'd had this conversation before. "That's right. They're beautiful, and they're all looking down at us."

"So if I do something bad, it isn't just God watching. Dad is too."

Mom tugged the knot closed. "What's wrong?"

"I yelled at Beth today. Then I said something really stupid to Davey Young."

He'd replayed the whole thing in his head many times, only to experience again the sting of screwing up. He'd failed his first test, and not only did Beth and the new kids know it, his dad knew it, and so did God. He wasn't good enough to be a preacher. The Reverend had told him to be himself, but he wasn't who he thought he was. He'd bet Jeremiah Peale, being perfect, never messed up the way he had. The Reverend didn't crack jokes to make himself important. He was a servant. He always worked hard to help others experience the same joy he did.

Mom inspected his jacket and pursed her lips at the dust on it. She whacked it a few times. "Do you know who's the spiritual warrior's toughest enemy?"

"The Devil?"

"Nope." She held up the jacket. "Himself. The impulse to sin he was born with. That we're all born with."

Deacon's eyes went wide as he allowed her to put it on him. "Oh." Mind blown.

"Did you say sorry?"

"To who?"

Mom smiled. "Beth and Davey."

"Sure, I did."

"That's half the battle," she said. "The other half is learning from your mistake. If you feel yourself about to do something bad, open your heart to the Spirit, and it will guide you. I'll pray for you, Deacon, as I always do."

Deacon was hazy on the rules of prayer, as most of the

things people prayed for didn't happen, but he liked that Mom would be talking to God about his welfare.

She straightened his collar. "And there we go. You ready?"

Outside, the singing had already started. Deacon ran out the door ahead of his mother. Hands linked in a human chain, the Family walked single file down the dirt road toward the baptismal stream. Children flanked the march, smiling with their hands raised the way they'd seen the adults do when taken by the Spirit, which was very much with them all on this beautiful blue-sky day.

Then came Jeremiah Peale, leading a beaming Mrs. Young by the hand and trailed by her reluctant children and Deacon's friends. His hair part had fallen into a sweaty tangle over his forehead. The Cheshire cat grin was going full force.

Behind them, the grim-faced church elders, the flock's shepherds, followed in their white shirts and black suits.

Deacon ran to join his friends.

The Reverend let up a fierce shout: "What should a *poor* sinner *do?*"

The congregation sang, *"Jesus said to go, down to the river."*

"Where should a *poor* sinner *go?*"

Deacon joined in this time. *"Jesus said to go, down to the river."*

"What can a *poor* sinner *gain?*"

"Wash away your sin, down at the river."

"Can a poor sinner *be saved?*"

"Wash away your sin, down at the river."

He marched along with pride, his funk now forgotten as he recalled the Spirit. As the procession passed the green fields, he checked out his new neighbors. David walked with his head down and hands in his pockets, while Angela scowled in a dress she obviously didn't like wearing.

Deacon nudged the boy. "You ready to be saved?"

The kid stared down at his feet. "I guess so."

"It's like swimming with your clothes on," Emily said. "We'll be there with you. Clapping like this." She broke out in manic applause. "You're going to be the star of the show!"

David looked up and smiled. "Really?"

"Really and truly."

They all followed the path through the dark oaks down to the stream where sinners were saved from eternal death. Deacon liked this part of the woods, where the big trees shaded the ground and the air was cool. While the congregation lined the shore to watch, Jeremiah baptized Mrs. Young and next Angela, and then it was David's turn. Resigned to his fate, the new kid plunged into the percolating stream. They splashed to the middle, where the water ran deep enough for a dunk. The Reverend kept a tight hold on the boy because of the current.

The congregation let up a choral hum that drowned out the forest's insects and birdsong. Mrs. Young cried with joy. Wrapped in a towel, Angela shivered and dripped. Out in the stream, Jeremiah had taken off his jacket and stood thigh deep in the water like a modern John the Baptist. One hand rested on the top of David's head while the other gripped a worn black Bible.

"The Book of John tells us we must be born of water," he cried. "And of the Holy Spirit! Peter told us to baptize in the name of Jesus. The water won't just clean dirt from his body but any sin from his soul!"

"Amen!" someone called out, and others echoed the sentiment.

Deacon did too. For him, this was more exciting than the cartoons he used to watch.

The Reverend raised his Bible. "David Young, do you accept the Lord Jesus Christ as your savior?"

David's eyes flickered across the congregation as if searching for a different kind of savior. They found Deacon, who gave him a thumbs-up. When they settled on Emily, he smiled. "Yeah."

"Do you love him with your whole heart?"

"Yes."

"Will you serve him all your days?"

"Okay."

"Let us pray for David." Eyes clenched shut, the Reverend bowed his head. "Lord, we thank you for this powerful encounter with the Living Spirit. This boy is ready to give his life to your service." He pressed his Bible against David's forehead. "David, on your profession of faith and obedience to the Word of God, I baptize you in the name of the Lord Jesus."

He cradled the base of David's skull with his big hand. "I *baptize* you!" He withdrew the Bible and pressed its worn cover against the boy's head a second time. "In the *name* of Jesus!" Again. "For the *remission* of *your* sins!"

This time, David disappeared into the water.

And came up sputtering and wiping at his eyes.

The Reverend rested his hand on the boy's shoulder. "David Young, in front of all these witnesses, you are now saved from death by the resurrection of Jesus Christ. You have emerged from the baptizing waters clothed in Christ, ready to serve the Lord!"

"Thank you, Jesus," David's mother sobbed.

Others applauded and added to the cries.

Deacon yelled, "Yes, Jesus!"

Emily whistled and clapped. Beth danced. Even Angela stopped scowling, impressed by the emotional display.

David blinked the last of the water away and responded to all this praise with a shy smile and wave.

The community celebrated the Young family's salvation with a lavish lunch eaten at picnic tables in the shade of a few ancient oak trees near the mess hall. Baked chicken, ham, potato salad, deviled eggs, fresh greens, apple cider, and more decked the tables, all harvested from the bountiful farm.

For special feasts like this, the women ate separate from the men, though the children all ate together. Of the one hundred and five people then living at the farm, nineteen were aged fourteen or younger. Deacon sat at a table with Beth, Emily, Josh, Wyatt, David, and Angela.

Josh and Wyatt were older kids like Angela was. Being fourteen, they neared manhood in the community with all its rights and privileges, and they never let the younger kids forget it.

When David reached to serve himself some fried chicken, Josh said, "Whoa, Trigger. We have to say grace first."

David looked around the faces for help, but Josh was right. The new kid had to learn how meals were done here.

He closed his eyes tight. "Jesus, thanks for this lunch. Amen."

Josh glanced at Wyatt, who burst out laughing. "Jesus wept."

"Hey," Angela said. "Big shot."

Josh's smirk faded. "Hey, what?"

The girl shook her head with slow menace, a look that said: *Don't test me.*

The big kid cocked his ear as if he was hard of hearing. "What's that?"

Beth raised her hands. "Lord Jesus—"

The kids all hurried to clasp hands in a circular chain around the table.

"—we are gathered here to share a meal in your honor. Thank you for bringing us together. Thank you for the food we're about to eat. Guide our hearts, words, and deeds so that we praise you in everything we do. And thank you for the new members of our congregation, they're really cool. In Jesus's name, amen."

"Amen," the kids said.

They all reached into the center of the table to pile plates with food.

"Hey, new girl," Josh said.

Now it was Angela's turn to cock her ear as if hard of hearing. "Say again?"

He gestured to the bench across from him and Wyatt. "Come sit with us."

She shrugged. "Okay."

Mrs. Young cackled at a nearby table. Angela winced as she settled into her new seat.

"What do you guys do all day?" David said.

"In the morning, we have to do our chores," Deacon told him.

The boy paused his chewing. "Chores?"

"Yup."

"Wait—all *morning*?"

"We peel potatoes, pull weeds, that sort of thing, wherever we're needed. We all work together. It's what keeps the farm going so we can live the way we want."

"Oh. Great." David was obviously a city kid.

"Then we get our schooling. After that, we can play."

He brightened at that. "What do you play?"

"We explore the woods," Emily jumped in. "We hunt for salamanders, fish the stream, play Kick the Can, whatever. Do you like trains?"

"Sure."

"After lunch, I'll take you somewhere that is super cool. You'll love it."

"Count me in," Deacon said.

"And me," Beth chimed in.

While he frowned at her, his mom appeared at the table holding a pitcher of iced lemonade. "I need a volunteer to bring this to the elders' table. How about you, Deacon?"

"Okay, Mom." He crammed as much food as he could into his mouth until his cheeks bulged. Hoisting the pitcher, he chewed his way to the elders' table and started filling glasses.

"Expansion," Jeremiah was saying. "If we buy the tracts next to us, we could clear enough farmland to support another hundred people."

"We might focus on better managing the folks we have here now." That was Shepherd Wright, fanning his craggy face with his wide-brimmed black hat.

The Reverend sighed. "We've talked about this."

"If we aren't vigilant," the old man said, "demons will tear this place down."

Deacon flinched. The men stopped talking. He froze, flushed to his ears and aware the shepherds now stared at him.

The Reverend gently gripped his arm in one large hand and took the pitcher away with the other. "I'll take it from here, boy. Go back and eat."

"Yes, sir."

As he made his way back to his seat, he overheard the Reverend tell Shepherd Wright that living with God was meant to bring joy. He missed the rest and didn't care to hear it. He shook with guilt that he'd peeked behind the curtain at machinery he wasn't allowed to see, and feared this somehow marked him.

The divisions among the elders were well-known. One couldn't live in a small, tight-knit community like this without gossip reaching even the kids, especially Beth, whose mom talked to everyone. Shepherd Wright and his allies thought Jeremiah was too liberal. He complained that the Family relied too much on medicine over faith, spared the rod too often in child-rearing, and had too much freedom to interpret God's will instead of relying on the elders' judgment.

But everyone loved the Reverend. He'd built this Eden in the wilderness with his bare hands. He'd furnished a home close to Heaven for more than a hundred lost sheep, and given this home a soul.

Without the Reverend, there was no Family.

Demons, though.

The idea made Deacon shudder.

His eyes swept the congregants talking and laughing around the picnic benches, the men in their suit jackets, the women in their dresses and headscarves, the kids decked out in their Sunday finest for the baptism. Even a single demon could ruin everything, could divide and scatter the community they'd built here. A shadow seemed to sweep across the farm, filling him with foreboding.

Demons will tear this place down.

Then he looked again at the Reverend.

No, he thought. *Not with him on our side.*

The very idea was laughable.

Deacon pitied the demon who would go toe to toe with Jeremiah Peale.

▲   ▲   ▲

The kids tramped through buckbrush until they found the deer trail winding through the oak woodland toward the Tehachapi Loop. Deacon marched along happily, finding a steady rhythm with a sturdy tree branch he'd scavenged from the forest floor as a walking stick. No chores and schooling today, just delicious food and singing and now plenty of free time to see and do and explore.

A gloomy Wyatt followed twenty yards behind. He was crazy about trains and wanted to come along, but Josh had stayed at the farm to hang around Angela. Emily asked her friends to pause a bit so he could catch up, but when they did, Wyatt stopped as well and kicked at the brush while chickadees sang in the high branches. They shrugged and carried on.

David gaped at the trees. "You guys aren't scared?"

"Oh, come on," Deacon said. "You've never been in the woods?"

"Wyatt said there are demons out here."

They turned as one to see the big kid laughing at them.

"You're a jerk, Wyatt Cornell," Beth said.

"What? Jeez, I was just kidding with him."

Emily studied David's face. "Do you hear that? No demons. Okay?"

"Okay."

"Bobcats, though," Wyatt said. "Mountain lions, wild pigs—"

"Ignore him," Emily said. "Let's go, people."

The group moved on down the trail. Deacon walked at Beth's side, intensely aware of her body next to his, though he stared straight ahead.

Annoying and enticing, but right now, she was just enticing.

He imagined holding hands with her, enjoying the butterflies racing between his heart and stomach. He didn't dare. There was something about a crush that found a delicious balance between wanting and having. Push and pull.

He bragged instead. "The Reverend visited again yesterday."

"What did he say?" Beth asked.

"He told me to be myself."

The kids oohed at this bit of grown-up wisdom.

"What's that supposed to mean?" Wyatt called out.

Deacon wheeled at the challenge. "It means I'm a good person."

"I think it means you're sweet on the preacher."

He blushed. "I am not. Take that back!"

Wyatt laughed. "You so are."

"Stop," Emily said in a loud voice.

The kids all froze.

She walked up to Wyatt, who straightened his shoulders and frowned down at her. After a few moments, he turned away, his face reddening.

"Come on," she said. "You're holding us up."

Wyatt followed her to the group, which set out again for the Loop.

Deacon tossed his walking stick into the brush.

"Hey, Deek," Beth said.

"What." Wyatt had ruined his mood, and she'd only make it worse.

"I think we need a song."

"I don't really feel like it."

She gave him a playful shove that almost knocked him over. "Sing!"

"Hey! Okay, jeez." He sang, "I may never march in the

infantry, ride in the cavalry, shoot the artillery. I may never shoot for the enemy, but I'm in the Lord's army!"

The kids joined in. *"I'm in the Lord's army!"*

"Yes, sir!"

"I'm in the Lord's army!"

"Yes, sir!"

They took turns as lead singer until they cleared the forest and mounted the hill, which crested at the overlook. Aside from some mountain mahogany, there was little shade from the blazing sun. At the top, they whooped and clambered over boulders in search of their favorite seats. From here, they had a sweeping view of the chaparral-covered Tehachapi Mountains and the Loop.

The Loop itself was a mile-long circular track. Trains going east emerged from a tunnel and swooped around the track to ease the grade getting through the Tehachapi Pass between Bakersfield and Mojave. Trains going west came down off the mountains and disappeared into the tunnel mouth. Sometimes, if a train was long enough, it circled itself like a coiled snake.

David pointed to the hill dominating the middle of the looped track. "Is that a white cross at the top?"

"That's a memorial for some railroad men who were killed," Emily said.

"Oh. So what happens now?"

She grinned. "Now we wait for a train. It's cool, you'll see."

"How long does it take?" The kid seemed flustered at the idea of waiting. He'd come from a world of instant gratification.

"Not too long," said Wyatt, the train buff. "About forty trains a day come through, so we'll probably see one. If we're lucky, we'll get to see two of them passing each other. That's really cool." He seemed to remember he was a bit of a bully, so he added, "I'm only telling you because you don't know anything."

The kids sat on the boulders and threw rocks down the slope. This became a contest to see who could throw the farthest, which Wyatt won.

A train emerged from the tunnel and looped sleepily around to the left.

Wyatt raised his hands in exultation. "Sweet baby Jesus, we thank you for this train we are about to receive."

Scandalized, the kids howled with laughter.

Emily said, "Amen."

Wyatt had warmed up to the younger kids and was establishing himself as a big shot in the group. Deacon liked it better when the kid sulked at a safe distance.

Beth shifted on the rock next to him, sitting so close they were almost touching. Her fingertips grazed his hand, and a strange thrill made him shiver. His gut flipped, pushed and pulled in different directions. Out of the corner of his eye, he spied her smiling at the distant train.

Was it an accident? Had she meant to touch him? Was she trying to tell him something?

Like Scripture, one could spend a lifetime pondering the meaning of that touch.

6

SING

The Wild Moon. Capacity: two hundred souls. A smaller concert venue, but when empty, the place seemed cavernous.

Cats Are Sad walked in like gunslingers, bladders aching from excess coffee and preshow jitters. They were professional musicians, and they had a paying gig. They acted bored anyway, faces going slack with disinterest, though their eyes scrutinized the box like climbers gazing up at Everest's summit.

"Hey-yo," Bart, the drummer, called out, doing his best Freddie Mercury. He flashed a grin, probably imagining a sea of screaming fans yelling it back at him.

To Deacon's ear, the acoustics sounded fine. Otherwise, he didn't mind the smaller venues. Christmas was Christmas, regardless of whether you got the impossible toy you imagined you'd be getting.

"And here we are," a voice said behind him. "Another glorious day."

The band manager strutted up and whipped off his sunglasses. He was built like a potato but always acted like the room's alpha male, making the most of the small part he'd accepted in LA's sprawling script.

Deacon didn't mind him either. The band often bitched about its rate of acceleration, believing themselves destined for great things now rather than later, but Frank ran a tight ship. He kept Cats Are Sad playing twice a week and had helped them score the storage facility so they could practice and try out new songs.

Otherwise, he handled the merchandise, facilitated a decent music video produced on a shoestring budget, and Whac-A-Moled all the bullshit involved in running a rock band as a business.

"I hope the help showed up this time," Laurie said.

Frank grinned and jerked his thumb over his shoulder. "See for yourself."

A pair of high schoolers grunted through the bright doorway, carrying armfuls of cymbals and extra stands from Bart's van to supplement the drums included as part of the Wild Moon's backline. Another long-haired boy hauled Laurie's pedalboard and gear. Members of a garage band Frank hired to help with the setup.

The kids grinned at the rockers they wanted to be when they grew up. The band scowled back to be cool, though it was more than that. They liked being idolized but didn't see themselves as worthy of it, not yet. They were all in their twenties except for Steve, the bassist, but these high schoolers made them feel old. Time had a way of flying, and one day, they might be opening for these kids.

"I'd better go talk to Jack," Frank said to nobody in particular. Jack Denton operated the club, booking gigs but staying away from the talent, whom he famously regarded as needy and ungrateful.

"See ya," Deacon said, watching the bustle of the loading.

The Wild Moon stage included a quality frontman cardioid dynamic microphone, so he had little to do until sound check. Waiting was part of the business as much as last-minute gig cancellations, failing lights, and sound problems. He sauntered to the green room. There, Laurie sat on the couch lighting incense, its scent struggling against the stench of spilled beer and flop sweat and general crud that had soaked into the very walls along with the graffiti.

"Incense." He wrinkled his nose. "Not very punk rock."

"Which *is* punk rock," she said, completing an old routine.

"You know that stuff gives Bart a headache."

"And this room's smell makes me want to puke. Take your pick."

He had a bit of a headache going himself. He'd stayed up most of the night polishing his songs. What little sleep he'd gained was plagued with dreams of Wyatt's father holding his son down and raising his knife. Over and over, Wyatt's screams turned into a wet, choking gargle.

"I have another sound challenge for you," he said.

Laurie snorted. His organ question had hardly been difficult. "Let's have it."

"The *Inception* sound."

She nodded sagely, satisfied to face a pitch worthy of her batting skills. "The *braaam*." The 2010 film *Inception* had popularized the sound, which even today was overused in movie trailers to convey drama and dread.

"Yeah, but more like an *om*." The primordial sound in the Hindu religion, the sound of God, ultimate reality, and the inner soul.

"The *braaam* is a wall of sound made of layered French horns, bassoons, trombones, tubas, and"—she snapped her fingers a few times to jog her memory—"yeah, timpani. Hit the drum and let it boom with a round sound. Instead of a bassoon, I'd recommend a contrabassoon. The vibrations are great."

"Cool, cool. Now how would you do it with bone?"

The first time Deacon heard a sound that reminded him of the horn blasting on Red Peak was a viewing of the movie *Godspell*, which opened with John the Baptist blowing a shofar to announce the coming of the Messiah.

The Jesus figure showed up soon after to be baptized, and most of the rest of the film was him teaching parables to a bunch of people who'd abandoned their lives to follow him. Deacon amused himself by pretending the lead character wasn't supposed to be Jesus, which turned the story into one about a hippie cult whose leader had a death wish.

When the Jesus figure told his followers if a part of them offended God, they were better off losing the part than eternal life, Deacon stopped watching. This scene was a little too close to home. He kept thinking about the horn, however. The pitch was wrong, but there was something familiar about the timbre.

The shofar was a horn, typically a ram's horn, used by the ancient Israelites for certain ceremonies. In the Book of Exodus, a shofar blasting from a smoke cloud over Mount Sinai made the Hebrews tremble in fear and awe. These were the slaves who'd furnished the bricks for vast pyramids, who'd witnessed the Nile turning to blood and a fog killing the Egyptian firstborn, who'd seen Pharaoh's chariots drown in the Red Sea.

That horn blast must have been quite a sound.

Deacon started playing around with whatever he could

find. Ram's horns, the vuvuzela, a didgeridoo. Some aboriginal peoples used a bullroarer, a wood instrument swung on a string that produced a ghostly sound like a giant cloud of flies, which represented the voice of spirits or ancestors. The closest he came was with the spiraled kudu, played at a very deep, rumbling pitch, though the sound he wanted was far bigger than that. It was the sound of everything.

For him, his search became a quest for theosony, the sound of God, represented by an alchemical mix of frequencies. He found it natural that music played a strong role in many religions around the world, from chanting and hymns to bells and gongs to drums and singing bowls. Music didn't pair with religion. Music was worship itself, a way to join reality and the divine realm.

This time, he'd find the sound he remembered and somehow re-create it.

His album depended on it.

Bart thrust his shaggy head into the green room to fetch them for sound check.

"Coming." Laurie eyed Deacon. "I don't know if you're being annoying or intriguing with this album idea."

"See for yourself." He handed her his black songbook.

She accepted it with something like reverence. "These are the songs?"

"The whole album. I finished it last night."

Laurie started to pull back the cover but restrained herself. "I'll take a look at it right after sound check."

They followed Bart's hulking silhouette back to the stage facing the cavernous empty space. Flanked by the house speaker enclosures and woofers, the band plugged in and tuned their instruments. Laurie on guitar, Bart behind the drum set, Joy on keyboard, Steve on bass. Deacon took his frontman position behind the microphone and adjusted the stand's height.

"Ready when you are," the sound engineer said from the control booth.

Cats Are Sad was a professional band. They had their amp settings pre-dialed, instruments tuned, and pedals calibrated and powered by fresh batteries. They'd given the engineer their input list and stage plot in advance. They had their emergency box on standby with tuning pegs and wire cutters and backup strings and electrical tape. They were ready to sing their loudest and softest songs and stay quiet during line check.

Laurie hoisted the first of her guitars and picked through the notes. She had spares, as well as guitars she swapped out between songs because retuning between extremes was difficult. She glanced at her bandmates, who nodded one by one as they settled in.

"We're ready, chief," she said.

First came the line check, where each musician played and sang until the engineer verified their equipment sent signals to his mixer. After that, the band started in on their most popular track, "Stood Up."

The room filled with blasting music.

Deacon closed his eyes and sang:

You gave me faith in a god I could not see.
You found something divine inside me.
When you walked away I thought it only fair,
Cuz what you saw inside me was never there.

"Okay, that'll do," the engineer blared over the PA system, which signaled the band to stop. "Thanks a lot, guys. My ears are bleeding."

Laurie grinned. "Too loud?"

"This is a small, tight venue. Let me turn the overall volume down."

"Whatever you say, chief."

To Deacon's ear, the music had sounded boomy, but that was common when playing to an empty room. When the place was packed, all those people would absorb sound, and everything would come together.

Next, the band played a snippet of "In Your Shadow," while the engineer walked around the space checking the sound mix. He returned to his booth, tweaked volumes and sound using an equalizer and other effects, and gave them a thumbs-up. They stopped playing.

"Does everything sound okay at your end?" he asked.

They worked out a few tweaks with him, and then they were done.

"I wish every band was as easy as you guys," the engineer said.

"They give you a hard time?" Laurie asked.

"You know how it is. Somebody almost always has some ridiculous request."

"We're cheap *and* easy."

"I've never met a quieter frontman. It's actually weird."

"Deacon gets PTSD from normal conversations," Joy said.

While the band laughed at his expense, the headliners burst through the doors like rock stars, glowering at Cats Are Sad for doing their sound check first instead of waiting for them. While they loaded in, Deacon went to the bar and pulled out his cell phone, along with a wrinkled business card.

Beth answered on the second ring. "Dr. Elizabeth Harris."

"I need a therapist," he said. "I'm crazy about a certain lady."

She laughed. "You shouldn't joke about mental illness."

"Who says I'm joking? Humanity's a spectrum disorder, remember."

Another rewarding laugh. "Right."

"Hey, listen. My band is playing tonight at the Wild Moon. It's on the Sunset Strip in West Hollywood. Want to come?"

"I wish I could, but I have to be up early tomorrow to catch a flight to a conference, and then I'll have patients waiting for me when I get back."

"I bet you're one of those go-getters who's always working."

"Something like that," she said.

"Well, physician, heal thyself. Take a break."

"I have patients, and you need to be patient. We'll do something soon."

"Okay." Deacon spotted a bottle cap the cleaners had missed and kicked it across the floor. "I'm glad we found each other again."

She was smiling at the other end, he could tell. "Me too, Deek."

"I don't know how I let so much time go by."

Beth didn't say anything. Her invisible smile retreated into the ether. He cursed his idiocy. They both knew when and how he'd lost her. Many years ago, he'd broken her heart. He'd broken it by refusing to even acknowledge its existence.

A powerful flashback manifested, threatening to envelop him in its painful grip. *Samurai Jack* playing on the TV while Beth cried in his peripheral vision.

"Well," he said in a loud voice to keep the memory at bay. He clenched his teeth in a forced smile that came out a grimace. "Let's do it soon, okay?"

"Soon," she agreed, though she didn't sound as sure now as she had only moments before. "Break a leg tonight."

"Thanks," he said, thinking: *You can leave the past behind, but the past always catches up, like some kind of zombie.*

Beth ended the call, leaving Deacon with a howl building in his chest that would have to wait a few more hours before he could release it onstage.

Crammed into a booth at Denny's, the band agreed on their set list over dinner. With only an hour allotted to them, they decided to pack the set with their most popular tracks, along with a few fresh numbers they wanted to vet.

"You guys do this right," said Frank, playing the big shot, "see if I don't book you at the Whisky or Roxy again by the end of the year."

The band's faces shifted into warped smiles as they tried to stay cool. Deacon shrugged, earning an irritated and anxious glance from their manager. Frank had never liked Deacon because he couldn't get a hook in his mouth.

"If *you* do it right," Joy said. She had a Junoesque figure and Frank was smitten with her, so she often spoke for the band. "We need that Frank Dean magic."

"And you shall have it," he said with solemn dignity, as if they were exchanging vows.

"We need to talk about the new album," Laurie chimed in. "Deacon had a crazy idea that got under my skin."

Frank's eyes roamed from her face to her bare arms as if searching for it, which made her reflexively cross her arms over her chest. "What is it?"

"The concept started out as a mind game," she said. "Something we've been tossing back and forth."

Deacon nodded, agreeing with the lie. Laurie knew if

Deacon tried to foist a finished product on the band, they'd attack it, and he'd give up. Best to make the album sound like *their* idea and let them have plenty of input.

He noticed everyone was staring at him, waiting for him to spill the beans. He looked down at the napkin in his hands, which he'd been tearing into strips. "I came up with a concept album about a cult that commits mass suicide."

"Sounds like fun," said Steve. A veteran of a dozen bands, the bassist was the group's old man and its storm's calm eye. He and Laurie had an on again, off again thing going, mostly because she couldn't have normal relationships with men who weren't musicians and didn't understand the life—the gruel and grind of touring and the lunging ups and downs of being an artist trying to make it.

"Right?" Laurie said. "We could—"

"Hang on." Steve raised his hands. "It sounds like fun, but I don't know if a concept album is the right move."

Frank snorted. "Yeah. Because it's a shit idea."

Laurie bristled. "Why?"

"Simple economics," Bart said, ignoring the collective groan that followed.

"We get it, you're a libertarian," Joy said. "That doesn't make you an expert."

"Long-tail economic theory, to be specific," the drummer pressed on. "We have a strong niche in fifty percent of the market shared by a million bands. We need to inch our way toward the handful of bands that dominate the other fifty percent. That's where the real money is."

"You make it sound easy."

Bart turned to Deacon. "Listen, brother, you write some freaky lyrics, and your performances helped build up a nice fan base, but we need to keep evolving. We need songs that indie rock stations will want to play. A little less nihilism."

Laurie glowered at him. "The art comes first."

"Why not have art *and* money? Radiohead—"

"Concept albums don't sell," Frank said. "They just *don't*. End of story."

"What about *Tommy*?" Laurie said. "*The Wall, Ziggy Stardust, American Idiot—*"

"All put out by bands who'd already made it."

"I just think concept albums are pretentious," Steve said. "For every *American Idiot*, there's a hundred tuneless wonders that go on and on." He raised his hands again, not wanting to offend anyone. "It's a real risk, is all I'm saying."

Laurie shot a look at Deacon, but he only sipped his tea, which he drank with honey before a show to lube his vocal cords, and went back to ripping his napkin into tiny pieces. She let out a loud sigh and sat back in her seat, the remains of her omelet forgotten on the table. She was apparently done trying.

Joy offered her and Deacon an apologetic smile. "It's a great idea, but maybe now's not the right time. I feel like we're close to something major breaking for us soon. We can see about doing it later."

"Later," Frank agreed, and muttered, "or never."

She raised her hand to silence him. "Okay, Laurie? Deacon?"

"Fine," Laurie growled.

In the rock business, an album was a major undertaking. Expensive in money, energy, stress, talent. Deacon knew they were just being practical. Committing to a concept album would be very risky during a time in their careers where a single misstep could sink their band or anchor it in obscurity.

He shrugged. "Fine. Whatever."

▲   ▲   ▲

They went back to the Wild Moon and cracked open beers in the green room to loosen up. The night's three bands were all there and pumped to perform. Laurie did her finger exercises and disappeared. Deacon sat on the couch nursing his beer and smiled and nodded while a roadie for Kung Fu Hip told animated stories from their last tour. The hours to showtime ground away to nothing.

At 9:40, the sound engineer played trip hop to warm up the crowd. Laurie reappeared, wiping her eyes until they bled black, and said she was *ready to play* and *go to hell, don't ask me why I'm sad.*

The band wrapped up their backstage prep and put on their game faces, determined to blow the roof off the house.

Laurie nudged Deacon. "You okay?"

"Why wouldn't I be?"

"You're smiling like the nice, quiet bandmate who turns out to have a dozen bodies buried in his basement."

He forced a chuckle. "Everything is just perfect."

"Showtime, guys," Frank said. "Go melt some faces."

The band swaggered onto the stage, playing it cool. Wearing the same dumb grin from the band poster, Deacon followed like some kid who'd wandered backstage and accidentally ended up in the show. He positioned himself behind the mic. The room was filled with people ready to rock, the vibes excellent.

When Cats Are Sad played, they did so for themselves, but when they *performed*, it was for total strangers wanting to bond with them and participate in the show, like a religious ritual. For however long the connection lasted, the audience became a mirror, and right now, the band loved what they saw. Right now, they saw gods. Deacon was ready to sing.

This gloomy club was his church, the Shure SM58 microphone under the harsh spotlight his pulpit.

Let the Gospel of Deacon begin.

The band launched into a strong rhythm played at blasting volume.

Deacon always kicked off "Shadow Boxer" with a long cry to rouse the blood, but this time, once it started to come out of him, he didn't stop. He had plenty of air in his lungs, a whole lot of scream to purge. Emily's death, David acting like a stranger, his old betrayal of Beth, the band rejecting his vision as unmarketable in an industry where art was product. His traumatic past, his future mortality. The cry built in strength and volume until he became the living shofar calling the faithful to rail at the universe for a crummy deal. The band rolled with it, shooting each other questioning looks while they jammed and Deacon went on howling.

It was so raw and over the top that the crowd went wild. Everyone in the band grinned now, all cool forgotten as they poured their hearts into the jam and followed their frontman to mad glory. The engineer got into the act and pulsed the lights.

Then Bart steered the rhythm into the song in the hopes it was all a spontaneous artistic eccentricity on Deacon's part, and not an onstage freak-out that would make them famous for the wrong reasons. On cue, Deacon sang:

Why do the young want to die?
Some fast
Some slow
Why do the old want to live?
It's too late
The story's told

Laurie launched a spectral glide for the chorus, rocking her pedal to crest it, adding turbo distortion to dirty the sound until its alien growl stained the walls. She frowned at the readouts at her feet, controlling the bends and swells, juggling frequencies. Together with the rest of the band, she was hacking brains, triggering oxytocin and cortisol and adrenaline, inviting the audience to join an infinite flow chasing the euphoric catharsis of falling in love while dying.

The pain so exquisite, Deacon gave the performance of his life.

The set had a hard close at eleven, no encore. Cats Are Sad ended their show with "Stood Up" and was cheered off the stage. Afterward, the band loaded up the van and covered the equipment with blankets before heading back inside to catch the headline act and enjoy a few postshow drinks. In the green room, they'd talk about how the show went, dart out to pose for selfies with fans, and find out how much merch Frank sold. Their stage high was about to crash, and they all wanted to bring the night in for a soft landing.

Laurie joined Deacon on the couch, where he sat staring into space while nursing the same beer he had earlier. "How are you?"

Drained and overexposed, his ears rang. "I'm awesome."

"What were you thinking about just now?"

Calling Beth to tell her he was sorry. "Nothing at all."

"I read your songs."

He perked up. "What did you think?"

She knocked back the rest of her Budweiser in several long, thirsty gulps, then came up for air. "It's personal for you, isn't it?"

Bart loomed over them, gripping a beer in one of his big

paws while the other combed his beard. "That opening, dude. That was something."

Deacon blinked. "Thanks."

"It was off the hook! Think we could build it into our act?"

"Probably."

Laurie leaned toward Deacon's ear, her breath warm and electric. "Do you want to split?"

He answered with a grateful nod.

She stood and took his hand. "We're gonna grab some fresh air, Bartman."

"Hurry back. That set was on fire. It must be analyzed, understood, bottled."

Deacon followed Laurie out to her ancient VW bug and folded himself into the little passenger seat. He accepted a bag full of pilfered beer in his lap and bent his head to light a Camel. "Where are we going?"

"My roommate's out for the night, so my place," she said. "We need to have a long, serious talk, my friend."

"Sure." He was still feeling strangely docile.

"You were wondering why I was crying before we went onstage? I was reading your shit, that's why. Nothing gets me anymore, but this did."

Deacon nodded, saying nothing.

"A long talk." She threw the transmission into gear, and the VW bug growled out of the parking lot. "Starting now. What's the story there?"

Deacon stared out the window at the endless city lights struggling with the inky blackness beyond. "Do you know about the Medford Mystery?"

"Dude." Of course she did.

"The Family of the Living Spirit?"

"Yeah, yeah. So, what, then? You had a family member in the cult?"

He blew smoke out the crack in the window. "Yup."

"Ha! That's what I thought."

"I was also in it myself."

She chuckled. "What, when you were a toddler?"

"I'll be thirty in September, Laurie."

"So you were..."

"My mom joined when I was eleven. I lived with the Family for four years."

The chuckling stopped. She turned with wide eyes. "What the hell, Deacon? Are you serious? You were *there* the last night? As a *kid*?"

"The funeral I went to was for Emily, another survivor. She killed herself. Only four of us there that night are still alive."

"Oh. My. God."

"Okay." Too tired to fake anything.

"So what's the inside scoop? About the last night?"

"I don't have the energy right now. Sorry."

Laurie bounced in her seat. "This album. This album! It needs to be made."

He shrugged. "You heard the others. They don't like it."

"Yeah, well, they're stupid."

Deacon closed his eyes and let the warm wind dry the sweat in his hair.

Then Laurie was shaking him. "Come on, we're here."

He followed her into the apartment building. The silence during the elevator ride became deafening as his ears struggled with post-performance reality.

They exited onto a corridor and stopped in front of a door.

"This is me," she said.

She unlocked it and walked into the messy living room, pulling her shirt over her head to toss onto the floor. A tiny skull and crossbones was tattooed on the pale flesh of her left shoulder.

Deacon closed the door behind him, hugging the plastic bag full of beer.

"Somehow, some way, we're going to make this album." Laurie turned, tugging at her belt buckle. "Let's fuck, and then we can get to work."

7

CONFABULATE

Dr. Elizabeth Harris poured herself a full, relaxing glass of expensive Cabernet Sauvignon while Mozart streamed from her Bluetooth speakers.

Just enough time to make everything right before she had to go.

A little early today, don't you think? It's not even ten in the morning.

"Yup," she said. "I earned it."

Even the pouring filled her with contentment. The glug of the wine, the thud of the bottle as she set it down. She scooped her glass and swirled it as she inspected her pristine condo from the comfort of her couch. Everything white with little splashes of color. A series of shelves crammed with books, mostly tomes documenting the vagaries of the human mind. The large picture windows offered a clear view of Santa Barbara and the Santa Ynez Mountains.

Not bad for a messed-up kid coughed out of the institutional system eleven years ago with a GED and few prospects, all thanks to hard work, scholarships, a supportive foster family, and a mountain of debt.

Now she was *Dr.* Harris, if you please.

Yes, you're quite an overachiever, aren't you. I mean, you "earn it" a lot.

Always her mother's voice slipping into her mind in the still moments of the day to try to knock her down.

Beth sipped her wine and said nothing. The vintage went down like silk. She *had* earned it. A little medicine to steady the nerves. In a few hours, she had to catch a commuter flight to San Francisco for a conference. Over the weekend, she'd buried a childhood friend, a girl she once believed held the best chance out of them all to enjoy a normal life.

And then there was Deacon.

Her mind flashed to a group of children exploring the baptismal stream to see where the water would take them. Beth could smell the moist earth, mineral-rich water, chlorophyll. *Wyatt turned over a rock and called out he'd found a salamander. The boy wondered if you pulled off its tail whether it would grow back. Deacon stomped over in helpless rage, demanding Wyatt leave it alone.*

The day she fell in love with Deacon. She left the memory with a gasp. So sudden and real, like she'd accidentally discovered a form of time travel. *Abreaction,* she thought, a term in her field used to describe reliving an experience to express repressed emotions.

She reached for her glass, which was almost empty. She didn't remember drinking it. She swirled the remains and took a deep breath. Soon, the alcohol would take the edge off, and then bye-bye, abreaction. At least for a while.

When they were kids, Deacon cared about every living thing, even plants and bugs. He used to care about Beth most of all. Now he didn't seem to give a crap about any-thing. Beth wondered if this was a self-defense mechanism.

Yeah? What's yours, Dr. Harris?

"Physician, heal thyself."

Her motto, dedicated to a life of mental surgery to fix her scars. She swilled the last of her wine with a bitter swallow.

There was a time when she'd loved him and believed she always would, forever and ever, amen. The childish fantasies of a young girl. Now he seemed to want to return to her life. Or maybe he didn't want her at all. She didn't know what he wanted. She didn't really know him anymore. Worse, maybe she did. Perhaps she knew him too well.

The last time she'd given him her heart, he'd tossed it like trash. Maybe David was right and the smart move was to leave the past alone.

That kiss, though.

She thought about pouring another glass and getting mel-low, numbing the past. Giving the kindling a thorough soak so it could never light.

You know that won't do.

At the airport lounge, then. A nice reward to help her sleep on the plane.

Beth brought the bottle and empty wineglass into the kitchen. She washed out the glass and put it in the sink. She killed the music and out of habit touched the little metal cross dangling from her throat, where for fifteen years she'd kept her memories of the Family close to her heart but sep-arate from herself. Then she grabbed the handle of her suit-case while reflexively popping an Altoids mint to mask the alcohol on her breath.

At the conference, she'd learn about trauma and how to treat it.

This made Beth chuckle all the way to the curb, where her taxi waited.

She checked into the hotel, dumped her bag in her room, and took the elevator down to the second floor, which was crowded with suited conference goers. She registered and received a program and badge with a little speaker ribbon attached.

Her panel was scheduled for tomorrow morning, giving her the afternoon to explore the other sessions. She went to the hotel bar and browsed the program while sipping a high-priced Cabernet, enjoying its clean, antiseptic scent.

Many of the sessions dealt with cognitive behavioral therapy, which had proven effective in treating post-traumatic stress disorder either through exposure therapy, which helped people to confront their trauma, or cognitive restructuring, which helped the patient understand the event and make sense of their feelings. A San Diego–based psychologist was presenting on the latest thinking in stress inoculation training, another on the need to update the ethics of hypnosis.

Beth gazed across the massive hotel lobby saturated with daylight streaming through large windows. Through this light, guests came and went, their voices absorbed by the cavernous space. Soothing piano music trilled from the bar speakers. She liked upscale hotels, the sound-absorbing carpets, the grand spaces, the chandeliers and general elegance. Everything under control, in its proper place, the guests doing their part to act distinguished and civilized.

An act she saw through. A spectrum disorder, indeed.

Humans were walking bags of base instincts and magical thinking, the latter being the more dangerous. From good luck charms to soul mates, delusion was a survival trait providing emotional comfort and even sanity, but it could be destructive.

Every woman who prayed over a dying child instead of taking him to the doctor, every man who gambled away his kids' college funds in Las Vegas, they weren't as deluded as the paranoid schizophrenic believing the CIA was remotely studying his brain, but they lived on the same basic spectrum.

You think you're better, but you're—

"I envy them," she murmured. "Now shut up and let me read."

She returned to her program. A game designer was giving a talk on using virtual reality to re-create fear-inducing environments, which sounded interesting.

The next session on the list made her burst out in a loud guffaw. Beth rarely laughed, but when she did, it sprang unbridled from the belly. Across the bar, heads turned in annoyance or curious amusement.

"Rockefeller Ballroom," she said, committing the name to memory. Third floor.

She checked her watch. Just enough time to catch the end. She drained her wineglass and shouldered her purse.

Crushing an Altoids mint between her teeth, she beelined to the elevators.

Beth entered the darkened ballroom and settled in a folding chair in the back. The speaker was wrapping things up in front of a projection screen loaded with bullet points under the headline, CALL TO ACTION.

The speaker was David Young, here to talk about cults.

"There may be as many as five thousand cultic groups operating in the USA alone," he said. "In the last forty years, over two million Americans joined cults."

The man in the next chair leaned toward her. "Could that dude be any hotter?"

Beth tilted her head and murmured, "Bad luck. He's married."

"And I'm straight. I'm just saying he's an attractive guy."

She turned and took in a smiling, youthful face, kind of handsome himself in a roguish sort of way. "He gets his looks from his mother," she told him. "You should see his sister. She was a real knockout back in the day."

"Can you introduce me?"

"She's a police detective with aggression issues."

The man chuckled. "Maybe not, then."

"Most people," David said, "do not wake up one day and decide to sign up for a cult. They are vulnerable. Searching for a home, hoping to make sense of a confusing world. There's nothing wrong with joining a group that provides truth and belonging. Even the word *cult*, which simply means a ritualistic devotion to a person, doctrine, deity, whatever, is not necessarily bad. What is wrong, what makes a cult the bad kind of cult, is if the group uses mind control, exploitation, blind obedience, and manipulated dependency against its members."

In other words, religious groups were a spectrum disorder as much as humanity was, Beth understood. Whether groups or people required intervention or treatment depended on the level of harm.

David wore a blue open-collared dress shirt and slacks, exuding confidence and passion as he hammered his presentation's major points. Beth smiled. *I knew that kid when he tripped over his own feet and was scared of going into the woods alone.* He seemed to glow in the light of the projection screen.

Her neighbor leaned toward her again. "I'm Carl, by the way."

"Beth."

"Are you in the field?"

"Yes. Let me guess." She took in his expensive suit. "You're a drug dealer."

He chuckled again. "Pharmaceutical sales, yup. We've got a hell of an antipsychotic for schizophrenics coming out this year. Works like a charm."

"Sounds wonderful, but I'm not a psychiatrist."

Clinical psychologists primarily dealt in psychotherapy, while as medical doctors, psychiatrists focused on serious mental illness and prescribed medications.

"You refer patients, though, right?"

"Of course." The two professions often collaborated for optimal treatment, depending on the patient.

"Then I find you incredibly interesting." Carl grinned. He struck Beth as the type of jerk whose principal charm resided in calling attention to what a jerk he was. "So, Dr. Beth, are you going to the Fab party?"

"I didn't know that still existed," she whispered. "Anyway, it's not my thing."

"Don't like to lose control, huh?"

"It's a terrible survival strategy."

"You should come. You and your friend."

David said, "While we don't know for sure how many leave cults each year, the good news is they do. My job is to help them think for themselves and make the decision to get out. The hard part comes after, when they return to the real world. By itself, just leaving the group is a traumatic experience. Many feel depressed, grieving, guilty, isolated, disconnected, and without purpose."

Hey, who does that remind you of?

Beth shrugged off her inner voice and listened. David had seen firsthand what magical thinking could do to people. The Family had taken its monopoly on truth to its logical dark extreme. She wondered if he'd replaced his own wishful thinking with a healthier alternative or had become a depressive realist, denying himself any comforting delusions at all. Then she remembered what he'd said about his family. Yes, they were his religion now.

"That's where you come in," David went on. "The more people leave cults, the greater the demand for therapy specifically aligned with their needs. We need a stronger relationship between our communities. A deeper exchange of information, dedicated treatments, more robust referral networks, data collection."

Beth found herself nodding.

People leaving cults often complained about the abuse they'd received, but blamed themselves and otherwise did not understand how thoroughly they'd been manipulated. They needed therapists who were more active and less reflective and who could differentiate between the individual's core issues and those stemming from long-term manipulation.

"Working together, we can help people escape cults and make sure they stay out to lead independent, healthy lives," David finished. "Thank you."

The audience broke into applause. Hands shot up for the Q&A while a steady stream of conference goers headed to the exits. After the last question, a throng gathered around David, some of them female admirers.

Carl gave Beth his card. He worked for Hippocratic Pharmaceuticals and was based in Los Angeles. He'd written a hotel suite number on the back of the card. "I'll see you tonight?"

She stood. "Maybe. Nice to meet you, Carl."

The crowd at the front of the room had thinned, and David was packing up his laptop and presentation notes.

She approached and waited until he noticed her. "We should so work together."

"Hey!" He laughed. "I should have guessed you'd come to this conference."

"You did great. I only caught the end, but what I heard was compelling."

"Thanks. I hate public speaking." He thrust his hands in his pockets and offered a lopsided grin. "Did you bring your flask?"

"How about we get a proper drink this time?"

Returned to the elegant comfort of the bar, Beth sat across from David. After fifteen years, she was seeing her old friend for a second time in just several days. She didn't put any stock in the notion of fate, but if she did, she'd believe the gods were trying to tell her something.

She sipped her wine and said, "You've come a long way, David."

He studied his scotch sweating on the table in front of him. "The work is meaningful. I care about it a lot. I feel like I'm making a difference."

So his family wasn't his sole religion. He'd filled the void left by the Family's destruction with a calling to save others from a similar fate.

One thing Beth missed about the Family was its sense of purpose. She admired that David had found something to replace it. Beth enjoyed helping people through their traumas, delusions, and addictions, but in the end, Deacon was probably right. To a large extent, she'd entered the field to learn how to fix herself.

"I couldn't do your job," she said. "Exit counseling sounds like pulling teeth."

"I couldn't be a therapist. I like that I only have a few days to make my case, and then they either make the decision to leave or they don't. Otherwise, I'd get too invested and go back to kidnapping people and deprogramming them. Being a shrink seems like getting paid to watch a hamster wheel go around."

"Ha," she said. "Therapy can sometimes feel like that, though you ask the hamster questions and bark at it every once in a while."

He smiled. "Well, I guess we can both agree it's better than being a musician."

Beth thought about Deacon tracing a lazy circle on her knee during the funeral service. A little jolt of excitement shot through her.

"I don't know," she said. "He makes it look appealing. He lives free. I'm just not sure what he's living *for*. What about you? How are you, really?"

"Uh-oh." He fidgeted with his wedding ring the way he had at Emily's funeral, apparently a nervous habit.

"What did I do?"

"I can never tell if it's personal or professional with you."

"It's always personal for me. Because I care about you."

"I'll make you a deal. I'll give you an honest answer, and then you drop it." When she nodded, he took a drink of his scotch as if to steel himself. "I'm all right, Beth, I really am. Before Emily's funeral, I hadn't had a panic attack since 2010. The nightmares are mostly gone too. The flashbacks still come and go, but I'm working on the triggers. Sometimes, I just get a feeling, a terrible feeling. I've learned to roll with it, one day at a time."

"As long as you're handling it and it's not handling you. What about Angela?"

David turned away with a grimace. "She seems to be okay.

I think even now, for some weird reason, she still blames me for what happened to Mom. Since she's trained on the use of lethal force, I usually leave her alone."

"Any plans on how you're going to deal with the fifteenth anniversary?"

"Kiss my wife and hug my kids," David answered. "Otherwise, I'm going to try not to think about it." He produced his wallet and pulled out a photo. "This is them."

Beth smiled. The photo had been taken in bright sunshine at a park. David's wife was beautiful and elegant, his grinning children flushed and beaming with youth and horseplay. "You have a gorgeous family."

"That's Claire, my wife. This is Alyssa, and that's Dexter."

"Alyssa looks a lot like your mom."

David's own smile turned into a grimace. Too late, Beth realized her mistake in bringing up how his mother looked.

"They keep me busy," he said. "They're my purpose. It's hard being away so much, but that's the job."

"So about the fifteenth anniversary, Deacon and I were talking, and we were thinking it might be interesting—"

His sigh interrupted her. "What?"

"I'm sorry. I don't mean to be rude. I just don't want to talk about the Family anymore. Emily's death brought back a lot of bad stuff."

"Hang on." Beth leaned on her elbows. "Hear me out. Exposure therapy is very effective in treating PTSD. One form of it is called *in vivo*, where a therapist guides you in a visit to the place that scares you so you can safely confront your fears."

His eyes widened. "You want to go back to Red Peak?"

"Deacon and I were thinking we should *all* go. It's been a very long time."

"What good could that possibly do?" His hand shook as he raised his glass to gulp the last of his scotch.

"Look, we're all functioning because we found a way to put what happened to us in a cage. I think we should try to purge it. You said you were working on your triggers. This is one way to do it."

He became thoughtful. "*You* want to go."

She smiled. "Why do you think I'd want to go?"

Beth had been trained to keep conversation directed away from herself and onto the other person. She could play this game all day, though she had a feeling it would get frustrating: David was an avoider, and she didn't know how to let things go.

He was right, however. Well, almost. She didn't *want* to go to Red Peak. She'd begun to believe they might *need* to go. All of them together. Whatever drove Emily to suicide possibly was inside them, waiting like a time bomb.

"I think you want me to be a part of some therapeutic experiment on yourself." He winced at his candor. "Sorry, I don't mean that to sound so harsh."

"David, let me be clear. I've gone through more therapy than you can imagine." Ego state therapy, abreactive hypnosis, rewind technique, emotional freedom tapping, eye movement desensitization reprocessing. Over time, all of it had calmed her brain's amygdala to a nagging inner critic. "I'm fine. I'll tell you why I want to go. You have your way of giving back. This is mine."

And the Academy Award goes to . . .

David said, "It was really nice to bump into you here, Beth."

He was shutting down, refusing to play the game. "I'm sorry if I—"

"I mean it," he added. "I'm proud of you. We should all be proud of ourselves. A bunch of major overachievers.

Whatever made Emily choose to end her life, the rest of us can look in the mirror and say we did more than survive, we made something of ourselves, and at a young age."

"Well." His speech got to her. He was right. Beth raised her glass to hide her blush. "Then let's drink to that."

She was used to getting her way. She'd learned how to negotiate past almost any obstacle. Patience was essential. Hamster wheel, indeed, only the wheel always stopped somewhere. She knew how to reach David and would find excuses to do it. Eventually, he'd come around.

David held up his empty glass to show he couldn't drink to anything.

"I'm heading up to my room," he said. "Apparently, there's this Fab party tonight. I may check it out and see if I can shore up my referral network for recovering cultists. Are you going?"

So Carl the drug pusher hadn't been putting her on. "I was thinking about it."

"Great, maybe I'll see you there."

Beth decided to go, if only to keep an eye on him. Even now, she wanted to protect him, as if a dormant instinct had awakened. She'd always believed the Fab was an urban legend. If the party was real, he had no idea what he was getting himself into.

The fabulous fabled Fab, the many-storied Confabulation Party, where prim and proper psychologists went to let their hair down. Nobody Beth knew had ever attended, but they all claimed to know someone who knew someone who had back in the day. With a judgmental yet envious gleam in their eye, they shared stories they'd heard about drugs, alcohol, quickies in the bathroom, an impromptu orgy in one of the bedrooms.

Carl the drug pusher opened the door. "You made it."

Beth entered the crowded suite and surveyed professional colleagues chatting on the generic hotel furniture or standing in groups. A bow-tied bartender served drinks at an open bar by a tabletop display promoting Hippocratic's new antipsychotic drug that promised relief from dangerous delusions.

The drug was called Fabula.

She belted out one of her belly laughs. "The joke's on us, I guess."

He offered a roguish grin. "You expected something different?"

"In a meta sense, not at all. I came to learn."

Carl swept his arm toward the Fabula display. "Then I shall instruct you. Hippocratic has a strong reputation for satisfying unmet needs related to the brain and central nervous system."

Beth waved him off. "Let me settle in and grab a drink first. I'll seek you out for your pitch later, though. You earned my time by giving me a good laugh."

She threaded the crowd and stepped up to the bar, where she ordered a red wine that wasn't up to her standards but would do in this pinch. Tired, old glam rock strutted from hidden speakers. She sipped her wine and surveyed the room. Her colleagues smiled and talked and glanced past each other's shoulders as if this were the actual fabled party and Bacchanalia would erupt. Like Beth, they'd come as tourists, prim and professional but not above a little voyeurism. Still playing their part in Carl's joke, as in psychiatry, confabulation was the act of inventing an imaginary experience to make up for a lack of memory.

No sign of David. Maybe he'd heard about the Fab's reputation and decided to stay in his room. She pictured him sitting on the bed with a TV remote, cruising the channels while twirling his wedding ring.

Perhaps he was right, and they should leave the past alone. The Family still haunted them, but they'd each accommodated their trauma. While they hadn't cured their disease, they'd made its symptoms manageable. In some cases, they'd even made the symptoms work for their benefit, such as in their respective careers. Beth had her young but profitable practice, her finely tuned life, a crutch she kept under control, and everything in its proper place.

Strange to realize that if she hadn't suffered, she'd be a different person. In a sense, she wouldn't exist.

Near the bar, Dr. James Chambliss, who'd recently won the American Psychological Association's International Humanitarian Award for his pro bono work with war refugees, pontificated to an admiring audience.

Though they both lived and worked in Santa Barbara, Beth hadn't seen him in years. Same astronaut build, though he'd shaved his thinning hair to go completely bald, a look that suited him. Years back, when she was a student at Pomona College, he'd been her mentor, therapist, and lover. She'd walked away from all three, the final stage in taking sole charge of her life, and she'd avoided him ever since.

She edged away from him again now and found herself tangled in another group, Dr. Tamara Wilke being admired possibly for different reasons, being young and prone to fidgeting gestures—tugging at her blouse collar and buttons—that suggested a repressed but itchy sexuality about to explode. Carl was there, nursing a drink while he devoured her with his eyes.

"Dr. Harris," she beamed. "I was just arguing that God is dead."

Beth offered a polite smile. "Psychology replaced him, I suppose."

"The human brain did." The woman appeared to be drunk, her gestures even more animated. "Quantum physics. The universe exists as it does because it is perceived. Without us, it might not exist at all. The materialist idea of consciousness being a projection of the physical is wrong. It may be the other way around. As for shrinks, we are merely priests of this invisible new religion."

Carl chimed in. "What about morality? Everybody would rape and pillage—"

"Don't be such a fucking pessimist," Tamara said. "Cooperation is a survival trait for our species. Morality precedes religion. It's part of the brain, just like the God spot that makes us hardwired for spirituality. Forget morality, though. I'm trying to say the entire universe may be conscious of itself."

"Speaking of God," Beth said, "I could use some advice with a patient."

All eyes turned to her now, ready for a challenge.

"His name is Ishmael. His dad is Abraham, whom he shares with his half brother, Isaac. One day, Abraham starts hearing a voice, which he believes is God. God tells him to kill Isaac and burn the body as a sacrificial offering."

Carl chuckled as he caught on. "The Book of Genesis, right?"

"In *my* story, God doesn't stop Abraham, who goes ahead with it. He kills his son."

"Seems to me Abraham should have taken Fabula."

"Here's my question," Beth said over the group's laughter. "Ishmael learns what his dad did, and suicidal ideation takes hold. The truth is unbearable. Either God doesn't exist, and Abraham murdered his son for nothing, or perhaps worse, God *does*, and Abraham killed his son because God wanted it."

Tugging at her collar, Tamara said, "Therapeutically, the answer is simple, which is it doesn't matter. You treat Ishmael's suicidal ideation and help him live with whatever truth he accepts. You can't treat a belief."

Beth pictured Emily in her casket and thought, *Sometimes, the belief treats you.* Maybe some things proved too big for therapy to fix.

"The biblical Old Testament God, on the other hand," said Tamara. "Him, I'd love to see on my couch. The vindictive, narcissistic, gaslighting bastard."

Beth glimpsed David on the far side of the room and excused herself, first stopping at the bar for another glass of the barely passable red.

Carl followed her. "Red pill or blue pill? I have free samples."

"Which is the one that gets you out of the Matrix, again?"

"Both of them." He jerked his thumb over his shoulder toward Tamara, who was cackling at some joke. "Why do you think they're talking about God?"

"I prefer the Matrix's orderly and comfortable design, thanks."

"You might benefit to loosen up a little."

She snorted. "Are you kidding?"

"To each their own." Again that grin, which she was starting to find grating. Beth suspected Carl valued mischief over sales.

The suite was packed with people now, a maze of groups radiating body heat in the airless room. The crowd's volume inched higher while AC/DC blasted from the speakers. Beth tried to work her way toward David but found herself

pulled into a half dozen conversations. She smiled and nodded along as she heard only half of what was being said,
much of which was nonsense anyway as many appeared to
have taken Carl up on his offer to escape the Matrix's con-
fines. Sweat dampened her armpits under her suit jacket. She
looked around for David, but he'd either left or disappeared
in the shifting throng. She needed a quick exit.

The bathroom door opened, and a woman left with a sheep-
ish smile, followed by a man whose face reddened as he realized
Beth recognized him. She went inside and locked the door.
The crowd rumbled and guffawed as if waiting for her outside.
Someone bumped against the door, which made her jump.

Take it easy, her other inner voice said.

Beth raised her glass and gulped the rest of her wine. Forcing down the last swallow with a gasp, she sat trembling on
the toilet. Something about the party was triggering her—the
gradual loss of control, perhaps, the undercurrent of hysteria.

David was right. Sometimes, the worst flashbacks came
on solely as a feeling, a terrible sensation of dread. Sometimes, they weren't triggered by what was happening but by
foreboding over what might.

Knuckles rapped on the door, followed by laughter. The
knock became pounding. Beth palmed a handful of Altoids
and chewed them into peppermint grist.

With a deep breath, she opened the door and darted into
the crowd. She glimpsed David across the room. He stood
with his back against the wall, twirling his wedding band
around his finger while a redhead leaned into his personal
space to make herself heard over the noise. Beth paused at
the sight of Tamara Wilke, PsyD, dancing on the couch,
several blouse buttons undone to reveal flashes of white skin
and black bra.

Arriving as tourists, the conference attendees were going native. They'd shown up expecting the Fab party, which had probably never existed, and created it from wishful thinking and imagination. Their belief was making it true.

Again finding herself near the bar, Beth ordered two more glasses of red and downed both of them like Kool-Aid while the bartender eyed her with a nervous smile. Her brain was starting to grow fuzzy and mellow enough to see her out the door and back to her room.

She reached David as the redhead leaned toward him again and this time flicked his ear with her tongue, making him flinch.

"Excuse me," Beth said, taking his hand. She led him toward the front door.

"Thank God," he said with relief.

In the hallway, the party evaporated to a throbbing bass that vibrated through the wall. Panting, he bent to rest his hands on his knees. "Give me a second."

Beth patted his back. "Are you okay?"

David wiped his sweaty forehead. "Crowds don't usually bother me, but..."

"Mobs do," Beth said.

"Yes. Right. That's exactly it."

She rubbed his back. "Remember your breathing."

He straightened with a long sigh. "I'm fine. You grabbed me just in time. Things had started getting a little hairy in there. You've always understood—"

Beth lunged to mash her lips against his. His body went rigid, but otherwise he didn't resist. She locked her arms around his neck and pressed against him, practically climbing him in a sudden burst of passion.

"You're real," she breathed.

Real like Deacon, real like nobody else seemed to be.

He turned away from her lips and firmly tugged her arms from his neck. "No, Beth. I have a *family*."

Shit. She wiped her eyes as she regained her composure. *What am I doing?* "David, I need you to listen to me very carefully. I sincerely apologize."

"I don't—"

"I'm sorry, David. I didn't mean any harm. I guess I had a few too many."

David breathed hard. "You know, Beth, you're good at getting into people's heads. You should peek inside your own once in a while."

He left without saying bye, leaving her flustered and pacing the corridor carpet in her high heels.

You messed up, gloated her inner voice, the mean one.

"I messed up big time," she muttered, no debate now.

Beth returned to the party and forced her way through the throng until she reached Carl, who was grinning at a trio of women dancing on the couch.

He acknowledged Beth with his rogue's grin and said, "The greater the repression, the bigger the explosion."

"Tell me what you're giving people."

He shrugged. "Placebos. Sugar pills. They're high because they want to be."

"You're lying."

The grin faded. "It's just Percocet."

Beth said, "Is the pharmacy still open?"

8

REBEL

2005

Beth crept through the woods. The trees sighed around her in the breeze, and Deacon was being extra annoying.

"Where are we going?" she hissed.

Wearing an impish smile, he hushed her and motioned for her to keep moving. School was done, and they had the rest of the afternoon to themselves until the supper bell rang. Deacon had told her he wanted to show her something.

"This had better be good," she breathed.

She used to enjoy antagonizing him for the ticklish thrill, but things had changed with age. Sometimes, she wanted to pinch him until he cried uncle. Others, she stared as if he was a well she could fall into and never hit bottom.

"You're gonna love it," he whispered back.

I'm gonna love you, Beth thought, but didn't say it. If it was, in fact, love. Whatever it was, it often hurt. But what a delicious pain.

"I'd better love it, or I'm going to pinch you." Make him hurt too.

She recognized this part of the woods. They were near the baptismal stream, where over the past week, they'd watched several new families receive the Holy Spirit as the Family expanded onto new land. The roof of a large rock outcropping lay ahead through the thinning oaks, providing a view overlooking the water.

Still in spy mode, Deacon pressed his finger over his lips and motioned for her to get down on her hands and knees to follow him onto the rock.

Beth crouched and started crawling after him on the tonalite, which was as coarse as sandpaper and as hard as, well, rock. It was like crawling on razor blades. The absurdity of it all made her snort, which threatened to become a giggle.

Deacon turned and shook his head slowly. The impish smile was gone. He swept his finger across his throat.

She nodded then hiccuped and clapped her hands over her mouth. A perverse hilarity welled up in her chest, threatening to burst.

Frantic now, he waved his hands at her. If she didn't laugh, she'd choke.

He backed up to whisper, "They'll *kill* us if they hear us."

This sobered her. She took a few deep breaths and nodded, truly curious now. Together, they crawled to the edge of the rock.

Deacon pointed down.

Beth peered over the edge and froze with her mouth stretched into a large *O*.

At the base, on a shelf worn into the rock that formed a natural bench, Josh and Angela were *kissing*.

Oh, my, God, she mouthed.

Deacon leaned close to murmur, "They come out here a *lot*."

His whisper tingled in her ear. She couldn't take her eyes off the couple. The vantage point wasn't very good, but she could see enough. Josh and Angela seemed to be devouring each other. Before Beth had come to the farm, she'd seen kissing but had always considered it gross.

This wasn't gross at all. It was something else. Beautiful. More delicious pain.

The supper bell rang through the woods. Stifling a scream, Beth flinched from the edge. Deacon was already retreating on his knobby knees, his eyes watery with fear. She followed, her knees on fire now from the coarse rock. It couldn't be suppertime yet. She didn't wear a watch, but her inner clock was nearly as reliable. The ring's pattern had called for an assembly, she realized, not supper.

Back in the trees, they sprinted toward the farm. Halfway, she started to giggle. Hilarity struck her again and shot out in a wild whoop. Deacon let out a guffaw, and then she was staggering along hugging her ribs and shaking with belly laughs.

"Come on, Beth!" He grabbed her hand and pulled her along, still cackling.

The woods gave way to the animal pens, beyond which the farm's green fields and cabins lay under a metallic blue sky. They stopped to catch their breath, his sweating hand still in hers.

The bell rang again, and they let go, as if shocked.

Deacon chuckled again. "Crazy, huh?"

The scene flashed through her mind. "Totally."

"I'm not going to tell on them. Are you?"

It hadn't occurred to her, but it was a practical question. Josh and Angela could get in a lot of trouble. "Maybe it should be our secret."

What they'd been doing was certainly sinful, though Beth wasn't sure how. The kissing had struck her as alien and subversive but also utterly normal. How could love be sinful, if it was pure and delivered joy?

So much had changed in the past year, making the world off-kilter.

At sixteen, Angela had grown enviable curves. Even Emily, who was a year younger than Beth, had started to bud. As Josh neared seventeen, his voice deepened, and his face became more angular and sprouted a wispy mustache. Soon, he'd claim all the rights of manhood and be allowed to build his own cabin and take a wife. As for Deacon, he seemed to grow taller by the minute, and his voice often cracked when he talked, as if it couldn't decide whether it wanted to be high or low.

At fourteen, Beth was on the same road to adulthood. Her monthly time started six months ago, which baffled her. When she looked in the mirror, however, she still saw a kid, except this kid had a tiny zit on the side of her nose. Mom called her a *late bloomer*, something else she didn't understand. At the farm, sex ed consisted of the basics of keeping herself clean and stern warnings about certain urges.

She liked the idea of sharing a secret with Deacon.

A crowd had gathered at the Temple. The bell stopped ringing. The congregation's anxious murmur filled the void.

"There's Mrs. Chapman," Beth said. "Let's ask her what's happening."

Their teacher was a hawk-faced widow with gray hair and sharp eyes. They called her *the prophet* behind her back, as she was always making predictions about what their lives would be like if they listened to her or didn't.

"The Reverend left," she told them.

"What? Why?"

"You'll find out when I do. You kids should find your parents."

The Family flowed into the Temple. Beth threaded the press of bodies until she located her parents. "Is the Reverend really gone?"

Daddy smiled at her. "Hey, honey. We're about to find that out."

"He's gone," her mother said. "I have it on good authority he packed up his truck and drove off. Just up and left."

Of course Mom would know. "He's coming back, though, right?"

"If he doesn't, things are going to change around here, mark my word."

They took their seats in their usual pew. Emily gave her a little wave as she passed in the aisle, but Beth barely responded with a nod. Things might change? What was that supposed to mean?

She didn't see a need for anything to change. And she hated that her mother appeared to be happy it might.

Dressed in their black jackets and hats, the shepherds sat on high-backed wood chairs arranged on each side of the chancel, facing the congregation. It was the first time Beth didn't see Jeremiah Peale up there, beaming and filling the room with excitement. The absence jarred her further. Worship was her favorite time, seeing the entire community come together in the Temple for worship, music, and to receive the many gifts of the Spirit. Here, she could pour out all her problems and worries in a seething flood and become filled with Jesus's strength and love. She'd surrender her body and mind to the Spirit and dance and sing and explode, and then leave energized with the kind of faith that could move mountains.

The Spirit felt far away right now, an unsafe, unsettling feeling.

Shepherd Wright rose and raised his hands for quiet. Bowing his head, he began a prayer, which Beth dutifully recited along with the rest of the congregation.

"Amen," he said. "I am honored to stand among you to tell you that Jeremiah will be away for some time to investigate an important spiritual matter."

The crowd stirred, waiting for details, but none came.

"In his absence, he entrusted the shepherds to guide the Family. He made us all promise we would run a tight ship." Wright had crossed the stage to stand behind the pulpit, a visual cue of who was really in charge. "There will be no idle hands while he's gone. We will work harder, fight harder, and love harder for the Lord every day until the Reverend returns."

Enthusiastic nods from the congregants, a few scattered amens.

"There will also be some new ordinances to clarify the true path," he added.

Beth shifted uneasily in her pew, wondering what that meant. In an instant, the world, already off-kilter, seemed to shift again under her feet.

The farm flourished in California sunlight. Under a bright blue sky, the moist, warm soil sprouted life across the green fields. Beth and the other children worked the lettuce rows, ferreting weeds from the dirt and dropping them into buckets.

"Yes, Jesus loves me!" they sang. *"The Bible tells me so . . ."*

The singing tapered off as they wilted in the heat, dead tired.

Beth didn't mind hard work. She'd always taken pride in contributing. For as long as she'd lived here, she provided helping hands every morning except Sunday, the day of rest. She weeded, peeled potatoes, churned butter, cleaned the chicken coop, watched over the little ones, and did myriad other jobs.

Late afternoons and weekends were for play, however, always had been at the farm. Until Shepherd Wright changed the rules.

"You guys are babies," Wyatt said. "It's only been a couple days."

"I don't hear you singing," Angela said, which made Josh laugh.

"'Spare the rod, spoil the child,' my dad always says." Mr. Cornell worked in the slaughterhouse and scared the kids with his scowl, though he favored the belt over the rod where his unruly son was concerned. "A little discipline will do you good."

Angela held up a clod of dirt and crushed it in her hand to watch the crumbs fall. "Our mom would never hit us. I'd like to see her try."

"She just yells," David chimed in.

"Mine never hits me either." Deacon grinned. "That's why we turned out nice."

Wyatt snorted. "Bunch of whiners is how you turned out."

Beth spotted a yellow-flowered dandelion and dug deep to remove the taproot along with the plant, all while casting a sidelong gaze at Deacon. Dressed in dirty shorts and a T-shirt, skinny arms tanned by the sun, he knelt in the soil and inspected a worm cupped in his hand.

"Got a new friend there, I see," she said.

"Yeah. He's a quiet little guy."

"What are you going to name him?"

A lopsided smile appeared under the tangled mop of brown hair. "Moses." He gestured toward Wyatt with the worm. "Let my people go."

"I'll bet you could turn water into whining," Wyatt said. "I should show you the rod myself one of these days. Toughen your backside up a little."

Deacon chuckled. "'Water into whining.' That's actually a good one."

"This all isn't so bad," Emily said.

Beth snorted. "Are you kidding?"

"We're all together. What's the big deal?"

"It sucks. For one."

Emily shrugged. "Good things come to those who wait. The Reverend will be back. Until then, all we have to do is say yes sir, no sir, and do what we're told."

Beth hoped Emily was right this time, because the wait was suffocating her. Last night, at supper, Mrs. Chapman sat with the children to enforce their silence. The grown-ups could talk, though they did so in hushed tones, as if afraid to laugh. Shepherd Wright's church was more God-fearing but far less joyful than Jeremiah's. This unsettled Beth less than the speed at which the transformation occurred, as if it was something they'd all secretly craved for a long time.

Deacon returned Moses to the dirt. "You're free."

"Why'd the Reverend leave, anyway?" David asked.

"He went camping," Wyatt said. Rumor had it the Reverend had loaded his truck with camping gear before he'd left. "The man needed a vacation."

"All by himself?"

"Why not? Not everybody's scared of everything like you, dumb-dumb."

Angela gave him an icy stare and raised her clenched fist. Wyatt grinned and blew her a kiss.

"What if he doesn't come back?" David said.

"He's coming back," Emily assured him.

"But how do you know?"

"Don't you think he would have said goodbye if he wasn't?"

Unless Shepherd Wright forced him to leave fast, Beth thought but didn't dare say aloud.

The bell clanged across the fields. The sound energized the kids with a second wind. They sprang to their feet and marched toward their cabins to wash.

"The shepherd didn't say anything about what we do after supper," Beth said. "I'll meet you guys at the trailhead. We'll go to the stream."

"I want to go to the Loop," Wyatt said.

"We don't have time. The trail, then?"

Everyone agreed. They'd have some time to themselves.

Ahead of her, Josh glanced at Angela and took her hand. Looking around in alarm, she wrenched from his grasp. Beth grunted as they parted, as if she was losing something herself.

After supper, Mom darned socks on the living room couch while Daddy studied his Bible in his easy chair. Mom was prattling about Mr. Cornell and the way he stared at Mrs. Durham—*he doesn't even hide what he wants! Her husband's only been dead six months, and him! He's married!* Sitting at the other end of the couch, Beth gazed out the window with longing. She'd bided her time, waiting for the right opportunity to ask to go out. With twilight on the way, it was now or never.

"Daddy, can I go out and play with my friends until bedtime?"

Mom kept on darning her socks. "Not tonight."

Daddy removed his reading glasses with a smile. "Sorry, honey."

He always called her their *miracle baby*, God's answer to their prayers when they couldn't conceive. For as long as she remembered, they'd had an unspoken deal. She followed the rules, and Daddy doted on her in return.

"I worked all day," she said. "Plus school. Why can't I go out?"

He attempted a conciliatory smile. "Just be patient—"

"When Jesus comes back," Mom cut in, "how do you want him to find you? Working hard to be a better Christian would be my guess."

"The Bible says to eat, drink, and be merry," Beth said.

Daddy frowned, trying to recall the passage until Mom gave him a knowing look, as if sharing an inside joke. "The Book of Ecclesiastes."

"Oh. Right. It's not a bad passage." He chuckled. "Words to live by."

Mom pinned him with her stare. "Are you serious?"

He went back to his Bible. "Never mind."

Let it go, Beth told herself, but couldn't. She was tired of how unfair her world had become, and her pious mother had grown increasingly irritating over the last year. "Maybe I should ask Shepherd Wright."

Mom's lips flattened into a stern line. "We're your parents. But while the Reverend is gone, the elders make the rules, and we must abide them."

This had nothing to do with the shepherd. This was just her mother being controlling. Mom valued order above everything. Which was one reason why she was such a gossip—she had to know everything so it wouldn't surprise her.

Beth's narrowed gaze crossed the living room into the kitchen. The cabin seemed to shrink until it became a jail cell. The whole world had become stunted and stifling. Outside the farm, kids attended enormous schools and wore nice clothes and had cell phones and didn't have to work all day. They went to the movies and chatted whenever they wanted and explored the wide world together.

Right now, that world was looking mighty appealing.

At the same time, she couldn't imagine leaving the farm. For over three years, she'd felt safe and loved here. She just didn't want anything to change. This made her unfair treatment all the more bitter and galling.

"This is supposed to be good." Beth's voice broke as she fought tears. "It shouldn't be mean."

"It *is* for your own good. You just don't understand that yet."

"We love you," Daddy told her. "You have to trust us. Your mother decided, and it's final. Just be patient—"

"Do you actually think I'll go to Hell if I hang out with my friends? Do you?"

"Elizabeth—"

"All my life," she shouted, "you've been letting me do just that while telling me Jesus loves me. Now you're saying he didn't love me all this time?"

They'd raised her with Christian love, but this was different, this was living a certain way because of fear.

"I don't know what's gotten into you," Mom said, "but I don't like it, and now's not the time for it. When the Reverend..."

She winced, as if she'd said something scandalous.

Beth leaned forward. "What? What about the Reverend?"

"We're not talking about the Reverend, we're talking about you."

"Just tell her," Daddy said.

"She's not ready."

"What are you talking about?" Beth asked. "Ready for what? Tell me."

"She's old enough," Daddy insisted.

Mom set down her knitting with a sigh. "The Reverend went to talk to God."

Beth guffawed. "What?"

"This is not in the slightest bit funny."

"I'm sorry," she said, bewildered now. "I just don't understand."

"One of the new arrivals told Jeremiah about a mountain where he'd seen a miracle," Daddy said. "The Reverend took it seriously enough to go look for himself."

"He thinks it may be the sign we've been waiting for," Mom added. "Do you understand what that means?"

Trembling, Beth stood. "Oh."

The apocalypse.

She bolted for the door.

The end of the world.

"Elizabeth!" her father called after her.

Sobbing, Beth ran across the commons. The distant woods were dark with twilight. Her bare feet slapped against stones, each footfall sending stabbing pains into her soles. Her father's cries echoed behind her, and then she disappeared into the trees.

She'd been raised to believe it was coming. The end times, the end of days. That's why they'd built a community in the wilderness. They'd come here to make ready for Jesus's return and prove themselves worthy of his mercy.

She'd never expected it actually would happen.

But what if?

If Jesus returned, she'd never grow up. She'd never enjoy everything the world had to offer. She'd never know what it'd be like to kiss Deacon on the lips.

Lord, if they all went to Heaven tomorrow, would she have to obey her mom forever and always, stuck at the same age? How did it work, exactly?

It wasn't fair. It shouldn't happen now, like this, when she was on the cusp of adulthood and finally gaining control of her own life.

She shivered in the chill. Around her, the bugs started their nightly song.

"Hey!" she yelled. "Emily! Deek!"

Nobody answered.

"Anybody?"

She'd missed them, and now they were gone.

And she was in big trouble.

She'd gained her freedom from her stifling parents, and she'd have to pay the price. Might as well stay out for a while, whether she had company or not, if for nothing else to delay facing her mother's anger.

Instead, Beth hurried back home, suddenly afraid the world might end while she was gone. That it had already ended, and everyone had left without her.

Wearing her best Sunday dress, Beth strolled with Emily along the dirt road that cut through the fields and wound through the wilderness all the way to Babylon.

"You said nothing ever bothers me," Emily said. "It's not

true. Plenty of stuff bothers me. The Reverend being gone, and these dumb rules, and Wyatt's a jerk, and I have a crush on Dave that keeps me up at night. I just don't let it get to me. You want to know my secret?"

Beth said nothing because of the big square of tape covering her mouth.

"Oh, sorry," Emily added. "I forgot."

"Mm-mm," she said, hoping it sounded enough like a *yes*.

After running away from her parents, she'd come back to plenty of yelling and punishments. Time after time over the following days, Beth had tried to put her feelings into words, only to fail. How could she explain wanting to gain Heaven, but not so soon? Her longing to break away from her family, while staying a part of it?

In the end, her mother's condescending sniping got her good and riled, and she'd discovered eloquence in telling Mom to screw herself.

That was last night. This morning, she had to wear the tape like a scarlet letter, marking her as an Unruly Child. Now everyone would see her with it at worship. She hated feeling like an outcast, but she'd wear it like a badge of honor out of pure stubbornness.

There should have been an extra commandment to listen to your kids.

"It's weird talking to somebody who doesn't talk back," Emily said. "I have to admit, though, I kind of like being able to do all the talking. Does it hurt?"

Beth shook her head. Not physically, anyway.

"You should draw a smiley face on it. If you want to make your mom really mad."

Beth chuckled, *hmm, hmm, hmm*, fighting back laughter.

"The thing is, none of this really matters," Emily explained.

"That's my secret. In the end, we'll be with God, so why sweat the small stuff? Why sweat anything?"

Beth could think of a lot of reasons to sweat but wasn't able to say them. She believed, but she didn't share her friend's simple, rock-hard faith. If Emily wrestled with the big questions, she never showed it.

In the end, Beth didn't care. She was simply glad someone was talking to her. She'd made everyone except Emily and Deacon angry. Her other friends were annoyed because her rebellion had made their parents extra strict.

"Especially now," Emily went on. "If the Reverend found a miracle and this is really the end, why would I care if I churn butter instead of play? That's what Jesus meant when he said turn the other cheek. He was saying the slap doesn't matter. He was saying the slap isn't even real. Think about *that*."

"Mm," Beth said.

If she could talk, she'd tell Emily she no longer believed the apocalypse was coming. She'd say the Reverend wouldn't find a miracle out there in the desert mountains. The world would go on as it always had.

That was the thing about rebelling. Once it started, it kept going.

Emily shrugged. "I don't know. Maybe if you say you're sorry…" She frowned into the distance. "Somebody's coming."

Beth turned as a truck emerged from the oaks, bouncing on the ruts and kicking up a rooster tail of dust and stones.

Emily grinned. "He's back! Hallelujah, he's back!"

Beth's smile strained against the tape.

The truck growled to a stop next to them. The morning sun burned orange on the dusty windshield. Jeremiah

Peale sat behind the wheel, his tanned, muscular arm draped out the window. His windswept hair hung tangled over his forehead.

"You girls headed to worship?"

"Yes, sir," Emily said.

The Reverend eyed Beth's face. "I guess I missed some drama."

"Beth and her mom had a fight. They—"

He raised his hand. "You can take that off, dear. Tell me what happened."

Beth pulled at the tape, but it didn't want to release its grip on her flesh. Her eyes watered. She pictured putting a whole roll of it over her mother's mouth. Clenching her eyes, she wrenched the rest of it from her face with a searing rip.

"Ow," she said, though it was a relief.

The words poured out of her in a flood. Shepherd Wright's new rules, the constant work and school, no talking allowed at the communal supper, Mom forcing her to stay in every evening to study her Bible, everybody acting so serious, losing control and ending up with her mouth taped shut... The rest dissolved in bawling as a week of frustration poured out.

The bell clanged, calling the Family to worship. The Reverend raised his hand. "I think I get the picture. I'll get it squared away as soon as I can."

"Thank you," Beth sobbed.

"If you were my little girl, we'd have a serious talk, and there'd be no need for the tape. But you're not my girl. So until we get this sorted out... Understand?"

She put the tape back on, good and tight.

"Good girl. It won't be long."

"Reverend?" Emily placed her hands on the window. "Where did you go, sir? Did you see a miracle?"

"Honey, I talked to the Spirit," Jeremiah said.

She goggled. "You did?"

"I sure did. You know what he told me?"

The girls shook their heads.

A grin filled his wide face. "He said to get ready. Now hop in the back."

Emily climbed onto the pickup and helped Beth get in. They'd barely settled among the camping gear when the old Ford lurched forward along the dirt road.

"Wow," she said. "Wow! Can you believe it?"

Beth was glad for the tape now. She wasn't sure what she believed. A miracle in the desert. A sign of the end times. What did it mean? There was a big difference between *the end is near* and *the end is here*. What did "get ready" mean? She'd been getting ready her whole life.

"Look at all this stuff." Emily reached into an open toolbox and raised a black marker. "Hey, come here."

Beth wagged her head.

"No smiley faces, I promise."

Another wag.

"I'm your friend. Have some faith."

She leaned forward with a groan. Cupping Beth's face to hold it steady, Emily scrawled something on the tape.

"Mm?" said Beth.

"I just wrote, 'I love you, Deacon.'"

She squealed.

"You do!" Her friend went into a mock swoon. "'Oh, Deacon! I want to kiss you and marry you and make babies—'"

Beth elbowed her. "MMMM!"

Emily laughed. "Just trust me, okay? I'm trying to get you out of Dodge."

The truck stopped in front of the Reverend's cabin. He got out and walked around to the back. "Down you go. Come on, I'll help you."

Still giggling, Emily took a flying leap at him, as if skydiving. The Reverend caught her and brought her in for a soft landing.

Then it was Beth's turn. He grabbed her by the waist and gave her a breathless twirl before setting her down.

Jeremiah chuckled at whatever Emily had drawn on her face. "Off you go before you get in even more trouble."

The girls dashed to the Temple while the bell rang. The Family flowed inside, filling the air with their excited babble as word spread of the Reverend's return. Beth spotted Mom and Daddy waiting for her outside the Temple doors.

Emily stopped to give her a hug. "Didn't I tell you everything would work out? Didn't I say it would all be perfect in the end?"

"Mm," Beth grunted. It wasn't perfect yet.

As she approached the doors, Mom inspected her face with a frown. "You can take that off for worship."

Ripping the tape off again, Beth looked down at it and read, *Sorry, Mom.*

They went inside and headed to their pew.

Daddy put his arm around her shoulders and kissed the top of her head. Then he whispered: "No, *I'm* sorry. Here, give it to me." He crumpled it into a ball and thrust it in his pocket. "Never again."

The Family settled into their pews, still babbling as they waited for something to happen. Beth and Emily were the only ones who knew the Reverend had found a miracle. She kept it to herself. For once, Mom wouldn't be the first to know.

Beth wasn't *that* sorry.

The doors crashed open. Dressed in his black blazer and a clean gray tee, the Reverend stomped up the aisle reaching for Heaven and declaring, "THANK YOU, JESUS, FOR THE CHANCE TO SERVE YOU."

The room burst into applause.

He strode to the altar and wheeled. "This is a celebration of the coming of Christ, so why aren't we celebrating? Where are my players?"

Mrs. Price warmed up the organ as those who wished to play took the stage and one by one joined in. Soon, Deacon was grinning over his guitar, Emily and her mom rattled tambourines, a red-faced Shepherd Ford blew his harmonica, and Mrs. Blanchard waved her arms as she led the joyous singing.

Across the seething mass of people, arms raised in exultation, eyes clenched tight, mouths spoke the angelic language or sang, feet tapped or danced. Already the Living Spirit was active among them, leading Mr. Preston to rave in tongues, while Mrs. Diaz, seized by prophecy, screamed that Jesus was coming, the sky was opening, he was in the clouds. Next to Beth, Mom jerked and twitched in otherworldly spasms, while Daddy did an awkward jig, as if square dancing with himself. Beth clapped along and waited for the Spirit to come, but it didn't.

Today, she just couldn't let go.

"Yes, Lord," Jeremiah called out. "Come, Jesus." Then he flung his arms wide and howled, "Wait! Hold it! Stop the music!"

The congregation faltered in confusion. He'd never interrupted the Spirit before. Usually, hymns didn't conclude so much as peter out from exhaustion.

"It's never boring, is it?" While they all chuckled, the Reverend went on, "That's because we worship God's way, with love and joy, an open door inviting Jesus to join us in the pews, and a room full of beautiful and fine people ready to take him back to their homes. I'm sorry to stop it. I had to stop it. I stopped it because I am bursting with good news. Bursting. But first, I need to talk about how things went while I was gone."

He bowed his head as if in silent prayer. When he looked up, he was a different man, the loving smile gone and his eyes blazing a bright blue. "I'll just say this. We worship God every day, and we do it with joy and love, not fear."

His eyes swept the congregation and settled on Beth, making her shiver. "If we must suffer, though, we do that with joy too. That's what being a Christian means. I've always believed if your faith comes easy, you're doing it wrong."

"Amen," someone said to fill the ensuing silence.

Beth wished she had enough tape to cover her entire face.

The Reverend's smile returned. "Now let me tell you about the miracle I saw."

The crowd sucked in its breath.

"As you all know, God judged us worthy to raise enough money to buy some neighboring land, enough to start work on cabins for twenty new families. One of our new arrivals came to tell me—Joe, are you out there?"

An old man waved from the pews.

"Joe told me about a miracle he saw while hiking in the mountains. No, not a 'You didn't eat your pie? It's a miracle!'" More laughter. "No, sir. This was a bona fide miracle, a once in a lifetime miracle, which I thought maybe, just maybe, could be the sign we've been waiting for. So off I went on a pilgrimage."

The Reverend hopped onto the altar and sat on it. A few people gasped in the pews. It was exactly the kind of thing he'd do. Scandalous, but reminding them altars and churches and rituals didn't matter, only God did.

"Red Peak," he went on in a quiet voice. "Mountain of the Great Spirit, the Natives call it. On the western side of Death Valley."

His eyes took on a dreamy cast as he recalled the journey. "You drive up 395 to a little town called Medford, dry desert all around, and then you keep going because you're still not there. You go up a dirt road into the Inyo range, and you get out and walk through the scrub, and then you find a mountain with a flat top the color of blood. You're still not there, no, you're not even close. Because you still have to make the climb, on foot, in the withering heat. The first summit is a false one. So is the second. Then you reach the crown…"

His eyes burned like blue coals now. "A massive stone sitting right in the middle of all that flat rock. And behind it a wood cross, older than old, planted tall off to the side of this natural altar. There, I was privy to mysterion."

The crowd oohed.

Mysterion. A word from the Greek New Testament. A mystery denied ordinary men but understood by the godly. God's counsel, hidden from nonbelievers and delivered only to the righteous chosen.

Jeremiah sprang back to his feet, producing a flurry of cries.

"There was no burning bush! Not for this servant. There was a burning *cross*! The cross burst into flame, angry and spitting sparks. It burned but was not consumed. I fell to my knees, but it was not enough. I pitched onto my face and hugged the earth, but it was not enough. I howled, I pleaded, I begged for mercy. That's when I fell to my *heart*, dear friends. And..."

He went quiet again for a long time.

The congregation remained rock still. Beth held her breath.

The Reverend said, "The Spirit talked to me in a clear, loud voice."

Mom sobbed. "Oh, my dear Lord."

"He said—" His voice cracked with emotion. "He commanded, '*O Man, deliver your tribe unto me in this place, for now is the time of purification. The time for the worthy to cross the black sea and ascend to the sacred place.*'"

"Praise God!" someone called out.

"That was what he said. 'Deliver your tribe unto me!' The time is now!"

The congregation leaped roaring to its feet, arms raised and fists clenched and eyes gaping as if trying to glimpse paradise through the steepled roof. Lifetimes of faith and prayer and supernatural hunger poured out all at once in an alarming clamor. They'd won the lottery, the ultimate lottery, and they'd won it all. They'd won eternity. The Spirit roamed among them, possessing them with its fury.

Beth alone remained sitting on her pew, crying tears lost in the clamor.

The ascension, he'd called it.

The world would die, only to be reborn.

Just as she would with it.

Then she laughed, a loud, cathartic squeal.

Emily was right. There was no fighting this. Nothing really mattered, not when faced by the sweep of such colossal divine events.

Beth had been raised her whole life to wait for this to

happen. She was one of the chosen few. And the time was now.

She would ascend with the Family and live forever.

Forever, in paradise.

"'DELIVER. Your TRIBE. Unto ME!'"

Beth leaped to her feet as the Spirit grabbed hold. Tearing at her hair and dress, it shot through her with a piercing scream of pure love and primordial terror.

9

REGRET

Beth flew back to Santa Barbara, not so much pursued by remorse as taking it home with her like a souvenir.

Everything in its proper place, she thought. *Everything.*

The words were more prayer than motto at this point, Pandora fretting over the box she'd opened, undoing decades of expensive therapy. Her recollections of last night remained hazy at best, flashes of a breakdown during the party.

James Chambliss had rescued her before she destroyed her reputation. He'd made sure she got back to her room, acting the perfect gentleman. He'd left his card, on which he'd scrawled, *We need to reconnect soon. It's important.*

He didn't miss her as a lover, she knew, but he'd never gotten over being inside her head.

This morning, she'd stumbled through her panel with a crushing hangover. As a depressant, alcohol plummeted serotonin levels, resulting in plenty of self-loathing.

No wine for you until tonight, the nice voice murmured in her head.

"If that," she murmured.

*And no more prescription opioids ever. What were you thinking?
Well, it's like this*, she thought. *I wasn't thinking.*

For the flight, she'd brought aboard a massive coffee, while
a bottle of Gatorade waited in the seat pocket. Her brain
throbbed in her skull. California sunshine flashed along the
wing, too bright.

And now everybody knows what you did, the mean voice
lashed out. There was no stopping it today.

"They were too busy doing it themselves." Her mouth
like cotton no matter how much water she drank. Her bow-
els rumbling.

The businessman sitting next to her glanced up from his
laptop. "Excuse me?"

"Sorry," Beth said. "I was just talking to myself."

"Been there, done that."

She turned to the window before he could take their
exchange beyond small talk. She was right about last night.
The behavior she'd seen some of her esteemed colleagues
engaging in was far worse than anything she did.

Which was fine for them. *She* was different. *She* was supposed to have her shit together.

What about David?

Plenty of regrets there. No big ones, though. The more
Beth considered it, touching him had been a homecoming
of sorts, warm and real and substantial. What touching Deacon again would be like.

Odd, how something bad could feel so correct. Even now,
she felt strangely energized and peaceful following her freak-
out, despite all the self-loathing.

She'd once wanted things. She'd once had faith that could
move mountains.

As the Canadair Regional Jet descended into Santa Barbara, Beth thought about the man who fifteen years ago had put her on the path of faith's alternative.

As a member of the Family, Beth was used to living under an open sky, close to nature. Now her world had shrunk to plain boxes coated in institutional green or white paint, her day similarly constricted into activities monitored by psychiatric nurses.

As for the Family, five still remained on the Earth, the only part of her new life that didn't give her painful vertigo. The rest had ascended a month earlier.

Left behind, Beth gazed through the wire mesh covering the rec room's windows into sunshine, wondering why the world was still here. A world that had become colorless since the Spirit abandoned her.

At night, she dreamed of red fire until her screams woke her.

During the day, she still cried, and once she started, she couldn't stop.

Dr. Klein had a stocky build and salt-and-pepper beard and wore a stodgy tweed suit. Even after numerous sessions, she didn't trust him. He wasn't a believer, which made him a sinner. Worse, he was Jewish and had rejected Jesus Christ as the Messiah. Beth often said she'd pray for him, intending it to sound cutting, but he only said, *Thank you.* When she said he was bound for Hell, he shrugged as if to say, *That's fine for you to believe, but not for me.* When she told him about the apocalypse, he gestured toward the barred window. Outside the lion's den, the Earth was still turning.

Gripping the little cross she wore around her neck for strength, Beth had declared that he could never understand her because he wasn't one of the chosen. He'd replied that was less important than her understanding the horrible things that had happened to her so she could process them.

What happened to Mom and Daddy.

No, Beth couldn't process that, not yet, maybe not ever.

Arguing with Dr. Klein was far more interesting. The psychiatrist fascinated her. He appeared immune to her beliefs, which made him an odd mix of monster and superhero. Statements that used to elicit amens and gasps in the Family succeeded only in producing one of his frustrating shrugs. She was Jacob, wrestling with the angel. He was always in control, sitting relaxed in his leather chair, his body language open and nonthreatening. She envied him.

One day, he showed up to their session with a book, which he thumbed to a bookmarked page and read aloud:

The lightning and thunder
They go and they come:
But the stars and the stillness
Are always at home.

Beth sat on the old couch facing him across the coffee table with its white box of generic tissues.

"What's that mean?" she asked.

"What do you think it means?"

"God abides," she answered without thinking.

The psychiatrist removed his glasses and cleaned them with one of the tissues. "That's a fair interpretation. How would you interpret it in regards to your life?"

"How would *you*?"

She enjoyed turning his questions back on him.

"I might interpret the poem to mean that big events, sometimes *bad* events, happen to us, but we can take comfort in remembering the calming things that remain. If I were in a storm, I might gain some peace in that."

Beth found this intriguing, producing a brief tug-of-war between playing this new game or sticking with the old.

"Read me another one," she said.

He returned the reading glasses to their perch and thumbed through the book. "George MacDonald wrote that last poem. It's called 'A Baby-Sermon.' Here's one by Stephen Crane you might find meaningful."

He read:

If I should cast off this tattered coat,
And go free into the mighty sky;
If I should find nothing there
But a vast blue,
Echoless, ignorant—
What then?

The words coalesced into a feeling that stirred her in a deep place. She imagined her mother flying through the Temple, a bizarre and unsettling image.

She turned away and said, "It means whoever wrote that is a sinner."

"Now I think you're deflecting," Dr. Klein said.

"What does that mean?"

"You don't want to feel certain things, so you redirect everything to the beliefs you were raised with or to our psychiatrist-patient relationship."

"How did you figure that?" she said.

"Because I'm trained to understand how people think."

"So you can change their beliefs."

"No," he said. "Well, yes, in some cases—for example,

if you intend to use your beliefs to harm yourself or others. Otherwise, I'm interested solely in your well-being. At Red Peak, you suffered a period of prolonged, extreme trauma that ended with events so tragic I can't imagine them."

"They happened for a reason." Her voice too loud.

"You need more than your beliefs. Because what happened wasn't normal, but very, very horrible. I was trained on how people think so I can help you understand your trauma and live with it."

Beth wiped her eyes with her palms. "They were *good people.*"

"Okay." He caught her expression and added, "I believe you, Beth."

"What they did makes me sad and angry. My mom…"

"Yes…" He waited. "Yes?"

"They're in Heaven, and you're a liar. You're fake. You're not even a real person." She glared at the psychiatrist.

Then she shuddered as she always did before losing control. A bottomless pit of despair awaited. The Spirit had abandoned her. She and her friends had betrayed the Family and let God down. They should have died too.

Mom, what are you doing with that knife?

Dr. Klein studied her. "Are you all right, Beth?"

She hugged her ribs and sighed, sorry she'd yelled at him. "Why did you read me poems today?"

"It's a form of therapy designed to stimulate growth and healing. The whole idea is to get people to identify with ideas and feelings in poems as a tool of self-learning for those whose thoughts and feelings are chaotic." Watching her closely, Dr. Klein continued. "The poem hits the brain's artistic and emotional right side, producing an instant trigger for feelings and memories—even traumatic events—

which can be viewed safely through the poem's objective filter."

She was barely listening. "Tell me what else you do. How you fix people."

"What do you want to know? I'm thinking we might play a game."

"What kind of game?"

"Let's pretend you are Dr. Beth. I come to you for advice about a patient raised in a religious group that committed mass suicide, which she witnessed. Before that, she saw everyone she loved subjected to systematic torture. And now she is struggling to cope with feelings of trauma, grief, and being left behind. What form of therapy would you recommend?"

This was an interesting game.

For the first time in months, her chaotic mind coalesced toward a sense of control, however fleeting.

"I'd tell her God still loves her," she said.

"That's good. What else?"

"I'd tell her to rid herself of the source of all her sin."

He sighed. "No, Beth."

She said, "I'd tell her to cut out her heart."

Dr. James Chambliss dimmed the lights and told her to relax.

Instead, she fidgeted on the couch. "I don't think this is going to work."

He sat in his chair facing her. "The odds are in our favor, if you give it a chance."

The year was 2012, and one out of ten Americans believed the reported completion of the Mayan calendar marked the end of the world. All the talk about the apocalypse had summoned old nightmares.

The congregation singing in the Temple, her mother silent.

The knife in Mom's hand.

What Beth remembered had actually occurred, or so she thought. She'd dreamed it so many times, she wasn't sure what was real anymore.

Today, she would find out. Seven years after the Family destroyed itself, she'd finally learn what happened the last night at Red Peak. Finally recall the memories she'd buried so deep.

"Abreactive hypnosis can be a valuable tool in ego state therapy," he said.

This therapy was based on the idea that the psyche was a mix of distinct personalities, such as a woman displaying a tough CEO in the boardroom but reverting to a petulant teen when visiting her mother.

"In your family of selves," he said, "we're targeting a vaded ego state. Specifically, teenaged Beth, who hasn't yet processed her trauma and needs to be calmed so she can rejoin the family."

Beth rolled her eyes. "You don't have to explain it."

"You're not a student here. You're my patient." His eyes gleamed with excitement.

James taught clinical psychology at Pomona College— where Beth was now in her senior year—and had become a mentor. They'd tried a spring–fall romance, but it had fizzled out due to a lack of any real feeling. Where their relationship ended up excelling was as therapist and patient.

And what a patient. James couldn't get enough of the Family of the Living Spirit. He scribbled lengthy notes during their sessions, as if planning to write a book.

"I just mean I'm too analytical," Beth explained. "I'll end up telling you how to hypnotize me."

She was also afraid of what he might find. Much of that last night on the mountain remained shrouded in repressed memory. What she did recall came through in fragments broadcast in dreams both strange and terrifying.

Hypnosis produced an altered state of consciousness in which memories were easier to access and sometimes surfaced in hyper vivid detail.

"That won't interfere with the hypnosis, though it would help if you'd try to relax," he said. "The key is if your left dorsolateral prefrontal cortex activates along with the dorsal anterior cingulate cortex." In other words, the executive control part of her brain lighting up in tandem with her attention-focusing network. "I've found that three out of four patients are able to go into a trance."

"Then let's roll the dice." She took a deep breath. "I'm ready."

The brain was an amazing organ, a primal cake coated in civilized icing. While the brain was capable of beautiful ideas, its primary purpose was to survive, and that survival was based on fear as much as reward. Events that threatened survival were remembered and often recalled without consent, while memories of some events were considered too threatening and might be repressed.

Plastic like Silly Putty, the brain could be remolded. It could be tricked into revealing repressed memories and rewired so that once recalled they weren't so visceral and terrifying, a process called cognitive restructuring.

James removed an antique bronze pocket watch from his suit jacket and dangled it at the end of its chain. "Okay—"

Beth laughed. "You're kidding me."

He reddened. "I realize eye fixation is no longer cred-
ited for its efficacy in hypnotherapy. Only verbal guidance
is required for induction. Patients see it in movies, though,
and expect the prop."

"Okay," she said. "I'm sorry. See how bad I am at this? I'm
ruining it already."

"You're doing fine."

"Just watch what you're doing when you're in my head. I
don't want you to accidentally implant any false memories or
induce split personality disorder."

Back in the 1980s and '90s, hypnosis yielded waves of
cases surfacing forgotten childhood sexual abuse, including
thousands of reports of Satanic ritual abuse that turned out
to be fabricated memories.

"I have enough to deal with in there," she added.

"I take it back," he said, seeming to remember she was
not only a patient but also a student and an ex. "You're right,
you're impossible."

She sat back and got herself comfortable. "Let's do this,
James."

"We're in a dim room that is *safe, warm, relaxing*," he
droned with a gentle cadence, his speech slow and deepening and emphasizing key words. "There is a part of you
listening to me talk. The part of you that *dreams*, that knows
how to *breathe*, that knows your body better than you and
how to *relax* every part of it. That part of you is focusing on
my words. That part of you is starting to feel *dreamy*. That
part of you is aware that your hands are *warm* and that your
arms are now completely *relaxed*. Your eyes are getting a little *heavier* as you picture sailboats on the bay. A gentle breeze
pushes them along. You're with them, and you're *drifting*..."

The room disintegrated. At peace with gravity, Beth

melted into the couch, which had become a peaceful and calm oasis.

"Imagine you're watching yourself on TV," he murmured. "Can you see yourself? It's early August, the year 2005. You're fourteen years old."

His voice sounded far away.

Time stretched as she considered his question and its answer.

On the TV in her mind, a girl walked through desert scrub dressed in a white choral gown.

Yes, she thought, unable to muster the energy to say the words aloud. *We sang during the purifications as the Family prepared to cross the black sea.*

"If you can't speak right now, you can nod. Can you see yourself? Good. Your TV has many channels, each having a different memory of your last night with the Family. You can change channels whenever you want. You will also fully experience the emotions in the scene while at the same time being completely safe with me. Okay? Very good. Now I want you to go back to the last night at Red Peak..."

So many stars filled the sky, they looked like static. The old cross burned high up on Red Peak's flat summit, visible only as a muted bloody glow. They'd all heard the screams. The Reverend had wanted to go first.

Mom walked next to her, silent. Dad hobbled on his crutches, his face a mask of pain. Beth's eyes roamed the procession but didn't see her friends. Had they escaped? The eyes of the congregants blazed back at her from the darkness.

Gaunt with hunger and stooped by suffering, they shuffled toward destiny. A different kind of hunger had seized them, seeking glory and relief. If any of them ever had qualms about quitting the Earth, they had none now.

They hummed a hymn as they approached the Temple.

James's voice was tinny and distant. "Find the event that hurt you the most. It's okay to feel the fear. Express yourself. Shout if you want to. Feel my wrist? You can squeeze it as hard as you need. I'm with you, and you are safe with me."

Shepherd Wright stood at the altar, on which rested scores of plastic cups filled with purple wine.

"The Reverend is dead," the elder said. "His example paved our road across the black sea. We will all be rejoined in the light of the sacred place."

Beth looked around but didn't see any of her friends. They'd followed the plan.

He sang: "Christian worker, be thou faithful, till life's toil and care be o'er; see a crown is waiting for thee, over on the other shore."

The congregation chanted: "When at last thy journey ended, thou shalt with the angels join, and a crown of fadeless glory, then, oh Christian, shall be thine."

The pews emptied as the Family shuffled toward the altar to receive the symbolic blood of Christ. The very real blood of dozens of sacrifices had stained the once-white cloth draped across its surface. The room still smelled like smoke and roasting meat from the burnt offerings.

Staring at the stains, Beth picked up her cup while Shepherd Wright smeared olive oil across her forehead to anoint her. She brought the wine back to her pew and stared into its purple depths, as if able to glimpse eternity if she only looked hard enough. It smelled like alcohol and bitter almonds.

Glory awaited, a bright, golden road to a place where pain didn't exist.

"It is Christ himself has promised," the Family sang, "and his word is ever sure. To reward the faithful servant, who shall to the end endure..."

People struggled in some of the pews. Shouts rang out. A woman screamed. A baby wailed. Daddy gazed back at her with wide eyes.

"Don't," he murmured.

"Mom," she said. "I don't want to do this."

Despite the familiar songs and trappings, this wasn't the religion she was raised with. The Spirit not the same ghost.

"Let your feelings out," James told her from far away. "Then you can forgive the people who hurt you. Forgive them so you can be free."

Mom turned toward her, tears streaming down her cheeks, a knife in her hand. She couldn't talk anymore, not after what they made her do, just as Dad couldn't walk anymore without crutches.

Gunshots boomed. Someone was shooting outside.

The singing faltered as the poison seized them all in its grip. One by one, the congregants doubled over and collapsed, heads banging on pews and bodies thumping to the floor. They arched their backs, arms clawing at the wood. The smell of pee and vomit filled the air. The baby stopped crying.

"Daddy, please stop this," Beth cried. "I believe you now. Let's go."

He gripped his stomach and groaned, shaking his head. "Can't."

"Daddy? You didn't . . ."

"I'm sorry," he said.

Mom had made sure he drank his at the altar.

"Daddy!"

"Now," he said. "Run as fast as you can."

"Beth!" James shouted from far away.

Daddy's crutches tumbled to the floor. He pitched forward into the pew in front of him, his body jerking and thrashing, growling like an animal being strangled. Foam boiled out of his mouth.

"Daddy!" Beth screamed and buried her face in her mother's chest. "He's dying!"

Mom held her close as she wailed, stroking her hair. Her hand settled on the back of Beth's neck.

"What are you doing?" Beth flinched as her mother's grip tightened. "Mom, don't."

Her mother looked down at her with a fierce love.

"I love you Mom please don't I'll be good I promise I'll be good I don't want to die—"

Mom raised the knife.

Beth was screaming and covered in blood—

"Stop," James howled.

The horn blared the judgment and the bodies flew spinning toward the Temple window in a colossal wind—

"Awake! Three, two, one, awake!"

Beth returned to the present, staggering at the sudden vertigo. James glared at her with wide, watery eyes, cupping his neck.

She looked down at her hands. Her nails red with his blood. Her throat hoarse from screaming.

"What the hell." He blinked in shock. "Christ, Beth. That's not supposed to happen. Do you know what you were doing?"

"James? Oh my God, I'm so sorry."

"Are you all right?" He breathed in rapid, shallow gasps. "Are you okay now?"

"Yes." She took quick stock and was surprised at how content she felt. "Are *you* okay? Did I do that to you?"

"I've never heard of this happening before," he said.

"I'm so sorry."

"Don't be." James pulled away his hand to inspect the blood on his fingers, revealing the scratch she'd made under his ear. He barked a nervous laugh. "You were talking the whole time. The things you shared. Beth, that was amazing!"

"I remembered things." Events she'd buried deep in the tar pits of her subconscious, where they'd boiled for years. "Some of the memories came out as abstractions, stuff my mind created." Freakish and creepy. Bodies smashing through the pews to tumble through the air, sucked toward the Temple window.

"We should keep going," he said. "Try again next week."

"I think you're right," she lied.

She'd never do this again. Beth wanted to find out what happened next, but she wasn't sure she'd believe it.

She wasn't sure she would survive it.

Returned to the comfort of Santa Barbara's familiar streets, Beth exited the taxi in front of her building. The clean, bright elevator delivered her to her air-conditioned floor. Her condo seemed to sigh as she entered.

Coming home had never felt so satisfying.

Once her luggage had been put away, Beth turned on her Mozart and went to the kitchen to open a bottle. She poured out a glass and swirled it before taking a sip that turned into a gulp.

Hair of the dog, I guess.

"You guessed right."

She settled on her couch and pulled a stack of research papers and presentation handouts onto her lap to read.

The Mozart seemed stifling. She switched to jazz.

She couldn't sit still. The handouts bored her. Even the condo seemed too still and confining. She set the papers aside and went to her bedroom to change into jogging attire. A long run at Shoreline Park would cure her restlessness.

Standing in her panties in front of the mirror, she ran her fingertips down the center of her chest to her belly as she thought again about kissing David.

Maybe she'd reach out to Deacon after all, despite the risks.

No, nothing romantic, however tempting that might be. No need to feed the monster. The episode at the conference hadn't taught her what she was missing, only that she had more work to do on herself. Unfinished business.

For fifteen years, Beth had lived with a time bomb. In 2005, Dr. Klein had shown her the bomb and where it was buried. In 2012, James Chambliss had tried to help her defuse it. Since then, she'd simply lived around it, which had required constant and extreme self-control. And over time, she'd come to believe she could have it both ways, a diminished past and a full present, but she was wrong.

There had to be an easier way to live than at the edge of one of two extremes. For most of her life, her mother had held a kitchen knife poised over her throat. Ridding herself of the past was the key to her future. Despite all the work she'd done on her brain, she had more ghosts in her head than a haunted house.

She needed to put them to rest forever, or else she might end up choosing a far easier path, the way Emily had. *I couldn't fight it anymore.*

As Beth pulled on her sports bra, she decided she'd reach out again, this time with a specific plan.

Deacon, David, Angela.

Together, they'd go to Red Peak on the fifteenth anniversary.

If the trip triggered anything, so be it. If she had a freak-out, even better. Either way, she'd come home a new woman, strong and complete and wanting nothing.

Dressed and ready to run, she went downstairs to the lobby, where the doorman intercepted her to hand her a box that had arrived minutes before.

The package was from Emily, as battered and heavy as the past.

Like her mother, her friend had reached out from the grave to present a mirage of some elusive, final truth. Holding the parcel, Beth sensed the answers it offered would only lead to more questions.

A chain that would only be solved by returning to Red Peak.

She opened it.

10

PROTECT

Behind the wheel of his Toyota, David sped south out of Modesto with the windows down to enjoy the invigorating rush of air. Every mile delivered him farther from chaos and closer to the security of home and work.

Only one task stood in his way.

"Damn it," he said. He rolled up the windows and thumbed a button on his cell phone. Then he set the phone on his lap while it dialed in speaker mode.

Angela answered. "I was wondering when you'd call."

"Hey, sis." He fished in his breast pocket for a Marlboro and bent his head to light it. One last cigarette, and then he could put them away for a while.

"Hey yourself, you little shit. What's up?"

"I'm driving home from a conference in San Francisco. How's life in Vegas?"

"I don't have all day, David," she grated. "Talk."

He forced a deep breath. "It was horrible."

"Which is why I told you not to go. Did you see Deacon and Beth?"

"Deek is like this hedonist rocker now, if you can believe it," David told her. "Beth is a psychologist." Thinking about her gave him a twinge of arousal and irritation. "She said we should all go back to the mountain."

The line went quiet for a while. "Why does she want to do that?"

He didn't want to tell her about the proposal, but Beth wasn't the type to let it go. Best his sister hear it from him before Beth got to her.

"She thinks we'll remember everything that happened and have a big catharsis and this will somehow make us happy instead of very, very sad."

"I've already been back," she said.

Here we go. Easy as pushing a button.

"I know."

Angela had her own special way of avoiding acceptance of the tragedy. She believed someone or something had duped the Family into destroying itself, and had returned to Red Peak numerous times to search for clues.

She'd never stopped seeking justice for Josh and Mom, and in so doing had become as obsessed with the Medford Mystery as its many fans and conspiracy theorists, people she otherwise despised.

"If you ever want to go, I'll take—"

"Thank you." He'd already known what she was going to say.

"Fine. I have to warn you about something. A production company called me. They're making a documentary about Medford. The fifteenth anniversary."

"What did you tell them?" He knew the answer to that as well, but he wanted to hear her say it.

"I told them if they came anywhere near me with a camera, the Las Vegas Police Department would bury them alive in the desert."

David chuckled. "That's my sis."

"Just a heads-up, they will probably try to hump your leg too."

"I'll just tell them you're my sister."

"It's not these documentary guys that worry me," Angela said. "The crystal anniversary is bringing out the weirdos, and we live in an age of zero privacy. Watch yourself."

His smile faded. "I will. Thanks."

"Give a visit out there some more thought, if only to go see Mom. That would be a good excuse to get us all out there."

Heat rose in his chest. *Where were you when we put Emily in the ground?*

"I just paid my respects to the dead."

"She wasn't family," Angela said. "Not to me. We owe Mom this much."

"My exit is coming up," David lied. "I have to go."

"Run along then, David."

"I love you, sis."

"You're all I have left." She hung up.

Angela said that whenever he told her he loved her, and every time, she made it sound like the most disappointing thing in the world.

David waited for his garage door to open with warm, calm satisfaction, like an explorer returning to the mother ship after a long journey in deep space. Once inside, he hauled his luggage out of the trunk and entered his house.

Comforting sounds and smells greeted him. Claire was cooking in the kitchen, and judging by the delicious smell, she was preparing spaghetti carbonara, a family favorite. His children were home. Alyssa nattered away at her mother while Dexter watched TV in the living room.

David smiled at the routine, completely content. He often found himself cowering in the lion's den of the chaotic outside world, but here, among his tribe, he was the lion, ready to tear apart anyone who threatened his blood.

The conversation in the kitchen stopped. "David, is that you?"

"I'm home," he called.

"Hi," Alyssa said.

David deflated a little. His kids used to come running to the door to hurl themselves laughing at him, but they'd grown a little old for that now. Dexter was starting third grade in the fall. At nine, Alyssa was an early bloomer the way her aunt Angela had been, and had grown moody.

He walked into the kitchen and gave Claire an obligatory kiss while she stirred the spaghetti in the boiling pot. "Hi, wife."

She was a tall woman, regal even when frying bacon, still trim and youthful after bringing two children into the world and living for them instead of herself. Her red hair was cut into a short, boyish bob, accentuating her slim neck, the sight of which had once filled him with a strange consumptive longing. She still wore her outfit from doing yoga, one of her addictions.

Claire turned to wrap her arms around him. "You're home for good?"

"Until the weekend."

"We missed you."

"I'm glad to be home." He gently stepped out of her

embrace and sat on one of the stools next to his daughter. "What are you doing there?"

"I'm drawing a cat," Alyssa said.

"I see that. You're so talented."

"He has little people for pets. See?"

"Very creative. How are you? Is everything okay?"

"Dex is really annoying and I wish I was an only child."

"Relationships come and go," David said. "But you'll always have your brother. Ten, twenty years from now, Dex will be your best friend. You'll see."

"No, I won't," his daughter deadpanned.

Based on his own relationship with Angela, he didn't really believe it either. "At least try to be kind. Never be cruel."

"A documentary film producer called while you were away," Claire said.

David flinched. "On the house phone? What'd they say?"

She poured out the boiling spaghetti into a colander. "He's doing a show on the Family of the Living Spirit cult and wanted to interview you."

"Right," he said. "He wants to talk to me about exit counseling."

"You'll be on TV, Daddy?" Alyssa asked him. "Are you famous?"

David gave her a smile. "No." Not in any way he might want to be, anyhow. "Is everything okay at camp?" Claire had enrolled her in a two-week drama camp. "Is Ellie still bothering you?"

"She's being nicer now."

"If she ever touches you again, I'll have to talk to her dad, and I won't be so nice about it. Make sure she knows that."

"It's all working itself out, Daddy." Alyssa went back to her drawing.

David watched his daughter flesh out her picture with a fierce love that poured from his body at the atomic level. He took the lion thing too far, he knew. He wasn't a helicopter parent, he was more like a helicopter with a squad of commandos aboard.

He understood he shouldn't try to solve all his daughter's problems nor fight his son's battles. He couldn't help himself; they were his world. Humanity might be alone in the universe, but if you had family, you weren't alone. She and Dexter were his real immortality. Just as he was everything to them, provider and protector, a responsibility he regarded as sacred. David's father had divorced his mom and now lived in Maine, about as far away from his errant progeny as he could get and still be in America. His mother joined the Family and died at Red Peak. In a few years, Alyssa would be David's age when he went to the mountain.

He'd vowed that what happened to him would never touch his kids. Soon, she and Dexter would leave the nest and have the rest of their lives to discover how cruel the world could be.

Until then, he'd show them its beauty, as all children deserved. In return, they would show him a childhood free from pain.

David curled up next to Dexter on the boy's little bed and read him his favorite book, a story about dog heaven. Claire had brought it home after they'd been forced to put down Gunner, the family's golden retriever, who'd developed bone cancer. Dexter loved seeing the dogs frolicking in open fields and eating their biscuits and took great pleasure in the idea Gunner was there too.

Tonight, his son turned thoughtful. "Daddy?"

"Yeah, Dex?"

"Is Heaven a real place?"

As Alyssa was growing up, David had expected this question. He'd dreaded it more than talking about the birds and the bees. While Claire had a spiritual bent and took the kids to various houses of worship to expose them to different religions and cultures, David was raising them to be skeptics. Eventually, they could form whatever religious beliefs they wanted, but at least these beliefs would be *theirs*. Other than having a skeptical, open mind, he refused to force anything on them.

So he answered Dexter the same way he had his daughter when she'd asked, the only way he knew how. "Some people believe it is, some people don't."

"So what about God. Is God real?"

"Same. Some people think so, others don't. What do you believe?"

Snug in his pajamas, his son nestled against him. Bedtime always made him extra affectionate. "I believe in everything."

David chuckled. "Heaven and God and even Zeus?"

"Yup."

"What about Thor?"

"Especially Thor."

"Well, I guess that makes you an omnitheist."

"What's that, Daddy?"

"It means you believe in everything."

"Om-knee-thee-ist," said Dexter. "That's me. Omni-me-ist."

"Some people are happy believing in things they can't see. Others want proof."

"You can't see love."

David smiled at the boy's cleverness. "Love is provable. It comes from the brain. The big question is whether God does too. Anyway, it's not what people believe that's a problem. If you ask me, the world needs more omni-me-ists. It's what they do with that belief, if they do bad things."

Dexter thought about it. "Like blow up a building."

Hearing his seven-year-old son describe religious terrorism was heartbreaking. "Yes, like that."

"God wants everybody to be good, though, right?"

"They say real change starts at home." David leaned closer to his son and said conspiratorially, "I think if God exists, he'd want you to be nicer to your sister."

Dexter gave him a devilish grin. "Yeah, but Thor told me I should be really annoying."

"That darn Thor. All right, Dex. Time for sleep." David kissed his son and tucked the blanket around the boy's chin. "Sleep tight."

"Good night, toilet seat."

He chuckled at their routine. "Good night, poopy diaper."

"Good night, stinky farts."

David went to the door. "Sleep tight, Dex. I'll be watching over you."

"You're the best daddy. Good night."

He turned out the light and shut the door. As always, his son's innocence and love filled him up until it turned into a strange melancholy. Sometimes, love hurt, but that was the best kind of love.

After putting Alyssa to bed, David headed to his living room, where Claire sat on the couch watching one of her TV shows.

She paused it with the remote. "Hey, stranger. How did everything go with your client?"

"Okay," he said and hated himself for lying.

"Do you think she'll leave?"

"No. I think she'll stay in the cult forever." The best lies always lay wrapped in the truth. "I just couldn't get through." Body tensed, he remained at the entrance, half in and half out of the room.

"That's too bad. I'm sorry to hear it." Claire patted the cushion next to her. "Do you want to talk about it? We could boil some tea. I'd like to hear how your conference went."

"I have to work." He just wanted to be alone. "Sorry."

His wife stared at him, then turned her show back on. "Fine."

"Tomorrow night, okay?"

"Yup." She'd stopped listening to him.

David walked off toward the den he'd converted into a home office, his chest burning with anger. He could tell she was irritated with him. He was *working*, providing for his family. His job wasn't nine to five like hers.

His desk and computer greeted him with the potential of hours of focus. He often retreated to his office at night and worked in solitude and the comforting fantasy everyone in the world was asleep except him. The surge of relief he felt quickly turned to more anger, this time directed at himself. He wasn't being fair to her, he knew. Lately, it seemed he was always working.

Sitting at his desk, David thought about going back and surprising her. Maybe in a few minutes. An hour, tops. Yes, that was a perfect compromise.

He pulled a notepad toward him to sketch out the intervention for his next client, a middle-aged couple here in Fresno who claimed their son Kyle was steadily isolating himself in a new religious movement. The couple couldn't tell him much about the group, only that it was called The Restoration and appeared to be a small Christian doomsday cult.

That meant his first step was to determine if Kyle was in fact actually in a cult. Only method separated a new religious movement and a cult. If the group used mind control to force obedience and dependency on its members, which it exploited, then it fit the popular definition of a cult. The difference was the level of harm.

No matter how much David learned, he still had a hard time determining whether Jeremiah Peale's Family of the Living Spirit was a cult. Yes, the group offered its members a pure ideal articulated by a beloved leader. It stifled critical thought by promoting a self-identity as being real Christians and regarding all other Christians as half-baked backsliders. New members were love-bombed. All had to obey a rigid orthodoxy, and those who didn't toe the line might be cast out.

All of which made the Family zealous, not a cult. Their brand of Christianity was charismatic, and they'd taken their God very seriously. Jeremiah Peale had started the community as a group of like-minded people who wanted to express their lives as a continual act of worship. They believed the Holy Spirit was real and could be drawn upon to strengthen and enlighten them in accepting God's rewards and tests. They'd believed God had chosen them and that they had to meet their creator halfway by purifying themselves, purify as in *repent*—to make oneself *righteous*, which in turn meant observing Christian doctrine and law. David recalled the community during the years at the farm as being rigid on rules but otherwise caring and joyful for a child. He'd always felt warm, safe, and loved.

At Red Peak, the community changed, and there was no doubt what it had become. Manipulation, group confessions, hard labor, starvation. Inducing trance states that cultivated suggestibility and furthered thought control. Mutilations, mass suicide, murder. In the desert, the Family became the worst sort of cult, joining a long, horrifying list with the likes of Peoples Temple and Heaven's Gate.

A Google search produced nothing about The Restoration, same with the cult databases. This wasn't surprising, as many cults consisted of a handful of members. A typical intervention lasted three to five days. He'd need the first day just to learn about the group from Kyle and profile its beliefs and techniques. Once he pinned all that down, he could follow his proven script.

Switching gears, David answered his emails, confirming with John and Amelia Turner that he'd see them Saturday morning for their son's session. He read an endless email from a mother terrified for her daughter, who she believed was in a sex cult, and replied to her questions about exit counseling, though the whole thing smelled like run-of-the-mill polyamory. Some therapists he'd met at the conference had written to him. An email from the producer making the Medford documentary he answered last, sending back a terse but polite no.

Claire had left his snail mail on the side of his cluttered desk. A handwritten thank-you letter from a grateful family, which he opened first. An invoice, junk mail, and finally a big box sealed in packing tape.

The sender was Emily Hayes, Bakersfield.

Her voice burst in his ears, as if she stood next to him.

We'll go to Heaven together.

His first thought was to put the package in the closet

he used to store office supplies, heave it onto the highest shelf, and revisit it when he was ready. Whatever Emily had sent him, he doubted it would make him happy. Curiosity didn't always kill the cat. Sometimes, instead, it gave the cat nightmares.

He'd be ready tomorrow. Always tomorrow.

Tear off the Band-Aid, he heard Beth say at the funeral home.

"Damn it."

David picked up his scissors and sliced the flaps open. He reached into the box and removed a rubber-banded stack of newspaper and magazine clippings, along with pages printed from the internet. The first headline read: 118 MISSING, FEARED DEAD IN MEDFORD.

Emily had done her homework. Everything one might want to learn about the official story of the Family's self-destruction was here, right up to articles written in anticipation of the fifteen-year anniversary.

Under that, he found another stack of paper bounded in a cross of rubber bands.

Microfiche-printed using a micrographic scanner, an article from the *Los Angeles Weekly Republican*, May 8, 1870, declared, 43 VANISH IN MEDFORD.

David blinked in surprise and started reading.

The article described how several years after the Civil War, a gold prospector named William Ward declared the imminent apocalypse and invited his followers, mostly German farmers settled in the San Joaquin Valley, to join him at Red Peak, where they suffered for three long months. Medford's citizens described rumors of starvation and self-mutilation among the Wardites, a strange fire visible from the town. Then the group disappeared, leaving behind all its worldly belongings, along with bloodstains testifying to terrible violence.

What happened in the summer of 2005 had occurred before, deepening the mystery while solving one small part of the puzzle. The Family had never figured out who'd come before them to plant the cross on Red Peak and build the tiny ghost town in its shadow. Emily had. But what happened to them?

One more sheet of paper lay at the bottom of the box, an article from the *Bakersfield Californian*, dated October 14, 2005, which reported, SHERIFF'S DEPUTY MISSING. David gasped at the photo, which showed the man who'd led him from his hiding place in the Temple.

In his memory, the deputy had looked as shocked as David felt. Apparently, the man had later returned to the mountain and vanished. Only his patrol car was found on the site, along with a blood trail proving a DNA match. The FBI had staged another massive search of the area, but turned up nothing but rocks and scrub.

"What the hell?" he murmured.

Why did people disappear there? What happened to the bodies?

Among all the paper, there was no letter from Emily, not even a single note. In her silence, however, David knew she was trying to tell him something.

An invitation, perhaps.

Look closer, she seemed to be saying. *Don't look away.*

Hours later, David got into bed and lay in the dark thinking about the mystery of Red Peak, which appeared solvable only by joining the mystery itself.

For years, he'd directed his rage at Jeremiah Peale, the

elders, the Family, his mother, himself. Even fifteen years later, he still sometimes fell into flashbacks at odd moments. He could be showering and find himself shouting at people who'd died long ago and existed only in memory.

Now he was angry at a place. Something about that place was evil.

"David," Claire whispered next to him. "David."

He stiffened but didn't answer.

"David?"

In his mind's eye, Red Peak loomed.

11

JOURNEY

2005

Outside the kitchen window, the first rays of morning revealed cabins and the distant smokehouse and green fields beyond, all of it still there after the long night. Nonetheless, David's world was ending.

"Glory," Mom said as she stuffed their kitchen into a handful of old cardboard boxes scavenged from the Dollar General Market in Tehachapi. She eyed her children at their small dining table. "Finish your eggs so I can pack these plates."

"Okay." David scooped cold scrambled eggs into his mouth.

"I'm not hungry," Angela said.

"Eat anyway," Mom told her. "You'll need your strength today. Glory!"

"Stop saying that. Seriously."

David chewed and chewed but couldn't force his dry throat to swallow. He pictured a great fire surging from the horizon.

His mother laughed. "Why am I even bothering to pack? Where we're going, we're not going to need anything."

He gulped his milk to push the food down. "Mom?"

"Yes, Dave?"

"What's going to happen?"

She smiled. "We're bound for Glory!"

Angela let out a labored sigh.

"Everybody's going to die." David's chin wobbled under an impossible weight. "What about Grandma? What about Dad?"

A satisfied smile flickered across Mom's beautiful face like an illusion, and he hated her right then, just as fleeting.

"What happens is between them and God. My sole concern is you kids."

"I don't understand why we can't just stay here," Angela said. "If God wants us, driving a couple of hours isn't going to make any difference."

"The Lord created everything, Miss Angela. The universe and everything in it. I don't think he owes you an explanation for his requests."

"What if God asked you to punch me in the face, Mom? Would I still be your sole concern?"

"I can't eat any more," David said.

Mom scanned their plates with a frown. "Fine. Go, then. Both of you. Go rain on somebody else's parade."

He brought his plate and glass to the sink. Tears stung his eyes.

Mom sang a Christian song as she went back to work, packing for Heaven.

Head down, David went outside. School buses and a tractor trailer waited in front of the Temple, ready to deliver the Family to the next step in its journey to another reality. Two men lurched out the doors, hauling a pew between them.

Sometimes, he felt strong in the knowledge he was on God's side. He liked stories about bad and selfish people getting their comeuppance, and felt safe knowing he was making better choices.

This was different, though. In a short time, everyone David knew from his life before the Family was going to burn in endless fire. Dad and Grandma and his cousins. Ajay and Sandy and Doug and all his teachers. Not just people, but all the animals and plants too. Everything. Soon, nobody new would ever be born. The Earth would be a smoking cinder in space. No longer needed, the entire universe might be switched off.

It was all too big for him. Too big and too scary.

Another truck squealed as it parked in a cloud of exhaust. He pictured one of them running him over, almost wanted it to happen. *Then* Mom would care how upset he was. *Then* she'd wish she'd paid attention to her son's feelings.

"Hey, stupid." Angela caught up to him. "Don't listen to Mom. She has no idea what's going to happen. It's all a story she likes telling herself so she's not sad."

The tears flowed freely now. "The Reverend told her. He's never wrong."

"I don't think he has any idea either."

Angela didn't believe the way Mom did. The way *he* did. She only liked the farm because Josh was here.

"Don't say that! You have to believe!"

"Excuse me for trying to make you feel better," Angela snapped.

His sister thought she was so tough. "When the fire comes, who's going to protect *you*?"

"You're such a stupid little—"

"You'll die forever!" David bolted.

"Fine, run away," Angela called after him. "I'm done watching out for you."

"I don't care!"

Driven by fear and anger, his legs kept pumping until he'd ditched her in the dust. He was mad at her—*after all this time, look who turned out to be the stupid one*—but Heaven might feel a lot like Hell if she didn't make it.

David ran into the Temple at breakneck speed and came to a stomping halt. The pews were gone. The altar, the wood dove mounted on the wall, all of it. The house of worship was large and cavernous now, stripped of its warmth. Dust hung drowsy in the morning light. His clomping footsteps echoed off the bare walls.

Just a few more steps brought him into the hallway, crowded with boxes. Like the nave, the supply closet had been emptied.

There, hugging his knees in the dusty dark, he wept as he did three years earlier, on his first day at the farm.

"Don't kill my sister," he prayed. "Please don't hurt anybody."

Angela had made herself the hero of her own story, one in which God would forgive her lack of faith. All she had to do was open her eyes to see Jesus was watching out for her, if only she'd let him.

It's not fair. God can do anything. Why doesn't he make everybody believe? Why does he have to destroy anybody? Why does sin have to exist at all?

Free will, David thought, answering his own question. A big subject at school. God gave his creation the power to choose.

Most people had forgotten God, and now they'd pay the price. He should have felt strong, being on God's good side.

Satisfied the way his mom was. Instead, he felt like a traitor, which, in itself, was a whole other kind of betrayal.

Sorry, God, he prayed. *I can't help it.*

The door opened, making him jump. He'd been so deep in his thoughts that he hadn't heard anyone approaching.

"I had a funny feeling!" Emily said. "Are you okay?"

He shrugged and turned his head to wipe his tears on his shoulder. Emily closed the door and sat next to him in the dim closet.

"Are you sad we're leaving?" she said.

Another shrug.

"Remember what the Reverend said? Wherever we go, that's our home, because we're all together?" She tucked her long hair behind her ears.

He sniffed. "That's not it."

"Then what's wrong?"

"You're not even a little scared of what's going to happen?"

"Why would I be?" Emily stood and dusted her knees. "Come on. Let's go."

"Don't want to."

"We're leaving today. Don't you want to say goodbye?"

David exploded with a sigh. "Fine." As usual, nobody wanted to take him seriously.

They left the church and went back into the heat and light. The Family hustled about their packing, lugging boxes and chairs and suitcases. Nobody worked the fields this morning, the crops abandoned. Freed by Mr. Preston, the sheep and pigs and chickens wandered among unpicked tomatoes and asparagus.

The farm was lush and beautiful, and it was home. He'd wanted to say goodbye like Emily wanted, but it was already gone.

"You always worry about what you're giving up," she said. "You should think about what you're getting."

"I wish I believed like you. You're really good at it."

"God has everything planned out." And one could either ride that bus or get crushed by it. "We'll go to Heaven together. You and me, Dave."

"God's going to kill everybody," David said. "Doesn't that bother you?"

"Remember when Mrs. Chapman taught us about the Flood? I think Noah was more scared of the rain than what would happen to all the wicked people."

David wondered how wicked they really were. "It just doesn't feel right to go to Heaven when so many aren't."

"That's why you deserve to go," Emily said. "See? You're good."

He didn't believe that. He'd tried his best, but he was no better than Ajay Patel back in Twin Falls, or any of his other old friends. The only difference was his mom believed in Jesus, so he did too. Being a Hindu, Ajay didn't.

"I'm not that good." How could he be? He'd *prayed* for this to happen.

"You're good to me," Emily said.

Blushing, he lost his train of thought. "Want to go to the stream one last time?"

"I see your sister!" Emily stood on her tiptoes to wave. "Let's see if she wants to come too. We'll all go together."

"Yeah, great." Angela could yell at him some more for being worried about her.

David thought of the Flood, how the rising water covered the Earth and killed every living thing on it. He wondered how Noah survived with his sanity intact while the world drowned all around him.

▲ ▲ ▲

The kids trooped through the woods toward the baptismal stream for the last time. The air hummed and chirped with insects and birdsong. David walked alongside Emily, his stride paced by a walking stick he decided he'd take to the desert. Deacon with Beth, Angela with Josh, two by two they'd march to the ark.

Wyatt moped behind them. "I wonder if you can get married in Heaven."

"We'll be happy there," Emily said. "That's all we need to know."

"Yeah, but can we eat blueberry pie?"

"I don't think we'll have bodies."

"I'd like to have pie one more time then. And see the trains."

"Stop trying to spoil everything," she scolded.

"I'm going to miss a lot, that's all."

Josh said, "Relax, bud. I'm sure they'll have blueberry pie in Heaven. All you can eat. You can swim in it. The trains bring it in."

"Make it hot fudge sundae then. This is Heaven we're talking about."

The kids laughed, a little too hard. Wyatt could be annoying, but his irreverence had a way of breaking the tension and making God feel a little more like a kindly Santa Claus and a lot less like Wyatt's stern father.

"You won't miss anything," Emily said. "You'll be happy. Nothing will hurt you."

"Huh." No doubt, Wyatt was picturing eternity without his dad's belt. "What about the birds? Are they going with us? What about all the cats and dogs?"

"There are no pets at the farm," Angela said with some surprise.

"It's a rule," Emily said. "Nothing to hold us back."

"We still don't know," Wyatt insisted. "I think they're all coming too. They didn't do anything wrong. They're innocent."

David had no idea. He found it strange that God was so explicit about his rules but had told his creation almost nothing about where they'd be living forever after they left this world. A thousand-plus-page book written by God, and barely a word.

"We can't understand it," Deacon said.

Wyatt spat in the dirt. "What's that supposed to mean?"

"It's impossible to describe or even imagine."

"Yeah?" The kid cackled. "Then how do we know it's even good?"

"Faith." Emily shook her head at him. "Obviously!"

"If you don't think it is, what are you doing here?" Angela said.

"I came for the pie."

Josh took Angela's hand and squeezed it as if to say, *Don't bother with him, you can't win.*

The trees broke to reveal the stream glittering in the morning light. Beautiful and cool and noisy with rushing water, this was their favorite place, where they swam and played and could be themselves. Their Eden within Eden.

For David, his journey as a Christian started here with his baptism. The shock of the freezing plunge. He'd risen to waves of love and applause. A bird had darted from the trees to disappear high up in the sun's glare. He remembered Emily on the bank, smiling in a blue dress, and for the first time since leaving Twin Falls, he'd thought, *This could be home.*

"We'll all be together," David said. "Right? That's the important part."

"Listening to you and Deacon whine for eternity," Wyatt said. "Sounds wonderful. Sign me up, Lord."

David's world blazed red. Soon, untold millions if not billions could be dead, destroyed in a great fire, including Ajay, and maybe even his dad, and this mean kid was getting a free pass and cracking jokes.

He lashed out in a clumsy swing. "Stop!"

Wyatt backpedaled, a terrified look on his face that made David feel sorry and powerful at the same time. It made him laugh, and Wyatt broke out in a nervous chuckle until David took another punch.

His fist bounced off the kid's chest, completely ineffectual, no energy behind it, as if he was fighting in a dream. Wyatt blinked in surprise, flinching as if he'd expected far more pain than he got.

Then his face went dark. "You little shit—"

Suddenly David was flying, up and over Josh's shoulder, where he squirmed shouting and kicking. The big kid splashed into the stream.

"Time to cool off, Davey boy." Josh flung him into the water.

He belly flopped with a loud splash and came up sputtering with shame and rage. His friends laughed as they ran into the stream splashing each other. Wyatt stood alone on the rocks, still looking angry and surprised.

"You'd better say you're sorry," Angela told him.

With a glum nod, David waded to shore. "Sorry."

Wyatt eyed him warily. "You done being a crazy animal?"

"You can hit me if you want. I deserve it."

"I'm not going to hit you, dummy. What the hell, though?"

"I was just mad," David said. "I have friends out there."

"Yeah, well, the next time you're mad at the man upstairs, don't take it out on me." The kid surprised him by thrusting out his hand. "Good fight, I guess."

They shook. "Thanks."

Wyatt surprised him again with a rough shove. "Jerk. Now let's go swimming."

David had friends here too.

Frolicking in the water, he forgot his burdens and laughed for the first time in days. Then Josh whistled and pointed. Time to go back.

Dripping on the shore, the pack gazed in silence across the stream, absorbing everything, as if they could take it with them.

"Bye, river," Deacon said.

"Bye, farm," Beth said.

"Bye, world," Emily chimed in.

"Goodbye, pie," Wyatt said, but nobody laughed now.

David climbed aboard the idling old bus and sat squeezed between his mom and Angela. He opened his backpack and found a bag lunch, bottle of water, and some books, including a Bible.

"How long is this trip gonna be?" he asked.

"I don't know," said Angela. "Mom, how long does it take to get to Glory?"

Mom frowned out the window. "Longer than my patience can last, I suspect." She was still annoyed at her kids returning soaked from their dip, which had required her to unpack towels and a fresh change of clothes.

"Mom?" David said. "I'm glad we came here to live."

She winked. "Wait till you see what comes next."

The babble died out as Jeremiah boarded to regard them

all with his trademark grin. "Welcome aboard the Heaven Express. How is everybody doing today?"

David raised his hands and cheered along with the rest, his thoughts no longer dwelling on those who wouldn't make it, but on his loved ones who would.

"This is it, brothers and sisters," the Reverend said. "We've traveled a long, hard road together. The road the world scorned and forgot about. The high road. It's led us here. Now it just needs to take us a little farther to our eternal reward."

The door closed with a pneumatic hiss. The bus rumbled onto the rutted dirt track that would deliver the Family out of the wilderness and back into a world that David recalled as a hazy dream after three long years.

He gazed for the last time across the green fields that had fed him. The cabins stood dark and empty as the Temple. His stomach flipped as he felt caught between leaving home and heading to an adventure. Regret and excitement.

And just like that, the farm was gone. Oaks filled the windows. David turned but saw only dust in their wake. Somewhere behind, the rest of the caravan followed. The congregants quieted as the bus rolled onto the main road and built up speed. Many hadn't set foot outside the farm in years.

Mrs. Blanchard sang, "Oh, this is a joy indeed, when from the Earth we've soared, to be from ill and sorrows freed, forever with the Lord!"

Across the bus, others joined in. "*In all that heaven of bliss, we never shall record, a sweeter, deeper joy than this, forever with the Lord.*"

David hummed and clapped along with the rhythm.

The hymn finished, and the Family settled in for the hundred-mile journey that would take them to Red Peak. Outside, the land turned brown and dry and patched with scrub. Hills covered in chaparral rolled into stark mountains. God was everywhere, but this was where he lived, in the deep wilderness far from the cities awash with sin. On desolate and windy peaks.

After driving two hours, the convoy crawled through a small town offering motels, gas stations, and restaurants. Murmurs passed the news that this was Medford, and they were close. When the bus stopped at a traffic light, David gazed out the window at a service station. An ordinary family gassed up their minivan, oblivious to the apocalypse rushing toward them.

The bus started moving again.

He tilted his head toward Angela. "Sorry I got mad at you this morning."

His sister patted his knee. "It's okay."

If he was going to Heaven, he wanted to go there with a clean slate.

"I like Josh," David said. "I'm glad you like each other."

"Josh has a good heart. I trust him."

"You're good too."

Good enough to enter Heaven, he hoped.

"Quit trying to score points with God." Angela crossed her arms.

At the front, Jeremiah rose from his seat. "Get ready!"

"Amen!" Mom whooped.

They left the highway and turned onto a dirt road that snaked east into the mountains. The atmosphere became thick and charged as the Family leaned toward the windows. The bus shuddered over the path where slopes of soaring hills joined to form a long gorge. Stones cracked against the undercarriage. Joshua trees dotted the dry, rocky soil, which David imagined as madmen running through the desert.

"There it is," the Reverend said. "On our left, you can see Red Peak."

David craned his neck for a view. From this vantage point, the mountain looked like a mesa with its flat top and cliff flanks defying all but the most experienced climbers. Much of it was dark, blackened by basalt outcroppings. Aztec sandstone girdled the crown in crimson bands.

As the bus crept closer, Red Peak appeared to grow in height and mass while revealing a long rocky slope providing a path to the summit, rippled with false summits like a giant's staircase. The Family's new home was no longer a lush, fertile valley, but a lifeless rock in the middle of a desert wilderness.

However majestic, the monolith struck him as foreboding. Not menacing or evil, but callous and uncaring. Whatever its promise, Red Peak inspired awe and something else—a deep, primordial fear.

Even at his age, David understood that the holy mountain would deliver tests before it bestowed its blessings.

12

HELP

David loaded his suitcase into his Toyota and started the short drive to the Holiday Inn near the airport. There, he'd meet the Turner family, which had rented a suite for the intervention staged to rescue their son Kyle.

Though this job was in Fresno, he'd decided to stay at the hotel instead of his house because of the typical intensity of counseling sessions. He'd never known one to be simple or easy. Eight hours a day, three to five days. Cults exerted mind control by discrediting all external information sources, redefining the past, and fostering emotional dependency. They convinced members that the group was the only real family they had.

While participation in an exit counseling meeting was voluntary, things could get heavy. Shouting, crying, the bitter airing of a family's dirty laundry. Sessions had a lot in common with drug addiction interventions.

At the end of it, he hoped to see Kyle leave The Restoration with strong bonds with his family and an awareness of what support he'd need to transition to an independent life. Leaving might subject the young man to withdrawal.

He parked in the hotel's spacious lot and smoked a Marlboro in the morning's rising heat, steeling himself for a grueling weekend. While he'd learned not to get too invested with his clients, it was exhausting work. Sometimes, when the cultist started to open up and David gained traction, the day's session might turn into a marathon of up to fourteen straight hours of talking.

He met the client at the restaurant's breakfast buffet. John and Amelia Turner were a handsome couple in their fifties and surprisingly chipper, more excited than anxious.

After ordering coffee, David said, "Did you learn anything new about the group?"

"It's religious," Amelia said.

"They believe the end of the world is coming," John added. "That's what has us thinking about him. It's changed him."

"I understand," David said.

"We don't want to talk him out of being Christian. Which makes us a little concerned about your own beliefs."

David wasn't surprised to hear this, as it was common in his field. "What I believe or don't believe is not important. My counseling separates belief from action. And what Kyle believes doesn't concern me. What concerns me is what Kyle does for the group, or allows the group to *make* him do."

John and Amelia exchanged a glance that was difficult to read.

Amelia said, "You were in a cult, is that right? Growing up?"

David waited until the server poured his coffee. "That's right."

"Then you understand," Amelia said.

"There are a lot of charlatans in your line of work," John added.

David sweetened the coffee and stirred. "I don't know about 'a lot.' Some, yes. The field isn't licensed, and reputation is the only thing that regulates us."

"We did our homework," John said. "You're the real deal."

"A basic thought reform approach will be to try to get Kyle thinking for himself and viewing his group from a different perspective. I'll ask lots of questions that will stimulate him to use critical thought, and anytime he does, I'll give him positive feedback. I'll educate him about how groups like this manipulate their members and encourage him to apply that knowledge to his own group." He drank his coffee. "Who else from the family will be here today?"

The man smiled. "Everybody. All the family and friends he's got."

"Well, they all need to be aware that Kyle may act different than they're used to," David warned. "Not just defensive, but hostile, on top of other personality changes. A group behaving like a cult brainwashes its members to depend on the leader and obey."

"We won't have any trouble with him," John said.

"The biggest problem is cultists are taught to discard anything outsiders might say. Right now, he might consider *you* outsiders."

"We're his family," Amelia assured him. "He loves us more than anything."

David hoped she was right.

After breakfast, they went upstairs to prepare the suite. David and John set up folding chairs to supplement the existing furniture while Amelia called room service to order a few pots of coffee.

The room filled with family and friends, sixteen people in all. They found somewhere to sit and eyed David with fawning smiles, as if he was a cult leader himself. Nobody spoke, the room quiet enough he heard the purr of the air-conditioning.

Unsettled by the attention, he again wondered why cult leaders put so much energy and effort into brainwashing others to love them. The only answer he'd ever been able to come up with was that they were narcissistic psychopaths—charming, manipulative, dishonest, and utterly lacking in empathy. Cult leaders demanded worship because they felt entitled to it as superior people, and created fantasies to justify their delusions of grandeur.

As David poured himself another coffee, he again reflected on Jeremiah Peale. The Reverend hadn't been a narcissist. If anything, he'd empathized with other people too much; he and the Deacon he remembered proved alike that way. Otherwise, every action he'd taken, he'd done with humility. While the Family starved at Red Peak, the Reverend had eaten less than anyone while working harder. On the last night, he'd even washed their feet as Christ had his disciples.

Peale was a good man. Of that, David had no doubt. But he'd heard the voice of God, and it told him to do terrible things.

The door to the suite opened to admit a handsome young man in a black T-shirt and jeans, his longish hair an unkempt mop, his smile open and disarming. John and Amelia hugged him and then turned to present David.

"This is him," Amelia said, her eyes bright.

"So you're David Young." Kyle held out his hand. "I've heard a lot about you."

"You have?" David hadn't expected the man to exude such confidence, cordiality, familiarity. He shook the offered hand. "What do you know, exactly?"

The young man gestured to the couch. "Please sit."

David's instincts went haywire. Something wasn't right. The friends and family grinned at him and Kyle as if they expected some type of entertainment rather than an intense emotional dialogue to sever ties with a destructive cult.

He sat with a frown. "You aren't a member of a religious group."

Kyle took his own seat on the couch, nestling between his parents. "Is that what you think? I guess we can all go home then."

"You're the leader, aren't you?"

"Excellent." Kyle laughed. "I'd like to tell you a story." He accepted a glass of water from one of his friends and sipped it. "It's about St. Thomas Aquinas."

"Okay," David said, disturbed he'd already lost control of the meeting.

"Thomas grew up in the Kingdom of Sicily in the 1200s. His family raised him to eventually run an abbey of monks, but he had other ideas. He wanted to join this new group called the Order of Preachers, what we now know as the Dominicans. These friars believed in bringing God's Word direct to the people. His mother didn't like it and arranged an intervention by his brothers, who imprisoned him. After some time, his family let him go, and he went on to produce writings in theology, metaphysics, and ethics that dominated Catholic philosophy for centuries. He was known to levitate in a state of ecstasy, and during one of these times, an icon of the crucified Christ spoke to him. The Pope made him a saint for it." He drank again from his glass and produced another charming smile.

"That's an interesting story," David said. "But I don't—"

"Bear with me, as I have another for you. Some years earlier, a contemporary of Thomas Aquinas, Francis of Assisi, founded the Order of Friars Minor, also called the Franciscans, the gray friars. Long before that, he was just another rich kid who liked fancy clothes and spending his dad's money. After selling some stuff from his dad's store to give to a church, his dad beat him, tied him up, and locked him in a small room. Francis renounced his inheritance and followed in Christ's footsteps by dedicating himself to a life of poverty, chastity, and charity. He was struck by a vision of a seraph on a cross and became the first man to receive the stigmata, the five wounds of Christ. They made him a saint too. Don't you see?"

David threw a questioning glance at John, who gave him a nod encouraging him to play along. "I'd like to hear you say it."

"You can't deprogram a man bound for sainthood."

"Well, that's what I want to talk to you about," David said, taking advantage of the break to wrestle back control of the conversation. He leaned forward on the couch. "This group of yours—"

Kyle guffawed, and to David's surprise, his family and friends laughed too.

"David, I'm afraid you don't see what's happening here."

He sat back in his chair. His gaze swept the smiling faces. Something was very, very wrong. "Why don't you tell me."

Kyle said, "We are The Restoration."

The surge of anger in David's chest evaporated. A cold, gnawing fear replaced it. "I don't understand."

"This is *your* intervention, David Young. We're here to rescue *you*."

▲　▲　▲

David swallowed hard. Past Kyle's beatific face, the suite's door seemed temptingly close yet too far for him to make a run for it.

If the leader of The Restoration didn't want him to leave, he wasn't going anywhere. The people surrounding Kyle weren't his real blood relations, but they were his family.

"Right now, I'm hoping I don't need to be rescued," David said, his body tingling.

"Fifteen years is a long time to wander the desert."

"People know I'm here. If I'm missed, the police will come."

Kyle chuckled. "This is an exit counseling session, not deprogramming."

"You want to talk to me. That's all."

"That's right."

"And I can leave anytime I want." David still didn't trust it.

"Would you have met with us otherwise?"

He considered. "It depends why you want so bad to talk to me."

"Why? Why." He laughed. "You're David Young!"

The room burst into applause. David flinched, bewildered.

Amelia said, "I'm sorry I lied about being Kyle's mother. It has been such an honor to finally meet you."

The rest called out similar sentiments.

David stared back at the smiling faces. "I still don't understand."

Kyle said, "Red Peak, of course."

"What about it?"

"I have to tell you one last story," the young man said. "May I?"

David leaned back on the couch and folded his arms. "Go ahead."

Kyle stood and wandered the room, sharing smiles with his followers. "For years, a group of people meets online in a private chat room to talk about the Medford Mystery, and coalesces around a theory, which takes on a life of its own. The voice, the strange lights and sounds, the missing bodies, the utter dedication to self-immolation. They do enough research and write enough posts to fill a library on the subject."

He paused to lay his hand on a woman's head before moving on. "Eventually, one of them proposes to take their group offline and put their theory to a very real test. At a hotel, they meet in person for the first time. They decide to follow in the Family of the Living Spirit's footsteps."

David twisted in his seat so he could keep his eyes on the man. "What's this theory?"

Kyle crossed in front of the couch until he stood over him. "That the Family actually *did* talk to God and went to Heaven. That's the first doctrine. The second is that the door is still open."

"Jesus Christ." These people weren't a cult. They were a bunch of cosplaying fans, but even that could be dangerous. "You should all go home."

They gazed back at him with fanatical intensity. They weren't a cult, but eager to become one, if that's what it took to solve the mystery. They'd found purpose in the Medford story, some kind of hope and meaning. Wanting to be a part of something bigger than oneself, something real, was a basic human trait. They weren't going back to their old lives, which they no doubt regarded as empty.

David tried a different tack.

"Look, everything you think you know about Medford came from police reports, and most of that came from the survivors. We were in shock. A handful of brainwashed kids. I honestly don't even remember what I told the police. I was hiding in a closet in the Temple while almost everybody I loved drank poison and stabbed or shot anybody who refused to die."

"I'll get straight to the point," Kyle said. "We're going to Red Peak and want you to come with us. We want you to lead us."

"Can I have some water?"

His mouth had turned to cotton. A beaming woman rushed to the sink to fill a glass and handed it to him with both hands like an offering. He gulped half of it, thinking hard about how to turn this around, how to perform exit counseling on an entire group of people.

"You want to follow in their footsteps?" David said. "Now I'm going to tell *you* a story."

Kyle resumed his seat between John and Amelia. "We're here to learn."

"The Family didn't just drive up there and go to Heaven. The Spirit told the Reverend we had to purify ourselves for the ascension first. Months of hunger and mutilations. Group confessions and hard labor until nobody could think for themselves anymore. Only then were we ready to die."

The would-be pilgrims shrank a little, and David was relieved to see doubt cross their blissful faces. They were obsessed with solving the mystery, not so interested in chopping off body parts.

Kyle said, "What did the Spirit promise in return?"

"Eternal life." He added bitterly, "Milk and honey. Seventy-two virgins."

"Eternal life," the man said, "is plenty enough."

"Then go at it like everybody else, and die of old age."

"Why wait? Compared to eternity, this so-called existence on Earth is an illusion. Don't you want to finish what
you started? See your mother again?"

"Jeremiah was the first to die," David said. "They crucified him. At dusk, they nailed him to a cross some long-lost
religious sect planted on the peak. I didn't see it from the
bottom of the mountain, but I heard him screaming. The
nails didn't kill him, though. The cross was set afire. He was
burned alive."

The faces around him morphed into something deeper
than doubt. Horror.

"Don't go," David begged them. "Please. There is something about that place that creeps into your head and changes
you. Something terrible. Something alive."

David opened his hotel room's door with trembling hands
and lurched inside, manually locking it behind him. He
flicked on every light until certain he was alone. His suit-
case rested on one of the double beds, untouched. He sat on
the other to think.

"Stupid," he growled, though he wasn't sure at whom he
was angrier right now. A bunch of lonely online wannabes
hoping to take their obsession to the next level, or himself
for failing to break through to them?

They'd talked all day and into the night. Caught off
guard, David had argued with them instead of using his
trained techniques to guide them away from harm and back
to reality. When Kyle started praising Emily's suicide and
lecturing him about what he owed the Family, David had
shut down for good.

They'd convinced themselves he had unfinished business with Red Peak and needed only a little prodding to

fulfill the covenant. While they followed Kyle's lead, they'd wanted *him* to be their leader. If he needed any proof of their madness, he had to look no further. They had no idea what they were playing with.

For some doomsday cults, the end became a self-fulfilling prophecy. And ideas, it turned out, were like viruses that infected human beings.

Inspired by this thought, he pulled out his phone, which he'd set to mute all day. Claire had called several times but left no messages. Her single text read, *Call me when you get this.* If it was related to the kids, she would have been more communicative. He decided it could wait.

He dialed Beth's number.

"David?" she said.

"Hi, I'm sorry to be calling so late."

"No, it's fine. I'm glad to hear from you. How are you?"

"Tell me about mass hysteria," David said.

"It's a big topic. What can I tell you?"

"Topline it for me."

"It's called mass psychogenic illness," Beth told him. "The illness starts in the mind but has very real symptoms. It passes into the mind through the eyes."

He rose from the bed and began to pace the room. "What does it do?"

"Often, it develops similarly to a severe stress reaction, but not always. In one famous case, a student marching band stopped in the middle of the field where they played, and three hundred collapsed. In another, a bunch of kids saw a TV show and reported the same symptoms as characters in the show." She paused to drink something, which David guessed was the red wine she favored. "In Tanzania, several schools suffered outbreaks of uncontrollable laughing. In the Middle Ages, there was a plague of dancing where they couldn't stop. There are tons of other documented cases."

David thought about it. It didn't quite fit.

"What about group hallucinations?"

"I guess we should know."

The fire writhing up to the heavens, the deafening horn blast.

David shook a cigarette out of its box and lit it, willing to pay the hotel's fine if he had to. "It's a common thing?"

"It's a verified phenomenon, and there are many cases of it. One famous case is the Miracle of the Sun in Fátima in Portugal in 1917. Three kids made a prophecy that the Virgin Mary would show up in the sky and perform miracles. Thousands came to see it. For about ten minutes, they saw the sun zigzag around, shooting colors."

"They stared at it for too long," he guessed.

"The point is thousands of people said they saw the same thing." She took another drink. "Is that enough? What else do you want to know?"

He found himself on his third circuit walking around the room, puffing away on his cigarette, nowhere to go except back where he started. "I'm not sure."

"Where are you going with this? Are you okay?"

"I'm fine. Did you get a package from Emily? Old articles?"

Beth's usual professional cool faltered. "I—yes, I did."

"It got to you, didn't it?"

"It's unsettling. Remember those old cabins we found? I'm still not sure yet what to make of it, to be honest."

David quit pacing in front of the window. He looked out across the glittering downtown. "I think Peale knew about the Wardites."

Beth gasped. "Oh my God."

The Reverend knew about the Wardites and had become obsessed with a religious mystery. The Family had followed in their footsteps, just as The Restoration wanted to follow in the Family's.

Jeremiah had heard the voice because he'd *expected* to hear it. He'd wanted to hear it so much that he'd denied his own senses. He'd burned toast and seen the face of Christ, only on a much bigger scale.

"For a long time," Beth said, "I wondered if Peale was a schizophrenic, bipolar, or a borderline personality, but I couldn't make it work. Now that I know the spark, I can. The voice, David. It was a projection of some suppressed narcissism. We might even be talking about multiple personality disorder."

Born from guilt and hardship, the voice had taken on a life of its own over time, demanding purity, blind obedience, and unconditional love. The Old Testament God. God as cult leader, or rather, a cult leader's projection of God.

"They all died because one man wanted to meet his maker," David said.

And failing to meet him, he'd created him.

"It still doesn't explain the bodies."

He thought of Angela. "I know exactly who can figure that out for us. I think we'll find Peale worked out a deal with some people in Medford."

If Beth was right about multiple personality disorder, it was possible the Reverend had set it up without any real awareness he was doing it.

If anyone could crack the final puzzle, his bulldog sister could. She'd find out where the bodies were buried. Fifteen years after the Medford Mystery, the survivors could lay the Family of the Living Spirit to final rest.

After a pause, Beth said, "I don't feel any better. Why don't I feel any better?"

He went to the bathroom and dropped his cigarette into the toilet. "Because there's nothing to feel happy about."

She sighed. "I wish Emily had sent us this stuff before she'd decided to exit."

David wasn't sure it would have made any difference. People believed what they wanted to believe. Emily had believed more than most.

He thought of The Restoration packing up for the long trip into the desert, and realized he'd made a colossal mistake. The articles had gotten into his head, and he'd argued with Kyle and his followers about avoiding Red Peak, as if the place had real power. As if something slumbered there, waiting.

There is something about that place that creeps into your head. Something terrible.

The exact wrong thing to say, he realized now.

At Red Peak, a voice would not call out to them, because that voice had been in Jeremiah's head. One of them would hear it anyway, maybe some or even all of them, because they *wanted* to hear it. Because not hearing it meant they'd have to go home, where life was hard and lacked meaning.

At Red Peak, they'd end up hurting themselves and their friends who didn't play along.

"I have to go," David said. "I'll talk to you soon."

"I hope so—"

He hung up and stared at his cell. His first thought was to get in touch with Angela, but he didn't want to see his sister mixed up in this, no matter how tough she was. He was on the right track, though. He'd contact the police in Medford and tell them what was coming their way.

His phone rang. Claire.

"Hi, hon," he said. "I was going to call you."

"David," she said, her voice cracking with stress.

"What's wrong? Are the kids okay?"

"That producer called back. He talked to me about you."

The temperature in the room plummeted.

"What did he say?"

"He told me about you and the Family of the Living Spirit cult."

13

CONFESS

With the windows closed and the fan kept off to minimize ambient sound, Laurie's room was sweltering and smelled like sex. Sitting cross-legged in boxers on her rumpled mattress, Deacon tinkered on a laptop. His bandmate lay on her stomach, glaring at her own computer and wearing nothing but a black T-shirt.

A chord progression trilled from her laptop. "Goddamn it."

"Let me hear it again."

"No. Focus on your own shit."

They hadn't left her apartment in three days. Between marathon stretches of work, Laurie pulled him onto her for some rough sex with plenty of biting. Deacon was starting to doubt she was human but rather some form of musical succubus.

Right now, she was obsessed with finding a perfect chord progression on her software. She said it would serve as a motif for the album to help tie the tracks together. Minor scale for a dark flavor. No power chords, Jesus chords, or the "epic" chord progression. She worked up a diminished chord, a dissonant sound that added tension and narrative drama.

When she dropped it into her progression, the whole thing leaned and fell over.

"Maybe not a dim chord," she muttered. "I could augment it. Resurrection instead of tragedy."

Deacon shrugged and went back to chasing his own white whale, the shofar of Exodus. He blinked at his screen trying to come up with a new direction, and ended up studying the perfect curvature of Laurie's ass and wondering what tone it would produce if he modeled it as a sound wave.

Time for a break. He pulled on his T-shirt and padded into the living room.

"Ugh," Charlotte said from the sofa. "When are you leaving?"

Laurie's roommate thumbed a text into her phone while a swiveling floor fan blasted air at her. Deacon stood behind the couch to enjoy the soothing wind.

"When my mistress releases me and gives me a ride," he said.

"What are you even doing in there?" Still staring at her phone, she extended her palm toward him. "Don't answer that."

"We're making a baby," Deacon said anyway.

She wrenched her eyes from her screen. "What?"

"We're working on an album together." He walked into the kitchen and filled a bowl with milk. "Can I eat some of this cereal?"

A loud, labored sigh. "Fine."

"Thanks." He sat and poured Cap'n Crunch. The fan

droned as it ponderously wagged its head. With each turn, the sound refracted.

As a general rule, musicians hated unwanted ambient noise. They might dirty their sound until it was good and wrecked, or shoot for a live performance atmosphere, but by design. They otherwise spent a great deal of effort filtering out anything that wasn't precisely engineered as part of the song.

God didn't live in recording studios. He lived on desolate peaks. His music was the never-ending song of entropy.

Inspired, Deacon wolfed down the rest of his cereal and hurried back to Laurie's bedroom, ignoring her roommate yelling at him to clean up his dishes.

On his laptop, he pulled a sample of a cimbasso, a brass mutant cross between a tuba and a trombone. He dropped the pitch a couple octaves, wet the signal, and then dirtied it up with a ten-second reverb until it was nice and meaty.

Next, he sifted through wind sound effects and found a lonely moan with the right pitch. He layered that into the background and played it back.

Laurie's head jerked like a cat sensing prey. "I like that."

"It's closer to what I remember. Not quite there, though."

She turned back to her screen. "Definitely a dim chord. We need conflict."

Deacon plugged in headphones and closed his eyes to let the horn rumble between his ears again.

A handful of bodies littered the dark slope around the cabins at the base of the mountain, the ones who'd tried to escape. The camp lay still. As far as he knew, everyone he loved was dead. From the summit, pulsing red fire boiled straight up into the sky, filling the night air with a ghostly murmur.

Then the horn boomed. Its vibrations drummed the boulder

behind which Deacon crouched shuddering in fear and shock. The roar built in volume until he couldn't hear his own breathless scream.

The bodies began to shift and stir on the ground—

"Deacon," Laurie yelled. "Answer your goddamn phone."

He came out of it with a gasp and wrenched off the headphones. His cell sang to him, wanting to be answered. He picked it up. "Yeah, yeah."

"Hey, it's me." Joy's voice. "We have a problem."

Deacon braced himself for being told that Honcy had been towed from the Wild Moon parking lot, where the car had sat for the past three days.

"Okay."

"Apparently, we made a big impression on a teen who caught our show," Joy said. "She went home and killed herself."

"Oh, shit." He couldn't think of anything else to say.

"Her suicide note was the lyrics to 'Shadow Boxer.'"

Laurie drove them to a Greek diner on Martin Luther King, where Frank had called an emergency meeting of the band.

"We can work with this." She leaned against the wheel like she always did, as if being a foot closer to the windshield helped her see the road better. "We could play up an angle about how some fans are like cultists themselves. Dedicate the album to this poor girl."

Deacon smoked in silence, still haunted by the vision of bodies bouncing around the ground until they'd started to tumble up the slope. As creepy as it was, nonetheless it served to distract him from the idea of a teenaged girl overdosing on sleeping pills because of a song he wrote.

"I'm not saying we exploit it," Laurie said. "I'm saying we let it inspire us."

She talked about the new album as if she'd poison herself too if that's what it took to create it.

Deacon watched Crenshaw's grimy gas stations and fast food joints rush past as he flicked ash out the window.

Laurie seemed to want him to say something, so he nodded. *Inspire us. Yes.*

"All right." She let go of the wheel to punch his thigh. "I feel like everything we've done so far has been playing at being a rock band so we can make money. I've got this impostor syndrome aftertaste in my mouth. Not with *this* album, though. This is real. It's fucking art. This album is going to be a statement."

"Yes," he said, though he didn't believe there was going to be an album.

The possibility seemed more remote than ever right now. He and Laurie had hoped that if they did the groundwork and shared the results with the group, their bandmates would get turned on and tune in.

A fan committing suicide was likely to make them lean even harder against Cats Are Sad's darker material. Hell, this was the kind of thing that could break up a band, produce a custodial fight over its soul.

They walked into the diner and found their bandmates waiting at a table.

Frank glared at them. "It's about time. What have you two been doing?"

"Working on a project," Laurie said.

Steve frowned at their hair, still wet from the shower they'd taken together. His shoulders sagged a little. He liked Laurie a lot, but he knew what she was like. She belonged to the music, not any man.

"We can talk about that later," the manager said. "Right

now, we need to discuss how we're going to respond to this suicide and the unwanted attention it's bringing us."

"We're not the first band with a fan who offed herself," Laurie said.

"Right. We can learn from what they did right and wrong. The first step is to post condolences to the family on social media, explain how our music is there to give hope and courage to people who don't fit into mainstream society, and offer an anti-suicide message. All of which I already took care of."

The server arrived to pour coffee for them. Joy ordered hot tea.

"That works," Bart said. "What else can we do?"

"Well, I also think you need to lay low for a while," Frank said. "Take a break and work on some new material, stuff that's a little less emo."

"Now you're talking."

Laurie frowned at Deacon, but he kept staring into the blackness in his mug.

"If you're going to be on social media, stay on message," Frank added. "If you say something stupid, you'll put you and your band on the wrong side of an internet mob. Optics are everything."

Deacon's phone rang. He turned away from the table to answer it. "Yeah?"

"Hi, this is Doug Winder with the *Intelligencer*," the voice said. "Is this Deacon Price with the band Cats Are Sad?"

He stuck his finger in his ear to mute the diner's noise. "Yup."

"I'm doing a piece on Alexandra Martinez. You're aware she took her own life after your last show at the, uh, Wild Moon?"

"We were just talking about that."

"What do you say to people who think your music caused her death?"

"I'd tell them they're stupid," Deacon said.

After a long pause, the reporter asked, "Why would you say that?"

"Music doesn't make you do anything. It's grease, not a wheel."

"What's the song about?"

Bart's eyes bugged. "Who's he talking to?"

Frank held out his hand. "Give me the goddamn phone."

Deacon stared at his manager as he said, "It's about religious frustration, Mr. Winder of the *Intelligencer*. Most of us are programmed to be spiritual, but there's nothing to connect with. I'm surprised we haven't all killed ourselves, but we're also programmed to survive. This conflict is driving the whole human race insane."

Bart groaned. "He's killing himself right now. And our careers."

"So life is hopeless," Winder said over the phone. "That's the message."

"No," Deacon told him, plugging his ear harder to shut out his bandmates. "*Death* is hopeless. If the human race stopped trying to find meaning in death, they'd find more meaning in life. We'd grow up and find our purpose. There are nearly eight billion people on the planet. We could do anything if we weren't a bunch of assholes."

"Stop talking," Frank growled. "Just shut the hell up."

Steve laughed. This wasn't his first trip to the imploding band rodeo.

Winder chuckled as well. "So what is the meaning of life?"

"You tell me," said Deacon. "The search itself is what's important."

"Fair enough. Last question. If Alexandra were still alive and you could say anything to her, what would it be?"

"I'd say I understand your pain, but you have to find your purpose so you can keep going. I'd say I know firsthand how hurtful taking your life can be to the ones you love, so if for nothing else, you go on for them."

"Firsthand, you said? What happened to you?"

"I grew up in a group called the Family of the Living Spirit that committed mass suicide fifteen years ago. My mother and almost everybody I loved died that night. More than a hundred people."

Another long pause from the reporter. "Seriously?"

Deacon glanced at his bandmates, who stared back at him with their mouths hanging open. "Yup. Foreal."

"How old were you?"

"Fourteen."

Joy gripped Laurie's arm. "Is he serious?"

Laurie nodded.

The reporter sucked in his breath. "Were you there the last night when—"

"We were talking about Alexandra," Deacon said. "The point I was trying to make was with all I'd survived, music didn't give me pain. It saved me. I wish it had saved Alexandra, because that's why we're doing this. If you can't find a purpose, you go on with this ridiculous charade because there's nothing else. Given the alternative of nonexistence, life is its own reason to live."

"That's very interesting," the reporter said. "Can I ask you a few more questions about the, uh, cult?"

"No," Deacon said and hung up.

"Well," Bart said.

The silence stretched.

"I can't believe it," Frank fumed. "You don't give a shit about anything, do you? I hope you know you just sunk this band."

Deacon stood. "I know I don't care about your bullshit, Frank."

He'd joined Cats Are Sad so he could bleed from his wrists for as large an audience as possible. Bare his soul for the mob so they could eat its flesh and drink its blood. Allow his love to be ritually crucified.

If the band didn't want him doing that anymore, he had no further use for it.

Laurie followed him outside, still gripping her mug of heavily sugared coffee. "Take it easy. They'll come around."

Deacon tilted his head and stared at the bright blue sky until he felt like he was falling into it. "They want to be rock stars."

She snorted. "Who doesn't? I still think you can have your cake and eat it."

"Why else have cake?" he said, completing an old routine.

"As long as the cake comes first. The art. I told Frank you were just speaking the plain truth to that reporter."

"What did he say?"

"He said, 'Nobody gives a shit about the truth.'" She fidgeted. "So. What now?"

He blinked away the brightness and came back to the earth. "I'd like to pick up my car. Then I'm gonna go away for a while."

"What about the album?"

"Soldier on without me. You have the story, and I trust you. I'll be back."

Laurie gulped down her coffee with a masochistic wince and tossed the mug into the bushes. "If that's what you need to do, then do it. Don't stay away too long, though."

They got into her VW Bug and drove to the Wild Moon. Honey was right where he'd left it, still covered in a film of dust and ash from his journey to Bakersfield.

"Hope you find your chill," she said.

Deacon sat behind Honey's wheel and started the car. "Hope you come up with some legendary chords."

As she sped off with a final wave, he glanced at two proverbs tattooed on his sweating arm: IMPERARE SIBI MAXIMUM IMPERIUM EST, which meant, *ruling yourself is the greatest power*, and upside down under it, MAKE PAIN YOUR FRIEND. Hope and reality in conflict. Pain and desire in collaboration.

Maybe the music wasn't the right path, this ongoing addiction to nurturing his hurt so he could release it, the exquisite and never-ending cycle of agony and catharsis in his own personal Passion play. Perhaps it was time to try to make the pain stop. He'd take a pilgrimage he should have pursued long ago.

He wanted to go home.

Driving north, he joined the flow of traffic on the freeway until he reached the coastal highway in Santa Monica. Lush green bluffs crowded the road on the right, while on his left, the endless Pacific yawned under a storm front. Towering palm trees leaned with the wind. Sunbeams burst through the approaching gray clouds to gleam along the rippling sea.

How great is God, Deacon thought. How ridiculously small was man.

How much like a dumb, spoiled little kid. God and man both, actually, proving God made man in his image.

Old memories stirred deep in his soul. Standing in the

desert at night, studying the stars crowding the black sky. The distances so impossible and vast, the light took hundreds and thousands of years to reach Earth. To view the stars was to visit the past. He wasn't going back nearly that far, but his origins felt as ancient to him.

While gazing up at the heavens, Deacon had once tried to imagine the scale of God but couldn't wrap his head around it. God seemed as remote as the stars at the time, and he'd felt like his suffering didn't matter. Now he doubted there was a God, and nothing had changed. His pain, his trauma, his memories, none of it mattered one damn bit in the big scheme. They mattered only to him.

The sunbeams died, swallowed by the clouds. He turned on the wipers as the first raindrops appeared on his windshield. The sky grew darker. Minutes later, the deluge arrived. Taillights of slowing traffic blazed mottled red. The palms shook in the wind gusts. With hope, the storm would travel east to extinguish the fires scouring the Sierra Nevadas.

Then, at last, he could revisit the mountain.

Soon. He'd do it soon.

First, he had something else he needed to do, what he hoped might be a one-step program to breaking his addiction to nihilism.

He took the first exit in Santa Barbara. At a red light, he inspected Beth's business card to double-check the address. The storm had passed, leaving the air cool and moist and clean. After parking Honey in a garage, he walked to her condo building, feeling even more out of place than he did at Emily's wake. Jeremiah Peale had once called America's cities teeming sewers of grime and sin, and that's just the way Deacon liked it. Instead, with its perfect planning and

Spanish-revival architecture, Santa Barbara looked like it had been designed as a Disney attraction.

In the lobby, the doorman eyed Deacon's rumpled T-shirt, wild hair, and stubbled face with disdain. "Can I help you?"

"I'm here to see Beth Harris."

The man bristled further. "Is Dr. Harris expecting you?"

"I'm a friend." Deacon turned away before any more judgment could be rained upon him. "Tell her Deacon is here."

He sat on a bench while the man returned to his desk to make the call. So tired, he could sleep right here. All he wanted was a nice, long rest, a chance to catch his breath. Decades ago, he'd run from Red Peak, and he felt like he'd never stopped.

"Deek?"

He opened his eyes, surprised he'd dozed off. He smiled. "Beth."

She crouched in front of him in a blouse and skirt, hair pulled back into an austere bun. Her bright, liquid eyes bored in his.

"What are you doing here? Are you okay?"

"I just wanted to see you."

The worry etched in her face softened. "I'm glad you came."

He said, "I wanted to tell you I'm sorry."

14

WORSHIP

2005

The Heaven Express reached the end of the line.

The bus parked on the side of the dirt road. The Family stood and stretched and gathered their belongings. Deacon peered out the window to see the first grinning people step into the sun's glare.

He'd squirmed with excitement the entire trip but now found it hard to move. "Do you think we'll get a warning when it happens?"

A voice, a trumpet blast, anything.

Mom pulled her bag onto her lap. "It won't hurt."

"We'll all go together, right?"

She ruffled his hair. "Hand in hand to meet the Lord."

"Okay." Deacon inspected his lean body, which now felt light and alien, as useless as clothes would be where he was headed. The idea that he could blink from flesh into a different state of existence still unnerved him.

He shouldered his backpack. "I'm ready for whatever happens, Mom."

"You're a kind and loving boy, Deacon." She leaned to plant a wet kiss on his cheek, which he accepted with a dramatic display of chafing. "I love you here, and I'll love you there. The love between a mother and her son is perfect. Everything else is going to change, but that won't ever change."

"*Mom*," he growled, embarrassed. "Jeez."

She giggled. "Let's settle in, and then I have to see to the organ. Don't forget to drink plenty of water today."

Deacon followed the excited pilgrims off the bus and blinked in the harsh sunlight and roasting heat that radiated from the ground and rocks.

The vanguard had been here for over a week, building their new settlement. A series of bare plywood shacks crowded a patch of dirt. The Temple and other communal buildings stood out as larger wood boxes. Red Peak loomed over it all.

He threaded the crowd to join David, who squinted at the scenery. He pointed to an outhouse. "That's your new crib right there, Dave. The bottom bunk is all yours."

The kid elbowed him with a grin. "Jerk."

The ramshackle camp wasn't much to see, little houses built to provide the bare minimum of space and shelter. Instead of doors, heavy wool blankets covered the entrances. The air smelled like minerals with a musky, bitter tang from the creosote and sagebrush patching the dusty ground.

"What a dump," Angela said behind them.

"It's all a matter of perspective." Deacon pointed up at the ocean of blue surrounding the mountain's rusty crown. "That's our real new home, right there."

The adults often one-upped each other with reminders that God was taking care of everything. Knowing nods answered optimism, and chummy reminders of God's plan and the power of prayer addressed complaints. Jokes were insider jokes. The Family never let themselves forget they'd been chosen and that whatever they said and did, Jesus stood there listening to every word.

"Shut up, Deacon." She surveyed the camp with an expression of utter misery. "Just shut your stupid face."

Josh approached with his thumbs hooked in the pockets of his jeans. He stared at Deacon. "Everything okay, Angel?"

"Everything is great," she grated. "Praise the Lord."

The couple walked off to join the human chain forming between the trucks and the new Temple. Boxes of clerical supplies bobbed down the line until swallowed in the Family's new house of worship.

"She'll come around," David said. "She'd better."

"Yeah." Angela's outburst had him a little shaken. "Man, it is really hot here."

"We're not staying long, right?"

Deacon gazed again at the cobalt sky, which seemed much farther away now. A bird circled overhead, a black glimmer in the pale blue.

A dove, he thought. *A sign? God is welcoming us.*

The bird soared up toward Red Peak's summit. He recognized the silhouette now. It wasn't a dove but a vulture, which vanished in the blazing sun.

The gang hiked through shad scale scrub girdling Red Peak's base. Deacon plodded along, wishing he'd brought a walking stick like David had, wore decent hiking boots instead of sneakers, and could drink the rest of the water warming in his pack. This wasn't any fun. In fact, in the parlance of his old life, it royally sucked.

"Anybody feel like going back?" he said.

Like the journey to Red Peak, the hike had started out as a grand adventure promising freedom. They'd climbed high enough to enjoy breathtaking views of the mountains to the east, beyond which lay Death Valley. Here, Deacon understood why the prophets found God deep in the wilderness. The very atmosphere invited a sense of connection with something bigger than himself.

The kids christened the camp New Jerusalem.

His elation didn't last long. The oven heat dried him out and left him light-headed, and biting black flies plagued his every step. No matter how much water he drank, the hot, parched air sucked it out of him. Nothing grew here except cactus and scrub that promised itchy, stinging pain. The lack of trails meant every footfall had to be mapped among rocks and boulders to avoid twisting an ankle. The spirit rejoiced in what the body rejected, but he was surprised and angry at how quickly the spirit wore out.

"Nobody's stopping you," Wyatt said. "Go back if you want."

Emily waved at a buzzing fly. "We need to find our spot."

Deacon frowned. He shouldn't have brought it up. He was weak. High pain threshold, but little endurance. Life wasn't much more comfortable back at the camp, melting during the day and shivering at night. Just hauling water from the spring a mile away was an exhausting trek.

With no farming to do, the adults spent much of the day praying on their knees at the Temple, waiting for God to come. What had started out as an adventure, like a camping trip, had already become grueling.

At the farm, the kids had their secret places to play with no grown-ups around. The woods and baptismal stream.

The Tehachapi Loop. They hadn't found a place here yet, and couldn't go back without it. They were on a mission.

After another mile of hiking, Josh stopped at the head of the group. "Check this out, you guys."

The kids gathered around to study a massive wall of black basalt that jutted from the slope, covered in hundreds of Native petroglyphs. A lip of rock provided a natural overhang that protected the carvings from the elements.

Deacon's eyes picked out bighorn sheep, zigzags representing mountain ranges, tall figures with shining heads. At the top, a massive petroglyph depicted what appeared to be an eye in a diamond. Under that, a creature spread its wings.

Along the periphery, someone had carved a wavy line of crosses.

Wyatt pointed at the eye. "I'm pretty sure that's *Tam Apo*, the Great Spirit."

This was a holy place for the Natives. Before the Europeans came, the whole region had been Paiute-Shoshone territory.

"What about the thing with the wings?" Emily said. "Is it supposed to be an owl?"

"I have no idea what it is," Wyatt answered. "From what I heard, though, that one was the key to a vision quest. Indians would come here, wash up, and hang out for days praying for a vision or a dream to show them their purpose. Then if the vision told them to share, they'd carve what they saw on the wall."

"How do you know all this?" David asked.

The big kid shrugged. "I grew up in Nevada, near a reservation. I had friends who told me some stuff. I don't remember most of it."

Deacon found the symbols stirring. They sang to him like poetry. History and scripture. Natives had come here to talk to the spiritual world and walked away with both power and purpose. These carvings recorded the testimonies of generations. The wide diversity in styles suggested differing artistic capabilities, or possibly the evolution of symbols over the centuries, or maybe the even more fascinating possibility that Natives from far away made pilgrimages to this site.

Red Peak had a weird aura of power around it, that was undeniable. Sometimes, at odd moments, Deacon sensed a rumbling hum in the atmosphere, but when he turned toward the sound, it either stopped or changed direction. There was something about this place.

A breeze crossed over them, providing a brief respite from the heat and flies.

"I think we found our spot," Emily said.

The kids nodded. It was a great place. As a bonus, the jutting rock face offered plenty of shade from the afternoon sun.

"Hey," Angela called behind them. "Take a look down here."

They turned and followed her gaze down the slope into the gorge below, where a ghost town lay in ruins. The kids gasped in delight.

"No way," Deacon said.

They picked their way down the rocks toward the crumbling skeletons of old wood cabins and a steepled church with a caved-in roof. The thick, twisted trunks of dead bristlecone pines stood among these structures.

"What's it doing here?" Beth yelled as she hustled down the slope.

"Gold rush town," Josh called out. "That's my guess."

The California Gold Rush had brought many settlements to the Sierra Nevada, subsequently abandoned after they'd drained all the gold.

Deacon, David, and Beth ran to a cabin that hadn't collapsed to its foundations, and found the dark, open doorway draped in cobwebs.

"I am so not going in there," Beth said. "Let's find another one to explore."

Deacon held out his hand. "Dave, let me see your walking stick for a second." He extended it to break the webbing. "Should we go in?"

David gaped into the darkness. "Be my guest."

Holding the stick like a spear, Deacon crept into the dusty interior, which was dimly lit by gaps in the clapboard roof. The bones of a mouse crunched under his foot, making him wince.

"This place is crazy," he whispered, as if afraid of waking something.

The cabin still had furniture. Crumbling books lined a shelf. Chairs surrounded a table set for a meal for four.

Beth looked around and murmured, "They just got up and walked away."

"With desert all around. Where did they go?"

"Like those towns you hear about," Wyatt said behind them, making them jump. "One day, everybody walks out and disappears." He held up a small glass bottle with an eyedropper in it. "Look what I found."

"Cool." Deacon overcame his fear of touching anything and poked around. He discovered a Bible, but it was wrecked. The rest was junk. A hairbrush, a basin for washing, a rusting can of Prince Albert tobacco, all covered in dust.

David grinned under a floppy hat. "Check it out."

"You know how dirty that is?" Wyatt said. "Mice probably crapped in it." He dropped the glass bottle on the table as if it too was contaminated.

David took off the hat and flung it to the floor. "They did not."

"They did too. Now you have mouse crap in your hair."

"Shut up, Wyatt."

Deacon ignored them as he opened a box and discovered a small metal cross on a chain. He picked it up and scratched at a tiny blemish.

"What'd you find?" Beth said.

He held it out for her to inspect. "Pretty cool, huh?"

"Way cool."

On impulse, he said, "It's for you."

"You sure?"

"Sure I'm sure."

"I mean, we can just take it?"

"I think so," he said. "I don't see why not. Finders keepers."

"Okay. Put it on me, will you?" Beth turned around and pulled her hair up to hold it piled against the top of her head.

Deacon draped it around her throat, the heat and his thirst forgotten. He eyed the back of her neck and remembered a movie he saw where a man put a necklace on a girl and then kissed the soft skin of her neck. Heart pounding in his ears, he fumbled with the clasp, but he couldn't get it hooked.

Unable to stand it anymore, he said, "I can't see in this light."

"I'll do it." Smiling, Beth reached up to clasp it in place. "How does it look?"

Every part of him ached now. "Really pretty."

Wyatt made puking noises and burst into laughter.

"Get a room, you two," David said uncertainly, repeating something he'd heard but didn't quite understand.

Josh poked his head in the doorway. "We should head back."

The kids marched back to New Jerusalem, tired but jubilant at their discovery. Their home had changed from a lush valley to a desert mountain, their parents had traded contentment for a forced cheerfulness, and God was still a no-show, but they'd found their oasis, a secret place where they could be themselves again.

For days, they waited. The Family prayed, toiled to gather water, ate canned food in the mess hall, and otherwise tried to remain cheerful while nothing happened.

The sky remained closed. The pearly gates stayed hidden. Each day, the sun burned across the encampment before the mountain cast it in shadow.

Dazed by the heat, the kids sat around a table in the otherwise empty mess hall. Their third day at New Jerusalem, and nobody was up for exploring.

David suggested a board game, but they'd left almost everything at the farm. They didn't think they'd need it.

Wyatt lay sprawled on one of the benches. "Never thought I'd miss chores."

The adults wouldn't let them do anything, and there wasn't much to do anyway. Every day, men and women trudged across two miles of baking rocks to fetch water from a spring, which provided just enough to keep them all hydrated. The rest of the time, they waited in the Temple.

"I can't stand this," Beth said. "I want it over with."

"This is part of the deal," Emily said. "We—"

"I *know* what the deal is, Em. Let me complain."

"Sorry."

Beth gripped her forehead as if she had a crippling headache. "No, I'm sorry. I'm just sick of it."

Deacon understood how she felt. He wondered if this was

a test. Like in school, only in this case he didn't even know what the question was.

"God changed his mind," Wyatt said.

"Shut up," Beth growled.

"He took one look—"

"Shut up," they all yelled while the kid chortled from his bench.

Deacon stood. "Well, that's it, then. I'm going to the top." He gazed back at their gaping faces with all the gravity he could muster. "Who's with me?"

This was his time to follow in the Reverend's footsteps and shine as a spiritual leader. He'd walk to the top and talk to God himself.

"What the heck do you want to do that for?" David said.

"I'm going to get some answers. So are you coming or not?"

Emily paled. "Not me." She was afraid of angering God.

"In this heat?" Beth said. "It's too far. No way."

"Right," Angela said. "No way I'm doing that."

"You too?" Deacon thought she'd jump at the chance. He'd been counting on the big kids to come along. "Why?"

"Suppose we hike all that way, and there's nothing there. No voice, nothing. Do we tell everybody? What do you think would happen if we did?"

David's sister had a rebellious streak, but she was smart enough to pick her battles. This wasn't one of them.

"Don't even look at me," Wyatt said. "I ain't going."

"If Angel goes, I go," Josh said. "If not . . . sorry, brother."

Deacon sagged. He didn't even bother asking David, who was, for lack of a better word, a coward—God bless him and all that, but he was. This was what he deserved for acting bigger than his britches. He'd wanted to prove himself, and now he'd have to climb alone. If he backed out, he'd never live it down.

"I guess I'll see you guys later." He headed for the door.

God never quit with the tests, even on the eve of apocalypse.

"Wait," David called after him. "I'll come."

Deacon grinned with relief. "You will?"

"I have some questions I'd like to ask."

"Good to have you along." That's what the Reverend would have said.

The kids jumped to their feet to follow them out the door and into the blazing sunshine. All eyes on him, Deacon made it look good. He gave orders to David, stuffed water bottles into a backpack, and gazed stoically up at the summit.

Wow, what a climb. The mountain appeared even taller now, every inch of it daunting and completely inhospitable to human life.

If the Reverend had done it, he could too.

David showed up wearing a ball cap and pacing himself with his walking stick, his tanned arms slathered with sun-tan lotion. "Ready."

"Time to get to the bottom of this then." The others were depending on him.

"You guys are nuts," Wyatt said, ruining the moment.

He rolled with it. "Yup." He smiled at David. "You ready, partner?"

David nodded, already out of breath from fear. Deacon was wrong about him. He wasn't a coward. Right now, he was maybe the bravest of the bunch.

They started walking. Angela shouted instructions and advice and warnings at her brother until the boys were out of earshot.

"Okay," David yelled back. "Okay!"

"Your sister's a handful," Deacon noted.

The kid sighed. "Welcome to my world."

They turned to give the others a last parting wave. Already, they appeared tiny. They all waved back, even Wyatt, who was probably still laughing at their expense. No matter, thought Deacon. His friends were counting on him.

Now it was just him and the mountain. The roasting sun. The prickly bushes that seemed to appear out of nowhere. The occasional burst of wind that blew blinding dust across the slope.

David huffed next to him.

"You okay?"

The boy nodded.

"Good. Because I'm not stopping until I get some answers for Beth."

"You don't have to try to impress her. She likes you."

"What? She does?" Deacon cleared his throat. "I mean, why would I care about that?"

David threw him a look.

He paused to take a swig from his water bottle, then passed it to his friend. "I guess it doesn't matter. The world's coming to an end."

"That makes it matter more," David said.

Deacon returned the bottle to his pack. "Let's keep going."

They toiled on. Shadows crept toward them from the crest as the sun crossed the peak. The summit appeared close now, but he knew this was only an illusion. It was only the first of the false peaks. Despite the heat, he shivered at the feeling the mountain was aware of him now and watching his every movement.

There was something about this place. A raw power. The mountain hummed with it. The closer he made it to the top, the more he worried about exactly what he was doing here. Down in the mess hall, his plan had flashed through his mind complete and shining with perfection. Since then, it had slipped away. If he met God, what would he say? Who was he to ask questions and demand answers, when he should have faith in the plan, like Emily had said he should?

Or worse, what if there was nothing up there?

He was starting to think this was a big mistake.

Gasping, he arrived at the top of the first summit, where the mountain plateaued before angling again toward the sky. He leaned on his knees, panting too hard to savor his victory.

David was no longer next to him.

He wheeled with a yelp to see the boy standing twenty yards behind, gaping up at the summit and shaking his head.

"Dave? You okay?"

The kid wagged his head again. "I'm going back."

Deacon walked back to join him. "What's wrong?"

"I'm sorry," the boy said. "I can't do it."

Above them, Red Peak's shadow crept closer, consuming the ground.

Deacon shivered again. "Don't worry about it. Maybe another time."

"You can go on without me, if you want."

"That's okay. I'll make sure you get back safe."

His legs trembled with exhaustion as they wound their way down the long slope through the rocks and thorns. He didn't stop to rest, though. Every step brought relief to be farther from the summit.

David whispered, "I've got the joy, joy, joy, joy, down in my heart."

Deacon joined in. "Down in my heart. Down in my heart."

"I've got the joy, joy, joy, joy, down in my heart, down in my heart to stay."

They sang the second verse, louder this time. They repeated the song all the way back to New Jerusalem, as if it were a spell that might protect them from the thing they'd come to seek.

The Family of the Living Spirit settled into old pews in the new Temple. The builders constructed the cabins as makeshift shelters but had lavished attention on the church's construction. Large windows flooded the nave with daylight. The familiar wood dove was mounted on the wall behind the altar. Deacon's mother welcomed the congregants from her organ, which filled the space with a plaintive hymn. Jeremiah sat on the left side of the chancel, waiting for his time to speak.

Seated next to David, Deacon watched his mom play and thought about how beautiful she was when she did, her delicate hands tumbling along the keys. A finger poked him in the back, which could only belong to Wyatt, who sat behind him at worship. Deacon turned to scowl at his grinning face.

"Are we there yet?" the kid said.

Deacon shook his head, trying not to laugh.

The organ lingered on a high note and then stopped.

Jeremiah rose to his feet in his usual black jacket and T-shirt, lean and tanned by the sun. "Brothers and sisters, welcome to the first Sunday worship in our new home, and one of our last before the ascension."

The congregation clapped and cheered, though it was hesitant as the words *one of our last* sank in. Paradise would continue to elude them a while longer.

"'Long is the way and hard, that out of Hell leads up to

the Light,'" he went on, and paused to let the words sink in. "John Milton wrote that. It's a daunting message but an inspiring one, if you think about it. And something to chew on for those wondering why we haven't crossed over already." The Reverend raised three fingers. "The Living Spirit told me there will be three tests."

The Family grew still, waiting.

"First, we will build a staircase leading all the way to the top of Red Peak. When we make it to the first summit, I will go again to the summit and receive the second test. While we go about this labor, we will daily confess our sins."

The congregation murmured at the idea of building stairs up a mountain. Deacon wondered at it himself. What was the point? God would only destroy it soon. But like the Reverend said, it was a test.

"You may think throwing stairs up a mountain in May will be hard, but that's the easy part," Jeremiah said. "In the good book, James tells us, 'Confess your sins to each other and pray for each other so that you may be healed.' Imagine winning a free one-way ticket to a tropical island. The catch is you can't bring a single suitcase. You learn real quick just how darn hard it is to let some things go."

While the Family chuckled, he went on.

"Tonight, we'll meet here again, and leave our children at home. Each of us will come prepared to confess his sins before the Family. But we won't be confessing that we talked back to Mom or flirted with another man's wife, no, sir. We'll be digging deep, straight to the root. Right to the core sin that defines you. Only by recognizing the sin can we make ourselves clean for God. In lieu of a sermon today, I'd like to go first and confess my own sin. It's a big one, the worst of all. Are you ready for it?"

Across the pews, the Family nodded.

"I was a big drinker back in the day," the Reverend said. "Yeah, you all know that story. Nothing wild to tell, nothing juicy, just a sad story about a selfish man. A man who lied to himself and everybody he cared about because he loved a drink more than himself, more than God. The Devil doesn't always throw a party for you. There isn't a big reward before he comes around to collect your soul. Because you'd given it away. Sometimes, sin just slips into your day like mail through a slot, mundane as brushing your teeth, and once it's inside, it takes over. Before you know it, all you care about is feeding it. You know I lost everything. You know I hit rock bottom. You know a higher power saved me, a newfound faith in Christ."

Deacon leaned forward in his pew, riveted as the first tears flowed down Jeremiah's broad face, tears he refused to hide.

"What you don't know is that is not my biggest sin, not by a long shot," the Reverend said. "My big sin was my faith sometimes seemed to me a fair-weather friend. It wasn't just fear that God would reject me after all the bad things I'd done in my sorry life. What I'm about to tell you is way worse than that. In moments of weakness, I wondered if anybody was listening to my prayers at all. If I'd only become saved as a crutch to kick the booze. I'd have terrors, three o'clock in the morning terrors, about the worst horror imaginable, that death is the end, that after a long, full life, you just wink out of existence forever without it meaning a thing. So much of my ministry was just me trying to convince myself it wasn't true." He looked up at the rafters, the tears still streaming. "It took hearing your voice, Lord, to give me the absolute certainty my faith should have already provided. It took you showing me the bright star in all that endless black sea.

I'm ashamed of this, and I beg your forgiveness." His gaze dropped. "I beg all your forgiveness."

The shocked silence only lasted seconds before Mrs. Blanchard called out: "I forgive you, Reverend!"

"Think about what you're saying. The man before you is a fraud and a liar."

David's mother jumped to her feet. "There's nothing to forgive, as far as I'm concerned. Without you and this family, I would never have found my path. You brought me closer to God, and you saved my children from eternal death."

"We all struggle with doubt, Reverend," Mrs. Chapman said. "There is no shame in it. That is the spiritual war."

"We forgive you!" Mrs. Diaz called out.

They all rose shouting, and those closest to the Reverend crowded around to lay their hands on him and proclaim their love and forgiveness. Deacon jumped with his hands in the air, yelling over and over he forgave him too.

One by one, Jeremiah hugged them back for all he was worth, bawling the whole time.

Deacon's mom began to play the first hymn, an uplifting song about tapping the strength of God, and the congregation sang with it.

Then the Spirit arrived like an electric current flowing through the Family, energizing them toward dance and proclamations and prophecy.

Deacon raised his hands with his eyes clenched shut as the raw music and its message soaked into his soul and set it alight with a love for humanity and God. This was his favorite time of worship, when he'd open wide and let the Spirit sing through him, filling the nave with his clear tenor, performing a one-man concert for his father looking down on him, for the angels, for God himself.

"I forgive you," he said through a smile so wide it hurt.

"*Ay-BRAY-mig a fafen!*" Mrs. Young cried.

Hands splayed, she gaped at something only she could see as the Spirit overtook her and spoke through her in tongues, the angelic language.

"*Ay-BRAY-mig a fafen!*"

"*Niis aqlo etharzi od moz,*" Freddie Shaw shouted.

Across the congregation, people raved. Gibberish, but they were chanting now, chanting in *unison*. This had never happened before. Nonsense words that nonetheless were loaded with meaning. An important message that Deacon couldn't understand, though he internalized it: *It's coming, get ready.*

"*Ay-BRAY-mig a fafen!*" they roared.

They jerked and danced like marionettes, grimacing as their bodies contorted. A wave of them collapsed to the floor, where they arched their backs and convulsed and clawed at the hardwood. The Reverend writhed in front of the altar, tumbling in place as if caught in an invisible clothes dryer.

His mouth yawning wide, Deacon did not sing. Instead, he gaped in alarm as more and more of the Family fell to thrash across the floor like fish yanked from water. This wasn't normal worship. This looked like pain, not ecstasy.

For a terrifying moment, he believed they were dying.

15

LOVE

Deacon awoke on a couch and bolted upright. Outside the large windows, the sun rose over Santa Barbara and the mountains. Beth's condo, he remembered. He checked his watch and discovered he'd slept sixteen hours, a record even for him. Despite the long rest, he remained exhausted by dreams of worship.

"*Ay-bray-mig a fafen,*" he whispered and shuddered. "Damn."

Slowly, the dreams released him from their syrupy grip, oozing back into the past. He visited the bathroom then returned. "Beth? Are you here?"

After living among musicians for the past ten years, he found the condo opulent but sterile. Bright and white and clean, as if Beth lived in a high-end modern furniture catalog. The only thing out of place was this scruffy musician.

She'd left his clothes freshly laundered and folded in a neat stack on the couch armrest. His phone vibrated, and he ignored it. He pulled on his T-shirt and jeans and padded barefoot into the kitchen.

"She does love me." There was hot coffee in the pot.

Deacon poured out a cup. The mug left a ring on the counter, which he decided to leave as a calling card. *Love, the Guy Who Makes a Mess Out of Everything.*

Maybe he'd go home. Figure things out with the band or find a new one if that's what it took to keep rocking his way.

Or maybe not. He was messed up. Stuck in an endless groove. Just because he'd made that work for him didn't mean he was any less messed up. He was tired of scratching the old itch until it bled, no matter how comforting it felt.

Beth could help him find a different way to live with the past. Putting it all on her was unfair, but he saw no other way.

At the foot of the stairs, he called again, "Beth?"

"I'm up here, Deek."

Deacon carried his mug up the exposed staircase and into the nearest room, which turned out to be her bedroom. Even here, everything was perfect. Uncluttered dressers, calming art on the walls. The bed appeared never slept in.

The room connected to an en suite bathroom, where she leaned over the sink in pajamas, applying makeup.

"Hey," he said. "What are you doing?"

"I'm getting ready for work."

Deacon's eyes caressed the slope of her back, then drank in the sight of her dabbing mascara around her eye. In the music world, he'd seen it all when it came to women, every brand of sex appeal expertly advertised, but it was the minor, mundane things that slew him. A beautiful woman in her jammies brushing her hair, putting on makeup, stepping into a pair of jeans.

He gazed at her with a fierce, longing ache and thought,

I should have put the necklace on you. Kissed you just like in the movies.

Her big brown eyes gazed back at him from the mirror. "What's wrong?"

"We should get married."

Beth shook with one of her belly laughs. "I thought you came to apologize for something."

"I didn't already?" Deacon couldn't remember. His arrival in Santa Barbara was a blur.

"All you've done since you showed up is snore on my couch."

"How about dinner tonight? I'll apologize properly."

She put on a finishing touch and stepped back to check her appearance. "For what?" Then held up her hand. "I know for what. It was a long time ago. I'm long over it. What's really bothering you?"

"God, you're good at this." Though he wasn't sure she *was* over it.

"What is it, Deek?"

He shrugged. "I'm tired of being me the way I'm being me."

Her eyes probed his as she made her educated guesses. "I can't save you."

"I don't want to relive the past. I just want to fix what I can from it. Clean my slate, so to speak. Like they do in the twelve-step programs. I've been thinking about some big changes in my life. Okay?"

Beth smiled. "All right."

"Now that we've got all that out of the way, how about dinner tonight?"

"It's a date. Now move aside so I can get dressed for work."

She'd always known how to give him something while making him want more.

▲   ▲   ▲

Dr. Klein smiled at the circle of children. "Who wants to go first?"

Notebooks in their laps, the survivors sat facing him on their folding chairs. At their last group therapy session, the psychiatrist gave them homework.

Nobody raised a hand.

He said, "Did everybody write a poem expressing something they're feeling?"

Deacon nodded along with his friends.

"Okay. We were going to read one and talk about it for an hour, but let's shelve that idea for now. Today, let's just read all the poems and see what happens. How does that sound?"

Another nod.

"Fantastic. Dave, you're usually the shy one, so I'm going to see if you're feeling brave—"

"David," the boy said.

"Excuse me?"

"My name is David. Not Dave."

"All right. David. How about you start us off?"

"I chose a tercet for mine." He read aloud:

Everything I learned from you,
The good and the bad, the glad and the sad,
Turned out to be untrue.
Everywhere you took me to,
Too cold, too hot, to gold and rot,
Is nothing I can't undo.

"That's very good," said Dr. Klein.

"That's all I have."

"Your poem is perfect. I heard a lot of strength in those words. Thank you, David." The psychiatrist then nodded to Deacon, who cleared his throat and read:

Make pain your friend
Is something they say,
Though love is better
In every way.
So make love your friend
But love, it can die,
So maybe pain's truer
And love is the lie.

"Very powerful quatrain," the psychiatrist said. "You're right that love is a better friend than pain, but you have to trust it again."

Or maybe they're the same thing, Deacon thought.

Dr. Klein focused on Beth. She blushed and read:

Someone screams out in the dark,
And I think how silence is cool.
I cry out to you and hear no answer,
And I think that silence is cruel.
Screams in my ears, I look at your eyes,
And I learn how silence can fool.

"There's so much we can talk about from these poems. Angela?"

She gave him a grin devoid of mirth. "I've got a limerick for you."

"Let's hear it."

There once was a bunch of people
Who built a church with a steeple,
I told them, "Don't blow it,"
But wouldn't you know it,
They killed themselves. The end.

"Yes," Dr. Klein said, as if she'd revealed something important despite her intention to do the opposite. "Thank you, Angela. Emily, your turn. What do you have?"

Emily read:

What if I tell you
To wait for me,
To be ready,
Because I am coming now.
You might be unhappy
If I don't show up
But you then remember
That I said to wait for me,
That I said to get ready,
That I was coming now.
So if you love me,
Truly love me,
You'll wait, you'll be ready,
And it will always be now.

"Thank you, Emily," Dr. Klein said, though he seemed unsettled by her poem. "Now, who wants to talk about what they wrote?"

Deacon gripped his notebook and thought about how satisfying it was to put his feelings on paper and speak them aloud. How much it hurt.

From then on, the two would forever be the same to him.

After Beth left, Deacon puttered around her condo while sipping her highbrow coffee. As in her bedroom, the art on the walls in the main living area was colorful and safe, with not a single personal photo to be found. Books about every manifestation of human madness and hurt lined extensive shelves. Delusion, addiction, trauma. Everything one needed to put Humpty Dumpty back together.

What he'd said at Emily's funeral about people becoming psychologists to learn how to fix themselves rang true when looking around this place. Beth had taken *physician, heal thyself* to a new level. Her whole lifestyle spoke of it. It screamed, *I've got my shit together*, but it was still a scream.

With his singing, Deacon went straight to the scream.

If he was going to change, he didn't want to become like her. He didn't want a psychologist. He needed his friend.

The spine of a book caught his eye. *Death in the Desert: The Family of the Living Spirit Cult* by E. L. Carter. Grisly mutilation, suicide, murder, and a mysterious mass disappearance packaged as entertainment, though Deacon had to admit this sensationalist piece of drivel was the most complete account of the Family's rise and fall he'd ever visited.

He remembered when Carter called him searching for insights, and only wanted to talk about the final night, which was all anyone wanted to hear about and why, long ago, he'd stopped telling people he'd grown up in the Family.

Deacon wondered if some poor soul had read the book and became inspired to follow in the Family's suicidal footsteps. Wondered if old E. L. blamed himself for it. A sad thing, sharing a horror as a warning just to see it repeated.

Maybe Deacon would become inspired himself. Write a book instead of sing. Share a story that would shock and titillate America. He'd tell everyone that before the Family went to Red Peak, they'd given him the best years of his life, years rich with love and purpose and wonder and meaning.

He returned to his wandering and ended up back in the kitchen for more java. This time, he noticed the large wine rack filled with corked bottles of Cabernet Sauvignon. Beth had an extensive collection of expensive wines. Empty long-stemmed glasses dried in the dish rack. It seemed the esteemed Dr. Harris needed some good old-fashioned lubrication when psychology failed to see her through the day. Rather than alarming him, this discovery made him strangely happy. They were still the same. They didn't need theory and lingo to understand each other.

His cell vibrated again, and this time he answered. "Yeah?"

"You don't know how to answer your fucking phone?" Laurie yelled.

"I'm taking a break. I thought you understood that."

"Drive your ass back to Crenshaw. We have work to do."

"Break," he repeated. "I can't do anything right now anyway."

Laurie sucked in her breath, which meant she was winding up to drill him a new hole, but hesitated.

"Wait," she said. "You have no idea what's going on, do you?"

Deacon poured his second mug of coffee. "Not a clue."

"Dude, that interview you gave is blowing up the internet."

"Everybody hates us, I get it." He blew across the mug and slurped.

"*Half* of everybody hates us," she corrected. "The *other* half are buying our songs online and watching our videos. Our social media is exploding."

He set his coffee down in surprise. "Huh."

"Frank got us a gig at Utopia." She let out a frustrated sigh when he didn't respond right away with an appropriate whoop. "*Utopia*, dude."

A premier LA venue. Capacity, five hundred. Long considered the launching pad of musical careers and dreams.

She seemed to expect him to say something, so he said, "That's great."

"Goddamn right it's great. Frank is working deals like crazy. Playing up the Medford anniversary, how you're the kid who lived to tell the tale and make music that comforts the afflicted, blah, blah, blah. Now he's bragging how he can turn shit into gold. But get this. The band changed their mind about the album."

"Wow," he said.

They wanted to do it for all the wrong reasons, but still.

"That's it? *Wow? That's great?* You know, it wouldn't kill you to be happy every once in a while."

"The last time I was truly happy, I almost *did* get killed."

"Poor you. When are you coming back?"

Perhaps God or the Devil did pull his life's strings to watch the monkey dance. The tests always arrived when you wanted something. The rewards always showed up when you were ready to walk away. You prayed not to be led into temptation, but the temptations came anyway, designed just for you.

He thought about Beth and hesitated. "Later this week, probably."

Laurie went quiet so long he wondered if she was still on the line.

"Hello?" he said.

"Where are you?"

"With an old friend. Another survivor."

"The 'we played so beautifully' girl?" Referencing the song he'd written.

"Yes."

"Just for inspiration, I hope."

Laurie wasn't jealous. The sex had been part of their working relationship and otherwise meant nothing to her. She lived to perform, and she performed because she could do nothing else. They were kindred spirits that way. She didn't want Beth to interfere with his return to the band.

He said, "I have to do something before I come back. Something important."

She exhaled through her nose like a kettle reaching the boiling point. "You know what I think is important? Getting everything you want. Eating that cake."

"Wait for me. If getting everything is that important to you, you'll do it."

"You've got one day." She meant it. Laurie made a steadfast ally but a savage and implacable enemy. "Then I'm coming for you."

"It'll take as long as it takes." He ended the call.

The phone started to vibrate seconds later, but he ignored it.

Deacon would give the Devil his due. He'd return to Los Angeles, resume the album, perform at Utopia, go back to the cycle of pain and purge. First, he wanted to clear the air with Beth. Kill the silence between them once and for all, a silence now older than he'd been when his world had ended.

At Beth's favorite restaurant at Stearns Wharf, the host seated them by the window, which offered stunning views of the harbor. Deacon barely noticed the natural beauty, instead focused on Beth in her sleeveless black dress.

After they ordered and the server poured her a glass of red wine, she relaxed. Then she told him about Emily's package and David's theory about the Wardites, wondering what he thought.

Deacon said, "I think it's just like David to put it back in the box as soon as it came out."

Beth sipped her wine. "What don't you agree with?"

"Something happened out there. The things I saw…"

Or thought you saw, he told himself.

"Like what? What did you see?"

Deacon sighed. "Why bother? You'll just come up with some educated way to say I'm crazy."

"This is the problem. We all keep secrets from each other."

"You want to hear it? Okay, here it is. I don't think what happened at Red Peak was a bunch of people losing their shit. Something else was going on. I think Emily understood it."

"Trying to find meaning in tragedy is natural," Beth said.

"There you go." He tossed his hands.

"Sorry. Let's say something *did* happen. Let's even say it was supernatural. In the end, you're still you. You still have to live with that and fix it."

"I just feel like something was done to us. I'd like to know why."

"Something *was* done to us," Beth said. "There might be no why."

"We'll find out when we get there."

"You still want to go back?"

Deacon nodded. "After my gig at Utopia, wildfires permitting. We're going together, right?"

She poured the rest of her wine down her throat, as if

steeling herself to give her answer. He watched her refill her glass. "Yes. I want to do it. I keep coming back to it as something I need to do."

"I'm glad you want to go. I don't want to do it alone."

"As soon as the forest fires burn themselves out."

Their meals arrived, and they ate while the harbor dimmed to black. Afterward, they walked out onto the pier, laughing at the kind of memories that didn't scar. Wyatt saying, *I'll bet you could turn water into whining.* Dr. Klein's habit of idly combing his beard when he talked. The way old Mrs. Kowalski would shout *Yes, Lord!* during sermons. Their discovery of the ghost town. The time they spied on Angela and Josh making out at the stream.

At the end of the pier, they stopped to listen to the sea's breathy roar. The wind carried its briny smell.

Beth leaned on the railing. "Deek?"

"Yeah?"

"Why did you kiss me? After the funeral?"

Deacon gazed into the darkness, imagining it stretched into eternity. "It was opposite day."

"What does that mean?"

"When we were kids, I thought about kissing you all the time but never had the nerve to do it. The longing became an end in itself. I was dumb."

"You said it yourself," Beth responded. "We were kids."

"When I saw you at Emily's funeral, I did the opposite. Ever since we left the hospital, in fact, every day has been opposite day."

The wind ruffled her hair. She shivered at the chill. "So it was just something to do. Unfinished business."

"That's one way of looking at it," he said. "Another is that I did it because I've always loved you."

"Oh." Her shoulders clenched a little. "Is that real, or another opposite?"

"The real deal. I'm sorry I hurt you, Beth. I am."

On the day she told him she was leaving the mental hospital to enter the foster care system, the pain had been overwhelming. They'd cried and hugged and promised they'd find each other on the other side, that they'd be together forever.

Then the day arrived. When she came to say goodbye, he pretended she'd already left and wasn't there. She'd begged and screamed for him to say something, anything. He'd stared at the TV until she was gone.

Simple as that, he shattered her heart.

Silence could be cruel.

Beth shrugged, but she still wouldn't look at him. "It's in the past."

"I wasn't trying to hurt you. I was using you to hurt *me*. I know that doesn't make it any better. It probably makes it worse. I just wanted you to know."

He'd preferred the pain, the ache of longing for something he couldn't have and therefore could never risk losing. An end in itself.

The Devil killed with comfort.

Beth turned to him, the glisten of tears on her cheeks. "I understand."

"Your turn," Deacon said. "Why did you kiss me back?"

"I'd just buried my childhood best friend, and I wanted to break something."

He smiled. "I understand too." All too well.

She wiped her eyes. "I might as well tell you that I never stopped loving you either."

"Even after what I did?"

"I still love you, but I can't figure out if it's you, or just a memory."

"We *are* our memories," Deacon said.

They made Beth real amid so much illusion.

He leaned in to kiss her again, this time for all the right reasons.

16

LOSE

The sex was incredible.

For Beth, sex had always been about scratching an itch, only to make it worse.

Tonight, the itch disappeared as if it never existed.

Deacon's pace quickened.

She raised her hips to push back against every thrust.

Oxytocin and endorphins, bonding and reward chemicals. The prefrontal cortex, insula, cingulate gyrus, and cerebellum lighting up with increased blood flow. The brain entering a trance state.

The whole so much bigger than the sum of these chemical parts.

Her mind flashed to Sunday worship in the Temple. The Spirit passing through her like electric current, leaving her raving and dancing.

Then her ego voided to the timeless place found in the singularity of a gunshot, what the Buddhists called Nirvana.

▲   ▲   ▲

After the third time, Beth lay sweating on her bed sheets, stretching to bask in the post-orgasm glow. Her digital clock told her dawn would arrive soon.

Deacon panted next to her in the dark. "Wow, lady."

"Amen," she purred.

Many of her patients came to her with delusions stemming from love. Jealousy, rationalization, shame, excusing abuse. It was enough to make Beth wonder why the human race bothered with it.

At last, she understood what the fuss was all about.

For all these years, Beth had been missing out, making love to placeholders. She'd had few sexual partners because she'd never been truly able to let go. She imagined Deacon had had many, because to him the act had been meaningless.

Love, it turned out, made all the difference.

He said, "You're still wearing it."

"Wearing what?"

"The necklace I gave you."

Beth fingered the little cross looped around her throat, which she'd worn for the past fifteen years. "It reminds me that there are some good, even wonderful, things I want to remember."

Right now, however, it made her think of the Wardites. The necklace, it turned out, had once belonged to a woman whose devotion to God had brought her to die at Red Peak more than a century before Deacon found it. Beth imagined a beautiful woman in a simple dress, hungry for food and God, taking it off and placing it in its box before ascending the mountain to die.

In all the years since, everything had changed except what made people tick.

"I can't believe you were here this whole time," he said. "I'm stupid."

"I told you I can't save you."

"No," he said. "But I'm thinking love could."

"The only thing that can save you is you. Take it from a shrink."

Deacon smiled. "That sounds like too much responsibility."

She shook with one of her belly laughs and drifted off to sleep.

Beth awoke the next morning more refreshed than she'd felt in years.

You got laid, her inner voice said. *Congratulations. You're a person.*

She sat up and stretched. "Shut up, mini-me."

Deacon was gone. Fifteen years in the making, their renewed connection made her feel reborn. At the same time, she was relieved to have her condo back. He trailed chaos wherever he went, oblivious to it.

The clock told her she didn't have time for her morning jog, but she didn't need one today.

Beth bounded out of bed to shower. Under the hot spray, she flashed to Deacon's sweaty arms. The mysterious tattoos covering his flesh like an instruction manual for a man chased by demons.

While she poured coffee, she remembered that electric kiss on the pier. As she spread creamy peanut butter on her toast, she pictured him licking her thighs.

Beth got into her Mercedes whistling a joyful tune, thinking maybe Deacon was right, that love was a catalyst for cognitive change. A different higher power to believe in, one that could empower her to take ultimate charge of her scarred brain.

You're still just the product of programming. You have no more real control of your life than you did yesterday, possibly less.

Sigmund Freud said humans were slaves to their subconscious conflicts. B. F. Skinner believed outside influences dominated behavior. Since then, scientists found genetics to be a major determinant in how people react. Some of them discovered brain activity increased before the conscious mind made a decision, suggesting the brain decided what to do an instant before its owner was aware that a decision was made.

In other words, maybe humans didn't have free will. Adam and Eve had no choice but to eat the apple and curse their race forever. Beth's parents could only choose to follow Jeremiah Peale into the desert and the grave. And Beth, the sum of genes and chemicals and experience, had no real control over her life, from Deacon breaking her heart to tumbling into bed with her a decade and a half later.

"That just means we're destined to be together," she murmured as she reached the building where she rented office space. She parked in the garage.

You could be destined to get hurt again.

"I can't fight fate, right? The decision's apparently already been made for me."

You remember what he did—

"God, there is no shutting you up, is there?"

Any other time, replying aloud startled her critic and made it recede back into the calm murmur of inner dialogue, but today was special, likely the result of her not getting enough sleep. To her relief, the voice at last shut up when she reached her office and settled at her desk.

She checked for cancellations and requests to reschedule, reviewed her bills, and spent a half hour on the phone fighting with an insurance company. This out of the way, she prepared for the day's one-hour sessions in her meeting room with its soft leather furniture, coffee table with a tissue box, healing-themed paintings on the walls, and gentle lighting from several floor lamps.

Gabe and Sara arrived on time to talk about their sixteen-year-old son, Jake, who ignored his parents, didn't care about school, and smoked pot every day. Beth worked with them to make sure they stood united in setting consistent boundaries and otherwise being predictable and firm in their parenting. After the meeting, she wrote up her notes on progress and next steps.

Janice arrived next to continue intervention therapy to treat her panic attacks, which had become so severe she thought she was having a heart attack. Beth had referred her to get a prescription for Zoloft, and they talked about how that was going before continuing their cognitive behavioral therapy, which involved identifying and altering the thought patterns that triggered fight-or-flight reactions.

Her third appointment was an assessment for Will, a new patient worn out by anxiety, which Beth traced to a series of childhood traumas. They agreed on a treatment plan and that they would meet again next week.

In all, it was a perfect morning in which everything went just right. People arrived, and they talked. She listened, and she talked. The air filled with words. Memories, feelings, desires, failures, and beliefs, all articulated, packaged, analyzed. Breakthroughs in understanding. The joy of realization and catharsis.

Over lunch, Beth caught up on her reading list and emails while thinking about going to Red Peak to again confront her own childhood, this time at the source. She pictured it as a romantic journey. She could drive down to Deacon's show in a few days. She hated rock concerts, which were too loud and unpredictable for her, but it would be fun to surprise him and hear him sing. Even the idea tickled her.

The afternoon didn't go as smoothly as her morning.

Beth had awoken flush with the love chemicals, oxytocin and dopamine, but these natural drugs were wearing off, and now her serotonin was dropping, elevating her anxiety.

This is your brain on love, she thought.

A different behavioral program.

The old itch had been replaced by another. The need to connect with Deacon. She dialed his cell and listened to it ring. When the phone went to voicemail, she terminated the call and tried again, and again.

Most nights, Beth stayed in to open a bottle of Cabernet and work, catch a movie over a bowl of popcorn, or both. She was used to being her own best friend, but tonight she felt alone in her condo. While the corn popped in the microwave, she stared at the spot on the gleaming counter where she'd wiped Deacon's coffee ring and wished it would reappear so she could wipe it again.

For the next few days, she'd tried many times to reach him, but he never answered, nor responded to her voicemails and texts. She'd played it cool at first, then gave in to worry.

Did something happen to you? Call me.

Her patience soon wore off, and she found herself leaving angry messages culminating in a cutting rant.

You think you're this boy who never grew up because his childhood was stolen, but I knew that kid. You're just a typical selfish man.

The next voicemail: *You blew it with the one woman who knew you. I'm done with you. Never call me again.*

And then the next: *I'm sorry about my last messages, I was upset. Can we at least talk about this?*

Beth was turning into the person she advised her clients not to be. She'd always had a hard time letting things go. She also hated the silent treatment, which was eating her from the inside out.

Tonight, Deacon's band was playing at Utopia. Cats Are Sad. He'd told her they'd named the band that because cats were independent creatures who didn't give a shit about anything, but nonetheless suffered from loneliness and existential despair. He'd be unreachable for the whole night, she knew.

The perfect time to shake him off. She wasn't a *program*, she was a woman armed with free will and a decade of self-actualization. To hell with mourning. She'd celebrate dodging a bus packed with chaos.

After a brief inspection of her wines, she selected her best, a 2007 Cabernet, a collectible. She removed the cork as the microwave dinged, and botched it. The screw ravaged the cork, which crumbled onto her counter.

Beth gritted her teeth at her handiwork. "Goddamn it."

No. She had this. She scraped out the loose bits and pushed the rest into the bottle, pausing to allow the bottle to breathe and herself with it. Positioning a coffee filter over her glass, she poured out a generous quantity and sipped.

Perfect.

She filled a large bowl with the hot popcorn and went to her living room to settle on the couch in front of the TV. A quick breathing exercise purged the last of her negativity.

Her cell rang.

The bowl in her lap slid and toppled to the floor as she lunged for the phone. Popcorn tumbled across her area rug.

Under the coffee table, under the couch. Her condo seemed covered in it.

"God*damn* it!" She answered. "Is this you, finally?"

"It is *me*," the voice said, "but probably not who you expected."

"James?" Dr. James Chambliss, still wanting inside her head.

"Is this not a good time?"

"James, listen—"

"We should finish what we started all those years ago. I can help you."

Beth gazed at the mess in despair. "I don't need to screw around with my head anymore."

He went silent, though she knew what he was thinking. He'd been the one to see her back to her room after the Fab party. Her head was already good and screwed.

"Our hypnosis work back in 2012 brought you to the brink of uncovering a major traumatic memory you'd repressed," he said. "Whatever you'd taken at the party almost brought it back. I can help you reach it, under safe conditions."

"I don't need to do anything, James."

"Don't you want to know what happened?"

"Everything in my life is perfect."

Another pause. Again, she could guess what he was thinking.

He said, "There's been a lot of innovation in the field since—"

Beth ended the call, shaking.

She couldn't stand this mess another second. As she got onto her knees to scoop up the popcorn, her arm jolted the coffee table. The wineglass rocked.

"Shit!" She made to grab it and instead shoved it across

the table to thud on the rug. A full glass of collectible Cabernet went flying with it.

Beth seized a throw pillow from her couch and screamed into it until she was gnawing on velvet. Tossing it aside, she stormed into the kitchen and returned with paper towels. She'd start over. She had this. Scoop the popcorn back into the bowl. Mop the wine. Roll the rug for the cleaners, or better yet, throw it away and call it a symbolic gesture of renewal. Refill her glass.

James actually could help if you—

"No," she grated. "Just no."

Beth started walking toward her front door. The spill could wait. She had a much bigger mess to clean up first. A giant coffee ring around her life that needed wiping until not a single trace of it remained.

Beth loathed rock concerts. Uniforms, groupthink, phony onstage antics, and a deafening wall of sound, all designed to produce euphoria that for the Family had been effortless thanks to loving worship and the boundless Spirit.

Utopia was packed to standing room only. The mood wild and cheerful and dangerous, somewhere between brotherhood and a riot. They'd all come to see the boy who survived the legendary final night. The kid who grew up in a cult that forced its members to mutilate themselves.

They wanted to hear him sing.

The stage stood empty under dimmed projector lights. The instruments awaited their players.

Petite and still wearing her suit jacket and skirt from work, Beth drew stares as she threaded the crowd with a plastic cup full of cheap red, searching for a decent sightline. Black T-shirts declared band names like ads for taste.

The DJ played trip hop to warm everyone up.

Beth found a spot near an emergency exit where she could put her back against the wall. The red was a little vinegary, but she drained it anyway.

The patrons cheered as the stage lights flared. Scowling with cool, the band walked out and got ready with their instruments.

Then Deacon wandered out and stood blinking at the microphone like a kid at a spelling bee asked to spell *Mississippi* backward. He broke into a grin.

He said, "If God is everything, he is also the Devil. The Adversary. The Accuser."

The crowd loved it.

Cats Are Sad launched into a heavy, pounding rhythm, and Deacon spread his arms like Christ and started to howl as the lights burned even brighter. It seemed to rise out of him like a soul departing a body still alive. Beth winced as the sound waves struck her ears at eleven hundred feet per second.

The Goth girl in front of her screamed and raised her fists. "Fucking yeah!"

The impressive freak-out rolled into "Shadow Boxer," which Beth recognized from YouTube, the song that inspired a suicide and resulting storm.

Standing on the extended stage surrounded by people raising cell phones, Deacon sang with his head bowed. The skinny guitarist with dyed blond pigtails stared at her Converse high-tops, stomping effects pedals. The Rob Zombie look-alike drummer grinned as he savaged his skins. The weathered bassist and buxom keyboardist exchanged a private smile before returning their cool gazes to the audience.

The next songs arrived, one following the other like

irresistible waves, each an ethereal, dreamlike mixture of searing lyrics and plaintive guitar distortion. The listeners settled into a trance state until Deacon paused to talk to them.

"I'm guessing most of you know by now where I grew up, and who I grew up with," he said into the microphone. "Do you want to hear about the mass suicide? The body parts on the altar? The missing bodies?"

The crowd rustled in anticipation.

Deacon smiled. "The fact you do is why Jeremiah founded the Family in the first place. I'm going to tell you a different story tonight. Before the Family went crazy, they were good people. My mother. The best friends I ever had. The one woman in my life I ever loved. You want to hear something else?"

The room remained silent.

He said, "What happened hurt so much, and hurts right now, because I was *happy*. You only know how much you have after somebody takes it from you. After it's all stripped away, the only thing you have left is life itself."

The band started playing again, piano chords and chainsaw guitar in breathy, swirling tones. The LED projectors tuned into a perfect simulation of moonlight.

Deacon said, "I wrote a song about it, which is going to be on our next album. 'We Played So Beautifully.'"

As he sang, the ersatz moonlight cast a ghostly halo around his tangled hair and pale, boyish face.

Beth's eyes watered as the words crossed the room and burrowed into her. He was singing to *her*. This was a song about *her*.

Too young to kiss,
But an old love so pure,

Of all I miss,
I'll never be as sure,
That we played so beautifully,
But the wall fell down.
How we played so beautifully,
But the wall came round.

Then Deacon was crying too, eyes bulging with tears streaming down his cheeks. A musician in Hell, singing his loss and sin in an endless concert for an audience of demons who'd come for the vicarious thrill.

Beth thought of a line of ancient Greek tattooed on his arm, which he'd explained meant, *What can't be said will be wept.*

The crowd gaped back at him, mesmerized. The song had hypnotized them, luring them into a guided meditation along a cult survivor's memories.

As the song reached its climax, he sang:

She played so beautifully.
She played so beautifully.
She played so beautifully.
She played so beautifully.

He was singing about his mother now, Beth knew. The warm, pure-hearted organist whose one sin was pride in her playing. A sin for which she'd atoned in the harshest way possible to prepare her spirit for its ascension.

A punishment she'd inflicted on herself out of belief that something bigger and better awaited her.

I wasn't trying to hurt you, he'd said on the pier. *I was using you to hurt me.*

"I understand," Beth murmured through tears.

They could never be together, but at least she now knew why.

Deacon couldn't stop his self-immolation. Neither could she. If he hadn't hurt her again with his silence, she would have found a way to drive him out of her life with her words, wipe at the stain until it never reappeared. Forever, they were doomed to suffer separately in the comfort of their coping routines. In the end, even love couldn't transcend their programs.

The crowd let out a frenzied cheer as the song ended with a roaring blast.

The horn she hadn't heard in fifteen years.

Lifeless forms rustled where they lay twisted and sprawling on the Temple floor. A pew groaned as it scraped along the hardwood.

The shofar called the dead home to paradise.

Mom was flying.

Beth reeled toward the exit while the horn vibrated through the air to rattle her heart and fill it with raving terror.

17

SUFFER

The clang of hammers and chisels echoed as the Family built their great stairway to the summit. The children went first, raking and sweeping loose stones from the path. In their wake, men hacked at the dry ground with pickaxes and shovels in a cloud of dust. Then the women came, hauling thick pieces of rough-hewn sandstone to form the broad treads, thinner stones to serve as risers.

After a month of hard labor, the Family neared the first false summit, where the mountainside leveled out a short distance before resuming its climb to the peak. Grueling misery in the hot sun, but they did it with zeal, happy to have something to do, to have some control. Paradise awaited them at the top.

Looking down at the great stairway from above, Beth was reminded of a wonder of the world, the building of the first railroad, or one of the big mysterious burial mounds that dotted the continent, visible as a serpent only from the heavens.

She scratched at the arid dirt with her rake. Her blistered hands stung and bled like stigmata. School had stopped, and even play was a luxury, as it was pointless to do anything other than finish the work they'd been tasked. Aside from sponge baths, she hadn't washed in weeks. Every morning, it took hours for them just to reach the highest part of the stairway and resume work.

"Just a little more," Deacon coaxed, "and then we can go back."

She nodded in the sun's glare and tottered, light-headed.

He handed her a bottle of water, which she gulped. "Not too much. You know it's hard to get more."

She pictured herself splashing in the baptismal stream. She licked dry, chapped lips. "I can't do it anymore."

"Sit down then. You can gather up the stones." The stones were mixed with sand and poured to form a base for the tread stones. "Or take a rest."

Still dizzy, Beth sat on a rock. "I don't feel very good."

Deacon gave her the bottle. "Finish it. I'll be okay until we get back."

She drank thirstily.

"The atonement is today," he went on. "We'll be in the Temple for the ceremony, and then we'll have the rest of the day off."

The Spirit had instructed the Family to confess their sins. Then it had told Jeremiah they'd all have to purify themselves for the ascension. Twelve of the grown-ups had volunteered, including Deacon's mom and David and Angela's.

Beth had no idea what purification entailed, only the children had a role to play in it. She'd pictured a celebratory ritual, like baptism.

"Fine," she said, hoping she had enough energy to walk back down.

An apparition appeared at the crest of the false summit, a black specter shimmering in the heat waves.

Beth raised her hand to shield her eyes from the blinding light. "What is that?"

The kids stopped work to gaze up the slope.

The specter solidified into the form of Jeremiah Peale.

Every few days, he climbed the mountain to talk to God and returned fired with new energy and determination. His infectious smile, however, was gone.

The Reverend sat in the dust. His blue eyes smoldered on his sunburned face. He drank from his canteen, swished it around his mouth, and spit.

"You kids," he rasped. "It's time."

"I want to atone too, Reverend," Deacon said.

Jeremiah sat unmoving with his head bowed, and Beth wondered if he'd fallen asleep. His eyes shot open. "You will. By watching and learning."

"And singing," Emily said.

A flicker of a smile passed the Reverend's face. "Just remember, if we suffer, we do it with joy. Abraham didn't complain when God asked him to give his foreskin. He obeyed. He circumcised his entire house."

"Okay," Deacon said uncertainly.

"Just as I obey, though I asked the Spirit that this burden could be lifted, or be given to me alone." He grimaced. "Yes, it's time."

The Reverend stood and dusted the seat of his pants. Then he set off back down the mountain, where the Family had stopped work and waited for him.

"What was that about?" Angela wondered. "That whole thing about Abraham?"

"I need to talk to my mom," said Deacon.

"Yeah. I'd better talk to mine too."

Beth heaved upright. Stars rushed into her vision. The earth wobbled. She closed her eyes and waited for it to pass. She had to wash up and put on her vestments. Then she had to sing.

She'd hoped the atonement would be a celebration, a relief from deprivation and hard labor, but now she wondered if things were about to get even worse.

Dressed in white choral gowns and holding hands, the Family's children crowded the sides of the nave. They sang as the first of the repentant entered the Temple and approached the altar, on which a smoking brazier rested.

There's a joy in my heart that shall ever abide
'Tis a joy to the world that unknown;
For in undying love Jesus came seeking me,
And he bro't me again to his own.

Deacon's mother had arrived first, scrubbed clean and wearing a white robe. A murmur rippled through the tense crowd. They waved fans to cool themselves. The pews creaked as they rustled with anticipation. Those nearest reached to lay hands on her as she moved up the aisle with an uncertain smile.

Beth leaned to hiss at Deacon, "Did you talk to her?"

Her friend was pale. "She told me to be strong."

"Do you know what they're going to do?"

He wagged his head. "I don't like this."

Whatever it was, she hoped it didn't last long. She was hungry and light-headed and wasn't sure how long she'd be able to keep standing. Though she was out of the sun now, the Temple was sweltering. Under her gown, her body was slick with sweat.

The Reverend raised his Bible as Mrs. Price reached the altar. "'If your right eye causes you to stumble, pluck it out and throw it away from you. For it is more profitable for you that one of your members should perish, than for your whole body to be cast into Gehenna.'"

"Amen," Mrs. Price said.

He turned his fierce gaze to the entire congregation, his eyes full of love. "And 'if your right hand causes you to stumble, cut it off, and throw it away from you. For it is more profitable for you that one of your members should perish, than for your whole body to be cast into Gehenna.' The Book of Matthew, chapter five, verses twenty-nine and thirty. This is the word of the Lord."

"Praise God," the crowd intoned.

The Reverend hugged the small, stout woman, his lips moving as he whispered private words of encouragement. She shook in his arms.

He kissed the top of her head and said, "Sherry, my oldest and dearest friend. Do you accept the Living Spirit in your heart?"

"I do, Reverend," she said in her small, shy voice.

"Do you love the Spirit more than anything?"

"I surely do."

"Have you come freely to purify yourself so you can ascend without sin?"

"I have."

"Declare your great sin before the Spirit," Jeremiah said.

Mrs. Price lifted her chin. "My sin is pride, Reverend."

He raised his hands in supplication. "Lord, we pray that you give this woman the strength to make herself ready." He smiled at her, though it wasn't his normal joyful smile, more like one reconciled to pain. "We forgive you and call you sister. You may atone. Shed your sin and become pure."

This was the signal to resume singing. While Deacon's mom rested her left hand on the altar, Beth sang:

O the sweet and precious joy he gives,
As I walk by his side day by day,

In my heart the blessed Savior lives,
And his love—

Mrs. Price raised a butcher's cleaver. The Family gasped and leaned forward in their pews. The singing faltered.

His love brightens all—

She swung the cleaver in a gleaming arc. The sharp blade sliced through the fingers of her left hand to thud against the wood.

Mrs. Price reared with a high-pitched scream. Blood sprayed across the altar and sizzled as it struck the brazier.

"Mom?" Deacon cried. "Mom!"

Grimacing with her left hand jammed into her armpit, she picked up her fingers one by one and tossed them onto the brazier, where they hissed. Smoke billowed into the air along with the sickeningly sweet stench of burning flesh.

"You are now one of the elect," the Reverend said.

Women rushed forward with bandages to help Mrs. Price to her seat. Deacon fell to his knees. Beth looked around wildly at the congregation and settled on her own mother, who stared at Sherry Price with a smile that gleamed with envy.

Mrs. Young was already walking up the aisle toward the altar.

The Temple began to spin. Beth twisted all the way to the floor and into utter darkness.

Beth awoke to a hand clasped over her mouth.

Hot breath in her ear. "Are you awake?"

Whimpering, she nodded.

"Come outside," her father said. "I'll meet you there."

Quietly, she left her bed and slipped on her shoes. Daddy waited outside in the moonlight.

"What's going on?" she whispered.

Three weeks had passed since the purifications began. After nearly two months of hard labor and surviving on what the Family had brought with them from the farm, Daddy's clothes hung on him like laundry drying on a line. The children no longer had to work on the stairway, but she knew the Family was now making steady progress to the second summit.

He motioned for her to follow him away from the cabins. The full moon hung over Red Peak. The air was silent and still and mercifully cold.

"Where are we going?"

Boots crunching on the stones, he kept walking until the cabins disappeared in the darkness. "I wanted to talk to you about something important."

"Okay." Her aching body protested at the walk, while her exhausted brain urged her to return to bed. "I'm listening."

"You're almost fifteen now. Old enough to understand. I don't have a choice."

"Daddy, stop. Tell me what's going on."

Her father's gait slowed to a halt. "Your mother. She's going to purify herself tomorrow."

Beth looked down at her body sheathed in its nightgown and wondered what Mom would sacrifice on the altar as a burnt offering. Which part of her offended the Spirit and needed to be removed to purge herself of sin.

Tears stung her eyes. "Okay."

"No," Daddy said. "Not okay."

She started in surprise. "What do you mean?"

"When your mother found this church, we almost got divorced. I just never believed the way she did. I went along with her because I didn't want to lose you."

"Daddy? What are you saying?"

He gazed into the darkness, no longer talking only to her, as if this were his own confession. "And she was right. The farm was good. I was even willing to go along with what was happening here for a while, as long as you were safe. This ascension business, though. I don't know if any of us are going to survive it."

"We're supposed to die." She felt sick now. "I don't understand."

"One day, you will die and go to Heaven, but the world is not coming to an end anytime soon. We're not going to just vanish and wake up in paradise."

"But that's how it's supposed to work. The Reverend talked to—"

"The Reverend isn't right in the head, and he's going to get all of us killed. That's the only way this can end."

Jeremiah hadn't purified yet, but he'd suffered more than most between barely eating and his labor on the stairs. He still climbed to the top of the mountain to beg the Spirit to deliver them now without any more suffering.

"The black sea?" her father added. "The ascension? Cutting off body parts? This isn't Christian anymore. It's something else. It's madness."

The Reverend never talked about God or Jesus anymore, only the Living Spirit, which he said lived on the mountain. When the Spirit came, no longer did it fill the Family with joy and make them dance and sing, only writhe on the floor chanting and howling and soiling themselves.

She thought of Deacon, who wouldn't leave his mother's side. David and Angela's mom, who'd cut up her face to destroy her beauty and stop inspiring love from men. She'd considered it horrible but also powerful, brave, breathtaking in its piety.

Was it all for nothing? They'd hurt themselves for a lie?

It hurt to even think about. She buried her face in her hands. "Stop it."

"I'm leaving," he said. "Right now. I'm going to get help."

"But..." Beth didn't know what to say. He was protecting her, as he always did, but she couldn't shake the dread he was betraying them all.

She thought again of David's mom, her once beautiful face held together by strips of medical tape. Deacon's, who'd taken too much pride in her musical talent and would never play the organ again. Emily's, who'd cut off one of her ears. Wyatt's father, who'd plucked out his left eye.

Tomorrow, her own mom would toss a body part onto the altar to burn into ash. What would it be? Her nose? A foot? Her lips?

"Okay, Daddy." The words surprising her. She wanted him to do it.

The elders had the keys to the trucks. He was going to have to walk out on foot and cross miles of desert to reach Medford.

He hugged her. "I love you, Beth. I'll come back for you. I promise."

Then he disappeared, leaving her shivering in the cold night.

The next morning, Beth awoke again to the sounds of her mother washing herself in a plastic basin.

"Where's Daddy?"

Humming to herself, Mom didn't answer.

For a moment, Beth wondered if walking with her father in the moonlight had all been a dream. His confession he'd only joined the Family so he could stay close to his daughter. His belief the Reverend was insane.

Hunger gnawed at her belly, but there'd be no breakfast

again today. She pictured Daddy returning with the police. They'd cure the Reverend of his madness and order them to stop hurting themselves. They'd feed her bacon and pancakes and ice-cold orange juice, and they'd take her back to the farm, where she'd return to Christian living close to the land and forget this ever happened.

Her choral gown lay folded on the edge of the bed.

"Mom?" No answer. "Mom, you don't have to do this."

Still no answer. She stepped out of bed and got dressed, ignoring her vestment. Mom was putting on her own, a white robe.

"You shouldn't have to hurt yourself to prove faith."

Nothing.

"Mom! Why don't you answer me?"

Her mother spread her arms and inspected herself. She flashed a brief smile. "Not everything must be spoken."

Outside, the bell rang, calling the Family to the Temple.

Beth crossed her arms. "I won't do it. I won't sing today."

Mom was already leaving.

"Mom!" Her anger melted into panic. "Please, don't."

The outside air was still chilly from the long desert night, the sunlight warm on her skin. Beth scanned the empty wastes surrounding the camp, expecting to see the flashing blue and red lights of patrol cars on the access road.

There was nothing but rocks and scrub and endless dust and the impossible stairway that snaked up the mountainside toward its bloody crown.

Where are you, Daddy?

The Family left their shacks to go to the Temple, gaunt and hungry, their cheeks sunken in their sunburned faces. They marched across crushed plastic and other garbage scattered in the dirt.

"Stop!" Beth raced to catch up to her mother. "Don't!"

Mrs. Blanchard scowled at her. "Disgraceful."

She froze, wilting under their stares. "Me?"

"She needs you now. You should be supporting her."

"If you can't," Mrs. Chapman said, "stay out of her path."

The Family had gone too far to think anything else might be true, right, or even possible. The only way to make the pain stop was to go all the way.

Even now, Beth felt pressure to go and sing her heart out while her mother mutilated her body. The Reverend said in order for her to atone, she had to bear witness, and without atonement, she'd be left behind to be destroyed in the great fire.

This was how the Family punished; they locked you out of Heaven.

Mrs. Young glared as she passed, her disfigured face making Beth shudder. David and Angela walked at her sides, holding her arms to support her. Her children didn't wear the robes today, as their parent had atoned.

"Meet us at the rock."

"What?"

Angela had appeared at her side, gripping her arm. "I said to meet us at the rock after it's over."

Beth broke down crying. "I have to take care of her."

"Get her settled, then come find us. Just an hour."

Wailing, she trailed after the Family members seeking purification, around twenty in all, dressed in their white robes. They filed inside the Temple.

Beth stayed outside, still crying. The doors thudded shut.

The singing started, muffled and discordant.

Mom needs me, she thought.

She didn't want to be cast out.

Nonetheless, Beth didn't move. She was stubborn. But

more than that, she couldn't bear to watch. She didn't think she could handle it.

Someone roared with pain inside, echoed by the Family's collective gasp and a smattering of applause.

The doors slammed open.

She flinched as Shepherd Wright staggered out, shaken and pale, cradling his left arm, which ended in a stump at the wrist, now wrapped in bloody bandages. He'd left his hand to burn on the altar. Freddie Shaw helped him stumble off in the direction of his shack as the doors swung shut again.

"Pray for him, Beth," Freddie said.

"I will."

Paralyzed, she wondered what the elder had done to deserve this. Had he been violent his whole life, or had he pushed someone important away? So far, the Temple confessions had all been summarized in a single word, one of the seven deadly sins. Only the grown-ups knew the full story from the group confessions.

Her mom knew, but for once, she wasn't telling.

Beth backed up again with a whimper. Shrieks of shock and pain emanated from the Temple, as if the building itself was screaming.

"Mom?" she whispered.

Then they stopped.

She gasped as the doors banged open again. Three men lurched into the sunlight, carrying an unconscious Mr. Preston, his pants bunched around his ankles, a bloodstain spreading around the crotch of his robe.

Beth turned away. She didn't want to see any more. She swayed on her feet as the heat and terror overwhelmed her. Exhausted, she sank to her knees.

The congregation let up a muffled cry inside the Temple.

Something big was happening. Then silence. Soon, the doors would open again, and another victim would stumble out trailing blood.

Beth hunched forward to dry heave into the dust.

The doors thundered wide. Her mother stood in the entrance, her face and the front of her robe covered in blood.

Beth gaped at her. "What did you do?"

Mom offered a weak, wincing smile that broadcast agony and relief. Blood stained her chin. Then she opened her mouth, and it poured out in a flood.

She'd cut out her tongue and fed it to the flames.

Beth screamed for her.

From Red Peak's summit came the distant echo of hammering. Today, it was an ominous sound, as if the men and women along the ridge were building coffins. Beth hurried along the rocky slope toward her friends, the only thing she still believed was real in this unending bad dream.

She found them in the shade of the petroglyphs. At the sight of her, they jumped to their feet clamoring about her mother.

"Mom's okay," Beth told them. "But I can't stay long."

Deacon hugged her. "Welcome to the club."

"Yeah." Too drained to think of anything else to say.

Aside from mealtimes, the kids rarely spent time together as they nursed their parents, who'd all made the burnt offering. Beth wondered if their true atonement wasn't bearing witness to their parents' sin but being forced to take care of them.

Angela resumed her seat on her favorite rock. "Now that Beth's here, I can tell you." She glanced at Josh next to her. "We both want to tell you."

"She's speaking for me too," Josh said. "Go ahead, Angel."

"This whole thing is wrong. You know it is. And the worst is yet to come. We should talk about getting out of here."

Beth squeezed her head in her hands. She was saying the same things as Daddy. If they were right, Mom cut out her tongue for nothing. They'd all suffered for *nothing*. Everything the Reverend said was a lie. Her entire childhood.

"We don't know it's wrong," Emily said. "God talks to the Reverend."

Angela flung a stone down the slope. "Does whatever that thing is on the mountain sound like the God we've been worshipping all these years? This Spirit?"

"Emily's right, though," David said. "How do we know?"

Beth wondered herself. God could be pretty mean in the Old Testament.

Angela narrowed her eyes at her brother. "We know because Mom cut up her face, Dave."

"Don't—"

"Because we're barely surviving on what they give us to eat. Because we have to walk two miles through hell just to get water. Because for a month and a half, everybody we know has been working themselves to death building a staircase going up a stupid mountain. Because there is *nothing here.*"

Wyatt guffawed. "It's about time somebody started talking sense."

"So my mom sacrificed her fingers for nothing," Deacon fumed. "That's what you're saying. My mom's a nutjob."

"What I'm saying," Angela grated, "is if God doesn't swoop down and take us all away, we might end up on the altar next."

"Mom wouldn't do that," David said.

"How do you know what she'd do if she thinks God told her to do it?"

"So what, then?" Deacon wondered. "We just leave? Where can we go?"

"Anywhere but here."

Beth opened her mouth to tell them Daddy had gone to Medford to get help and would be back soon, but hesitated, unable to trust her friends to keep the secret. Another betrayal.

"I don't like this either," Emily said. "But that's the whole idea, right? We're being tested. It's supposed to hurt. We're supposed to suffer with joy..." Her voice trailed off, as if even she didn't believe it anymore.

"You're just repeating what you've been told," Angela said.

Emily blanched, fighting tears. "I don't know anything else."

"I can't leave my mom," Deacon said. "I won't."

Aside from Josh and Wyatt, Angela had no takers.

"Okay," she snarled. "Then we'll climb the mountain."

Deacon and David exchanged a terrified glance.

"If God talks to us, we'll do whatever he says, no matter what it is. If he doesn't, we leave right then and there."

Nobody said anything this time. Again, she had no takers.

"Fine," Angela said. "We're going all the way. If things get really bad, I'll go to the bottom of the staircase and wait there for you for one hour. After that, I'm gone."

Josh rubbed her back. "I'll be there. I'm with you, Angel."

"I'll be there too," said Wyatt. "With bells on. I don't think it's God up on that rock. I think it's something else." He glared at them. "If any of you tell on me, I'll punch your lights out."

Emily stared at him. "The Devil?"

"Forget it."

Deacon blew out a sigh and stood. "Fine. I have to get back to Mom."

"Me too," Beth said.

The kids rose to their feet for the long walk back to the

camp. Weak with hunger, Deacon stumbled and gripped his stomach with a wince. Beth wanted to reach out and hold him. They were running out of time. Some things had to be said, now or never. Angela and Josh walked ahead of them, holding hands. Beth envied them, how they loved each other and made it look all so easy.

She said nothing. Now was the best time to tell him how she felt, but it was also the worst time to risk ruining what she had. Instead, she took his hand. Deacon started in surprise then grinned straight ahead. Energy flowed along the circuit they'd made, surging until it filled her heart and then burst into the air as something bigger than herself. It wasn't romantic, not now, but it was love.

"If things get bad, will you leave with Angela?" he asked her.

"I hope it won't come to that." She still held out hope Daddy would come back to put an end to all this, and she wouldn't have to decide.

Deacon pointed. "Somebody parked a truck outside your house."

Beth smiled. "I'll see you later, okay?"

She ran toward her cabin, the horrors of her life forgotten. Her father was back, and everything was going to be okay.

She swept aside the blanket covering the door to her home. "Daddy?"

Daddy groaned on his bed, his clothes soaked through with sweat. Her pale mother slept next to him. She'd spit out her gauze and dyed her pillow with a massive dark red bloodstain.

Beth took a step toward him and froze at the sight of his right foot, which was bare, swollen, and bloody.

Someone had driven a large black nail into his body between the shinbone and the top of his foot. The nail was still there.

18

DREAM

Dr. James Chambliss was waiting outside her building when she pulled up.

Beth leaned across to open the passenger door. "Get in."

He climbed in and shook water from his raincoat. "I don't see why this couldn't wait. It's one o'clock in the goddamn morning and raining like hell."

She'd called him on the way back from West Hollywood, still fresh from the swirling, fragmented vision she'd experienced after hearing Deacon's song and the blasting horn at its end.

Beth drove them into the underground parking garage and pulled into her stall, where she cut the engine. "I almost remembered it all on my own tonight. It's now or never."

"Repressed memories never go away," he said.

"They can be harder to retrieve, though. It's been a long time."

No hard scientific evidence even supported they existed at all. If an event overwhelmed coping mechanisms, it imprinted trauma on the brain. If the trauma was too over-whelming, the brain might blank it out, though it was still there somewhere. That was the theory.

Freud was never proven wrong about dissociative amnesia, but he was never definitively proven right either.

"Only for you," he growled.

"Because you love me."

He turned to scrutinize her through his round spectacles. "Because I've treated war refugees, and I've never found a patient as interesting as you."

Beth very much doubted that. "What makes *me* so interesting?"

"Do you realize what you've got locked in your head somewhere?"

"A knot that can unravel my life," she answered, remembering his catchphrase from his lectures back at Pomona.

"No." He smiled. "The answer to the Medford Mystery."

She shook her head as she got out of the car. So that explained his continued persistence over the years in trying to convince her to resume treatment. Why he'd dutifully shown up at her doorstep drenched at one o'clock in the morning at her request. He didn't care about her. He'd never gotten over his fascination with the Family of the Living Spirit. Dr. James Chambliss wanted to be the man who cracked the bizarre mystery.

And in so doing, gain fame and professional standing.

Book deal, talk shows, cable news consulting gigs, the works.

Beth had always regarded his interest in her as touching but mildly alarming in its intensity. She was relieved to understand it at last, even if the explanation was a bit disappointing.

In the end, it didn't matter. He could have his talk shows.

They rode her elevator up to her floor and entered her condo, where he shucked his dripping trench coat to reveal a professorial cardigan sweater buttoned over a pajama shirt. He seemed to take mental notes, scrutinizing her pristine home. Then he focused on the mess she'd made at the coffee table.

"Interesting," he said.

"I'll clean it up." Beth hurried to the kitchen for more paper towels. She couldn't stand the sight of it.

"Don't bother on my account. I don't have all night."

"Then you can help. I won't be able to relax with it there."

Together, they swept the popcorn back in its bowl. This done, she considered soaking the red wine stains on the white area rug with club soda, but found them too unsettling. James moved the coffee table so Beth could roll up the carpet, then made himself comfortable on the couch.

"You know," he said as she disappeared back into the kitchen. "Recalling repressed memories may benefit your mental state, but it may not completely heal you. You'll need cognitive therapy so you can handle your triggers."

Beth poured two glasses of wine and brought them into the living room. "I've already done a lot of work in that direction."

James accepted his and set it untasted on the coffee table. "Beth, I tell you this as a friend and colleague. Everything is a trigger for you. Anything you can't control. Unpredictability is like a burning match for your kindling. Like that party at the conference. It forces you to live in a box."

She sat on the couch next to him and sipped her Cabernet. "I thought you only wanted to solve the mystery and find out where the bodies are buried."

"The primary purpose here is treatment." She'd offended him.

"What if nothing is there? They killed themselves, and that's it?"

"Then we still learned something."

Beth stared at him. "You won't try to *plant* anything."

He sighed. "If you didn't trust me, you wouldn't have asked me to help you."

"Fair enough."

With Deacon out of the picture, she wasn't sure she'd ever make it back to Red Peak in the flesh. This might be her last chance. She gulped her wine and set it down.

"Okay. Let's do it."

"We're in a dim room—"

"No pocket watch this time?"

James sighed. "You're still impossible, you know that?"

She settled into the couch, suppressing a shiver. "I know."

"We're in a dim room that is safe, warm, relaxing."

The room bled away as he droned on until only James remained, and then he too disintegrated to become words floating in the air.

"It's the summer of 2005, and you're fourteen years old."

The bell called the faithful to the evening meal. Beth told her parents she would bring food back for them, but Mom pushed herself upright.

"You need to rest," Beth said.

Her mother answered with a wag of her head that triggered a feverish wince.

Mom had once filled the house with her talking. Beth often prayed she'd shut up for once. For just one night, she'd hoped, she wouldn't have to hear everyone's personal business and her mom's authoritative opinion about it.

This silence was far worse.

At twilight, the Family had shambled down the stairway, exhausted and starving but jubilant. The stairway was complete. They'd finished the test the Spirit had given them just as they'd passed the test of the purifications. Still God's chosen, earning their way.

Only one test remained. Tonight, the Reverend promised, he'd reveal it.

"*I'll bring you supper, Daddy.*"

"*No,*" *he said.* "*Not tonight. I'd better go too.*"

Whoever had hurt him weeks earlier had left crutches propped against the wall. Beth helped him sit up and positioned the crutches in front of him so he could grab hold.

The nail was still there.

She'd offered to pull it out, but her father had told her they'd promised to put it right back. Because they loved him, he'd said. They wanted him to be saved.

He gained his feet with the heartbreaking wail of a dying animal.

Mom edged toward the door with a determined smile, tottering from starvation. She'd put on her white robe again, its front still mottled by bloodstains.

"*Let me help you,*" *Beth said in a firm voice.*

She nestled against her mother, who placed her hand on her daughter's shoulder for support.

Thank you, *she imagined Mom saying.* You're a good Christian girl, Beth, even if you do always keep one little part of you for yourself and away from the Lord.

Yep, that was Mom, all right.

The sun bled into Red Peak's crown. The final test awaited. Angela had told her to be ready to run. Beth shivered. She didn't want a nail in her foot. Her parents were suffering, and she hated the idea of leaving them uncared for, even a single night. She still wasn't even sure Daddy and Angela were right.

Mom shuffled across the ground in silent determination. Beth guessed the only thing keeping her on her feet was her faith.

In the mess hall, the congregation sat in an exhausted silence at their tables. Almost all missed parts of themselves. A hand, a foot, an eye. Faces pale or feverish. The wounds wept and emitted a sour, rotten stench.

Beth helped her parents sit with David's family. Angela caught her eye and nodded. David stared at his lap and breathed in shallow gasps, ready to bolt at the slightest provocation. Beth glanced at what was left of their mother's face and turned away in horror.

Flanked by the elders, Jeremiah Peale rose from his seat. His trademark grin had departed long ago, his hair a tangled mess on his forehead. "Brothers and sisters, friends of the Spirit, I welcome you to our last supper."

The Family stirred at these words. Beth and Angela exchanged a wide-eyed glance. The elders stood to serve the day's meal.

"We have taken a long, hard journey together," he boomed. "I look around this room, I see so many good people, so much sacrifice and strength. Your faith fills me with awe. I have spoken to the Spirit, and it is pleased. The time has come for you to claim your heavenly prize. You did it. I love you all so much."

The congregation broke into smiles. Many wept.

"All along, we weren't waiting for God," he went on. "He was waiting for us. After supper, you will go to the Temple, shed your mortal coil, and ascend."

"It's happening," Daddy murmured. "They're going to kill us."

"You have purified yourselves for the ascension. All except me. You may have wondered how I would repent for my great sin. You may have wondered what I would sacrifice. You may have wondered if I was shirking my duty. There is no need to wonder any longer. The Spirit told me how I am to atone for my sin."

Tears streamed down the man's broad face.

Even from where she sat, Beth could see the man shaking.

"I'm not coming with you," he said. "Like Moses, who led the chosen people to the Promised Land, only to be denied himself. This is to be my punishment for my lack of faith. Tonight, I will enter the black sea, but I will not reach the other side."

Wails filled the room.

"Do not cry for me! I will obey the Spirit now as I did then. When we suffer, we do it with joy. We obey. After supper, I will make the last climb up the holy mountain. I need three strong men to help me. Who will help their pastor?"

Nobody answered.

Everyone wanted to help, but they knew what he was asking.

"Please," he said.

He needed three men to help him die.

At last, Mr. Sumner stood. "I'll go with you, Reverend."

Jeremiah offered a weak smile. "Thank you, Phil. And bless you."

A plate clattered in front of Beth. A handful of cold ravioli. She swept her fork from the table and wolfed it down, finishing by licking the plate clean.

Her mother pushed her own meal toward Beth, who didn't want to take it but did. She devoured that meager portion too, unable to control herself. Then her father's, while Daddy rubbed her back and watched her eat with a pained smile.

"You'll need your strength," he murmured in her ear. "You'll know what to do. When you get the chance to go, you take it. You run and don't stop running."

Beth nodded, but he was wrong. She wasn't at all sure what she would do.

Jeremiah's voice cracked with emotion as he thanked his last volunteer. "I love you all. Because of you, I will enter paradise in your hearts. Pray for me then as you do now. I have two more tasks, and then my ministry is complete."

He hauled a bucket in front of the nearest table and bent down. Soaking a sponge, he began to wash his weeping congregants' feet.

This was his goodbye.

Beth cried and couldn't stop, even when it was her turn, as he gently washed her feet for her last walk to the Temple.

She put her hands on his head. "I love you, Reverend."

Insane or not, she did.

He smiled and moved on to Deacon, who lunged at him for a hug.

The rest played out like a familiar dream. The Reverend left with three strong men to make his final climb up the finished stairs. Hammering rang through the night, followed by a distant scream carried on the wind. A crimson glow appeared like a signal along Red Peak's summit. Shepherd Wright led the congregation to the Temple, where they accepted the blood of Christ.

Then almost everyone she knew died.

The Family of the Living Spirit fell where they stood, thudding to the floor to convulse in agony as the cyanide crushed their organs. The air filled with choking, breathless gasps. Mr. Preston exploded with vomit and pitched forward. Mrs. Chapman lay in the aisle, mouth foaming, slapping and kicking at the floor as the poison squeezed her life from her. Mrs. Blanchard bolted to slam her face into a wall.

"Now," her father said. "Run as fast as you can."

His last words.

Mom put her arm around Beth's shoulders and hugged her as Daddy fell, thrashing and keening through clenched teeth. Her hand settled on the back of Beth's neck. Her grip tightened.

Beth gasped. "I love you Mom please don't I'll be good I promise I'll be good I don't want to die—"

Mom raised the knife to deliver her to Heaven.

"Don't." Beth struggled, but Mom but wouldn't let go of the tight hold she had on her neck. "Please, don't."

Mom didn't answer. Couldn't answer.

Gunshots roared outside.

"I'm begging you, Mom. Please stop. Please. I don't want this."

The blaze in her mother's eyes clouded, turned to love and something else, disappointment. Hand trembling, she lowered the knife.

Then swept it across her own throat.

Hot blood sprayed across Beth's face, and she lunged forward to hug her mother, screaming for help.

Beth collapsed with her to the floor, Mom's body like a blanket. Blood seeped into Beth's ears, muting the final agonizing, strangled cries of the Family of the Living Spirit.

She blanked out.

She had no idea how long she lay there. Covered by her mother, there was no need to ever move again.

After a while, a pair of boots thudded on the floorboards. A gun banged, impossibly loud. Then more steps, followed by another shot.

At last, the gun banged a final time, and a body toppled to the floor.

Silence returned, deafening from the ring in her ears.

More time passed, but Beth didn't sleep nor was she fully awake, instead caught suspended in time, unable to face the past or the future. Frozen like the dead around her.

Her mother stirred.

Mom?

The body trembled until it was shaking, as if seized by the Spirit one last time.

Mom was alive.

The weight lifted from Beth as the body began to rise. She gaped in terror and awe as her mother hovered above her, long hair streaming down, eyes closed in beatific sleep, the deep slash along her throat winking and dripping.

Beth rose to her knees and wiped blood from her eyes. All around her, the bodies of the Family ascended in a blinding red light throbbing through the windows.

Slowly, she reached for her mother. "Mom?"

The Temple shook as the horn blasted the Judgment.

Beth cried out, her voice lost in the roar.

The end of the world.

Eyes fixed in sightless stares or closed as if in sleep, hands splayed or waving, bodies arched or curled or floating face down, the Family of the Living Spirit bobbed in the air for one final moment.

Then they hurtled crashing through pews and spinning through space to burst through the window and disappear in the night.

Beth emerged from her trance shaking. "Oh, God. Oh my God."

James handed her his wineglass. "Drink some of this."

She was in Santa Barbara. This was her condo. She was nearly thirty years old, a clinical psychologist with a budding, successful practice. For fifteen years, she'd repressed what had happened at the Temple and with meticulous care built a life on top of it, one in which she had control and rarely looked back at her beginning.

It was all a lie.

She gulped the wine and came up for air with a gasp. "Do you know?"

"You talked the entire time," James said. "The mystery does not want to come out. You substituted a very real ascension for what happened. An incredibly vivid hallucination. Fascinating."

"Fascinating," she muttered, a dull echo.

"Your mother took her own life instead of yours. In the end, she just couldn't do it. Her faith so strong she finished the job on herself, her maternal instinct so strong she couldn't hurt you. That had an incredible impact on you."

"Impact." She chewed on the word and tasted ash.

He jumped to his feet, pacing. "We have two choices, Beth. We can keep digging until the truth breaks through the fantasy, or we can grind down the fantasy at the edges by trying to interpret it. What do you think?"

"What do *I* think?"

James stopped and peered at her through his glasses. "I need to hear from you how you'd like to proceed. Personally, I recommend another dig."

She stared at him. "You want me to proceed."

"Yes." Studying her blank expression, he seemed less certain now. "I assume you're still committed to your treatment?"

Beth wagged her head as she stood and looked around again at her condo. Clean and antiseptic. Calming art on the walls, the furniture arranged for feng shui. Everything in its proper place.

"Hey, talk to me. Are you okay?"

The wineglass snapped in her grip. The bulb and stem shattered on the floor. She gazed in fascination as wine and blood mixed together in her palm.

"I'll get you..." He took a step toward the kitchen but stopped. "Beth, I need to know if you're all right."

Outside, the lights of Santa Barbara glittered in front of a horizon black with dark mountains. She caught her reflection in the glass, ethereal as a ghost, as she crossed to her bookshelves. Wine and blood dripped from her fist.

The blood of Christ. The Reverend's voice now. *Shed for you.*

Books crammed the shelves, venerable tomes that together provided an evolving instruction manual for the mechanics and malfunctions of the human mind. A defective mind that created the universe by perceiving it.

Beth gripped a handful of this knowledge and flung it to the floor.

"Liars," she said.

"What?"

Reaching behind the row of books, she swept it all in a crash of paper. "Lies. All of it. Bullshit and lies."

He raised his hands in a defensive posture. "You're scaring me, Beth."

She straightened her back. "James. James? Listen to me."

"Okay. I'm listening."

"I am upset by what I saw, and I need to act out."

"Yes, but we should—"

"No," she said. "We shouldn't. I need to be alone so I can come to terms with what I experienced. Then I will phone you next week to discuss treatment options."

James eyed her warily. "That sounds reasonable."

"Because it is. Now please leave so I can process my feelings in a safe environment."

"You'll call me next week?"

"Absolutely. This was a breakthrough. I'll consider the options you outlined."

"Okay." He pulled on his coat and hesitated. "Your hand..."

"I'll be fine, James. Good night. Thank you for everything."

He nodded. "Good night."

The door closed.

With calm, methodical precision, Beth walked along her bookshelves and toppled the rest of the false prophets to the floor.

She'd never call James again. She had no further use for

him. The man had achieved a solution to the mystery only to ignore it staring him right in the face, because it didn't fit his reality.

She'd ignore it no longer. The Reverend had been right all along. The Family had ascended, just as they'd planned. Their faith had taken them all to paradise.

She had to go back to Red Peak, and do it now. Nothing else mattered in this illusion she'd constructed. For fifteen years, the truth had tried to chew its way out of her. On the holy mountain, she'd discover it once and for all.

Beth hadn't survived the Family of the Living Spirit's final night.

She might have been left behind.

19

ATONE

Cradling a Nerf football, David walked along the sidewalk with his kids skipping behind him. They needed a little exercise away from their screens. He needed to avoid Claire and the conversation she wanted to have with him.

The sun beat down on Fresno, its heat rippling over the street. Birds and insects hummed in trees and flower beds. Water sprinklers shimmied on lawns dotted with palm trees. Otherwise, the neighborhood was quiet, this being a weekday. He hated being away from his children, but one of the good things about his and Claire's jobs was when they weren't traveling, they were home.

As August wore on, the kids had started to go feral after weeks of summer camps and trips to the water park and neighborhood pool, the result of too much of a good thing. They were ready to go back to school and its structured routines. Now they bickered over nothing as usual, simply for the fun of it even though it would likely end in tears. He hoped they'd be better friends later in life, and not end tense phone calls with, *You're all I have left.*

As their voices escalated to draw him into their fight, he said, "You know, it doesn't get any better than this."

"It'd be way better if Dexter would shut up," Alyssa muttered.

"Or if you weren't so stupid," her brother shot back.

"I'm serious," David said. "It's a beautiful day, and we have nothing to do except have some fun. When you're my age, you'll remember every bad thing that ever happened to you. Try to remember today."

"If it's so good, why do you look so sad?" Alyssa asked him.

"Because the good doesn't always last." When he was her age, he'd watched trains disappear into the tunnel at the Tehachapi Loop. "That's why you should enjoy it."

"I have a great life, Daddy," Dexter said.

Alyssa guffawed. "It'd be perfect—"

The boy shot into the park, yelling, "I'm open!"

The park was actually the fenced grounds of a school, which offered its broad lawn and playground to the public. A few small children played on the jungle gyms and swings. David waited for the right moment and then fired the Nerf across the lawn. The football arced into the sun before bouncing off the boy's face. Arms flailing, Dexter went down in a comical tumble.

After glancing over his son to make sure he was all right, David chuckled. "Catch with your hands next time, Dex."

Laughing, the kid hurled the ball, which landed near David's feet. He scooped it up, enjoying himself already. Nothing like some honest exercise to flush the noise out of his head, and he had plenty of noise to clear. The imminent anniversary of the Medford Mystery seemed to loom over him. Then there was Claire's anger, and his guilt at shutting down when she'd confronted him about the documentary producer's claim he'd been a member of the Family.

She was mad enough to give him the silent treatment ever

since he'd left the hotel. So mad that he'd begun to worry if she'd had enough. When he'd married her, he'd thought that since all his faults were in the open, there wouldn't be any buyer's remorse. After all, they'd met in the confessional of group therapy. She'd already known the product was a little broken when she bought it.

He'd been wrong. Marrying someone from his group also meant she was able to describe his faults with laser precision, such as his tendency to avoid stillness and get overwhelmed, which triggered her own resume of wounds, notably her fear of abandonment. He and Claire were experts at criticizing each other and terrible at speaking up for what they wanted.

For years, he'd kept his past and present separate, but that wall was now crumbling. His family had always been a sanctuary from the world. It was the one thing he couldn't run from.

His son raced across his line of sight. "Hey, Daddy! I'm open!"

David turned to Alyssa and motioned for her to run. "Go long, lady."

"Can I play on the swings?"

He threw the ball again to Dexter, who caught and spiked it with a whoop. "Of course you can."

His son threw it back, and they passed it back and forth until he noticed Alyssa was sitting motionless on one of the swings, her back to him.

"I'll be right back, Dex."

David jogged over to his daughter, who was texting on her phone, as he'd thought. "Hey. Come and join us."

"I don't feel like it."

He crouched in front of her. "What's wrong?"

She cast a glum look around the playground. "Everybody here is little. None of my friends are here."

"When you're my age, you won't remember a single minute of your life spent staring at a screen." He'd gotten her the phone for safety, but her tendency to use it to shut down alarmed him, even more so because he recognized it in himself. "Come on. Give me five minutes."

David enticed her out onto the lawn and lobbed her the ball to get her engaged.

"Aww," she said. "Look. We need a new ball."

Alyssa showed him the canine teeth marks that had scored little chunks out of the soft material. Gunner used to snatch the football up and run off with it.

"That's why we still have it," David said. "It reminds us of him. When we play with it, we can think of all the fun we had together."

Not what they'd lost, but what they'd gained.

He was self-aware enough to realize this was more *do as I say, not as I do* parenting, but he wanted Alyssa and Dexter to avoid his mistakes, not repeat them. He wanted them to be better than him, not become him.

His daughter smiled. "I'm going to keep this ball forever then."

A car honked on the street next to the park. David looked over and recognized Claire's Toyota. "There's Mommy. Let's go see what she wants."

The kids ran ahead, David lagging behind. By the time he got there, they were already climbing into the backseat.

"I'm taking the kids to my mother's," Claire said from behind the wheel. She wore sunglasses that hid her eyes and made him anxious.

On the phone with her at the hotel, he'd told her the documentary producer was lying. He had nothing to do with the Family of the Living Spirit.

I'm done trying, she'd said and hung up.

"For a visit?" David licked dry lips. "See you around dinnertime, then?"

She turned and shifted the car into drive. "Yes."

"Bye, Daddy!" Dexter yelled as the Toyota sped off.

He waved them out of sight. The car's growl faded into birdsong. He suddenly felt small and alone and resentful. He wanted to blame Claire for not leaving his past alone, but in the end, he couldn't. She couldn't be blamed for being upset he'd kept an incredible secret during their entire marriage, even if it was for everyone's good. He felt sorry for her. He'd been losing his connection to her for years, but the idea he might lose her nearly immobilized him with despair. At the same time, he wanted to *do* something. Something that would fix this.

Inspired by a brainstorm, he decided he'd finally get to the yard work and lose himself in the labor. When Claire returned, she'd find everything perfect and be reminded that he was a provider who would go on providing. She'd understand that his past wasn't the man he was today, and therefore didn't matter.

For an hour, he paced his lawn with his reel mower, grooming the grass to just the right length. This done, he got down on his knees to weed the flower beds in front of the porch. Sweat soaked his T-shirt, not the sour flop sweat of anxiety but the clean, honest sweat of hard work. Once done with the beds, he intended to expand his garden in the backyard by planting herbs in wood boxes.

Kneeling in the mulch pulling weeds, he heard a car humming down the street. His kids were back, which brought a smile to his face.

He raised his head to squint at sunlight glaring along a dusty windshield. Not his wife's car, but another parking in front of his house. His smile turned to surprise as the door opened.

Angela stepped out and slammed the door. As usual, she wore a simple black T-shirt and jeans, no makeup, her wavy hair tied in a sloppy ponytail, her face and toned arms tanned by the Nevada sun.

David rose to his feet. "Hey. What are you doing here?"

She stopped in the middle of his manicured lawn and scowled at him. "You fucked things up real good, little brother."

His sister marched past him and sat on one of the reading chairs on the porch. He was curious what she wanted, but a ritual had to be completed first.

He went into the house, pulled bottles of cold beer from the refrigerator, and returned to hand one over.

"You drove all this way just to tell me that? Tell me something I don't know."

"We need to talk."

He sat on the other chair and popped the cap. "Okay, what did I do?"

She said, "They're all dead."

His stomach lurched. "What do you mean? *Who* is dead?"

"The group you talked to. The Restoration."

"Oh. Jesus." It lurched again. "How do you know?"

"I keep tabs on the mountain. The sheriff called me."

"So stupid," he raged. "I tried to talk them out of it. They wouldn't listen."

"You should have called me."

"They were role-playing, but crazy enough to take it very seriously. I didn't want you mixed up in it." He grimaced. "Are they going to want me to go out there and make a statement? Help them identify the remains or anything?"

Angela barked out something approximating a laugh.

"There are no remains," she said.

She shared the story from the police report. The Restoration had rumbled into Medford in a happy caravan, stopping for snacks and to top their gas tanks. They'd disappeared into the Inyo Mountains, searching for their mystery.

The sheriff's department had missed their arrival. Tourists and other travelers passed through Medford all the time, but because of David's warning, a deputy drove out every few days to check on the site, but not that day, nor the next.

That night, the sky glowed over the mountain, a sliver of crimson visible for miles. The fire department rushed to Red Peak to investigate what they believed was another wildfire that might spread and devastate the area.

The firefighters found cars and minivans at the base. The stairs leading to the top, sections of it in disrepair. On the summit, dawn revealed blood splatter everywhere, but no bodies.

Kyle had gotten his wish. He'd solved the Medford Mystery by becoming part of it.

"Somebody in that town is screwing with us," David said.

Angela took a long pull on her bottle. "How do you figure?"

He shared his theory about the Wardites and Beth's diagnosis of narcissism and split personality disorder. Knowing the Wardites' story, Jeremiah Peale had heard a voice in the wilderness because he'd wanted to hear it. That voice became a second personality he'd projected as God, and then—

"Bullshit." His sister barked another harsh laugh.

"I know, I know. The bodies. Peale was obviously working with somebody in Medford, who disposed of them. That's where you come in. You can—"

"No, David. Whatever you're about to propose, I'm not doing that."

He couldn't believe what he was hearing. "Don't you want to...?"

"I already know what happened to the bodies. I've known all along."

His bottle thudded against the porch to spin foaming across the floor. He snatched it up and poured the rest onto the flowers.

"What..." He struggled for words.

Claire pulled into the driveway with the kids. Alyssa and Dexter flew out of the car clamoring to see their aunt.

Whatever Angela had to tell him, it would have to wait.

Claire had brought pizzas home for dinner, which the family shared around the dining table. Alyssa and Dexter hadn't seen their aunt since Christmas and bombed her with questions about the police and life in Las Vegas, which she answered with tall tales. David gazed at them all with an indulgent smile, though he wasn't listening.

The kids adored Angela, who was beautiful like their grandmother had been. On the rare occasion David saw his sister, he tried to recall what Mom looked like before she'd cut herself with a knife. All he could ever remember now was her disfigurement. For weeks, he'd had to look at that scarred mask and pretend it wasn't hideous and terrifying until one day, it became normal.

"Do you want to watch a movie with us after dinner?" Dexter asked.

"Not tonight," Angela told him. "I have to get back on the road."

"Aww."

"Sorry, Dex. I hope we can do it next time."

"It's okay."

At the end of the meal, the kids ran off to watch their movie.

Claire turned to Angela and said, "So what brings you all the way to Fresno?"

"I had to see my little brother about something."

"It must be a painful time for you."

"Why do you say that?"

"The fifteenth anniversary is Friday, isn't it?"

David flinched but knew Angela would cover for him.

"That's right," his sister said. "I'd like to go to Medford and drive out to the site to visit Mom. I'm hoping David will come with me."

He stiffened, ready to jump to his feet and walk out, but Claire beat him to it.

After she'd gone, he wheeled on his sister. "Why did you do that?"

This was his *home* she was messing with. His *family*. His castle and sanctuary. He was dug in here.

"I'm done lying to protect you," Angela said.

"You're screwing with my life," he fumed.

The Family, Red Peak, the Medford Mystery, it was all a bad dream nobody would ever let him forget.

He was sick of ghosts.

Angela stared at the pizza crusts on her plate. "On the last night, I knew what was going to happen. I told Mom I didn't want to die. We argued until she was literally dragging me toward the Temple, with me fighting her every step of the way. I told her she was murdering her own child. In the end, she just broke down. She told me she'd let me go. She'd even help me leave."

"It's in the past." He crossed his arms. "I don't want to hear it."

She stared past his shoulder into the nightmare of memory. "Josh was with us. We found Anna Tibbs, who also wanted to escape. She'd gotten the key to one of the trucks from her father. Mom was pushing me into the truck, but I wanted to find you and get you out too. I had to find you and then convince Mom to come with us. Josh was yelling at me to hurry. Freddie Shaw came over and asked what we were doing." She clasped her hands over her chest. "He shot Mom right here."

"*What?* You told me Mom drank the poison along with everybody else."

"I told you," she said. "I'm done lying."

"Freddie killed her?" David bowed his head, fighting tears, struggling to process this sweeping revision of his past.

"Josh had the truck running. He yelled again, but I didn't hear it, I was screaming. He was trying to distract Freddie from shooting me. Freddie fired every bullet he had left in his gun at him and Anna. Josh's head just flew apart." Angela splayed her hands and grimaced with an insane giggle. "I can still see it. It's still happening. Every day, he dies again. His head explodes onto the windshield. If I hadn't argued with Mom, he would have survived. But I wouldn't leave without you. And you hid in the one place I couldn't look."

"I was scared," he said. "I was *twelve*."

"I ran. I thought maybe you'd followed the plan and were waiting for me at the bottom of the stairs." She glared at him. "You weren't there. Nobody was."

David was sobbing. "I'm sorry! I didn't know—"

"It was too late to go for help. I thought everybody was dead. So I went up. I climbed the mountain. I went all the way to the top."

"I didn't know." He needed her to understand.

"It was horrible." Angela's face had gone blank again. "They'd crucified the Reverend and lit him on fire, and he was somehow still burning. The men who'd nailed him up there had drunk cyanide and died around a big stone cut in the shape of an altar. That's when it happened." Her eyes blazed at him. "I was going to tell you what happened to the bodies. I saw it with my own eyes. Are you ready for the truth?"

He buried his face in his hands. He didn't want to hear it, not really.

Then he nodded. The mystery. He had to know. It was the key to everything.

"The stone burst into fire. The fire reached up and up and up into the sky. I knew right then I was seeing the thing that talked to the Reverend."

David jerked his head to look at her through a blur of tears. She'd gone back to staring over his shoulder, her face transfixed by her private horror.

"I stood there, mesmerized," she whispered. "The most beautiful light. The shooting had stopped, and it was so quiet. Then that fucking horn ripped straight through me and pushed me right off my feet. I had no control of my body. I pissed myself. I thought I was dying. After it quit, the bodies of the three men who'd crucified the Reverend rose in the air. Their arms and legs and heads wagging around. Like some invisible force hauled them up by their belts."

"Emily and Deacon saw something similar," he said. "It was some kind of mass hallucination—"

"I got back on my feet and thought about grabbing them and pulling them back. I thought if I did that, I could save them." She cackled without mirth. "I wasn't thinking straight. It didn't matter. I couldn't move. I was too petrified.

Then a hand brushed my hair. I jumped away as Mrs. Kowalski floated past. Behind her, all the bodies rose out of the dark and into the light. I saw Deacon's mom, then Mrs. Chapman and Shepherd Wright, then Beth's mom and dad, and Mom and Anna and Josh. They were dead, David, but they *flew*. They whirled and tumbled through the air around the fire, always up and up, like moths around a flame. That's when the Reverend broke free of the cross and shot up after them."

David shook his head. "See? That's not right. It proves it was all a hallucination. Peale said the Spirit told him he wasn't allowed to ascend."

"Another fucking test," she said. "Whatever that thing was, and I doubt it was really God, it had mercy on the Reverend. It wanted him too."

If his sister was right, the mystery wasn't a mystery at all. The answer had been staring him in the face all these years, if only he'd accepted the impossible.

He heard sobbing behind him and turned to see Claire standing in the hallway. Angela had told her story to her as much as David, and in so doing, David's story as well.

"Claire!" His chair crashed to the floor as he jumped to his feet.

His wife was gone.

He glared helplessly at his sister. "Get out."

"David," she said. "Listen to me."

"Just get out of here. Get out! *GET OUT!*"

"Tonight, I'm going to Bakersfield. I'll wait for you until Friday. Beth is meeting me, and she's working on getting Deacon to go. We're all going to Red Peak. I'm going to visit Mom. I'll climb the mountain again. And I'll find the thing that did this to her and Josh and finish it."

"Count me out. You need help. Nothing is out there except bad memories."

"It's there. We're still the Family of the Living Spirit, and we made a deal. It's waiting for us, and it wants us all there together."

"Even if that's true, why do what it wants? What good would that do?"

"Because I want it to suffer the way it made *us* suffer," Angela said. "Whether it's God, Satan, or something else, I don't really give a shit. If there's a way to kill it, I'll find it."

David found Claire dressed in workout attire, sitting in front of her vanity in their bedroom. He thrust his hands in his pockets, unsure what to say to her.

"Are you going out to the gym tonight?"

"Yes."

"I'm sorry you heard all that."

Her vacant eyes settled on his reflection. "She doesn't seem to be well."

David wasn't so sure this was true. In fact, he had a sneaking suspicion Angela might be the only sane one among the survivors.

"I can tell you that if it wasn't for her, I wouldn't be here right now."

"How so?"

If Claire knew about the last night, she might as well know all of it. He wanted to keep her talking, afraid of what would happen if she stopped. "Angela warned us. She wanted to save us. She always protected me. If she hadn't planted the idea that what the Family was doing was wrong, I would have drunk cyanide with the rest of them. I was just a kid. I didn't know any better."

"How could she have seen what she thinks she saw?"

"I don't know. A false memory, maybe."

"The other things she said, though. That part was true, wasn't it?"

David sighed. "I wasn't with her, but yes, it was like that."

"Josh was her boyfriend?"

"He was."

Claire wiped away another tear. "I'm so sorry. Why did you keep it a secret all these years? Why did you shut me out?"

"I don't know." He sat on the edge of their bed, twisting his wedding ring. "You had a hard life, and I didn't want you to ever worry about me. I thought I was protecting you."

Liar, he thought. *You know exactly who you were protecting all these years.*

Her eyes probed his. "Will you tell me what happened now? Everything, from the beginning?"

He turned away. "Wasn't that enough?"

"David, you need help. I want to help you."

Heat filled his chest. "I'm fine. I'm not broken. Whatever happened, it made me, and I made it work for me."

"Oh, David. It's not working. Not anymore. Don't you see that?"

"It helped make this life for us. A *good* life."

"And ever since we got it, you started shutting me out."

"That's not fair. You escape plenty." Over the years, she'd channeled her own angst into obsessive exercise and chasing spiritual and self-help fads that sometimes alarmed him because he knew a charlatan when he saw one.

"When I'm with you, though, I'm *present*. I'm not scared of my own life." Claire turned on the bench to finally speak for what she wanted. "The kids have a father, but I need my husband. I *need* you. Something needs to change, David, before you start shutting out the kids too."

"I can..." He shivered as an overwhelming helpless exhaustion overtook him, leaving him barely able to keep his eyes open. "I don't know what you want."

You're doing it right now, he told himself. *You're shutting down. You're going to blow up everything that's important to you.*

"I want you to do something about it," she said. "I want to be in your life."

"I love you." He did, desperately, even if it was sometimes too heavy for him to carry day after day. In the end, perhaps his son was right that love was something you had to believe in, a constant act of faith. "I love our kids. Okay?"

"David..."

"You're my wife. I don't want anybody else except you. That has to count for something. That has to be enough."

She was right to be irritated. He just didn't know how to change. More than that, he didn't *want* to change. What Claire had begun to see as stifling and empty, David found comforting and safe.

She stared at him a moment longer before giving up and turning back to the mirror. "Are you going to go to Red Peak with Angela?"

"I don't know about that either. No, I don't think so."

"You owe her your life. You said so yourself."

David's body broke out in a sweat. "Yes."

"She always protected you. Maybe she needs you to protect her now."

He cried, unable to control it. "I'm scared." He was twenty-seven years old, talking to his wife in a house they owned in a nice neighborhood, yet he felt twelve again, helpless and terrified. "I'm really scared."

Of Red Peak, the past. Of opening up to Claire. Of everything.

She stood and sat on the bed next to him. "Come here."

David melted into her hug, still sobbing for everything he'd lost. "It just grinds me down. Every minute, every day. It never stops."

"Go find your sister. Try to make peace with what happened to you out there. Then come back to me. I still love you. We need you whole."

"I don't think I'm strong enough."

"You are," she murmured.

"Maybe I'm not." He pictured Emily in her casket. She'd written, *I couldn't fight it anymore.* He wondered if the same fate awaited him.

"You are." Claire wiped the tears from his cheeks and offered him an encouraging smile. "Remember what they told us in group therapy?"

He shook his head.

She said, "If you can't outrun the past, turn around and kick its ass."

Claire's strength poured into him. Yes, love was something that required constant faith. But it was also a higher power that made change possible.

If you can't outrun the past, turn around and kick its ass.

Holding on to her, David felt himself drawn toward it, one way or the other.

For months, he'd dreamed of leaving the mental hospital. No more therapists, social workers, police. No drugs that gave him headaches and stern orderlies barking orders and angry glares from Angela that made him hate himself.

Then Dr. Klein told him a foster family would soon take him home.

"Careful what you wish for, I guess," he told Emily.

"It doesn't matter," she said. "We'll always be together."

They paced the courtyard, awash in sunshine but surrounded by walls. After living close to the land for years, he'd found the institution stifling, but now that he was leaving, its confinement proved comforting.

For the first time, Emily offered no comfort herself. He wanted his mom to come hug him and tell him it was okay. He wanted his sister to stop glaring at him as if this was all his fault. He wanted to set out to find the Family.

"I don't need a new family," he said. "I already have a mom."

"I know."

"*Alive.* She's alive out there, somewhere."

Emily touched his back. "I know she is. But you're lucky. I can't wait to get out of here."

"Don't you miss your mom and dad?"

"They're in a better place."

They completed their circuit of the courtyard with its picnic benches and flowers and a few trees offering shade. He didn't want to hear it. He was in a safe place, and all he had to do was wait, and his mom would come for him.

Even as he thought it, he knew it wasn't true. He didn't know where to hide, didn't even know anymore what he should be running from.

David wrung his hands. "What are we gonna do, Em?"

"We'll go back," she said.

"Go back?" He thought about the farm.

"We'll go back to Red Peak. We'll start again. We'll finish it."

"Yeah." Maybe she was right; he didn't know anything else.

"But only if you come too. We'll go to Heaven together."

"Yes," he said, but he was lying.

He wasn't going back. No way would he ever return to Red Peak. The place was evil. Just thinking about it overrode the drugs and made him shake. A plan was already starting to take shape in his mind.

He'd put it all behind him.

Jeremiah Peale, the farm, Red Peak, the last night. He'd simply forget it ever happened.

David had the rest of his life to hide in.

He made sure Dexter changed into his pajamas and brushed his teeth and flushed the toilet. The boy crawled into bed, and David lay next to him to read him his favorite story before kissing his forehead.

"Good night, Dex. Time for sleep."

"I liked seeing Aunt Angela again, Daddy."

"Me too."

"I wish she could have played with us."

"Next time," said David. "We'll all play together."

"Daddy?"

"Yeah?"

"What was Grandma and Grandpa like? Your mommy and daddy?"

David once dreaded questions from his kids about their grandparents as much as he did about God. His dad, who walked out on his family and lived far away with a new family. His mom, with her intense yearning for a spiritual life that led her children into the depths of horror. He found it easier to answer now.

"I don't really remember much about Grandpa. Your grandma was beautiful, like your aunt, and just as stubborn. And even tougher, if you can imagine that."

As a kid, he'd been a little jealous of God. After Dad left, Mom was always putting God above everything, even her kids. Because God made Mom happy, this was the same as prioritizing her own happiness over her children's. He'd always pictured her dying in the Temple, wondering where her children had gone but pouring the cyanide down her throat anyway, because God told her to do it.

Angela had revealed a different story.

In the end, Mom had chosen her kids over Heaven.

He said, "Grandma was a good person, and she loved me and your aunt."

And she was fallible, he now understood as an adult. Tormented. Facing her trials by searching for something better, something that would give her life meaning, and dragging her children along for the ride. But good and loving.

Dexter nestled into his pillow and said, "She's in human Heaven."

"That's right. She protected us the way I protect you. Then she passed away. Bad things sometimes happen to good people, Dex. Sometimes, good people do bad things. That's a truth I can't protect you from forever."

The boy's eyelids fluttered. "You're a good daddy."

David kissed his forehead. "Night, poopy head."

Too tired for their old game, his son didn't answer, already drifting away. Just once, David wished he could fall asleep as easily. He switched off the light, plunging the room into darkness.

After putting Alyssa to bed, David went to the kitchen to pour himself a few fingers of scotch. He retreated to his office, where the usual correspondence, bills, and other business tasks awaited him. A never-ending to-do list that most nights satisfied him in its ability to make time go by and keep his restless mind from wandering. The safety of this cocoon tempted him to stay here forever.

He ignored it all, sitting and sipping his scotch. Memories stirred in his subconscious. He reached into this toxic pool and snatched a pearl.

Among the pea stalks, Beth taught Deacon a dance that was all the rage before she arrived at the farm. Arms thrashing, hips swooshing like she was rolling an invisible hula hoop. Deacon grinned as he tried to follow along. Emily laughed and clapped her hands while Wyatt played the peanut gallery. Angela shook her head until she stepped in to show them all how it was done.

The memory turned sour, but David shrugged it away and found another that made him smile. At last, he put them all away and picked up his phone.

He texted Angela, *I'm coming.*

This done, he went to his bedroom and climbed into bed with Claire. For the first time in months, he felt his consciousness begin to slip away within moments of lying down.

"David," his wife whispered. "David?"

He turned and opened his eyes to gaze at her dim outline. Then he reached to take her in his arms.

20
LEAP

Stage lights and the pounding 4/4 beat of the DJ's house music had turned an old industrial warehouse in the heart of Los Angeles into an impromptu dance club and concert hall. Cats Are Sad swept through the open bar and found a spot against the wall where they could see and be seen, though the vast space was almost empty.

"I knew we shouldn't have come early," Bart shouted over the music.

Joy squinted at the scenery. "I think I went to a rave here once."

Holding his plastic cup of generic white wine like a prop, Deacon braced himself for a long night. The start of a headache was already blooming in his skull from the sweet, chemical smell of the fog machines misting the colorful light beams.

"What are we doing here?" Laurie fumed. "We should be working on the album."

"Are you kidding?" Frank said. "They love you guys."

They being the nu metal band Gray Rainbow, which was throwing this party to celebrate the launch of their fresh LP, *The Secret Life of Seraphim.*

"If they love us so much, why aren't we on the bill?"

Mono No Aware, Spank the Imp, and Sweet Fetish would all be playing short sets tonight before Gray Rainbow took the stage.

Frank shrugged. "They only started loving you after Utopia. They booked these bands months ago. The world doesn't turn on a dime for anybody."

"So we're here to make Gray Rainbow look cool," Bart growled.

"They already *are* cool," Steve said. "They have a deal with Roadrunner. They released 'Fool's Gold' before the album as a single, and it made *Billboard.*"

"Yeah, for like one week."

"*Billboard,*" Steve repeated with even more emphasis.

"We're here to network," Frank lectured. "My advice is drink little, be cool, and make a nice impression."

Deacon's phone vibrated in his jeans. He pulled it out in the irrational hope someone was calling to yank him out of this. Surprisingly, it was Beth, who'd given up trying to contact him a few days ago. Seeing her name in his caller ID again both thrilled and shredded him. He let it go to voicemail and wished he could take his stabbing regret into a studio right now.

A shaggy giant in a leather jacket stomped through the chemical fog to grin at them. "Cats Are freaking Sad!" Cage, Gray Rainbow's frontman. He enveloped Steve in a bear hug. "Stevie! Been a long time. So happy you could join the party."

"So how does it feel?" the bass player said.

"Right now, I feel like my throat just ran a goddamn marathon."

Steve smiled in vicarious pleasure. "Hit the studio hard, huh?"

"Six weeks bashing tracks, my man, singing my heart out and surviving on coffee and dreams."

"Nice. Not up and coming anymore, looks like. You've made it."

"I'm always up and coming, Stevie." Cage winked at Joy.

"Well, congrats."

"Thanks." The giant's dark eyes roamed across Laurie's lanky body before settling on Deacon. "So this is the boy who survived." He reached to crush him against his barrel chest. "Welcome, my brother."

Deacon slid his phone back in his pocket. "Thanks, Cage." It felt strange calling the man by his stage name, but Deacon didn't know his real one.

"I see your name everywhere. The press is fantastic. You're blowing up the freaking internet, man." His breath smelled like Jack Daniel's. "You should come to the after-party. I need to hear your story firsthand."

"Okay."

"Okay!" Cage echoed and laughed. "You're hilarious. So y'all are working on a concept album about the Family of the Living Spirit. Art is the deep, dark secrets we tell everybody, am I right? What are you calling it?"

"Right now, we're settled on *Gnosis*," Laurie said. The band had nixed *The Gospel of the Sad Cat* as not edgy enough.

"Whose-is?"

"*Gnosis*. As in spiritual secrets known only to a privileged few."

Cage belched. "Love it. When does it drop?"

Frank deftly took over. "We're rehearsing now and shopping producers."

"You going indie, or looking for a label?"

"All options are on the table."

"Holler at me later, manager guy. You should be talking to Roadrunner."

While they talked shop, Laurie leaned toward Deacon and said, "What do you think of signing with a label?"

Deacon shrugged. "I think whatever you think."

"I like the idea of doing it ourselves. I can do the mastering myself."

Joy jumped at Cage for a selfie, squealing as he pulled her close for the shot. Interrupted, Frank scowled while Bart beamed an awkward grin at the man he wanted to be.

Deacon said to Laurie, "We should try to deal with a label at least to push stores and radio play, though, right?" Repeating stuff he'd heard Frank say.

"Whatever milks this cow while it still moos," Laurie agreed. "We can't give up control of the product, though. Not for this one. This one is gonna be pure art."

Cats Are Sad had found itself riding a wave to the unknown. Deacon's notoriety, which had gone viral and was being fed by a string of interviews following the Utopia show, generated a spike in sales and bookings, enough income to finance an album or tour. The question was where to go from here.

In the wake of their budding success, existential terror had set in among his bandmates, the paralyzing epiphany they could shape their own destiny combined with the fear that it could all end tomorrow. They knew Deacon's personal history was a meme of the week, a novelty in a busy world that had largely forgotten the Family of the Living Spirit even existed, not the basis for a musical group. They woke up each morning wondering if the person in the mirror was talented enough.

Frank wanted them to take advantage by touring their last album and building their fan base. The band decided instead to make Deacon's concept album and cash in all the way. Frank said that would work if it meant a deal with a label they could leverage into a follow-up album. Laurie wanted to master it herself, having the final say on everything from relative track volumes to equalization and gain.

Around and around it went. The usual politics, but this was bigger than who was short on paying their fair share of the bill at Denny's after a show. For his part, Deacon didn't care how the album was produced, as long as it got made.

The clock was ticking. Right now, they worked hard every day to nail down the tracks, rehearse them to the point of being able to play them in their dreams, and order them in a list with beats per minute locked down so the engineer would have the tempo before recording. Then they could get into a studio, one with excellent outboard gear, a live room with great sound so Bart could lay down his drum tracks, and a top-quality mic and isolation booth for Deacon to howl his vocals.

Laurie added, "You should start thinking about the liner notes."

"Me?" Deacon said.

Liner notes were little facts and observations about the tracks, sometimes printed in the CD packaging as bonus content.

"Memories about the cult. People would eat it up."

"Okay." His phone vibrated again.

Cage noticed he'd lost his audience and left Frank's latest question to wander in the house music's droning beat. "Y'all have a great time, okay? Pretty please, come to the after-party. In the meantime, drink up and enjoy the sounds." Backing away, he pointed at Laurie. "Ask for our signature drink called Fool's Gold at the bar. It'll knock you on your fantastic ass." His pointer finger's aim shifted to Deacon. "Love you, man. We'll talk later."

"Christ," Laurie said after he'd gone. "Do all musicians have to be like that?"

"Like what?" Frank said. "Successful?"

"Cocky and desperate."

"It's all in the game, sweetie."

Deacon shrugged. "He seemed nice enough to me."

"Fool's Gold," Laurie growled. "Sounds perfect right now." She walked off toward the open bar.

Deacon reached into his pocket to check his phone, but the band manager grabbed his arm.

"You want to do your gimmick album instead of tour, that's fine by me," Frank said. "That's your call. It's your band. This is too important for DIY, though. I don't care how prodigious she is at mixing. Roadrunner could put you guys on a whole new level. If not them, one of the other labels I'm talking to."

"Okay."

"We're done begging our way into some college music department and having some pimple-faced kid engineer our product. Praying we sell enough merch at our live shows for gas money and investing everything we've got into busking on YouTube and Bandcamp. We actually have a shot at something real."

"Okay."

"'Okay,' you agree with me? Say the word, and I'll push for a deal."

"Okay, whatever," Deacon said. "I told you I don't care about your bullshit. Laurie's either. You guys fight it out and let me know what we're doing."

Frank released him, nose wrinkling in disgust. "I just can't read you. You're the only musician I've ever known who isn't hungry for it."

He was hungry, all right. Just not for the things Frank valued.

The warehouse had filled with partygoers who flocked to the bar for drinks. On the stage, Mono No Aware tuned up for their short set. The vibe was great, making Deacon wish he was performing tonight. Third in line just before the headliner would be perfect, right when the crowd overcame its shyness and was drunk or high enough to groove with a band. By the time Gray Rainbow took the stage, it would be surly and starting to thin.

"I can't believe I didn't say a single word to him," Bart fumed.

"You can see him at the after-party," Joy said. "Just be yourself."

Deacon pulled out his phone, which had three unread texts from Beth.

Coming to LA. Driving to Bakersfield tonight to meet
Angela and David
We're going to Red Peak
Text me in the next hour if you want in

He thumbed his reply.

Yes
Pick me up?
I'm in Industry southeast of El Monte

Moments later, a message flashed:

K
Txt address
Will txt when close

Deacon wasn't sure where the hell he was. Under LED lights sweeping the stage in slow, colorful arcs, Mono No Aware started its first trippy song, alternating stretches of placid swirl with sudden, furious bursts of metal madness. He loved this band, but he was barely listening. He opened his GPS and texted Beth the address before pocketing his phone.

And that was that. He was going back to Red Peak.

Laurie returned with her drink. "Cage wasn't lying." She held her plastic cup high to inspect the yellow liquid. "Tastes like horse piss, but it has a real kick."

"I need to talk to you," Deacon shouted back. "Outside, where I can hear."

She scowled. "Goddamn Frank. Right? Okay, let's go."

They wound their way to the exit and distanced themselves from the crowd of smokers outside. Laurie took out her earplugs, specially designed musician plugs that allowed her to hear the music but at a lower sound level. Deacon looked around for a trash can for his unfinished wine.

"I'll help you with that."

She swiped the wine from his hand, tossed it back, and flung the cup onto the ground among other litter. "So what did Frank say?"

Deacon lit a Camel. "You know what he said."

"Asshole." Laurie took one of his cigs and bent her head to accept a light from him. "He doesn't understand the art."

"That's not what I wanted to talk to you about," he said. "I'm leaving town for a couple days."

"Of course you are."

"I'll be back Saturday, Sunday at the latest."

"Sure." She blew an angry cloud of smoke and flung the cigarette onto the street, where it landed with a burst of sparks. "Next, Bart will find Jesus, and Steve will catch butt cancer. Oh, and Joy's gonna be a mommy."

"It's not like that—"

"I mean, why would we actually want to succeed as a band when we've been struggling for years? Who needs a fucking holy grail, anyway? Who actually *likes* cake?"

"I'm going to Red Peak."

Laurie shrugged. "And you think that means something to me."

"I can't sing without it. The worse it is, the better I sing."

Her glare softened. "You're pathetic."

"Probably."

"Why can't you just get hooked on heroin like everybody else?"

The closest thing to a blessing Deacon would get out of her. He smiled and dropped his own cigarette to grind out with his heel.

"There has to be a better way to make art," she said. "I mean, to feel something, anything. To be a whole person."

"I don't know how to be anybody else."

"You going back inside?"

He shook his head. "I'm leaving now. Answering the call."

"The 'we played so beautifully' girl."

"All of us. We're going back. Tomorrow is the big fifteen."

Laurie's irritation morphed into an envious expression. She wished she was going. Whatever he suffered, she'd gladly take it on to be a part of it. Her hands twitched at her sides, the start of a hug, but hugging wasn't in her nature.

He hugged her instead. "If something bad happens to me and I don't come back, the album is all yours. You'll know what to do with it."

She pushed him away. "Piss off. Go do your vision quest. And get your ass back here by Sunday, or I'll hunt you down."

"Have fun with your networking. Give Frank hell."

"You can count on *that*."

Then she was gone. Deacon waited in the cool night under the glaring streetlight, chain-smoking. Mono No Aware finished their set, and the house music returned until Sweet Fetish started banging out its first song. Soon, Beth would arrive to take him into the unknown. Whatever happened next, it'd be a relief to get away from the band for a while. Laurie and Frank could fight without him.

His phone vibrated with an incoming text.

Here, it said.

Beth's Mercedes flashed onto the street. He waved at the headlights, smiling in a brief burst of joy. This was happiness the way he was used to it. Fleeting.

The car stopped. Deacon climbed in, and she took off back to the I-5.

He studied her profile as she drove, wondering what he was in for during the trip. She no longer wore a corporate jacket and skirt, but instead a gray T-shirt tucked into jeans. Her long hair flowed free around her shoulders. The car's interior smelled like alcohol and breath mints.

He said, "I'm sorry I've been unreachable."

Sorrier than she knew. Beth's voicemails and texts had savaged him, all of which he'd taken on stage to deliver his greatest performance ever at Utopia.

Like he'd told Laurie, he couldn't sing without it.

"I understand," she said.

"You do?" It hardly made sense to him.

"If you hadn't done it to me, I would have done it to you. I would have boxed you up and drowned you until you saved yourself by running. If I'm mad, it's only because you beat me to the punch. Bastard."

"I didn't want to do it."

Beth nodded behind the wheel. "You did what you needed to do. What I'd need to do." She smirked. "Which is screwed up. I'm tired of pretending otherwise."

"You won't believe this, but I do love you."

"Why wouldn't I believe it?"

"I'll never love anybody else."

She patted his knee. "Sometimes, silence is cool."

They drove in that silence to the I–5, which took them north into endless fog.

Rare in August, tule fog formed when the interior became very hot and pulled cool air from the coast. Something about it stirred Deacon's soul. It was pleasing to see a metaphor for his life manifest itself on this pilgrimage.

Beth stayed quiet the entire ride up from Los Angeles, staring out the windshield into the swirling mist while classical music lilted from the speakers. Deacon glanced at her GPS, which told him they were getting close to Bakersfield.

She said, "You're going to need sunscreen and a jacket."

"Why?"

"Because, as you know, where we're going will be blazing hot in the day and very cold at night."

"I'm going as I am," he said. "If I suffer, I suffer."

"Why?"

"If something's there, it wants me to." The Spirit, God, or

whatever it was. Deacon thought about it more and added, "The suffering could be a means, not an end. It wants us to love it more than we love ourselves."

Then again, he didn't have a clue what God wanted. His upbringing should have made him an expert. Years spent studying a book written over centuries by men claiming a secret knowledge of the divine, an invisible world populated by fantastic beings that defied human comprehension. As a child, he'd absorbed the stories with wonder and accepted the simple truths they told.

As an adult, however, he found the book to be filled with vague rules and contradictions, betraying an imperfect understanding and defying the notion of direct divine authorship. And it was one religion among thousands through the ages, progressively evolving to shape the divine from natural to superhuman to abstract, all groping at the same questions: Who made us? Why are we here? What happens after death? The answers guiding behavior, often forming covenants that changed the course of history. Many peoples, many different covenants.

All things considered, Deacon didn't know a damn thing about God, not really, and even less about the thing that lived on the mountain.

"I wonder if we're anthropomorphizing it," Beth said. "Whatever it is. Maybe it's unknowable. Maybe it's a force like a hurricane or gravity, and not an intelligent being."

"I guess there's only one way to find out." Make the climb on faith. Maybe whatever was up there couldn't be defined by rules, but he still believed it was comprehensible.

She tightened her grip on the wheel. "What if there's no *it* there at all?"

"What if we're following in the Rev's footsteps, confusing hope with reality?"

"Creating a story so it all means something. Right down to false memories."

Deacon shrugged. "I'm not sure which is worse. That I actually saw dead people roll up a hill and fly into a pillar of fire, or that I made it up."

The car crawled along the highway. Fog swirled in the headlights, shrouding the road. The morning sun would burn it away, and all would be revealed.

21

RETURN

At sunrise, Beth drove them from the hotel to the cemetery where Emily rested. She got out of the car holding a hot cup of Starbucks while Deacon lit a cigarette and pondered the rows of tombstones stretching into the thinning mist.

"I caught your show," she said. "At Utopia."

A smile flickered across his face. "You did?"

"The song you wrote. I liked it. It made me remember the good stuff."

"The good stuff hurts too."

"Not to me," Beth said. "The good stuff is everything."

Headlights glimmered in the fog. David's Toyota hummed onto the lot and parked next to Beth's car.

Angela got out first. "Jesus, look at you two. You went and grew up."

Deacon hugged her. "Real good to see you, Detective."

She gave his back an indulgent pat. "Okay, Deek."

Beth hugged her next. "I can't believe it. You look great."

"Good to see you. Why are we meeting here?"

"Emily's death brought us to this journey." It seemed so long ago, though it'd been less than a month since they'd buried her here. "It seemed appropriate."

David got out of the car. "So I guess we're doing this after all."

Deacon shook his hand. "Welcome back, Dave."

Beth tensed to embrace him but hesitated.

He hugged her. "I'm happy to see you."

"Thank you," she whispered.

He'd forgiven her for making a pass at him at the conference, as she'd forgiven Deacon. No stones in these glass houses. They'd go to Red Peak with a clean slate.

Beth led the survivors into the graveyard and found Emily's headstone. There, they stood in silent recollection while the strengthening sun burned away the fog to reveal rows of tombstones shaded by mesquites and palms. Beth once considered Emily her best friend. Her mind raced through fragments of memories, little moments of shared secrets and laughter.

"For Pete's sake, just tell him you like him."

"Are you crazy?"

Emily rolled her eyes. "Everybody knows already."

Beth shoved her. "Shut up, 'everybody knows'!"

"You should do it soon. I'm being serious now. Time is running out."

"I know she'd love seeing us together again," David said.

Beth nodded and wondered if this had been Emily's plan all along.

Deacon turned to Angela. "What now?"

Though the difference in their ages was now negligible, they defaulted to viewing David's big sister as older and wiser and therefore the leader.

Angela said, "We go to Red Peak and find out if we're crazy or there really is something there that took our families and friends."

"If we're crazy," David said, "we'll put all this behind us for good, right?"

If nothing happened, he wanted to see them all free themselves of the rabbit hole instead of doubling down on their beliefs.

"You still don't buy it," Deacon said.

"No. Maybe. I don't know. I didn't see what you saw. I'm going into this with an open mind. That's all you're gonna get from me."

"I think we're all on the same page," Beth said. "Let's grab some breakfast and hit the road. On the way, we can talk. No more secrets."

Angela said, "You heard the lady. Let's go."

On the long drive to Medford in David's mini SUV, they shared their stories. The ritual, the pillar of fire shooting up from Red Peak's summit, the awful horn, the bodies tumbling up the slope to fly into the flames. The fate of loved ones. Josh dying in the truck. Wyatt making a run for it until caught by his father, who cut his throat. The Wardites, the deputy, and The Restoration, who all disappeared on the same site.

The stories coalesced into a single account of what happened at Red Peak the last night and since. The separate accounts so similar even David, the skeptic, grew quiet behind the wheel as he took it all in.

In Medford, they stopped at a gas station and piled out to stretch their legs. Deacon went inside to buy cigarettes. Angela walked off to call the sheriff's department and tell them their plan to visit Red Peak.

Beth stood with her back against the car's warm metal and watched people drive past, living their own stories, oblivious to the mysteries that lay mere miles away.

David unscrewed his gas cap and started pumping. "So we're going to find out if something is at Red Peak. Some weird force."

"That's the plan," Beth told him.

"What if there is? What then?"

"We get answers." Know the thing that had taken her parents, as much as it was knowable, and hopefully learn what it had done with them.

"Okay, great. Then what?"

"Answers aren't enough?" She hadn't thought beyond that.

"Everybody wants something besides answers," David said. "Angela wants to find something up there so she can punish it. What do you want?"

They sought Oz the Great and Powerful, who might grant them all a wish.

Beth considered her answer. Just going to Red Peak had been enough for the moment, a cathartic release that had silenced the scathing voice in her head. What else did she want?

She said, "I don't want to end up like Emily."

He blinked in surprise. "Do you think about it? You know..."

"It's still in me."

David shivered. "Okay."

It was in him too, apparently. She didn't tell him that she believed she hadn't been left behind after all. That she'd chosen to stay. That she now hoped she might be given another choice.

Beth doubted he'd understand the difference.

He removed the nozzle and screwed the cap back on. "I hope we get the answers you want."

"What about you? What do you want?"

"I guess I want to stop being afraid of it."

Deacon returned cradling an armful of bottled water, Angela right behind him.

She pocketed her phone. "The search for The Restoration is over. There are no police at the site. We'll be on our own out there."

David looked at them. "This is it, then."

Angela nodded. "Everybody ready for this?"

Beth wasn't sure, but she said she was anyway. Ever since James had helped her surface her memories, she'd steadily given up control to Red Peak. Chosen a psychic path far less traveled.

She was about to find out where both would take her.

The car rocked on the rutted track that snaked through the foothills and gorges at the edge of the Inyo range. Nobody spoke during this final stage of their journey.

Beth remembered the long bus ride to the holy mountain and felt the same excitement now, a mix of anticipation and relief.

In 2005, the apocalypse was imminent, but she'd spent half the trip staring at the back of Deacon's head several rows ahead. Young love, so ridiculous and beautiful and powerful. She'd gotten off the bus feeling both let down and relieved that the world didn't end then and there.

Beth now gasped as Red Peak came into view and triggered a flood of emotions. It was smaller than she remembered. The first time she'd seen the mountain, it had inspired awe, as if it were a very real Olympus. Now it seemed lonely and desolate. Angry rather than hopeful, ominous instead of majestic.

Then the camp appeared, still standing where they'd left it, waiting to tell her that in all endings there is a beginning. The stairs still there to welcome pilgrims wishing to make the climb.

David parked near the Temple, and they got out, taking their time, as if they no longer trusted their balance. The sun glared down on them, the desert heat an almost physical force.

Beth broke out in instant sweat.

The elements had scarred the shacks, but otherwise they stood eerily intact, as if the Family had all gone to pray or fetch water. Beth could see them in her mind, excitedly spilling off the buses carrying their luggage and crying babies, the children bolting amid laughter to explore their new home.

"We'll make the best of it," Daddy said.

"The 'best of it'?" Mom laughed. "It's perfect."

Now it was sad and pathetic.

Beth gazed down the slight incline toward the shack where she'd lived for three long, hot months. While it briefly had been her home, it wasn't the right place to say goodbye to her parents. Beth gravitated toward the Temple. The door was ajar, a dark maw emitting a musty stench. A large crack like a black lightning bolt ran down the front of it.

She turned to her friends with a questioning look, though she wasn't sure she wanted to go inside.

David paled. "I'm not going in there. No goddamn way."

His sister walked off a short distance and knelt to touch the ground. "This is where Mom died. Josh too."

He turned away. "Yeah."

Deacon stared off at some distant point, wiped his eyes, and sniffed.

"You okay?" Beth asked him.

He pointed. "See that boulder? I hid behind it most of the night. From there, I saw Wyatt's dad hold him down and..." He pointed again. "Right there."

Angela stood and clapped dust from her hands.

She said, "If you want to say goodbye, come with me."

▲   ▲   ▲

Beth followed without question. She was satisfied to be moving again, to be doing something, anything. Memories haunted the camp, vengeful and needy, both happy and horrifying. The musky, bitter smells of the creosote and sagebrush threatened to bring them to life in her mind.

Angela led them across Red Peak's northern flank, and after a few steps Beth knew where they were headed.

The black basalt wall and its petroglyphs jutted from the slope where she remembered. Hundreds of carvings spoke prophecies and dreams. Stick men with shining heads received enlightenment. The winged creature promised a vision quest to the hungry and patient. The Great Spirit presided over it all.

Down the rocky incline, the Wardites' camp had suffered over the intervening years, its cabins reduced to their foundations, the steepled church with its broken back wilted further toward its center.

Beth studied the carvings. "Something's wrong with it."

Deacon squinted. "What?"

"There are way more crosses than I remember. Aren't there?"

Crosses had once dotted the wall face's periphery. Someone had carved scores of fresh symbols along the edge.

"Yes." Angela crouched next to the black rock. "I carved them." She ran her fingers along a series of the crosses. "One for every member of the Family. This is their memorial."

"How many times have you come back here?" Deacon asked.

"Once a year, around this time, so this makes fifteen. Emily wanted to come too, but she wouldn't go without the rest of you."

"Did you ever, you know, go up?"

Beth tilted her gaze toward Red Peak's summit looming above them. On this slope, no false summits blocked one's view all the way to the top.

"Yup," Angela said.

"Nothing happened, apparently," Deacon said.

David sighed, though Beth couldn't tell if it was from exasperation or relief. "Well, that's pretty telling."

"What it tells me is the thing up there doesn't like me very much," Angela said.

"You have to want it," Deacon said. "You have to *love* it."

David shook his head. "That kind of thinking is how this whole thing started."

"How about we go up with an open mind, then?"

He sighed again, this time in resignation. "Fine."

Angela said, "If you have anything to say to your loved ones, do it now. We have a long climb ahead of us."

Beth touched two of the crosses, claiming them for her parents. Mom and her nonstop chatter about God and the other members, keeping her world turning by defining it with words. Mom, whose silence and sacrifice had haunted Beth for so long. Daddy and his quiet, patient suffering to keep his family together so he could go on protecting his only daughter, his miracle baby girl. Daddy, who'd tried to escape in search of rescue but in the end crossed over with his wife, the father who'd given Beth the final push to run instead of drink.

She'd waited for her mother to speak ever since.

Goodbye, she thought. *I love you. I miss you. I forgive you.*

Then she stepped back from the rock, ready to make the climb to the top of the holy mountain, where she hoped to stop running long enough to listen.

22

ASCEND (1)

The sandstone stairway wound up from the camp to the first false summit. Drenched with sweat, David labored toward the top in the afternoon sun's oven heat.

This place. God, what a mistake, coming back here.

For a short time, it had once been something like home, but it now struck him as sinister, producing a sense of unease that clung like a foul aftertaste. Seeing the Temple had triggered a menacing flashback. The Family hobbling out of the dark, their eyes shining with a manic, hopeful light. A strange, alien feeling overtaking him, the idea he didn't know them anymore and they were coming to drag him to the mountaintop and kill him. Now, as then, he wanted to hide.

He took another step. Another, huffing and puffing.

Then he faltered, the same as he had when long ago he'd tried to climb Red Peak with Deacon. The closer one crept to the top, the more threatening and powerful the mountain seemed to become. The angrier.

When he was twelve, he'd trekked up the slopes to ask God not to destroy the world, only to be stunned into flight by a single heretical thought. That he didn't want to meet a God who would kill most of the world. That such a God was something to be feared, not loved.

That was when he still believed with all his heart. A long time ago, but he remembered what it felt like.

Ahead of him, Angela turned with a warning stare. "Keep going."

"We should stop and rest."

"At the first summit."

"This is stupid. You understand that, right? We're wasting our time."

Worse, what they were doing was dangerous. David had studied cult behavior long enough to believe that his friends inched toward taking over for their parents. How wonderful, not to have to think. To surrender control to an all-powerful, invisible being. To have a simple and irrefutable worldview handed to you. To be solely privy to mysterion, the ritual secrets God shared with his chosen.

Just as faith could move mountains, it could also level them.

His sister waited until he started moving again, matching his stride. She'd reached a point of no return. If he ran, he had no doubt she'd force him up the slope, frog-marching him if she had to. She wore her service weapon holstered on her hip, a reminder who was in charge.

"I always hated the saccharine bullshit," Angela said. "Praise the little baby Jesus and all the phony insider jokes and everybody talking like they were performing for an audience of one, Jesus Christ himself."

David shrugged. "I kind of liked it." It had once been a source of pride, in fact.

"Yeah? That's nice for you. Me, I was one *a-men!* from blowing my brains out. Mom was the worst. So goddamn smug about the sinners getting theirs. The way she'd say *Jesus* like she was gushing about her new boyfriend. The way she'd talk about God killing everybody like it was cool."

"Yeah." David had detested that last part as well.

"After she cut up her face, I hated her. I hated her stupid faith that got us mixed up with a bunch of goddamn lunatics who were going to get us all killed. The love she had for some invisible guy who made her happier than her own kids did."

This time, he said nothing, letting her push it off her chest.

"It wasn't until years later that I got over my bullshit," Angela said. "I couldn't imagine how hard it was for her, alone with two kids. Dad sneaking off to hotel rooms with another woman until one day he didn't come back."

David nodded. "He was having an affair."

"How did you know? I never told you that."

"I pieced it together way later."

"Her faith saved her," she went on. "The church gave her a new life and a reason to wake up in the morning, besides feeding two kids. Her belief in God turned the whole stupid show into a test that actually meant something. She took it all too far, but I get it now, where it came from. She was broken."

He nodded again. He remembered wishing he could see what his mother saw when she beheld Eden in the woods. She hadn't seen paradise, apparently, but her own personal salvation.

"But you know what?" she said. "In the end, even though she'd gone all in, she put us first. When push came to shove, Mom chose *us* over what she believed. She tried to get us out."

"Why are you telling me this?" David asked.

"We owe her. She died for us." Angela glared, still radiating anger. "The least we can do is find out what happened
to her and maybe even why."

His sister was right. What they were doing here wasn't
stupid. Wasn't a waste of time. Was the least they could do.
Was, in fact, the right thing to do.

This time, there could be no hiding. With all his excuses
gone, all he had left was his dread. "Just give me one minute."

He stopped to slide one of his Marlboros from its box. His
hands trembled as he lit it. The smoke burned his stretched
lungs, and he coughed into his fist. Sweat poured off him
from the heat and the climb.

Angela paused with him, directing her gaze down the
mountainside to make sure the rest of her ducklings were in
line. Beth and Deacon plodded up the slope about fifty yards
behind, taking their time.

"I'm no better than Mom," David said. "I should be home
playing with my kids. Making things right with Claire. But
here I am, looking for God."

"You'll be home with them soon."

"You don't know that."

"Isn't that what you wanted me to say?" Angela took a nip
from her canteen and spat. "I thought you didn't believe this
was anything but a wilderness hike."

David unzipped his backpack and yanked out a towel. His
body continued to sweat in waves in the desert's furnace
heat, and stopping had only made him hotter. He wiped
his face and looked up at the false summit, which appeared
much nearer now. The truth seemed to hover just out of
reach up there. He wasn't so sure anymore that this was only
a hike. He was beginning to doubt his doubt.

"I don't know what this is," he admitted.

Above him, the false summit brooded in afternoon sunshine. Mountaintops always evoked a sense of awe, but this one was special. An atmosphere of power blanketed it. In all the bright, empty glare above Red Peak, something seemed to wait. The dead rocks and dirt appeared alive, pulsing in the heat.

Or maybe he was simply projecting his fears onto this place. Giving it a personality. Maybe the truth, begging to be known, also waited for him to write it. With all its vast nothing, the mountain provided a blank slate for yearning souls. The emptiness did not like being ignored. It demanded translation. It wanted meaning, could not exist without a human brain to create and complete it.

The Wardites, the Family, and now him.

"There's only one way to find out," Angela said.

David tested another drag on his cigarette and decided to put it out in favor of taking a swig from his own water bottle. He returned his towel and bottle to his backpack and shouldered it. He caught his breath.

"Okay," he said. "I'm ready."

In the past few weeks, he'd suffered watching almost all his Band-Aids tear away one by one, exposing his wounds to air and light, scrutiny and judgment. Only one remained.

Angela studied him. "You sure? I know this is hard for you."

He'd keep going, not because of what he might owe his mother, but because of what he knew he owed his sister.

Maybe she'd forgive him after this. Maybe he'd forgive himself.

"I'm saying you can back out if you want," she said. "I know you want to."

David didn't answer her. Instead, he put his foot forward. Did it again.

Step by step, he ascended his past to an uncertain future.

23

ASCEND (2)

Deacon staggered up the last steps to the first summit, which revealed another long slope leading to the second. The group stopped to rest. Too much smoking over the years had him wheezing, though that didn't prevent him craving a cigarette now. He dug into his pocket for his pack before withdrawing empty-handed. This pilgrimage, he reminded himself, demanded a sense of sacrifice.

He sat on the rock ledge and took a long pull from his water bottle. The Family's derelict camp appeared tiny from this height. Already light-headed from the sun's heat and blinding light, he was starting to feel sick, his stomach churning. He didn't know what he'd find at the final summit, but he knew what he might.

Up there, something that defied human comprehension could be waiting.

The same as when he'd tried to make the climb as a kid, the mountain seemed to shift without actually moving, as if taking notice of him.

Yes, there was likely nothing. All in his head. They were probably all crazy. Occam's razor strikes again. It was also possible they weren't crazy at all, or rather, that they'd finally become sane again after so long.

A refreshing breeze washed over the mountain, drying the sweat that covered him and replenishing him with a second wind. He glanced at Beth sitting nearby, eyes closed, her face raised to catch the breeze.

"We'd better get back to it," Angela said, triggering a flurry of groans.

Deacon watched her athletic body arch in a stretch. "I never could believe you ran the whole way up, but now I'm starting to get it. You're a machine."

She hadn't just jogged up the mountain back in 2005. She'd also walked all the way to the sheriff's substation in Medford, making the desert trek without food and water on sheer willpower alone.

He'd been right to be a little afraid of her when they were kids.

"It's like Mom always said. A little exercise would do me a world of good." She shrugged. "I was young and on a mission that night."

"You're still young."

"Still on a mission," she corrected him. "That I can wholeheartedly agree with. After the second false summit, a short walk will take us to the top."

With that, she started up the next set of stairs.

Deacon worked his way back onto his feet. "Where's a decent walking stick when you need one, huh?"

David returned a brief smile. "Up Shepherd Wright's ass." Completing a very old routine.

Deacon laughed. "I missed you, man."

His friend's smile strengthened. "Yeah."

"Talk to me." He grunted as his muscles protested at resuming the climb. "Take my mind off my sore feet."

"Tell me what it's like being on a stage performing," David said.

"When the vibe is pumped and the crowd is connecting with the band, I feel like God." Starving for love and getting it in spades, not to mention the sense of power. "When the audience isn't happy, I feel like Satan." Ruining everyone's night but plowing ahead anyway. "Either way, it's the greatest thing I ever did."

"Your mom loved music. I know she'd be proud of you."

Deacon's face hardened. "My mom." Everything led back to the Family.

David caught his expression. "Sorry if I—"

"No problem. I'll tell you something about Mom, though. She was my first fan. Music was big around my house. My first memories are of her singing at the kitchen sink. Can I tell you something funny?"

"Sure," David said.

"The last night, when everybody left the mess hall and was heading over to the Temple, she was a wreck. She'd always had a thing for the old Reverend. Which I didn't mind, not one bit. My real dad's dead, and the Rev was like a dad to me. I told her we should get away, like Angela said. You know what she told me?"

His friend shook his head, grunting with the exertion of the climb.

"Mom told me I should run, but she was staying. If God wanted her to die, then that's what she'd do. If the Rev was dying, then so was she. She stopped crying while she said it. She actually looked happy. She couldn't wait to rid herself of the body she hated and become spirit. She couldn't live without the man she loved. In the end, Mom chose suicide over her own son."

"Come on," David said. "She loved you."

"Sure, she did. My first fan. She just loved Jesus more. Maybe even the Rev."

"In seven years, I'll be my mom's age when she died. Maybe it's because I'm getting older, maybe it's because I have kids, but I feel like I understand her now."

"My mom made me what I am today," Deacon said.

Someone who put himself first.

A man who didn't know how to truly love because he couldn't love himself.

Screw it. To hell with suffering and sacrifice. He took out his crumpled pack of Camels, extracted a wilted cigarette, and torched its tip with his lighter.

It was the best he ever had. "Do you want one?"

David shook his head. "No, thanks."

He turned to see Beth toiling behind them. "You go ahead. I'm gonna take a break."

"Already?" David caught him staring at Beth and smiled. "Ah. Sure. Can I tell you something I learned the hard way?"

"Sure, man."

"It's never too late."

Something shifted in his chest. "You might be right."

"You should get that tattooed on your arm."

His friend marched off, leaving Deacon chuckling. He smoked while Beth crossed the distance separating them and stopped panting a few feet downslope.

Resting her hands on her knees to catch her breath, she cast an irritated eye at him. "I thought we said everything that needed saying."

That wasn't remotely true, but Deacon understood that words didn't matter anymore. She already knew he loved her but that it wasn't enough for him to change. They couldn't be together, not in the way they both wanted.

What she didn't know was how beautiful she was to him and that he'd never belong to another, something words couldn't express, not a tattoo, not even a song.

He smiled. "What makes you think I want to say anything?"

"You've got that look. Like a dam about to break, and there's a marriage proposal or a speech about human nature or a song on the other side of it."

He said, "Silence can fool, you know."

Her irritation deepened before it gave way to a smile, the smile to one of those belly guffaws that had always made him laugh along with her. Her laugh turned into a coughing fit from all the dust in the air.

"You," she rasped, "are a piece of work."

That Deacon already knew, no reminders needed. It was tattooed on his life.

He extended his hand. She took it, and they resumed their climb holding on to each other, onward and upward toward the next false summit.

While they weren't equipped to ever be a couple, they'd be together during this journey, right to the end.

24

ASCEND (3)

Drawing strength from Deacon's sweating hand, Beth forced herself to climb the last steps to the second summit, which provided a view to a short series of stairs leading up to the mountain's red crown.

There, they let go of each other to catch their breath. She spread her arms and swayed in the breeze, her limbs slick and sunburned, her clothes dusty.

To the west, the sun plunged toward the Sierra Nevadas.

"I think you're right," she gasped.

Sweat dripped from Deacon's tangled hair into the dirt. "About what?"

"It wants us to suffer."

She wasn't joking. The stairway had a purpose, she saw that now. Along the way, she'd shed everything that slowed her down. Her memories, her tangled feelings about Deacon, her worry of what they'd find at the top. Her very sense of self. The harsh climb purged all of it. She'd sweated it out of her.

And along the way, the silence had reached inside her mind. Beth would be making the last part of the climb without any cares other than finishing it. Her mind and body a stripped-down, empty vessel.

"Long is the way, and hard," Deacon said.

David completed the quote. "That out of Hell leads up to the Light."

Or night, Beth thought, watching the sun bleed into the mountains.

She shrugged off her pack and chugged the last of her water. The air was cooler here. The final summit wasn't far. Small mercies, and maybe a promise of bigger mercies to come.

"We're almost there," Angela said, still looking surprisingly rested. "Let's make the most of the daylight."

Deacon held out his hand again. "Shall we?"

Beth took it. She marched with renewed vigor, pulling him along. After her hypnosis session, she believed she'd been left behind, and this feeling had returned. That she'd come too late, and everyone had ascended. With each step, the mountain's true summit appeared to recede farther out of reach.

Deacon squeezed her hand. "Can you feel it?"

"What?" she managed.

He either didn't have enough breath to answer, or there was simply no way to put it into words. The latter more likely, because she felt it now too.

The mountain's powerful atmosphere seemed to respond to her attention by almost physically pushing back. Judging by the loud grunting, all of them were having the same experience. Angela struggled in particular, snarling at each step. David cried out in panic.

We were invited, Beth thought.

Her mind flashed to the raucous worship at their Tehachapi church, the Family singing and waving and opening themselves to inhabitation by the Spirit.

We invite you.

Beth drew a deep breath and opened herself to the energy, which reversed from resisting to fill and flow through her. The mountain seemed to sing, a single vibrating *om* that resonated in her chest.

The pilgrimage ended with her staggering onto the summit, bathed in the dying sun's red glare. The others arrived gasping moments later.

"Wow," Deacon said.

Beth nodded, still fighting to catch her breath. The barrier defied comprehension. But that wasn't what impressed them now.

Under a dimming sky, the mountain's desolate flat peak stretched to the horizon, charcoal-black rock vined with rust. At the center of the otherwise empty crown, a large cubical stone stood like an altar, similarly rusted with iron oxides and hematite. Behind it, a tall, old wood cross thrust from the ground at an angle, the famous cross that had burned but was not consumed.

Whatever happened to the people they loved, it had all started here.

She shuddered. The cross still had old spikes jutting from its arms and stem.

"Does anybody else think that was weird?" David said. "That wasn't in our heads. There was something going on."

"Something," Beth agreed.

"So why aren't we getting the hell out of here while we can?"

Nobody answered. They'd all come too far to turn back now.

"I'm staying," Deacon said.

He started forward, hesitantly at first but with greater determination as nothing strange happened.

Angela looked at her brother. "You coming or going?"

David looked back down the slope with longing. "Damn it." He turned to glare at his sister. "You could have warned us. You've been here before."

"Would you have believed me?"

Beth held out her hand. "Come on, David. Remember to breathe."

He took her hand, and together they walked across the open ground to join Deacon at the altar and cross.

Angela crouched in front of the altar. "This was made. See?"

She was right. The stone had been roughly hewn into a cubic shape with primitive tools. Deep grooves radiated from the center down each of its four sides like a falling cross. Beth imagined blood flowing along these channels from a sacrifice, making her shudder again.

"Look closer." David's sister pointed. "These are petroglyphs."

The stone was dense with them, neatly arranged in rows, unlike the haphazard Native carvings of their childhood hangout. Time had worn them to an almost illegible smoothness. Beth's mind fleshed out the detail, producing a snapshot of rich symbols that looked vaguely Mesoamerican, Aztec, or Mayan, but far cruder. Then they collapsed into a meaningless pattern in her mind's eye.

Beth shifted her attention to the cross behind the altar, planted by the Wardites a century earlier. Old-time religion paired with something far more ancient. Their shadows seemed impossibly long in the dying light, as if grasping for something.

"Amazing, how it survived being burned," Deacon murmured, running his hand along the cross's charred, fireblackened skin.

The shadows disappeared as the sun bled into the mountains and became a glimmer on the horizon. The anniversary mere hours away. Beth didn't care about the cross. She opened her mind to the energy that permeated this place, trying to silence her thoughts so she could hear its song again.

The mountain remained silent, as if ignoring her.

"Yeah, amazing." David agreed with Deacon, then looked up in alarm at the darkening sky. "Can we head back now? There's nobody home."

Deacon frowned at the cross like he wanted to kick it. "That's it?"

"It was always *it*, if you ask me. All in their heads."

This was Beth's cue to say they'd gained something valuable by coming here. Catharsis and reflection. They'd confronted their collective past and flooded its dark corners with the light of rational scrutiny. They'd go home better equipped to live in the present. Years of psychological training provided the framework and the words. She'd tell them that not every mystery had to be solved. That the important thing was to let the dead rest and go on with life.

No. Beth wasn't going to say any of it.

She hadn't come here to define what had happened, package it in a way she could accept it. She'd come to see it define itself on its own terms.

She wanted the god of Red Peak to reveal itself at last.

The wind moaned across the mountaintop, whistled in its crevasses.

She raised her hands and said in a loud, clear voice, "We invite you."

The altar exploded in a rush of fire.

25

CHOOSE

Red flames danced around the altar before hurtling into the atmosphere in a blinding eruption. David screamed as his friends disappeared in the flash. He crumpled to his knees, covering his eyes with his arm, his heart ringing in alarm.

Impossible. Insane. Unbelievable, though he himself had witnessed it.

He curled in a fetal ball on the dirt, quivering with mindless terror.

IT was here. The thing the Family worshipped. Something he couldn't believe existed, yet undeniably real, vast and ancient and powerful.

David struggled against its presence like a fly pinned to a wall, scrutinized by a primordial force that could destroy with a mere thought.

The light dimmed. His breathing steadied.

He ventured to open his eyes.

His friends were gone. The pillar of fire had extinguished, though the sky glowed like a hot coal in its aftermath.

A boy stood on the altar, fists clenched at his sides, his unruly hair a shining crimson halo framing his face.

"Hello," said the boy.

David blinked at him in further disbelief. "Dex?"

It was his son in almost every respect, right down to his Minecraft T-shirt.

The boy grinned. "Guess again."

"Who are you?"

"You don't know? You came a long way to see me."

David pushed himself onto his knees but was still too weak to stand. "You're putting all this into my head. It's a trick."

"You tricked yourself," Dexter told him.

"What does that mean?"

"You see me as you want to see me. You hear my thoughts in words of your choosing. You could not bear to see or hear me as I really am."

"You can't be real." He slapped himself as if trying to wake himself up from a dream. "I'm hallucinating."

A psychotic break, shredding the reality he could no longer process.

"Want to see a magic trick?" Chuckling, the boy tossed a coin and slapped it against his forearm. "Madness or belief?"

David covered his face in his hands. "No. I'm not doing this."

"You don't need to do anything, Daddy."

He dropped his hands to gape at his daughter. "Please stop."

"Then stop yourself." Alyssa hopped off the altar and reached for him, making him flinch. She cupped his face in her hands. "You always take care of us and protect us. Let me help you for once."

"What are you? Are you God?"

"If God is everything, I am God," his daughter said.

"You trick people. You hurt them. You're the Devil."

She shrugged. "If God is everything, I am the Devil."

Both and neither. "What are you?"

"I am what I am, as you name me," the girl said.

"Did we . . . create you?"

She laughed, Alyssa's adorable *hee, hee, hee,* though edged with a deep bass that rumbled across the sky. "I have always been. If you made me out of wishes, you made me as I am, both alpha and omega."

David wagged his head to make her release him. His friends had come here to know the entity that had destroyed their families, but it stubbornly remained unknowable, inviting him to come up with any understanding that satisfied him.

No wonder Jeremiah Peale had fallen under its spell. He'd probably seen Jesus in a white robe or an angel complete with halo and wings, commanding him to deliver his tribe for salvation.

David stood and gazed across the desolate ground, dark under the glowing sky. Where was Angela? Where were his friends?

What did this thing want from him?

"Where's my mom now?" he said. "Did you take Emily too?"

"David."

Dressed in her yoga attire, Claire reached for him. He knew it was an illusion, another trick, but he couldn't refuse her touch. She enveloped him in a hug.

And he understood. The creature wanted him to obey it.

Like Claire, it wanted unconditional love, the same as it loved David with all its heart.

What he didn't understand was why this was so important to the entity. If it was so powerful, what did it gain from human pain, and why did he have a choice?

"We complete each other," Claire murmured into his ear. "Namaste."

"What you made Mom do wasn't love."

"It's the purest love in existence," she whispered.

She melted into him, the skin of her soft arms sliding against his shoulders as her hands caressed the back of his neck. Her breath hot against his cheek.

Gritting his teeth, he turned his head away from her. "You hurt them for nothing. Just because you could."

"They sacrificed. They gave up desire and meat. Do you want to see your mother again? Emily?" She writhed against him. "Is that what you want?"

"Of course I do."

"You know what to do. To be with them forever." Her words tickled his ear. "A leap of faith."

"You want me to trust you, after what you did?"

Claire stepped back from him and crossed her arms with a glare David knew all too well, speaking words he also recognized. "You're disappointing."

She could erase his existence with a sigh.

She said, "Do you know who I am? What you are compared to me?"

"I don't want it. I..."

He was tired of the tricks, but the entity wasn't tricking him. David had conjured Dexter, Alyssa, Claire himself. Through them, he'd expressed to himself his innate desire to run and hide. To simply walk away from the pain of his life.

He was also telling himself what he wanted most in the world. Something he already had, if only he'd accept it.

"Why did you come to Oz, then?" she said. "What do you want from me?"

David wanted to stop being afraid. "What I want, I have to give myself."

"You want nothing I can give?"

"I just want to go home." To the thing he wanted most of all, his family.

His wife's eyes blazed like twin pools of black fire.

"Then earn it," she said in a voice that thundered across the ether.

26

SEEK

Alone, Deacon lay cowering in the dust while the fire soared overhead.

A figure emerged from the writhing flames to grin down at him.

"Well, look at you," the man said. "You went and grew up."

Deacon cried out. "Reverend? Is that you?"

The same suit jacket worn over a black T-shirt and jeans. The same leather boots. The side part coming undone in a tangle over his forehead. Cheshire cat smile beaming. Half rascal, half choir boy.

Jeremiah Peale hopped off the altar. The terrifying jet of fire seemed to reverse direction and collapse, pouring back into the stone until it expired. In its place, the Wardite cross ignited to burn with surprising energy.

Deacon rose onto his elbows, still gaping. "It is you."

Theories flitted through his brain. Peale had harnessed a great power. The Family was still alive, living somewhere near the mountain. He was seeing a ghost.

"No, son," the man said. "I'm not who you think I am. Sorry about that."

All his theories collapsed into a singular idea. "You're it, aren't you? You're..." The monster? The god? God?

"I am that which I am. You wanted me to appear this way."

Deacon looked around at the alien sky. "And I'm hallucinating all this."

"It's real enough. Just different, is all." Peale extended one of his big paws. "Stand up, boy. Let me have a look at you."

Deacon took the man's hand and grunted in surprise at the strong, substantial grip. The Reverend hauled him up to stand on trembling legs.

"You left a boy and came back a man," Peale said. "The prodigal son returns."

"What are you doing? What do you want from me?"

The man chuckled. "You came to me, remember? You called, I answered."

"I can't believe this is happening," Deacon said.

"Of course you do. If you didn't, you wouldn't have come to visit. I suppose you want to talk a bit about your mama."

He shook his head and decided to roll with it. "Is she alive? Is she happy?"

"You think she ditched you, her own blood, all those years back, and that's what you want to know, if she's happy."

"Is she?"

"She is indeed." He tilted his head. "Let's walk and talk."

Deacon followed the man across black rock under a rust sky. "I'm glad it's you, you know."

"Him," the thing corrected. "Think of it as a mask so you can talk to me without losing a few screws."

"I missed him. Is he there too? On the other side?"

"He suffered more than most, and he earned his place. Like your mama, now he longs to hear your joyful singing again."

Deacon shot a glance over his shoulder toward the cross burning behind the altar. He shuddered. "I'm glad he made it. I always thought he did."

"See that?" The Reverend winked. "I told you that you believed."

Enough, apparently, to take it in stride that he was talking to a dead man, a dead man who might have been God, a dead man who might still be alive in a world of light on the other side of a vast, empty void.

"How does it all work, Rev?"

Heaven and Hell, good and evil, free will and the Plan, why bad things happened to good people, and whether there was such a thing as the divine sound, the frequencies still echoing from the primordial thought that created everything.

"You want it all, huh?" Peale chuckled again. "Does it matter? You didn't come to talk theology. Anyway, it'd hardly be called faith if you had all the answers. Understanding comes on the other side, and by then, it won't be nearly as important."

"How about the end of the world? Does it happen? Can you tell me that?"

"Oh, sure. You do it to yourselves. It's already started. But your world already ended long ago, didn't it, boy?"

They reached the eastern edge of the peak, where Deacon expected to see the Wardite settlement rotting at the base of the mountain. Instead, gently rolling clouds girdled the peak, thicker than tule fog and pulsing with light and mysteries.

The Reverend didn't say why he was showing him this, but one message seemed clear. Outside of Red Peak, everything was fog, a fleeting, meaningless dream. Deacon knew nothing, and he'd die knowing nothing. The only thing that mattered was here, now, and the choice he knew he'd have to make.

"You think your mama didn't love you," the Reverend said. "She did and does now. She loved you enough to let you go and wander the Earth until you returned."

"You said she's there. She made it across the black sea."

"As promised. You scratch my back, I scratch yours." His smile returned. *"She's waiting for you, boy. She misses you."*

Deacon pictured his mother playing an organ in a green meadow awash in bright Technicolor sunlight. The entire Family was there, dressed in shining white and waving their arms as they sang about the glory of the Lord.

"It's not like that," Peale said. *"Not even close."*

"Show me. Please. I want to see."

"You wouldn't understand it even if I was willing to do that. You wouldn't even survive it. Your mind wouldn't."

Deacon shifted his feet, restless. *"Can I at least see Mom? Talk to her?"*

The grin evaporated in an instant. *"You know there's only one way. You have to sacrifice to gain eternity. I give, you give. What they call a covenant."*

"You want me to suffer," he said. *"What would I have to do, exactly?"*

The Reverend guffawed. *"Good Lord, haven't you suffered enough already? There's only one thing left for you and your friends. You have to shuck your mortal coil. You must shed time itself."*

Deacon turned from the edge. *"Why are you doing this?"*

"Another thing I shouldn't have to spell out for you. You know why."

"I want to hear you say it."

"We're like two peas in a pod, you and me. If I were to make you in my image, wouldn't that make me Father? Does a father not want love as much as the son?"

"If you're the real God, did you create us?"

"Think about it, Deacon."

Whether the entity had created his flesh out of nothing didn't matter. In every way, it had shaped Deacon's life and made him who he was now.

"But why suffering and death, though?" he asked. "How is that love?"

"What better way to prove love than to face the unknown on faith?" Peale shrugged his broad shoulders. "Anyway, they came looking for a shortcut to paradise. The only way to gain it was to shed their flesh and worldly desires."

"Shed," Deacon echoed with disgust. "They killed themselves. They chopped off parts of themselves. They murdered the ones who didn't want to go."

"It's like killing during war. It isn't bad if it's done with a loving heart."

"It was bad for me." Deacon turned back toward the clouds, knowing it was his only way out. Either way, it seemed, he'd be facing the unknown.

The fog or the black sea.

The endless wandering of his old life, or the chance for a new life rejoined with the Family.

All it took was an ultimate act of faith. Faith in something he couldn't see or understand with his mortal brain, something that if he even got to see, he couldn't tell was real or just another illusion, like the Jeremiah who stood before him.

"So what are you, boy?" the Reverend said. "Wheat or chaff?"

"You want me to die."

"I want you to choose." The grin returned full force. "And you won't die. You will become. Amen."

Deacon wondered what the others thought of what the entity was offering.

What choice Beth would make.

27

DIE

The world disappeared in fire. Beth cried out in the blinding glare.

A voice spoke from the flames. "I waited so long for you, honey."

"Daddy?" She raised her hand to shield her eyes. "Daddy! Is that you?"

The light began to dim. Beth wiped at her watery eyes, struggling with sight. A vague shape formed in the fire, dancing in it.

A second voice spoke.

"He wants you to know he was wrong. He never should have told you to run. None of it was your fault."

The voice tore a sob from her. "Mom?"

"She wants you to know she should have stopped talking long enough to listen to you," her father said.

As the glare continued to fade, the shape crystallized, still dancing.

Beth screamed.

The giant mouth stretched into a smile, flames pouring between massive lips.

"Do not be afraid," it said in her parents' voices.

She took another step back, her hand still raised as if this could protect her. "Are you real, or in my head?"

"Yes."

"*Both?*"

"*I am here. You also created me, so we can finally talk.*"

"*But is it really you, Mom?*"

"*No,*" her mother said.

Her father added, "*And yes.*"

"*I am the Living Spirit—*"

"*Which you seek, and—*"

"*I manifested as your—*"

"*Mind wished, as the—*"

"*People you love, as the—*"

"*Voice that must—*"

"*Break the—*"

"*Long—*"

"*Silence.*"

Another sob shook her, and then she was crying, joy and mourning and horror and catharsis all mixed together. Real or not, she didn't care.

Her hand dropped to her side. "It's good to hear your voices."

A chorus poured from the mouth. "*Don't cry for them, Beth. Rejoice.*"

She heard them all talking now—Reverend Peale, Josh, Wyatt, Emily, Mrs. Young, Mrs. Chapman, Freddie Shaw, Shepherd Wright, Anna Tibbs, Mrs. Blanchard, and all the rest, speaking in unison.

They said, "*The Family wants you to come home.*"

"Where are you?" Beth said and shook her head, knowing she was talking to the entity, not the real Family. "Where are they?"

"*Behold . . .*"

The bright, rust-colored sky faded to total night. Gasping, she raised her arms again to protect herself. This wasn't night but a complete and terrifying emptiness, a black void that stretched on forever, infinity itself.

The black sea.

She pictured it filled with cosmic leviathans, eager to consume helpless souls, but this was only her imagination. The truth of its utter emptiness was far worse. Gazing into the endless void's depths, she fell from a terrifying height into herself, fragile flesh and blood, tiny and insignificant as a mote of dust. Everything she'd done or would ever do, every frustration and joy, every love and hate, every dream and memory, the dark revealed as meaningless illusion and worse, delusion.

The darkness devoured all of it, even the fire. It was nothingness. Annihilation.

Her scream caught in her throat as she began to fall into the void—

"The light, Beth," the voices called.

The flaming pillar lanced up into the infernal night, where the darkness swallowed it. Then she saw the fire didn't matter. It was merely pointing the way.

Far off in the void, a single star blazed, an eternal beacon.

"They're waiting," the voices said. "Pass through the door, and return to the Family."

The star opened to another universe of light.

To reach it, all she had to do was ascend.

Her flesh rebelled at the idea of its extinction. Of all grief's phases over one's own demise, denial started at birth. Still, she was sick of feeling left behind. Exhausted from the endless silence that had defined her life for fifteen years.

To ascend across the black sea, she'd have to surrender her life. But was this so bad? What was her life worth? It was hardly being used. The idea of dying repelled her while at the same time offering relief. She could just surrender.

"Are they happy?" she said.

"Yes," the spirit said.

Beth took a ragged breath. "I want to come home."

"You are welcome, Beth."

"Welcome." She laughed as the weight of years of quiet suffering lifted from her heart. "I'm welcome. Yes, I'm ready to go."

"It has already begun."

In a blink, Deacon, David, and Angela appeared at her side.

"Beth," Deacon yelled. "Thank God, are you—"

Angela raised her Glock and fired at the smiling mouth, emptying the magazine with a long howl of fury.

Beth flinched away from the deafening shots. The great mouth shimmered in the flames, still wearing its patient smile.

Flushed and breathing hard, Angela lowered the smoking gun. "We aren't toys for you to fucking play with."

The mouth morphed into the Reverend's Cheshire cat smile.

"Screw you." She turned to the others. "Is everybody ready to go? If this thing isn't going to kill me, I'm getting out of here."

"If it lets us go," David said. "Can we just leave?"

Deacon stared at Beth. He gave her a slight nod.

"I think I might stay awhile," she said.

"Me too," said Deacon.

Angela wheeled on them. "No. You're not."

"If you're staying, I'm staying," Deacon told Beth. "I love you. It's the only thing that's real to me, the only thing I really have that's good."

David gasped. "You'd better think this through—"

"He's right, Deek," Beth said. "Don't do it for me."

"Oh, I'm going to cross anyway." Deacon looked up at the bright star in the endless night. "I'd really like to see it. And I want to see Mom and the Rev again."

Beth smiled at him. "I love you too, Deek. To the end."

He beamed back. "This is how we can be together."

"Bullshit." Angela's beautiful face had turned scarlet and mean. She reloaded the gun, chambered a round, and aimed it at Deacon. "I said we're leaving. Now."

He didn't flinch, though he was shaking. "Make it quick."

She lowered the gun. "What?" As if surprised he thought she'd actually make good on her threat. "Please. Don't do this."

"Are you really sure?" David said.

"Are you sure you don't want to take the deal? It's a good deal."

"If it's telling the truth. If any of this is real."

Deacon sighed. "I'm done with doubt."

Beth held out her hand. "Give me the gun and go. I'll do it."

Crying, Angela shook her head. Josh, her mother, the other kids, even David, she hadn't been able to protect any of them.

Because, Beth knew, one couldn't protect people from themselves, not really. After years of self-medicating and maintaining strict control over every aspect of her life, she'd become an expert on the subject.

David said, "I got this, sis. It's on me."

For the first time, he was protecting her. Gently, he took the Glock from her hand. Still weeping, she didn't resist.

"Give it to me, David," Beth said.

She couldn't ask Deacon to do it. He looked pale and terrified, barely able to stand up. She wasn't sure she had the strength to do it either, though she wanted it.

David stared at the gun in his hand. For an alarming moment, Beth thought he might fling it away, into the fire.

He said, "I can do it."

"It has to be me," Beth said, though she was crying now too, with relief.

He offered her a weak smile. "You're my friends. And if I do it, the spirit will let Angela and me go. It'll let me go back to my family."

"Thank you," she said. "I'm sorry, David. For everything."

"I want you to tell Mom that Angela and I love and miss her. That we're sorry. Tell her we understand, and we hope she will too."

"Josh," Angela managed through her tears. "Tell him I'll always love him."

"Tell Emily. Tell them all."

"I will," Beth promised.

David turned toward the apparition, which still waited in the flames. "Suffering for you doesn't make us love you. Being forced to do things we hate doesn't make us love you. Killing and dying doesn't make us love you."

The entity didn't reply.

David aimed the gun with trembling hands. "Forgive me."

Beth closed her eyes. "We'll see you on the other—"

The horn sounded like the roar of Creation.

28

FORGIVE

David clung to his sister as the shofar's blast ripped through them in powerful and convulsive waves of force, threatening to hurl them from the mountain. He screamed into the tumult, unable to hear his own voice.

His friends were *flying*.

Framed by cascading sheets of fire, they jerked and rolled in the air, limbs twirling. Together, they pirouetted in spirals around the flaming geyser, up and up and up, rising and dancing and tumbling until he lost sight of them.

Then they flared out of existence.

The horn stopped. The fire died in a flurry of sparks that one by one winked out. Darkness returned to Red Peak as if a cosmic curtain had closed.

Angela shuddered and released him. "It's over. Oh God, it's done."

Only the altar and cross remained in utter stillness.

David held the gun. He stared at it vacantly, still dazed by the awful horn that even now purred in unsettling vibrations in his core, like the echo of a sonic boom. He hadn't fired it. As his finger tensed against the trigger, his friends had vaulted into the air.

He'd passed his test, and for it, the entity had spared him the pain of murder. Abraham's knife had been stilled, but he'd lost Isaac anyway.

"I'm still not sure that really happened," she said.

When they were kids, Deacon once told him the divine defied human comprehension. After seeing the supernatural firsthand, David still believed that to be true. For the rest of his days, he'd struggle to grasp what he'd experienced.

He understood the choices he'd made, however.

"This is yours." He extended the gun toward her.

She took her service weapon, felt its familiar grip, and holstered it. "Thanks."

"Are you okay?"

Angela shook her head. "What do you think?"

He looked up at the night sky, which now flared with not one but millions of stars. "Do you think...?"

"They got what they wanted."

They'd gone to a better place, where their souls would at last find peace. They'd reached their loved ones at last. They'd tell his mother she was remembered and loved by her children. They'd tell Emily he was sorry.

Like his sister, he chose to believe it.

"They wanted to be there more than they wanted to be here," she added. "In a way, I can't blame them."

"You could have gone too, you know. If you wanted."

"No. I couldn't."

"Why not?"

Angela's face returned to the stubborn, angry scowl he

knew all too well. "Because we deserved better. What about you? Why did you stay?"

For the man who liked a way out, it was the ultimate exit, but he'd chosen a different, more difficult road.

"Let's go home," David said.

Together, the last living survivors of the Family of the Living Spirit threaded the mountain in reverse, navigating the stairway by starlight. They didn't talk the entire way down, too exhausted to speak, their thoughts and feelings too big to put into words. At the bottom, they stumbled through the ruins. They ignored the derelict Temple and shacks, as the buildings no longer had any power over them. The car sat where they'd left it, substantial and normal and promising a return to reality.

David sank into the seat behind the wheel and started the engine, ready to put Red Peak behind him for good. He drove until the mountain disappeared in his rearview. He no longer feared it, its grip on him gone. There was nothing to run from anymore.

He drove into Bakersfield, his car low on gas and his body running on fumes. He found a parking place in the lot of Angela's motel and cut the engine.

She went on gaping out the windshield as she had the entire drive down from Medford. "Did that really happen?"

David thought about it. The more distance he gained from it in time and miles, the more like a dream it seemed. "I don't know."

He didn't trust anything as real anymore. A part of him feared he was still on the mountain, imagining all this. His friends were gone, of that he was absolutely certain. Other than that, he wasn't sure. Anything else was an act of faith.

Outside, the sun blazed on the car and motel. A maid

with a cleaning cart knocked on one of the blue doors and went into the room.

Angela nodded, as if he'd said all that could be said. "I'm going home."

"I'll call you soon." A promise he intended to keep.

"Okay." She opened the door.

"Wait." He tightened his grip on the wheel. "I'm sorry. About Mom."

She rested her hand on his shoulder. "It wasn't your fault."

"I wasn't as strong as you. I put myself first—"

"*David.* It wasn't your fault. I'm sorry for ever making you think it was."

He sighed as his final burden slipped away. He let go of the wheel and rested his hands on his lap. "Thank you."

Angela said nothing.

He added, "You may not know this, but you did save me. You saved all of us. I love you, sis."

"I love you, too." She smirked as she got out of the car. "You little shit."

Once she'd gone, he began to feel shaky. Now that he was alone, the shock set in. He gritted his teeth through a wave of nausea and restarted the car, driving on autopilot. The world around him pulsed in sunshine and bright colors, still insubstantial. How could all this exist in the same world as the thing at Red Peak?

After missing his turn onto the road to Fresno, he knew where he was going. David drove into the cemetery parking lot and parked facing the rows of tombstones, where Emily's body rested.

Finally, he allowed himself to mourn.

He wept for Emily, Deacon and Beth, his mother, and the Family. He recalled the old pastor's comforting platitudes at

Emily's funeral, which didn't seem so empty now but instead the only truths that mattered. One cried not because loved ones were dead but because they were gone. The loss hurt because their lives had touched his life, either in some small way or by completely transforming it.

The car devoured the miles to Fresno. Stomach rolling with mounting excitement, David drove onto his neighborhood's familiar streets. He passed trees and mailboxes, houses and a teenaged girl walking her dog.

Home had never appeared so warm and welcoming.

And real, more real with each passing moment.

For the first time, he wasn't running from something but toward it.

His pulse quickened as he sighted his house. Glowing in the bright sunlight, Alyssa and Dexter frolicked in his front yard. He pulled over and parked across the street to watch them dart shrieking and laughing through the spray of a water sprinkler. Happy and innocent and believing they were immortal.

Their play made him think of Deacon and Beth. Did they still exist? Was it as beautiful as this? Were they as happy to be home?

David wanted to think so, but he couldn't be sure. Even after everything he'd witnessed, the same uncertainty would dog him to his final days, when it was time for him to discover the fate of his own mortal remains.

He was okay with that.

The afterlife would take care of itself. The only thing that mattered was here and now. What else had the pastor said? The Tree of Life goes on.

David got out of his car.

His children stopped playing at the sight of him. Alyssa waved.

"Daddy, watch me!" Dexter cried.

David smiled as his son lunged across the sprinkler to land in a somersault.

"That's nothing," Alyssa said. "Check this out."

He chuckled as they competed to see who could pull off the most outrageous stunt. Cartwheels, somersaults, soaring leaps. He applauded, his heart swelling with love and pride and meaning.

The front door of the house opened, and Claire stepped out, her face etched in worry and relief.

"David," she called to him.

He smiled. "I'm here, Claire. I'm home."

Unbidden, Emily's poem flashed through his mind:

So if you love me,
Truly love me,
You'll wait, you'll be ready,
And it will always be now.

David crossed the street without fear, making his own leap of faith.

ACKNOWLEDGMENTS

Writing a novel about the search for the meaning of life and the yearning for existence beyond death had me many times reflecting on the people for whom I'm grateful, who give my life meaning: my wonderful children and my partner, Chris Marrs. They keep my days and my heart full and the demons at bay.

I'd also like to express my gratitude to those who shaped me as a writer: Eileen and Chris DiLouie, John Dixon, Peter Clines, David Moody, Ron Bender, Ella Beaumont, Timothy W. Long, Randy Heller, Jonathan Moon, Timothy Johnson, Eloise Knapp, all my IFWA and HWA friends, and many others. A special thanks goes to Michael Bailey, who helped polish an early draft.

To you all, I'd like to say: Live well and long. Eat, drink, and be merry. And I hope you find meaning in every minute of the journey.

Finally, I'd like to thank David Fugate, my terrific agent, and my fantastic editor Bradley Englert, whose faith continues to fuel a dream partnership.

meet the author

Photo Credit: Jodi O

CRAIG DILOUIE is an acclaimed American-Canadian author of literary dark fantasy and other fiction. Formerly a magazine editor and advertising executive, he also works as a journalist and educator covering the North American lighting industry. Craig is a member of the Imaginative Fiction Writers Association, the International Thriller Writers, and the Horror Writers Association. He currently lives in Calgary, Canada, with his two wonderful children.

if you enjoyed
THE CHILDREN OF RED PEAK
look out for

ONE OF US
by
Craig DiLouie

"This is not a kind book, or a gentle book, or a book that pulls its punches. But it's a powerful book, and it will change you."
—*Seanan McGuire*

They've called him a monster from the day he was born.

Abandoned by his family, Enoch Bryant now lives in a run-down orphanage with other teenagers just like him. He loves his friends, even if the teachers are terrified of them. They're members of the rising plague generation. Each bearing their own extreme genetic mutation.

The people in the nearby town hate Enoch, but he doesn't know why. He's never harmed anyone. Works hard and doesn't make trouble. Never even gets mad when they glare at him anymore. He believes one day he'll be a respected man.

But hatred dies hard. The tension between Enoch's world and those of the "normal" townspeople is ready to burst. And when a body is found, it may be the spark that ignites a horrifying revolution.

1

On the principal's desk, a copy of *Time*. A fourteen-year-old girl smiled on the cover. Pigtails tied in blue ribbon. Freckles and big white teeth. Rubbery, barbed appendages extending from her eye sockets.

Under that, a single word: WHY?

Why did this happen?

Or, maybe, why did the world allow a child like this to live?

What Dog wanted to know was why she smiled.

Maybe it was just reflex, seeing somebody pointing a camera at her. Maybe she liked the attention, even if it wasn't the nice kind.

Maybe, if only for a few seconds, she felt special.

The Georgia sun glared through filmy barred windows. A steel fan whirred in the corner, barely moving the warm, thick air. Out the window, Dog spied the old rusted pickup sunk in a riot of wildflowers. Somebody loved it once then parked it here and left it to die. If Dog owned it, he would have kept driving and never stopped.

The door opened. The government man came in wearing a black suit, white shirt, and blue-and-yellow tie. His shiny shoes clicked across the grimy floor. He sat in Principal Willard's creaking chair and lit a cigarette. Dropped a file folder on the desk and studied Dog through a blue haze.

"They call you Dog," he said.

"Yes, sir, they do. The other kids, I mean."

Dog growled when he talked but took care to form each word right. The teachers made sure he spoke good and proper. Brain once told him these signs of humanity were the only thing keeping the children alive.

"Your Christian name is Enoch. Enoch Davis Bryant."

"Yes, sir."

Enoch was the name the teachers at the Home used. Brain said it was his slave name. Dog liked hearing it, though. He felt lucky to have one. His mama had loved him enough to at least do that for him. Many parents had named their kids XYZ before abandoning them to the Homes.

"I'm Agent Shackleton," the government man said through another cloud of smoke. "Bureau of Teratological Affairs. You know the drill, don't you, by now?"

Every year, the government sent somebody to ask the kids questions. Trying to find out if they were still human. Did they want to hurt people, ever have carnal thoughts about normal girls and boys, that sort of thing.

"I know the drill," Dog said.

"Not this year," the man told him. "This year is different. I'm here to find out if you're special."

"I don't quite follow, sir."

Agent Shackleton planted his elbows on the desk. "You're a

ward of the state. More than a million of you. Living high on the hog for the past fourteen years in the Homes. Some of you are beginning to show certain capabilities."

"Like what kind?"

"I saw a kid once who had gills and could breathe underwater. Another who could hear somebody talking a mile away."

"No kidding," Dog said.

"That's right."

"You mean like a superhero."

"Yeah. Like Spider-Man, if Spider-Man half looked like a real spider."

"I never heard of such a thing," Dog said.

"If you, Enoch, have capabilities, you could prove you're worth the food you eat. This is your opportunity to pay it back. Do you follow me?"

"Sure, I guess."

Satisfied, Shackleton sat back in the chair and planted his feet on the desk. He set the file folder on his thighs, licked his finger, and flipped it open.

"Pretty good grades," the man said. "You got your math and spelling. You stay out of trouble. All right. Tell me what you can do. Better yet, show me something."

"What I can do, sir?"

"You do for me, I can do plenty for you. Take you to a special place."

Dog glanced at the red door at the side of the room before returning his gaze to Shackleton. Even looking at it was bad luck. The red door led downstairs to a basement room called Discipline, where the problem kids went.

He'd never been inside it, but he knew the stories. All the kids knew them. Principal Willard wanted them to know. It was part of their education.

He said, "What kind of place would that be?"

"A place with lots of food and TV. A place nobody can ever bother you."

Brain always said to play along with the normals so you didn't get caught up in their system. They wrote the rules in such a way to trick you into Discipline. More than that, though, Dog wanted to prove himself. He wanted to be special.

"Well, I'm a real fast runner. Ask anybody."

"That's your special talent. You can run fast."

"Real fast. Does that count?"

The agent smiled. "Running fast isn't special. It isn't special at all."

"Ask anybody how fast I run. Ask the—"

"You're not special. You'll never be special, Dog."

"I don't know what you want from me, sir."

Shackleton's smile disappeared along with Dog's file. "I want you to get the hell out of my sight. Send the next monster in on your way out."

2

Pollution. Infections. Drugs. Radiation. All these things, Mr. Benson said from the chalkboard, can produce mutations in embryos.

A bacterium caused the plague generation. The other kids, the plague kids, who lived in the Homes.

Amy Green shifted in her desk chair. The top of her head was itching again. Mama said she'd worry it bald if she kept scratching at it. She settled on twirling her long, dark hair around her finger and tugging. Savored the needles of pain along her scalp.

"The plague is a sexually transmitted disease," Mr. Benson told the class.

She already knew part of the story from American History and from what Mama told her. The plague started in 1968, two years before she was born, back when love was still free. Then the disease named teratogenesis raced around the world, and the plague children came.

One out of ten thousand babies born in 1968 were monsters, and most died. One in six in 1969, and half of these died. One in three in 1970, the year scientists came up with a test to see if you had it. Most of them lived. After a neonatal nurse got arrested for killing thirty babies in Texas, the survival rate jumped.

More than a million monster babies screaming to be fed. By then, Congress had already funded the Home system.

Fourteen years later, and still no cure. If you caught the germ, the only surefire way to stop spreading it was abstinence, which they taught right here in health class. If you got pregnant with it, abortion was mandatory.

Amy flipped her textbook open and bent to sniff its cheesy new-book smell. Books, sharpened pencils, lined paper; she associated their bitter scents with school. The page showed a drawing of a woman's reproductive system. The baby comes out there. Sitting next to her, her boyfriend Jake glanced at the page and smiled, his face reddening. Like her, fascinated and embarrassed by it all.

In junior high, sex ed was mandatory, no ifs or buts. Amy and her friends were stumbling through puberty. Tampons, budding breasts, aching midnight thoughts, long conversations about what boys liked and what they wanted.

She already had a good idea what they wanted. Girls always complimented her about how pretty she was. Boys stared at her when she walked down the hall. Everybody so nice to her all the time. She didn't trust any of it.

When she stood naked in the mirror, she only saw flaws. Amy spotted a zit last week and stared at it for an hour, hating her ugliness. It took her over an hour every morning to get ready for school. She didn't leave the house until she looked perfect.

She flipped the page again. A monster grinned up at her. She slammed the book shut.

Mr. Benson asked if anybody in the class had actually seen a plague child. Not on TV or in a magazine, but up close and personal.

A few kids raised their hands. Amy kept hers planted on her desk.

"I have two big goals for you kids this year," the teacher said. "The main thing is teach you how to avoid spreading the disease. We'll be talking a lot about safe sex and all the regulations about whether and how you do it. How to get tested and how to access a safe abortion. I also aim to help you become accustomed to the plague children already born and who are now the same age as you."

For Amy's entire life, the plague children had lived in group homes out in the country, away from people. One was located just eight miles from Huntsville, though it might as well have been on the moon. The monsters never came to town. Out of sight meant out of mind, though one could never entirely forget them.

"Let's start with the plague kids," Mr. Benson said. "What do all y'all think about them? Tell the truth."

Rob Rowland raised his hand. "They ain't human. They're just animals."

"Is that right? Would you shoot one and eat it? Mount its head on your wall?"

The kids laughed as they pictured Rob so hungry he would eat a monster. Rob was obese, smart, and sweated a lot, one of the unpopular kids.

Amy shuddered with sudden loathing. "I hate them something awful."

The laughter died. Which was good, because the plague wasn't funny.

The teacher crossed his arms. "Go ahead, Amy. No need to holler, though. Why do you hate them?"

"They're monsters. I hate them because they're monsters."

Mr. Benson turned and hacked at the blackboard with a piece of chalk: MONSTRUM, a VIOLATION OF NATURE. From MONEO, which means TO WARN. In this case, a warning God is angry. Punishment for taboo.

"Teratogenesis is nature out of whack," he said. "It rewrote the body. Changed the rules. Monsters, maybe. But does a monster have to be evil? Is a human being what you look like, or what you do? What makes a man a man?"

Bonnie Fields raised her hand. "I saw one once. I couldn't even tell if it was a boy or girl. I didn't stick around to get to know it."

"But did you see it as evil?"

"I don't know about that, but looking the way some of them do, I can't imagine why the doctors let them all live. It would have been a mercy to let them die."

"Mercy on us," somebody behind Amy muttered.

The kids laughed again.

Sally Albod's hand shot up. "I'm surprised at all y'all being so scared. I see the kids all the time at my daddy's farm. They're weird, but there ain't nothing to them. They work hard and don't make trouble. They're fine."

370

"That's good, Sally," the teacher said. "I'd like to show all y'all something."

He opened a cabinet and pulled out a big glass jar. He set it on his desk. Inside, a baby floated in yellowish fluid. A tiny penis jutted between its legs. Its little arms grasped at nothing. It had a single slitted eye over a cleft where its nose should be.

The class sucked in its breath as one. Half the kids recoiled as the rest leaned forward for a better look. Fascination and revulsion. Amy alone didn't move. She sat frozen, shot through with the horror of it.

She hated the little thing. Even dead, she hated it.

"This is Tony," Mr. Benson said. "And guess what, he isn't one of the plague kids. Just some poor boy born with a birth defect. About three percent of newborns are born this way every year. It causes one out of five infant deaths."

Tony, some of the kids chuckled. They thought it weird it had a name.

"We used to believe embryos developed in isolation in the uterus," the teacher said. "Then back in the Sixties, a company sold thalidomide to pregnant women in Germany to help them with morning sickness. Ten thousand kids born with deformed limbs. Half died. What did scientists learn from that? Anybody?"

"A medicine a lady takes can hurt her baby even if it don't hurt her," Jake said.

"Bingo," Mr. Benson said. "Medicine, toxins, viruses, we call these things environmental factors. Most times, though, doctors have no idea why a baby like Tony is born. It just happens, like a dice roll. So is Tony a monster? What about a kid who's retarded, or born with legs that don't work? Is a kid in a wheelchair a monster too? A baby born deaf or blind?"

He got no takers. The class sat quiet and thoughtful. Satisfied,

Mr. Benson carried the jar back to the cabinet. More gasps as baby Tony bobbed in the fluid, like he was trying to get out.

The teacher frowned as he returned the jar to its shelf. "I'm surprised just this upsets you. If this gets you so worked up, how will you live with the plague children? When they're adults, they'll have the same rights as you. They'll live among you."

Amy stiffened at her desk, neck clenched with tension at the idea. A question formed in her mind. "What if we don't want to live with them?"

Mr. Benson pointed at the jar. "This baby is you. And something not you. If Tony had survived, he would be different, yes. But he would be you."

"I think we have a responsibility to them," Jake said.

"Who's we?" Amy said.

His contradicting her had stung a little, but she knew how Jake had his own mind and liked to argue. He wore leather jackets, black T-shirts advertising obscure bands, ripped jeans. Troy and Michelle, his best friends, were Black.

He was popular because being unpopular didn't scare him. Amy liked him for that, the way he flouted junior high's iron rules. The way he refused to suck up to her like the other boys all did.

"You know who I mean," he said. "The human race. We made them, and that gives us responsibility. It's that simple."

"I didn't make anything. The older generation did. Why are they my problem?"

"Because they have it bad. We all know they do. Imagine being one of them."

"I don't want things to be bad for them," Amy said. "I really don't. I just don't want them around me. Why does that make me a bad person?"

"I never said it makes you a bad person," Jake said.

Archie Gaines raised his hand. "Amy has a good point, Mr. Benson. They're a mess to stomach, looking at them. I mean, I can live with it, I guess. But all this love and understanding is a lot to ask."

"Fair enough," Mr. Benson said.

Archie turned to look back at Amy. She nodded her thanks. His face lit up with a leering smile. He believed he'd rescued her and now she owed him.

She gave him a practiced frown to shut down his hopes. He turned away as if slapped.

"I'm just curious about them," Jake said. "More curious than scared. It's like you said, Mr. Benson. However they look, they're still our brothers. I wouldn't refuse help to a blind man, I guess I wouldn't to a plague kid neither."

The teacher nodded. "Okay. Good. That's enough discussion for today. We're getting somewhere, don't you think? Again, my goal for you kids this year is two things. One is to get used to the plague children. Distinguishing between a book and its cover. The other is to learn how to avoid making more of them."

Jake turned to Amy and winked. Her cheeks burned, all her annoyance with him forgotten.

She hoped there was a lot more sex ed and a lot less monster talk in her future. While Mr. Benson droned on, she glanced through the first few pages of her book. A chapter headline caught her eye: KISSING.

She already knew the law regarding sex. Germ or no germ, the legal age of consent was still fourteen in the State of Georgia. But another law said if you wanted to have sex, you had to get tested for the germ first. If you were under eighteen, your parents had to give written consent for the testing.

Kissing, though, that you could do without any fuss. It said so right here in black and white. You could do it all you wanted. Her scalp tingled at the thought. She tugged at her hair and savored the stabbing needles.

She risked a hungering glance at Jake's handsome profile. Though she hoped one day to go further than that, she could never do more than kissing. She could never know what it'd be like to scratch the real itch.

Nobody but her mama knew Amy was a plague child.